DETECTIVES 2

DETECTIVES 2

LOVEDAY BROOKE

CATHERINE LOUISA PIRKIS

LADY MOLLY
OF SCOTLAND YARD

BARONESS EMMA ORCZY

COACHWHIP PUBLICATIONS

Landisville, Pennsylvania

2 Detectives: Loveday Brooke / Lady Molly of Scotland Yard
Loveday Brooke, by Catherine Louisa Pirkis (1841-1910), published 1894.
Lady Molly of Scotland Yard, by Baroness Emma Orczy (1865-1947),
    published 1910.
Copyright © 2012 Coachwhip Publications
No claims made on public domain material.

ISBN 1-61646-112-8
ISBN-13 978-1-61646-112-6

CoachwhipBooks.com

CONTENTS

LOVEDAY BROOKE

LADY MOLLY OF SCOTLAND YARD

LOVEDAY BROOKE

THE BLACK BAG LEFT ON A DOOR-STEP

"It's a big thing," said Loveday Brooke, addressing Ebenezer Dyer, chief of the well-known detective agency in Lynch Court, Fleet Street; "Lady Cathrow has lost £30,000 worth of jewellery, if the newspaper accounts are to be trusted."

"They are fairly accurate this time. The robbery differs in few respects from the usual run of country-house robberies. The time chosen, of course, was the dinner-hour, when the family and guests were at table and the servants not on duty were amusing themselves in their own quarters. The fact of its being Christmas Eve would also of necessity add to the business and consequent distraction of the household. The entry to the house, however, in this case was not effected in the usual manner by a ladder to the dressing-room window, but through the window of a room on the ground floor—a small room with one window and two doors, one of which opens into the hall, and the other into a passage that leads by the back stairs to the bedroom floor. It is used, I believe, as a sort of hat and coat room by the gentlemen of the house."

"It was, I suppose, the weak point of the house?"

"Quite so. A very weak point indeed. Craigen Court, the residence of Sir George and Lady Cathrow, is an oddly-built old place, jutting out in all directions, and as this window looked out upon a blank wall, it was filled in with stained glass, kept fastened by a strong brass catch, and never opened, day or night, ventilation being obtained by means of a glass ventilator fitted in the upper panes. It seems absurd to think that this window, being only about four feet from the ground, should have had neither iron bars nor shutters added to it; such, however, was the case. On the night of the robbery, someone within the house must have deliberately, and of intention, unfastened its only protection, the brass catch, and thus given the thieves easy entrance to the house."

"Your suspicions, I suppose, centre upon the servants?"

"Undoubtedly; and it is in the servants' hall that your services will be required. The thieves, whoever they were, were perfectly cognizant of the ways of the house. Lady Cathrow's jewellery was kept in a safe in her dressing-room, and as the dressing-room was over the dining-room, Sir George was in the habit of saying that it was the 'safest' room in the house. (Note the pun, please; Sir George is rather proud of it.) By his orders the window of the dining-room immediately under the dressing-room window was always left unshuttered and without blind during dinner, and as a full stream of light thus fell through it on to the outside terrace, it would have been impossible for anyone to have placed a ladder there unseen."

"I see from the newspapers that it was Sir George's invariable custom to fill his house and give a large dinner on Christmas Eve."

"Yes. Sir George and Lady Cathrow are elderly people, with no family and few relatives, and have consequently a large amount of time to spend on their friends."

"I suppose the key of the safe was frequently left in the possession of Lady Cathrow's maid?"

"Yes. She is a young French girl, Stephanie Delcroix by name. It was her duty to clear the dressing-room directly after her mistress left it; put away any jewellery that might be lying about, lock the safe, and keep the key till her mistress came up to bed. On the night of the robbery, however, she admits that, instead of so doing, directly her mistress left the dressing-room, she ran down to the housekeeper's room to see if any letters had come for her, and remained chatting with the other servants for some time—she could not say for how long. It was by the half-past-seven post that her letters generally arrived from St. Omer, where her home is."

"Oh, then, she was in the habit of thus running down to en-quire for her letters, no doubt, and the thieves, who appear to be so thoroughly cognizant of the house, would know this also."

"Perhaps; though at the present moment I must say things look very black against the girl. Her manner, too, when questioned, is not calculated to remove suspicion. She goes from one fit of hysterics into another; contradicts herself nearly every time she opens her mouth, then lays it to the charge of her ignorance of our language; breaks into voluble French; becomes theatrical in action, and then goes off into hysterics once more."

"All that is quite Français, you know," said Loveday. "Do the authorities at Scotland Yard lay much stress on the safe being left unlocked that night?"

"They do, and they are instituting a keen enquiry as to the possible lovers the girl may have. For this purpose they have sent Bates down to stay in the village and collect all the information he can outside the house. But they want someone within the walls to hobnob with the maids generally, and to find out if she has taken any of them into her confidence respecting her lovers. So they sent to me to know if I would send down for this purpose one of the shrewdest and most clear-headed of my female detectives. I, in my turn, Miss Brooke, have sent for you—you may take it as a compliment if you like. So please now get out your note-book, and I'll give you sailing orders."

Loveday Brooke, at this period of her career, was a little over thirty years of age, and could be best described in a series of negations.

She was not tall, she was not short; she was not dark, she was not fair; she was neither handsome nor ugly. Her features were altogether nondescript; her one noticeable trait was a habit she had, when absorbed in thought, of dropping her eyelids over her eyes till only a line of eyeball showed, and she appeared to be looking out at the world through a slit, instead of through a window.

Her dress was invariably black, and was almost Quaker-like in its neat primness.

Some five or six years previously, by a jerk of Fortune's wheel, Loveday had been thrown upon the world penniless and all but friendless. Marketable accomplishments she had found she had none, so she had forthwith defied convention, and had chosen for herself a career that had cut her off sharply from her former

associates and her position in society. For five or six years she
drudged away patiently in the lower walks of her profession; then
chance, or, to speak more precisely, an intricate criminal case,
threw her in the way of the experienced head of the flourishing
detective agency in Lynch Court. He quickly enough found out the
stuff she was made of, and threw her in the way of better-class
work—work, indeed, that brought increase of pay and of reputation alike to him and to Loveday.

Ebenezer Dyer was not, as a rule, given to enthusiasm; but he
would at times wax eloquent over Miss Brooke's qualifications for
the profession she had chosen.

"Too much of a lady, do you say?" he would say to anyone who
chanced to call in question those qualifications. "I don't care
twopence-halfpenny whether she is or is not a lady. I only know
she is the most sensible and practical woman I ever met. In the
first place, she has the faculty—so rare among women—of carrying
out orders to the very letter: in the second place, she has a clear,
shrewd brain, unhampered by any hard-and-fast theories; thirdly,
and most important item of all, she has so much common sense
that it amounts to genius—positively to genius, sir."

But although Loveday and her chief as a rule, worked together
upon an easy and friendly footing, there were occasions on which
they were wont, so to speak, to snarl at each other.

Such an occasion was at hand now.

Loveday showed no disposition to take out her note-book and
receive her "sailing orders."

"I want to know," she said, "If what I saw in one newspaper is
true—that one of the thieves before leaving, took the trouble to
close the safe-door, and to write across it in chalk: 'To be let, unfurnished'?"

"Perfectly true; but I do not see that stress need be laid on the
fact. The scoundrels often do that sort of thing out of insolence or
bravado. In that robbery at Reigate, the other day, they went to a
lady's Davenport, took a sheet of her note-paper, and wrote their
thanks on it for her kindness in not having had the lock of her safe
repaired. Now, if you will get out your note-book—"

"Don't be in such a hurry," said Loveday calmly: "I want to know if you have seen this?" She leaned across the writing-table at which they sat, one either side, and handed to him a newspaper cutting which she took from her letter-case.

Mr. Dyer was a tall, powerfully-built man with a large head, benevolent bald forehead and a genial smile. That smile, however, often proved a trap to the unwary, for he owned a temper so irritable that a child with a chance word might ruffle it.

The genial smile vanished as he took the newspaper cutting from Loveday's hand.

"I would have you to remember, Miss Brooke," he said severely, "that although I am in the habit of using dispatch in my business, I am never known to be in a hurry; hurry in affairs I take to be the especial mark of the slovenly and unpunctual."

Then, as if still further to give contradiction to her words, he very deliberately unfolded her slip of newspaper and slowly, accentuating each word and syllable, read as follows:—

"SINGULAR DISCOVERY.

"A black leather bag, or portmanteau, was found early yesterday morning by one of Smith's newspaper boys on the doorstep of a house in the road running between Easterbrook and Wreford, and inhabited by an elderly spinster lady. The contents of the bag include a clerical collar and necktie, a Church Service, a book of sermons, a copy of the works of Virgil, a *facsimile* of Magna Charta, with translations, a pair of black kid gloves, a brush and comb, some newspapers, and several small articles suggesting clerical ownership. On the top of the bag the following extraordinary letter, written in pencil on a long slip of paper, was found:

"'The fatal day has arrived. I can exist no longer. I go hence and shall be no more seen. But I would have Coroner and Jury know that I am a sane man, and a verdict of temporary insanity in my case would be an error most gross after this intimation. I care not if it is *felo de se*, as I shall have passed all suffering. Search diligently for my poor lifeless body in the immediate neighbourhood—on the cold heath, the rail, or the river by yonder bridge—a few moments will decide how I shall depart. If I had walked aright I might have been a power in the Church of which I am now an unworthy member and priest; but the damnable sin of gambling got hold on me, and betting has been my ruin, as it has been the ruin of thousands who have preceded me. Young man, shun the bookmaker and the race-course as you would shun the devil and hell. Farewell, chums of Magdalen. Farewell, and take warning. Though I can claim relationship with a Duke, a Marquess, and a Bishop, and though I am the son of a noble woman, yet am I a tramp and an outcast, verily and indeed. Sweet death, I greet thee. I dare not sign my name. To one and all, farewell. O, my poor Marchioness mother, a dying kiss to thee. R.I.P.'

"The police and some of the railway officials have made a 'diligent search' in the neighbourhood of the railway station, but no 'poor lifeless body' has been found. The police authorities are inclined to the belief that the letter is a hoax, though they are still investigating the matter."

In the same deliberate fashion as he had opened and read the cutting, Mr. Dyer folded and returned it to Loveday.

"May I ask," he said sarcastically, "what you see in that silly hoax to waste your and my valuable time over?"

"I wanted to know," said Loveday, in the same level tones as before, "if you saw anything in it that might in some way connect this discovery with the robbery at Craigen Court?"

Mr. Dyer stared at her in utter, blank astonishment.

"When I was a boy," he said sarcastically as before, "I used to play at a game called 'what is my thought like?' Someone would think of something absurd—say the top of the monument—and someone else would hazard a guess that his thought might be—say the toe of his left boot, and that unfortunate individual would have to show the connection between the toe of his left boot and the top of the monument. Miss Brooke, I have no wish to repeat the silly game this evening for your benefit and mine."

"Oh, very well," said Loveday, calmly; "I fancied you might like to talk it over, that was all. Give me my 'sailing orders,' as you call them, and I'll endeavour to concentrate my attention on the little French maid and her various lovers."

Mr. Dyer grew amiable again.

"That's the point on which I wish you to fix your thoughts," he said; "you had better start for Craigen Court by the first train to-morrow—it's about sixty miles down the Great Eastern line. Huxwell is the station you must land at. There one of the grooms from the Court will meet you, and drive you to the house. I have arranged with the housekeeper there—Mrs. Williams, a very worthy and discreet person—that you shall pass in the house for a niece of hers, on a visit to recruit, after severe study in order to pass board-school teachers' exams. Naturally you have injured your eyes as well as your health with overwork; and so you can wear your blue spectacles. Your name, by the way, will be Jane Smith—better write it down. All your work will be among the servants of the establishment, and there will be no necessity for you to see either Sir George or Lady Cathrow—in fact, neither of them have been apprised of your intended visit—the fewer we take into our confidence the better. I've no doubt, however, that Bates will hear from Scotland Yard that you are in the house, and will make a point of seeing you."

"Has Bates unearthed anything of importance?"

"Not as yet. He has discovered one of the girl's lovers, a young farmer of the name of Holt; but as he seems to be an honest, respectable young fellow, and entirely above suspicion, the discovery does not count for much."

"I think there's nothing else to ask," said Loveday, rising to take her departure. "Of course, I'll telegraph, should need arise, in our usual cipher."

The first train that left Bishopsgate for Huxwell on the following morning included, among its passengers, Loveday Brooke, dressed in the neat black supposed to be appropriate to servants of the upper class. The only literature with which she had provided herself in order to beguile the tedium of her journey was a small volume bound in paper boards, and entitled, *The Reciter's Treasury*. It was published at the low price of one shilling, and seemed specially designed to meet the requirements of third-rate amateur reciters at penny readings.

Miss Brooke appeared to be all-absorbed in the contents of this book during the first half of her journey. During the second, she lay back in the carriage with closed eyes, and motionless as if asleep or lost in deep thought.

The stopping of the train at Huxwell aroused her, and set her collecting together her wraps.

It was easy to single out the trim groom from Craigen Court from among the country loafers on the platform. Someone else beside the trim groom at the same moment caught her eye—Bates, from Scotland Yard, got up in the style of a commercial traveler, and carrying the orthodox "commercial bag" in his hand. He was a small, wiry man, with red hair and whiskers, and an eager, hungry expression of countenance.

"I am half-frozen with cold," said Loveday, addressing Sir George's groom; "if you'll kindly take charge of my portmanteau, I'd prefer walking to driving to the Court."

The man gave her a few directions as to the road she was to follow, and then drove off with her box, leaving her free to indulge Mr. Bate's evident wish for a walk and confidential talk along the country road.

Bates seemed to be in a happy frame of mind that morning.

"Quite a simple affair, this, Miss Brooke," he said: "a walk over the course, I take it, with you working inside the castle walls and I unearthing without. No complications as yet have arisen, and if that girl does not find herself in jail before another week is over her head, my name is not Jeremiah Bates."

"You mean the French maid?"

"Why, yes, of course. I take it there's little doubt but what she performed the double duty of unlocking the safe and the window too. You see I look at it this way, Miss Brooke: all girls have lovers, I say to myself, but a pretty girl like that French maid, is bound to have double the number of lovers than the plain ones. Now, of course, the greater the number of lovers, the greater the chance there is of a criminal being found among them. That's plain as a pikestaff, isn't it?"

"Just as plain."

Bates felt encouraged to proceed.

"Well, then, arguing on the same lines, I say to myself, this girl is only a pretty, silly thing, not an accomplished criminal, or she wouldn't have admitted leaving open the safe door; give her rope enough and she'll hang herself. In a day or two, if we let her alone, she'll be bolting off to join the fellow whose nest she has helped to feather, and we shall catch the pair of them 'twixt here and Dover Straits, and also possibly get a clue that will bring us on the traces of their accomplices. Eh, Miss Brooke, that'll be a thing worth doing?"

"Undoubtedly. Who is this coming along in this buggy at such a good pace?"

The question was added as the sound of wheels behind them made her look round.

Bates turned also. "Oh, this is young Holt; his father farms land about a couple of miles from here. He is one of Stephanie's lovers, and I should imagine about the best of the lot. But he does not appear to be first favourite; from what I hear someone else must have made the running on the sly. Ever since the robbery I'm told the young woman has given him the cold shoulder."

As the young man came nearer in his buggy he slackened pace, and Loveday could not but admire his frank, honest expression of countenance.

"Room for one—can I give you a lift?" he said, as he came alongside of them.

And to the ineffable disgust of Bates, who had counted upon at least an hour's confidential talk with her, Miss Brooke accepted the young farmer's offer, and mounted beside him in his buggy.

As they went swiftly along the country road, Loveday explained to the young man that her destination was Craigen Court, and that as she was a stranger to the place, she must trust to him to put her down at the nearest point to it that he would pass.

At the mention of Craigen Court his face clouded.

"They're in trouble there, and their trouble has brought trouble on others," he said a little bitterly.

"I know," said Loveday sympathetically; "it is often so. In such circumstances as these suspicions frequently fastens on an entirely innocent person."

"That's it! that's it!" he cried excitedly; "if you go into that house you'll hear all sorts of wicked things said of her, and see everything setting in dead against her. But she's innocent. I swear to you she is as innocent as you or I are."

His voice rang out above the clatter of his horse's hoots. He seemed to forget that he had mentioned no name, and that Loveday, as a stranger, might be at a loss to know to whom he referred.

"Who is guilty Heaven only knows," he went on after a moment's pause; "it isn't for me to give an ill name to anyone in that house; but I only say she is innocent, and that I'll stake my life on."

"She is a lucky girl to have found one to believe in her, and trust her as you do," said Loveday, even more sympathetically than before.

"Is she? I wish she'd take advantage of her luck, then," he answered bitterly. "Most girls in her position would be glad to have a man to stand by them through thick and thin. But not she! Ever since the night of that accursed robbery she has refused to see me—won't answer my letters—won't even send me a message. And, great Heavens! I'd marry her to-morrow, if I had the chance, and dare the world to say a word against her."

He whipped up his pony. The hedges seemed to fly on either side of them, and before Loveday realized that half her drive was over, he had drawn rein, and was helping her to alight at the servants' entrance to Craigen Court.

"You'll tell her what I've said to you, if you get the opportunity, and beg her to see me, if only for five minutes?" he petitioned before he re-mounted his buggy. And Loveday, as she thanked the young man for his kind attention, promised to make an opportunity to give his message to the girl.

Mrs. Williams, the housekeeper, welcomed Loveday in the servants' hall, and then took her to her own room to pull off her wraps. Mrs. Williams was the widow of a London tradesman, and a little beyond the average housekeeper in speech and manner.

She was a genial, pleasant woman, and readily entered into conversation with Loveday. Tea was brought in, and each seemed to feel at home with the other. Loveday in the course of this easy, pleasant talk, elicited from her the whole history of the events of the day of the robbery, the number and names of the guests who sat down to dinner that night, together with some other apparently trivial details.

The housekeeper made no attempt to disguise the painful position in which she and every one of the servants of the house felt themselves to be at the present moment.

"We are none of us at our ease with each other now," she said, as she poured out hot tea for Loveday, and piled up a blazing fire. "Everyone fancies that everyone else is suspecting him or her, and trying to rake up past words or deeds to bring in as evidence. The whole house seems under a cloud. And at this time of year, too; just when everything as a rule is at its merriest!" and here she gave a doleful glance to the big bunch of holly and mistletoe hanging from the ceiling.

"I suppose you are generally very merry downstairs at Christmas time?" said Loveday. "Servants' balls, theatricals, and all that sort of thing?"

"I should think we were! When I think of this time last year and the fun we all had, I can scarcely believe it is the same house. Our ball always follows my lady's ball, and we have permission to ask our friends to it, and we keep it up as late as ever we please.

We begin our evening with a concert and recitations in character, then we have a supper and then we dance right on till morning; but this year!"—she broke off, giving a long, melancholy shake of her head that spoke volumes.

"I suppose," said Loveday, "some of your friends are very clever as musicians or reciters?"

"Very clever indeed. Sir George and my lady are always present during the early part of the evening, and I should like you to have seen Sir George last year laughing fit to kill himself at Harry Emmett dressed in prison dress with a bit of oakum in his hand, reciting the 'Noble Convict!' Sir George said if the young man had gone on the stage, he would have been bound to make his fortune."

"Half a cup, please," said Loveday, presenting her cup. "Who was this Harry Emmett then—a sweetheart of one of the maids?"

"Oh, he would flirt with them all, but he was sweetheart to none. He was footman to Colonel James, who is a great friend of Sir George's, and Harry was constantly backwards and forwards bringing messages from his master. His father, I think, drove a cab in London, and Harry for a time did so also; then he took it into his head to be a gentleman's servant, and great satisfaction he gave as such. He was always such a bright, handsome young fellow and so full of fun, that everyone liked him. But I shall tire you with all this; and you, of course, want to talk about something so different;" and the housekeeper sighed again, as the thought of the dreadful robbery entered her brain once more.

"Not at all. I am greatly interested in you and your festivities. Is Emmett still in the neighbourhood? I should amazingly like to hear him recite myself."

"I'm sorry to say he left Colonel James about six months ago. We all missed him very much at first. He was a good, kind-hearted young man, and I remember he told me he was going away to look after his dear old grandmother, who had a sweet-stuff shop somewhere or other, but where I can't remember."

Loveday was leaning back in her chair now, with eyelids drooped so low that she literally looked out through "slits" instead of eyes.

Suddenly and abruptly she changed the conversation.

"When will it be convenient for me to see Lady Cathrow's dressing-room?" she asked.

The housekeeper looked at her watch. "Now, at once," she answered: "it's a quarter to five now and my lady sometimes goes up to her room to rest for half an hour before she dresses for dinner."

"Is Stephanie still in attendance on Lady Cathrow?" Miss Brooke asked as she followed the housekeeper up the back stairs to the bedroom floor.

"Yes, Sir George and my lady have been goodness itself to us through this trying time, and they say we are all innocent till we are proved guilty, and will have it that none of our duties are to be in any way altered."

"Stephanie is scarcely fit to perform hers, I should imagine?"

"Scarcely. She was in hysterics nearly from morning till night for the first two or three days after the detectives came down, but now she has grown sullen, eats nothing and never speaks a word to any of us except when she is obliged. This is my lady's dressing-room, walk in please."

Loveday entered a large, luxuriously furnished room, and naturally made her way straight to the chief point of attraction in it— the iron safe fitted into the wall that separated the dressing-room from the bedroom.

It was a safe of the ordinary description, fitted with a strong iron door and Chubb lock. And across this door was written with chalk in characters that seemed defiant in their size and boldness, the words: "To be let, unfurnished."

Loveday spent about five minutes in front of this safe, all her attention concentrated upon the big, bold writing.

She took from her pocket-book a narrow strip of tracing-paper and compared the writing on it, letter by letter, with that on the safe door. This done she turned to Mrs. Williams and professed herself ready to follow her to the room below.

Mrs. Williams looked surprised. Her opinion of Miss Brooke's professional capabilities suffered considerable diminution.

"The gentlemen detectives," she said, "spent over an hour in this room; they paced the floor, they measured the candles, they—"

"Mrs. Williams," interrupted Loveday, "I am quite ready to look at the room below." Her manner had changed from gossiping friendliness to that of the business woman hard at work at her profession.

Without another word, Mrs. Williams led the way to the little room which had proved itself to be the "weak point" of the house.

They entered it by the door which opened into a passage leading to the back-stairs of the house. Loveday found the room exactly what it had been described to her by Mr. Dyer. It needed no second glance at the window to see the ease with which anyone could open it from the outside, and swing themselves into the room, when once the brass catch had been unfastened.

Loveday wasted no time here. In fact, much to Mrs. Williams's surprise and disappointment, she merely walked across the room, in at one door and out at the opposite one, which opened into the large inner hall of the house.

Here, however, she paused to ask a question:

"Is that chair always placed exactly in that position?" she said, pointing to an oak chair that stood immediately outside the room they had just quitted.

The housekeeper answered in the affirmative. It was a warm corner. "My lady" was particular that everyone who came to the house on messages should have a comfortable place to wait in.

"I shall be glad if you will show me to my room now," said Loveday, a little abruptly; "and will you kindly send up to me a county trade directory, if, that is, you have such a thing in the house?"

Mrs. Williams, with an air of offended dignity, led the way to the bedroom quarters once more. The worthy housekeeper felt as if her own dignity had, in some sort, been injured by the want of interest Miss Brooke had evinced in the rooms which, at the present moment, she considered the "show" rooms of the house.

"Shall I send someone to help you unpack?" she asked, a little stiffly, at the door of Loveday's room.

"No, thank you; there will not be much unpacking to do. I must leave here by the first up-train to-morrow morning."

"To-morrow morning! Why, I have told everyone you will be here at least a fortnight!"

"Ah, then you must explain that I have been suddenly summoned home by telegram. I'm sure I can trust you to make excuses for me. Do not, however, make them before supper-time. I shall like to sit down to that meal with you. I suppose I shall see Stephanie then?"

The housekeeper answered in the affirmative, and went her way, wondering over the strange manners of the lady whom, at first, she had been disposed to consider "such a nice, pleasant, conversable person!"

At supper-time, however, when the upper-servants assembled at what was, to them, the pleasantest meal of the day, a great surprise was to greet them.

Stephanie did not take her usual place at table, and a fellow-servant, sent to her room to summon her returned, saying that the room was empty, and Stephanie was nowhere to be found.

Loveday and Mrs. Williams together went to the girl's bedroom. It bore its usual appearance: no packing had been done in it, and, beyond her hat and jacket, the girl appeared to have taken nothing away with her.

On enquiry, it transpired that Stephanie had, as usual, assisted Lady Cathrow to dress for dinner; but after that not a soul in the house appeared to have seen her.

Mrs. Williams thought the matter of sufficient importance to be at once reported to her master and mistress; and Sir George, in his turn, promptly dispatched a messenger to Mr. Bates, at the "King's Head," to summon him to an immediate consultation.

Loveday dispatched a messenger in another direction—to young Mr. Holt, at his farm, giving him particulars of the girl's disappearance.

Mr. Bates had a brief interview with Sir George in his study, from which he emerged radiant. He made a point of seeing Loveday before he left the Court, sending a special request to her that she would speak to him for a minute in the outside drive.

Loveday put her hat on, and went out to him. She found him almost dancing for glee.

"Told you so! told you so! Now, didn't I, Miss Brooke?" he exclaimed. "We'll come upon her traces before morning, never fear. I'm quite prepared. I knew what was in her mind all along. I said to myself, when that girl bolts it will be after she has dressed my lady for dinner—when she has two good clear hours all to herself, and her absence from the house won't be noticed, and when, without much difficulty, she can catch a train leaving Huxwell for Wreford. Well, she'll get to Wreford safe enough; but from Wreford she'll be followed every step of the way she goes. Only yesterday I set a man on there—a keen fellow at this sort of thing—and gave him full directions; and he'll hunt her down to her hole properly. Taken nothing with her, do you say? What does that matter? She thinks she'll find all she wants where she's going—'the feathered nest' I spoke to you about this morning. Ha! ha! Well, instead of stepping into it, as she fancies she will, she'll walk straight into a detective's arms, and land her pal there into the bargain. There'll be two of them netted before another forty-eight hours are over our heads, or my name's not Jeremiah Bates."

"What are you going to do now?" asked Loveday, as the man finished his long speech.

"Now! I'm back to the 'King's Head' to wait for a telegram from my colleague at Wreford. Once he's got her in front of him he'll give me instructions at what point to meet him. You see, Huxwell being such an out-of-the-way place, and only one train leaving between 7.30 and 10.15, makes us really positive that Wreford must be the girl's destination and relieves my mind from all anxiety on the matter."

"Does it?" answered Loveday gravely. "I can see another possible destination for the girl—the stream that runs through the wood we drove past this morning. Good night, Mr. Bates, it's cold out here. Of course so soon as you have any news you'll send it up to Sir George."

The household sat up late that night, but no news was received of Stephanie from any quarter. Mr. Bates had impressed upon Sir

George the ill-advisability of setting up a hue and cry after the girl that might possibly reach her ears and scare her from joining the person whom he was pleased to designate as her "pal."

"We want to follow her silently, Sir George, silently as, the shadow follows the man," he had said grandiloquently, "and then we shall come upon the two, and I trust upon their booty also." Sir George in his turn had impressed Mr. Bates's wishes upon his household, and if it had not been for Loveday's message, dispatched early in the evening to young Holt, not a soul outside the house would have known of Stephanie's disappearance.

Loveday was stirring early the next morning, and the eight o'clock train for Wreford numbered her among its passengers. Before starting, she dispatched a telegram to her chief in Lynch Court. It read rather oddly, as follows:—

"Cracker fired. Am just starting for Wreford. Will wire to you from there. L. B."

Oddly though it might read, Mr. Dyer did not need to refer to his cipher book to interpret it. "Cracker fired" was the easily remembered equivalent for "clue found" in the detective phraseology of the office.

"Well, she has been quick enough about it this time!" he soliquised as he speculated in his own mind over what the purport of the next telegram might be.

Half an hour later there came to him a constable from Scotland Yard to tell him of Stephanie's disappearance and the conjectures that were rife on the matter, and he then, not unnaturally, read Loveday's telegram by the light of this information, and concluded that the clue in her hands related to the discovery of Stephanie's whereabouts as well as to that of her guilt.

A telegram received a little later on, however, was to turn this theory upside down. It was, like the former one, worded in the enigmatic language current in the Lynch Court establishment, but as it was a lengthier and more intricate message, it sent Mr. Dyer at once to his cipher book.

"Wonderful! She has cut them all out this time!" was Mr. Dyer's exclamation as he read and interpreted the final word.

In another ten minutes he had given over his office to the charge of his head clerk for the day, and was rattling along the streets in a hansom in the direction of Bishopsgate Station.

There he was lucky enough to catch a train just starting for Wreford.

"The event of the day," he muttered, as he settled himself comfortably in a corner seat, "will be the return journey when she tells me, bit by bit, how she has worked it all out."

It was not until close upon three o'clock in the afternoon that he arrived at the old-fashioned market town of Wreford. It chanced to be cattle-market day, and the station was crowded with drovers and farmers. Outside the station Loveday was waiting for him, as she had told him in her telegram that she would, in a four-wheeler.

"It's all right," she said to him as he got in; "he can't get away, even if he had an idea that we were after him. Two of the local police are waiting outside the house door with a warrant for his arrest, signed by a magistrate. I did not, however, see why the Lynch Court office should not have the credit of the thing, and so telegraphed to you to conduct the arrest."

They drove through the High Street to the outskirts of the town, where the shops became intermixed with private houses let out in offices. The cab pulled up outside one of these, and two policemen in plain clothes came forward, and touched their hats to Mr. Dyer.

"He's in there now, sir, doing his office work," said one of the men pointing to a door, just within the entrance, on which was printed in black letters, "The United Kingdom Cab-drivers' Beneficent Association." "I hear however, that this is the last time he will be found there, as a week ago he gave notice to leave."

As the man finished speaking, a man, evidently of the cab-driving fraternity, came up the steps. He stared curiously at the little group just within the entrance, and then chinking his money in his hand, passed on to the office as if to pay his subscription.

"Will you be good enough to tell Mr. Emmett in there," said Mr. Dyer, addressing the man, "that a gentleman outside wishes to speak with him."

The man nodded and passed into the office. As the door opened, it disclosed to view an old gentleman seated at a desk apparently writing receipts for money. A little in his rear at his right hand, sat a young and decidedly good-looking man, at a table on which were placed various little piles of silver and pence. The get-up of this young man was gentleman-like, and his manner was affable and pleasant as he responded, with a nod and a smile, to the cab-driver's message.

"I sha'n't be a minute," he said to his colleague at the other desk, as he rose and crossed the room towards the door.

But once outside that door it was closed firmly behind him, and he found himself in the centre of three stalwart individuals, one of whom informed him that he held in his hand a warrant for the arrest of Harry Emmett on the charge of complicity in the Craigen Court robbery, and that he had "better come along quietly, for resistance would be useless."

Emmett seemed convinced of the latter fact. He grew deadly white for a moment, then recovered himself.

"Will someone have the kindness to fetch my hat and coat," he said in a lofty manner. "I don't see why I should be made to catch my death of cold because some other people have seen fit to make asses of themselves."

His hat and coat were fetched, and he was handed into the cab between the two officials.

"Let me give you a word of warning, young man," said Mr. Dyer, closing the cab door and looking in for a moment through the window at Emmett. "I don't suppose it's a punishable offence to leave a black bag on an old maid's doorstep, but let me tell you, if it had not been for that black bag you might have got clean off with your spoil."

Emmett, the irrepressible, had his answer ready. He lifted his hat ironically to Mr. Dyer; "You might have put it more neatly, guv'nor," he said; "if I had been in your place I would have said: 'Young man, you are being justly punished for your misdeeds; you have been taking off your fellow-creatures all your life long, and now they are taking off you.'"

Mr. Dyer's duty that day did not end with the depositing of Harry Emmett in the local jail. The search through Emmett's lodgings and effects had to be made, and at this he was naturally present. About a third of the lost jewellery was found there, and from this it was consequently concluded that his accomplices in the crime had considered that he had borne a third of the risk and of the danger of it.

Letters and various memoranda discovered in the rooms, eventually led to the detection of those accomplices, and although Lady Cathrow was doomed to lose the greater part of her valuable property, she had ultimately the satisfaction of knowing that each one of the thieves received a sentence proportionate to his crime.

It was not until close upon midnight that Mr. Dyer found himself seated in the train, facing Miss Brooke, and had leisure to ask for the links in the chain of reasoning that had led her in so remarkable a manner to connect the finding of a black bag, with insignificant contents, with an extensive robbery of valuable jewellery.

Loveday explained the whole thing, easily, naturally, step by step in her usual methodical manner.

"I read," she said, "as I dare say a great many other people did, the account of the two things in the same newspaper, on the same day, and I detected, as I dare say a great many other people did not, a sense of fun in the principal actor in each incident. I notice while all people are agreed as to the variety of motives that instigate crime, very few allow sufficient margin for variety of character in the criminal. We are apt to imagine that he stalks about the world with a bundle of deadly motives under his arm, and cannot picture him at his work with a twinkle in his eye and a keen sense of fun, such as honest folk have sometimes when at work at their calling."

Here Mr. Dyer gave a little grunt; it might have been either of assent or dissent.

Loveday went on:

"Of course, the ludicrousness of the diction of the letter found in the bag would be apparent to the most casual reader; to me the high falutin sentences sounded in addition strangely familiar; I had heard or read them somewhere I felt sure, although where I could not at first remember. They rang in my ears, and it was not altogether out of idle curiosity that I went to Scotland Yard to see the bag and its contents, and to copy, with a slip of tracing paper, a line or two of the letter. When I found that the handwriting of this letter was not identical with that of the translations found in the bag, I was confirmed in my impression that the owner of the bag was not the writer of the letter; that possibly the bag and its contents had been appropriated from some railway station for some distinct purpose; and, that purpose accomplished, the appropriator no longer wished to be burthened with it, and disposed of it in the readiest fashion that suggested itself. The letter, it seemed to me, had been begun with the intention of throwing the police off the scent, but the irrepressible spirit of fun that had induced the writer to deposit his clerical adjuncts upon an old maid's doorstep had proved too strong for him here, and had carried him away, and the letter that was intended to be pathetic ended in being comic."

"Very ingenious, so far," murmured Mr. Dyer: "I've no doubt when the contents of the bag are widely made known through advertisements a claimant will come forward, and your theory be found correct."

"When I returned from Scotland Yard," Loveday continued, "I found your note, asking me to go round and see you respecting the big jewel robbery. Before I did so I thought it best to read once more the newspaper account of the case, so that I might be well up in its details. When I came to the words that the thief had written across the door of the safe, 'To be Let, Unfurnished,' they at once connected themselves in my mind with the 'dying kiss to my Marchioness Mother,' and the solemn warning against the race-course and the book-maker, of the black-bag letter-writer. Then, all in a flash, the whole thing became clear to me. Some two or three years back my professional duties necessitated my frequent attendance at certain low class penny-readings, given in the South London slums. At these penny-readings young shop-assistants, and others of their class, glad of an opportunity for exhibiting their accomplishments, declaim with great vigour; and, as a rule, select pieces which their very mixed audience might be supposed to appreciate. During my attendance at these meetings, it seemed to me that one book of selected readings was a great favourite among the reciters, and I took the trouble to buy it. Here it is."

Here Loveday took from her cloak-pocket *The Reciter's Treasury*, and handed it to her companion.

"Now," she said, "if you will run your eye down the index column you will find the titles of those pieces to which I wish to draw your attention. The first is 'The Suicide's Farewell;' the second, 'The Noble Convict;' the third, 'To be Let, Unfurnished.'"

"By Jove! so it is!" ejaculated Mr. Dyer.

"In the first of these pieces, 'The Suicide's Farewell,' occur the expressions with which the black-bag letter begins—'The fatal day has arrived,' etc., the warnings against gambling, and the allusions to the 'poor lifeless body.' In the second, 'The Noble Convict,' occur the allusions to the aristocratic relations and the dying kiss to the marchioness mother. The third piece, 'To be Let, Unfurnished,' is a foolish little poem enough, although I dare say it has often raised a laugh in a not too-discriminating audience. It tells how a bachelor, calling at a house to enquire after rooms to be let unfurnished, falls in love with the daughter of the house, and offers her his heart, which, he says, is to be let unfurnished. She declines his offer, and retorts that she thinks his head must be to let unfurnished, too. With these three pieces before me, it was not difficult to see a thread of connection between the writer of the black-bag letter and the thief who wrote across the empty safe at Craigen Court. Following this thread, I unearthed the story of Harry Emmett—footman, reciter, general lover and scamp. Subsequently I compared the writing on my tracing paper with that on the safe-door, and, allowing for the difference between a bit of chalk and a steel nib, came to the conclusion that there could be but little doubt but what both were written by the same hand. Before that, however, I had obtained another, and what I consider the most important, link in my chain of evidence—how Emmett brought his clerical dress into use."

"Ah, how did you find out that now?" asked Mr. Dyer, leaning forward with his elbows on his knees.

"In the course of conversation with Mrs. Williams, whom I found to be a most communicative person, I elicited the names of the guests who had sat down to dinner on Christmas Eve. They were all people of undoubted respectability in the neighbourhood. Just before dinner was announced, she said, a young clergyman had presented himself at the front door, asking to speak with the Rector of the parish. The Rector, it seems, always dines at Craigen Court on Christmas Eve. The young clergyman's story was that he had been told by a certain clergyman, whose name he mentioned, that a curate was wanted in the parish, and he had traveled down from London to offer his services. He had been, he said, to the Rectory and had been told by the servants where the Rector was dining, and fearing to lose his chance of the curacy, had followed him to the Court. Now the Rector had been wanting a curate and had filled the vacancy only the previous week; he was a little inclined to be irate at this interruption to the evening's festivities, and told the young man that he didn't want a curate. When, however, he saw how disappointed the poor young fellow looked—I believe he shed a tear or two—his heart softened; he told him to sit down and rest in the hall before he attempted the walk back to the station, and said he would ask Sir George to send him out a glass of wine. The young man sat down in a chair immediately outside the room by which the thieves entered. Now I need not tell you who that young man was, nor suggest to your mind, I am sure, the idea that while the servant went to fetch him his wine, or, indeed, so soon as he saw the coast clear, he slipped into that little room and pulled back the catch of the window that admitted his confederates, who, no doubt, at that very moment were in hiding in the grounds. The housekeeper did not know whether this meek young curate had a black bag with him. Personally I have no doubt of the fact, nor that it contained the cap, cuffs, collar, and outer garments

of Harry Emmett, which were most likely redonned before he returned to his lodgings at Wreford, where I should say he repacked
the bag with its clerical contents, and wrote his serio-comic letter.
This bag, I suppose, he must have deposited in the very early morning, before anyone was stirring, on the door-step of the house in
the Easterbrook Road."

Mr. Dyer drew a long breath. In his heart was unmitigated admiration for his colleague's skill, which seemed to him to fall little
short of inspiration. By-and-by, no doubt, he would sing her praises
to the first person who came along with a hearty good will; he had
not, however, the slightest intention of so singing them in her own
ears—excessive praise was apt to have a bad effect on the rising
practitioner.

So he contented himself with saying:

"Yes, very satisfactory. Now tell me how you hunted the fellow
down to his diggings?"

"Oh, that was mere ABC work," answered Loveday. "Mrs. Williams told me he had left his place at Colonel James's about six
months previously, and had told her he was going to look after his
dear old grandmother, who kept a sweet stuff-shop; but where she
could not remember. Having heard that Emmett's father was a cab-
driver, my thoughts at once flew to the cabman's vernacular—you
know something of it, no doubt—in which their provident association is designated by the phase, 'the dear old grandmother,' and
the office where they make and receive their payments is styled
'the sweet stuff-shop.'"

"Ha, ha, ha! And good Mrs. Williams took it all literally, no
doubt?"

"She did; and thought what a dear, kind-hearted fellow the
young man was. Naturally I supposed there would be a branch
of the association in the nearest market town, and a local trades'
directory confirmed my supposition that there was one at Wreford.
Bearing in mind where the black bag was found, it was not difficult to believe that young Emmett, possibly through his father's
influence and his own prepossessing manners and appearance, had
attained to some position of trust in the Wreford branch. I must

confess I scarcely expected to find him as I did, on reaching the place, installed as receiver of the weekly moneys. Of course, I immediately put myself in communication with the police there, and the rest I think you know."

Mr. Dyer's enthusiasm refused to be longer restrained.

"It's capital, from first to last," he cried; "you've surpassed yourself this time!"

"The only thing that saddens me," said Loveday, "is the thought of the possible fate of that poor little Stephanie."

Loveday's anxieties on Stephanie's behalf were, however, to be put to flight before another twenty-four hours had passed. The first post on the following morning brought a letter from Mrs. Williams telling how the girl had been found before the night was over, half dead with cold and fright, on the verge of the stream running through Craigen Wood—"found too"—wrote the housekeeper, "by the very person who ought to have found her, young Holt, who was, and is so desperately in love with her. Thank goodness! at the last moment her courage failed her, and instead of throwing herself into the stream, she sank down, half-fainting, beside it. Holt took her straight home to his mother, and there, at the farm, she is now, being taken care of and petted generally by everyone."

THE MURDER AT TROYTE'S HILL

"Griffiths, of the Newcastle Constabulary, has the case in hand," said Mr. Dyer; "those Newcastle men are keen-witted, shrewd fellows, and very jealous of outside interference. They only sent to me under protest, as it were, because they wanted your sharp wits at work inside the house."

"I suppose throughout I am to work with Griffiths, not with you?" said Miss Brooke.

"Yes; when I have given you in outline the facts of the case, I simply have nothing more to do with it, and you must depend on Griffiths for any assistance of any sort that you may require."

Here, with a swing, Mr. Dyer opened his big ledger and turned rapidly over its leaves till he came to the heading "Troyte's Hill" and the date "September 6th."

"I'm all attention," said Loveday, leaning back in her chair in the attitude of a listener.

"The murdered man," resumed Mr. Dyer, "is a certain Alexander Henderson—usually known as old Sandy—lodge-keeper to Mr. Craven, of Troyte's Hill, Cumberland. The lodge consists merely of two rooms on the ground floor, a bedroom and a sitting-room; these Sandy occupied alone, having neither kith nor kin of any degree. On the morning of September 6th, some children going up to the house with milk from the farm, noticed that Sandy's bed-room window stood wide open. Curiosity prompted them to peep in; and then, to their horror, they saw old Sandy, in his night-shirt, lying dead on the floor, as if he had fallen backwards from the window. They raised an alarm; and on examination, it was found that death had ensued from a heavy blow on the temple, given either by a strong fist or some blunt instrument. The room, on being entered, presented a curious appearance. It was as if a herd of monkeys had been turned into it and allowed to work their impish will. Not an article of furniture remained in its place: the bed-clothes had been rolled into a bundle and stuffed into the chimney; the bed-stead—a small iron one—lay on its side; the one chair in the room stood on the top of the table; fender and fire-irons lay across the washstand, whose basin was to be found in a farther corner, hold-ing bolster and pillow. The clock stood on its head in the middle of the mantelpiece; and the small vases and ornaments, which flanked it on either side, were walking, as it were, in a straight line to-wards the door. The old man's clothes had been rolled into a ball and thrown on the top of a high cupboard in which he kept his savings and whatever valuables he had. This cupboard, however, had not been meddled with, and its contents remained intact, so it was evident that robbery was not the motive for the crime. At the inquest, subsequently held, a verdict of 'willful murder' against some person or persons unknown was returned. The local police are diligently investigating the affair, but, as yet, no arrests have been made. The opinion that at present prevails in the neigh-bourhood is that the crime has been perpetrated by some lunatic, escaped or otherwise, and enquiries are being made at the local asylums as to missing or lately released inmates. Griffiths, how-ever, tells me that his suspicions set in another direction."

"Did anything of importance transpire at the inquest?"

"Nothing specially important. Mr. Craven broke down in giving his evidence when he alluded to the confidential relations that had always subsisted between Sandy and himself, and spoke of the last time that he had seen him alive. The evidence of the butler, and one or two of the female servants, seems clear enough, and they let fall something of a hint that Sandy was not altogether a favourite among them, on account of the overbearing manner in which he used his influence with his master. Young Mr. Craven, a youth of about nineteen, home from Oxford for the long vacation, was not present at the inquest; a doctor's certificate was put in stating that he was suffering from typhoid fever, and could not leave his bed without risk to his life. Now this young man is a thoroughly bad sort, and as much a gentleman-blackleg as it is possible for such a young fellow to be. It seems to Griffiths that there is something suspicious about this illness of his. He came back from Oxford on the verge of delirium tremens, pulled round from that, and then suddenly, on the day after the murder, Mrs. Craven rings the bell, announces that he has developed typhoid fever and orders a doctor to be sent for."

"What sort of man is Mr. Craven senior?"

"He seems to be a quiet old fellow, a scholar and learned philologist. Neither his neighbours nor his family see much of him; he almost lives in his study, writing a treatise, in seven or eight volumes, on comparative philology. He is not a rich man. Troyte's Hill, though it carries position in the county, is not a paying property, and Mr. Craven is unable to keep it up properly. I am told he has had to cut down expenses in all directions in order to send his son to college, and his daughter from first to last has been entirely educated by her mother. Mr. Craven was originally intended for the church, but for some reason or other, when his college career came to an end, he did not present himself for ordination—went out to Natal instead, where he obtained some civil appointment and where he remained for about fifteen years. Henderson was his servant during the latter portion of his Oxford career, and must have been greatly respected by him, for although the remuneration derived from his appointment at Natal was small, he paid Sandy a regular yearly allowance out of it. When, about ten years ago, he succeeded to Troyte's Hill, on the death of his elder brother, and returned home with his family, Sandy was immediately installed as lodge-keeper, and at so high a rate of pay that the butler's wages were cut down to meet it."

"Ah, that wouldn't improve the butler's feelings towards him," ejaculated Loveday.

Mr. Dyer went on: "But, in spite of his high wages, he doesn't appear to have troubled much about his duties as lodge-keeper, for they were performed, as a rule, by the gardener's boy, while he took his meals and passed his time at the house, and, speaking generally, put his finger into every pie. You know the old adage respecting the servant of twenty-one years' standing: 'Seven years my servant, seven years my equal, seven years my master.' Well, it appears to have held good in the case of Mr. Craven and Sandy. The old gentleman, absorbed in his philological studies, evidently let the reins slip through his fingers, and Sandy seems to have taken easy possession of them. The servants frequently had to go to him for orders, and he carried things, as a rule, with a high hand."

"Did Mrs. Craven never have a word to say on the matter?"

"I've not heard much about her. She seems to be a quiet sort of person. She is a Scotch missionary's daughter; perhaps she spends her time working for the Cape mission and that sort of thing."

"And young Mr. Craven: did he knock under to Sandy's rule?"

"Ah, now you're hitting the bull's eye and we come to Griffiths' theory. The young man and Sandy appear to have been at loggerheads ever since the Cravens took possession of Troyte's Hill. As a schoolboy Master Harry defied Sandy and threatened him with his hunting-crop; and subsequently, as a young man, has used strenuous endeavours to put the old servant in his place. On the day before the murder, Griffiths says, there was a terrible scene between the two, in which the young gentleman, in the presence of several witnesses, made use of strong language and threatened the old man's life. Now, Miss Brooke, I have told you all the circumstances of the case so far as I know them. For fuller particulars I must refer you to Griffiths. He, no doubt, will meet you at Grenfell—the nearest station to Troyte's Hill, and tell you in what capacity he has procured for you an entrance into the house. By-the-way, he has wired to me this morning that he hopes you will be able to save the Scotch express to-night."

Loveday expressed her readiness to comply with Mr. Griffiths' wishes.

"I shall be glad," said Mr. Dyer, as he shook hands with her at the office door, "to see you immediately on your return—that, however, I suppose, will not be yet awhile. This promises, I fancy, to be a longish affair?" This was said interrogatively.

"I haven't the least idea on the matter," answered Loveday. "I start on my work without theory of any sort—in fact, I may say, with my mind a perfect blank."

And anyone who had caught a glimpse of her blank, expressionless features, as she said this, would have taken her at her word.

Grenfell, the nearest post-town to Troyte's Hill, is a fairly busy, populous little town—looking south towards the black country, and northwards to low, barren hills. Pre-eminent among these stands Troyte's Hill, famed in the old days as a border keep, and possibly at a still earlier date as a Druid stronghold.

At a small inn at Grenfell, dignified by the title of "The Station Hotel," Mr. Griffiths, of the Newcastle constabulary, met Loveday and still further initiated her into the mysteries of the Troyte's Hill murder.

"A little of the first excitement has subsided," he said, after preliminary greetings had been exchanged; "but still the wildest rumours are flying about and repeated as solemnly as if they were Gospel truths. My chief here and my colleagues generally adhere to their first conviction, that the criminal is some suddenly crazed tramp or else an escaped lunatic, and they are confident that sooner or later we shall come upon his traces. Their theory is that Sandy, hearing some strange noise at the Park Gates, put his head out of the window to ascertain the cause and immediately had his death blow dealt him; then they suppose that the lunatic scrambled into the room through the window and exhausted his frenzy by turning things generally upside down. They refuse altogether to share my suspicions respecting young Mr. Craven."

Mr. Griffiths was a tall, thin-featured man, with iron-grey hair, but so close to his head that it refused to do anything but stand on end. This gave a somewhat comic expression to the upper portion of his face and clashed oddly with the melancholy look that his mouth habitually wore.

"I have made all smooth for you at Troyte's Hill," he presently went on. "Mr. Craven is not wealthy enough to allow himself the luxury of a family lawyer, so he occasionally employs the services of Messrs. Wells and Sugden, lawyers in this place, and who, as it happens, have, off and on, done a good deal of business for me. It was through them I heard that Mr. Craven was anxious to secure the assistance of an amanuensis. I immediately offered your services, stating that you were a friend of mine, a lady of impoverished means, who would gladly undertake the duties for the munificent sum of a guinea a month, with board and lodging. The old gentleman at once jumped at the offer, and is anxious for you to be at Troyte's Hill at once."

Loveday expressed her satisfaction with the programme that Mr. Griffiths had sketched for her, then she had a few questions to ask.

"Tell me," she said, "what led you, in the first instance, to suspect young Mr. Craven of the crime?"

"The footing on which he and Sandy stood towards each other, and the terrible scene that occurred between them only the day before the murder," answered Griffiths, promptly. "Nothing of this, however, was elicited at the inquest, where a very fair face was put on Sandy's relations with the whole of the Craven family. I have subsequently unearthed a good deal respecting the private life of Mr. Harry Craven, and, among other things, I have found out that on the night of the murder he left the house shortly after ten o'clock, and no one, so far as I have been able to ascertain, knows at what hour he returned. Now I must draw your attention, Miss Brooke, to the fact that at the inquest the medical evidence went to prove that the murder had been committed between ten and eleven at night."

"Do you surmise, then, that the murder was a planned thing on the part of this young man?"

"I do. I believe that he wandered about the grounds until Sandy shut himself in for the night, then aroused him by some outside noise, and, when the old man looked out to ascertain the cause, dealt him a blow with a bludgeon or loaded stick, that caused his death."

"A cold-blooded crime that, for a boy of nineteen?"

"Yes. He's a good-looking, gentlemanly youngster, too, with manners as mild as milk, but from all accounts is as full of wickedness as an egg is full of meat. Now, to come to another point—if, in connection with these ugly facts, you take into consideration the suddenness of his illness, I think you'll admit that it bears a suspicious appearance and might reasonably give rise to the surmise that it was a plant on his part, in order to get out of the inquest."

"Who is the doctor attending him?"

"A man called Waters; not much of a practitioner, from all accounts, and no doubt he feels himself highly honoured in being summoned to Troyte's Hill. The Cravens, it seems, have no family doctor. Mrs. Craven, with her missionary experience, is half a doctor herself, and never calls in one except in a serious emergency."

"The certificate was in order, I suppose?"

"Undoubtedly. And, as if to give colour to the gravity of the case, Mrs. Craven sent a message down to the servants, that if any of them were afraid of the infection they could at once go to their homes. Several of the maids, I believe, took advantage of her permission, and packed their boxes. Miss Craven, who is a delicate girl, was sent away with her maid to stay with friends at Newcastle, and Mrs. Craven isolated herself with her patient in one of the disused wings of the house."

"Has anyone ascertained whether Miss Craven arrived at her destination at Newcastle?"

Griffiths drew his brows together in thought.

"I did not see any necessity for such a thing," he answered. "I don't quite follow you. What do you mean to imply?"

"Oh, nothing. I don't suppose it matters much: it might have been interesting as a side-issue." She broke off for a moment, then added:

"Now tell me a little about the butler, the man whose wages were cut down to increase Sandy's pay."

"Old John Hales? He's a thoroughly worthy, respectable man; he was butler for five or six years to Mr. Craven's brother, when he was master of Troyte's Hill, and then took duty under this Mr.

Craven. There's no ground for suspicion in that quarter. Hales's exclamation when he heard of the murder is quite enough to stamp him as an innocent man: 'Serve the old idiot right,' he cried: 'I couldn't pump up a tear for him if I tried for a month of Sundays!' Now I take it, Miss Brooke, a guilty man wouldn't dare make such a speech as that!"

"You think not?"

Griffiths stared at her. "I'm a little disappointed in her," he thought. "I'm afraid her powers have been slightly exaggerated if she can't see such a straight-forward thing as that."

Aloud he said, a little sharply, "Well, I don't stand alone in my thinking. No one yet has breathed a word against Hales, and if they did, I've no doubt he could prove an *alibi* without any trouble, for he lives in the house, and everyone has a good word for him."

"I suppose Sandy's lodge has been put into order by this time?"

"Yes; after the inquest, and when all possible evidence had been taken, everything was put straight."

"At the inquest it was stated that no marks of footsteps could be traced in any direction?"

"The long drought we've had would render such a thing impossible, let alone the fact that Sandy's lodge stands right on the graveled drive, without flower-beds or grass borders of any sort around it. But look here, Miss Brooke, don't you be wasting your time over the lodge and its surroundings. Every iota of fact on that matter has been gone through over and over again by me and my chief. What we want you to do is to go straight into the house and concentrate attention on Master Harry's sick-room, and find out what's going on there. What he did outside the house on the night of the 6th, I've no doubt I shall be able to find out for myself. Now, Miss Brooke, you've asked me no end of questions, to which I have replied as fully as it was in my power to do; will you be good enough to answer one question that I wish to put, as straightforwardly as I have answered yours? You have had fullest particulars given you of the condition of Sandy's room when the police entered it on the morning after the murder. No doubt, at the present moment, you can see it all in your mind's eye—the bedstead on its side, the clock on its head, the bed-clothes half-way up the chimney, the little vases and ornaments walking in a straight line towards the door?"

Loveday bowed her head.

"Very well, Now will you be good enough to tell me what this scene of confusion recalls to your mind before anything else?"

"The room of an unpopular Oxford freshman after a raid upon it by undergrads," answered Loveday promptly.

Mr. Griffiths rubbed his hands.

"Quite so!" he ejaculated. "I see, after all, we are one at heart in this matter, in spite of a little surface disagreement of ideas. Depend upon it, by-and-bye, like the engineers tunneling from different quarters under the Alps, we shall meet at the same point and shake hands. By-the-way, I have arranged for daily communication between us through the postboy who takes the letters to Troyte's Hill. He is trustworthy, and any letter you give him for me will find its way into my hands within the hour."

It was about three o'clock in the afternoon when Loveday drove in through the park gates of Troyte's Hill, past the lodge where old Sandy had met with his death. It was a pretty little cottage, covered with Virginia creeper and wild honeysuckle, and showing no outward sign of the tragedy that had been enacted within.

The park and pleasure-grounds of Troyte's Hill were extensive, and the house itself was a somewhat imposing red brick structure, built, possibly, at the time when Dutch William's taste had grown popular in the country. Its frontage presented a somewhat forlorn appearance, its centre windows—a square of eight—alone seeming to show signs of occupation. With the exception of two windows at the extreme end of the bedroom floor of the north wing, where, possibly, the invalid and his mother were located, and two windows at the extreme end of the ground floor of the south wing, which Loveday ascertained subsequently were those of Mr. Craven's study, not a single window in either wing owned blind or curtain. The wings were extensive, and it was easy to understand that at the extreme end of the one the fever patient would be isolated from the rest of the household, and that at the extreme end of the other Mr. Craven could secure the quiet and freedom from interruption which, no doubt, were essential to the due prosecution of his philological studies.

Alike on the house and ill-kept grounds were present the stamp of the smallness of the income of the master and owner of the place. The terrace, which ran the length of the house in front, and on to which every window on the ground floor opened, was miserably out of repair: not a lintel or door-post, window-ledge or balcony but what seemed to cry aloud for the touch of the painter. "Pity me! I have seen better days," Loveday could fancy written as a legend across the red-brick porch that gave entrance to the old house.

The butler, John Hales, admitted Loveday, shouldered her portmanteau and told her he would show her to her room. He was a tall, powerfully-built man, with a ruddy face and dogged expression of countenance. It was easy to understand that, off and on, there must have been many a sharp encounter between him and old Sandy. He treated Loveday in an easy, familiar fashion, evidently considering that an amanuensis took much the same rank as a nursery governess—that is to say, a little below a lady's maid and a little above a house-maid.

"We're short of hands, just now," he said, in broad Cumberland dialect, as he led the way up the wide staircase. "Some of the lasses downstairs took fright at the fever and went home. Cook and I are single-handed, for Moggie, the only maid left, has been told off to wait on Madam and Master Harry. I hope you're not afeared of fever?"

Loveday explained that she was not, and asked if the room at the extreme end of the north wing was the one assigned to "Madam and Master Harry."

"Yes," said the man; "it's convenient for sick nursing; there's a flight of stairs runs straight down from it to the kitchen quarters. We put all Madam wants at the foot of those stairs and Moggie herself never enters the sick-room. I take it you'll not be seeing Madam for many a day, yet awhile."

"When shall I see Mr. Craven? At dinner to-night?"

"That's what naebody could say," answered Hales. "He may not come out of his study till past midnight; sometimes he sits there

till two or three in the morning. Shouldn't advise you to wait till
he wants his dinner—better have a cup of tea and a chop sent up to
you. Madam never waits for him at any meal."

As he finished speaking he deposited the portmanteau outside
one of the many doors opening into the gallery.

"This is Miss Craven's room," he went on; "cook and me thought
you'd better have it, as it would want less getting ready than the
other rooms, and work is work when there are so few hands to do
it. Oh, my stars! I do declare there is cook putting it straight for
you now." The last sentence was added as the opened door laid
bare to view, the cook, with a duster in her hand, polishing a mirror; the bed had been made, it is true, but otherwise the room must
have been much as Miss Craven left it, after a hurried packing up.

To the surprise of the two servants Loveday took the matter
very lightly.

"I have a special talent for arranging rooms and would prefer
getting this one straight for myself," she said. "Now, if you will go
and get ready that chop and cup of tea we were talking about just
now, I shall think it much kinder than if you stayed here doing
what I can so easily do for myself."

When, however, the cook and butler had departed in company,
Loveday showed no disposition to exercise the "special talent" of
which she had boasted.

She first carefully turned the key in the lock and then proceeded
to make a thorough and minute investigation of every corner of
the room. Not an article of furniture, not an ornament or toilet
accessory, but what was lifted from its place and carefully scrutinized. Even the ashes in the grate, the debris of the last fire made
there, were raked over and well looked through.

This careful investigation of Miss Craven's late surroundings
occupied in all about three quarters of an hour, and Loveday, with
her hat in her hand, descended the stairs to see Hales crossing the
hall to the dining-room with the promised cup of tea and chop.

In silence and solitude she partook of the simple repast in a
dining-hall that could with ease have banqueted a hundred and
fifty guests.

"Now for the grounds before it gets dark," she said to herself, as she noted that already the outside shadows were beginning to slant.

The dining-hall was at the back of the house; and here, as in the front, the windows, reaching to the ground, presented easy means of egress. The flower-garden was on this side of the house and sloped downhill to a pretty stretch of well-wooded country.

Loveday did not linger here even to admire, but passed at once round the south corner of the house to the windows which she had ascertained, by a careless question to the butler, were those of Mr. Craven's study.

Very cautiously she drew near them, for the blinds were up, the curtains drawn back. A side glance, however, relieved her apprehensions, for it showed her the occupant of the room, seated in an easy-chair, with his back to the windows. From the length of his outstretched limbs he was evidently a tall man. His hair was silvery and curly, the lower part of his face was hidden from her view by the chair, but she could see one hand was pressed tightly across his eyes and brows. The whole attitude was that of a man absorbed in deep thought. The room was comfortably furnished, but presented an appearance of disorder from the books and manuscripts scattered in all directions. A whole pile of torn fragments of foolscap sheets, overflowing from a waste-paper basket beside the writing-table, seemed to proclaim the fact that the scholar had of late grown weary of, or else dissatisfied with his work, and had condemned it freely.

Although Loveday stood looking in at this window for over five minutes, not the faintest sign of life did that tall, reclining figure give, and it would have been as easy to believe him locked in sleep as in thought.

From here she turned her steps in the direction of Sandy's lodge. As Griffiths had said, it was graveled up to its doorstep. The blinds were closely drawn, and it presented the ordinary appearance of a disused cottage.

A narrow path beneath over-arching boughs of cherry-laurel and arbutus, immediately facing the lodge, caught her eye, and down this she at once turned her footsteps.

This path led, with many a wind and turn, through a belt of shrubbery that skirted the frontage of Mr. Craven's grounds, and eventually, after much zig-zagging, ended in close proximity to the stables. As Loveday entered it, she seemed literally to leave day-light behind her.

"I feel as if I were following the course of a circuitous mind," she said to herself as the shadows closed around her. "I could not fancy Sir Isaac Newton or Bacon planning or delighting in such a wind-about-alley as this!"

The path showed greyly in front of her out of the dimness. On and on she followed it; here and there the roots of the old laurels, struggling out of the ground, threatened to trip her up. Her eyes, however, had now grown accustomed to the half-gloom, and not a detail of her surroundings escaped her as she went along.

A bird flew from out the thicket on her right hand with a startled cry. A dainty little frog leaped out of her way into the shriveled leaves lying below the laurels. Following the movements of this frog, her eye was caught by something black and solid among those leaves. What was it? A bundle—a shiny black coat? Loveday knelt down, and using her hands to assist her eyes, found that they came into contact with the dead, stiffened body of a beautiful black re-triever. She parted, as well as she was able, the lower boughs of the evergreens, and minutely examined the poor animal. Its eyes were still open, though glazed and bleared, and its death had, un-doubtedly, been caused by the blow of some blunt, heavy instru-ment, for on one side its skull was almost battered in.

"Exactly the death that was dealt to Sandy," she thought, as she groped hither and thither beneath the trees in hopes of light-ing upon the weapon of destruction.

She searched until increasing darkness warned her that search was useless. Then, still following the zig-zagging path, she made her way out by the stables and thence back to the house.

She went to bed that night without having spoken to a soul be-yond the cook and butler. The next morning, however, Mr. Craven introduced himself to her across the breakfast-table. He was a man of really handsome personal appearance, with a fine carriage of the head and shoulders, and eyes that had a forlorn, appealing look in them. He entered the room with an air of great energy, apologized to Loveday for the absence of his wife, and for his own remissness in not being in the way to receive her on the previous day. Then he bade her make herself at home at the breakfast-table, and expressed his delight in having found a coadjutor in his work.

"I hope you understand what a great—a stupendous work it is?" he added, as he sank into a chair. "It is a work that will leave its impress upon thought in all the ages to come. Only a man who has studied comparative philology as I have for the past thirty years, could gauge the magnitude of the task I have set myself."

With the last remark, his energy seemed spent, and he sank back in his chair, covering his eyes with his hand in precisely the same attitude as that in which Loveday had seen him over-night, and utterly oblivious of the fact that breakfast was before him and a stranger-guest seated at table. The butler entered with another dish. "Better go on with your breakfast," he whispered to Loveday, "he may sit like that for another hour."

He placed his dish in front of his master.

"Captain hasn't come back yet, sir," he said, making an effort to arouse him from his reverie.

"Eh, what?" said Mr. Craven, for a moment lifting his hand from his eyes.

"Captain, sir—the black retriever," repeated the man.

The pathetic look in Mr. Craven's eyes deepened.

"Ah, poor Captain!" he murmured; "the best dog I ever had."

Then he again sank back in his chair, putting his hand to his forehead.

The butler made one more effort to arouse him.

"Madam sent you down a newspaper, sir, that she thought you would like to see," he shouted almost into his master's ear, and at the same time laid the morning's paper on the table beside his plate.

"Confound you! leave it there," said Mr. Craven irritably. "Fools! dolts that you all are! With your trivialities and interruptions you are sending me out of the world with my work undone!"

And again he sank back in his chair, closed his eyes and became lost to his surroundings.

Loveday went on with her breakfast. She changed her place at table to one on Mr. Craven's right hand, so that the newspaper sent down for his perusal lay between his plate and hers. It was folded into an oblong shape, as if it were wished to direct attention to a certain portion of a certain column.

A clock in a corner of the room struck the hour with a loud, resonant stroke. Mr. Craven gave a start and rubbed his eyes.

"Eh, what's this?" he said. "What meal are we at?" He looked around with a bewildered air. "Eh!—who are you?" he went on, staring hard at Loveday. "What are you doing here? Where's Nina?—Where's Harry?"

Loveday began to explain, and gradually recollection seemed to come back to him.

"Ah, yes, yes," he said. "I remember; you've come to assist me with my great work. You promised, you know, to help me out of the hole I've got into. Very enthusiastic, I remember they said you were, on certain abstruse points in comparative philology. Now, Miss—Miss—I've forgotten your name—tell me a little of what you know about the elemental sounds of speech that are common to all languages. Now, to how many would you reduce those elemental sounds—to six, eight, nine? No, we won't discuss the matter here, the cups and saucers distract me. Come into my den at the other end of the house; we'll have perfect quiet there."

And utterly ignoring the fact that he had not as yet broken his fast, he rose from the table, seized Loveday by the wrist, and led her out of the room and down the long corridor that led through the south wing to his study.

But seated in that study his energy once more speedily exhausted itself.

He placed Loveday in a comfortable chair at his writing-table, consulted her taste as to pens, and spread a sheet of foolscap before her. Then he settled himself in his easy-chair, with his back to the light, as if he were about to dictate folios to her.

In a loud, distinct voice he repeated the title of his learned work, then its sub-division, then the number and heading of the chapter that was at present engaging his attention. Then he put his hand to his head. "It's the elemental sounds that are my stumbling-block," he said. "Now, how on earth is it possible to get a notion of a sound of agony that is not in part a sound of terror? or a sound of surprise that is not in part a sound of either joy or sorrow?"

With this his energies were spent, and although Loveday remained seated in that study from early morning till daylight began to fade, she had not ten sentences to show for her day's work as amanuensis.

Loveday in all spent only two clear days at Troyte's Hill.

On the evening of the first of those days Detective Griffiths received, through the trustworthy post-boy, the following brief note from her:

> "I have found out that Hales owed Sandy close
> upon a hundred pounds, which he had borrowed at
> various times. I don't know whether you will think
> this fact of any importance.—L. B."

Mr. Griffiths repeated the last sentence blankly. "If Harry Craven were put upon his defence, his counsel, I take it, would consider the fact of first importance," he muttered. And for the remainder of that day Mr. Griffiths went about his work in a perturbed state of mind, doubtful whether to hold or to let go his theory concerning Harry Craven's guilt.

The next morning there came another brief note from Loveday which ran thus:

> "As a matter of collateral interest, find out if a
> person, calling himself Harold Cousins, sailed two
> days ago from London Docks for Natal in the *Bonnie
> Dundee?*"

To this missive Loveday received, in reply, the following somewhat lengthy dispatch:

"I do not quite see the drift of your last note, but have wired to our agents in London to carry out its suggestion. On my part, I have important news to communicate. I have found out what Harry Craven's business out of doors was on the night of the murder, and at my instance a warrant has been issued for his arrest. This warrant it will be my duty to serve on him in the course of to-day. Things are beginning to look very black against him, and I am convinced his illness is all a sham. I have seen Waters, the man who is supposed to be attending him, and have driven him into a corner and made him admit that he has only seen young Craven once—on the first day of his illness—and that he gave his certificate entirely on the strength of what Mrs. Craven told him of her son's condition. On the occasion of this, his first and only visit, the lady, it seems, also told him that it would not be necessary for him to continue his attendance, as she quite felt herself competent to treat the case, having had so much experience in fever cases among the blacks at Natal.

"As I left Waters's house, after eliciting this important information, I was accosted by a man who keeps a low-class inn in the place, McQueen by name. He said that he wished to speak to me on a matter of importance. To make a long story short, this McQueen stated that on the night of the sixth, shortly after eleven o'clock, Harry Craven came to his house, bringing with him a valuable piece of plate—a handsome epergne—and requested him to lend him a hundred pounds on it, as he hadn't a penny in his pocket. McQueen complied with his request to the extent of ten sovereigns, and now, in

a fit of nervous terror, comes to me to confess himself a receiver of stolen goods and play the honest
man! He says he noticed that the young gentleman
was very much agitated as he made the request, and
he also begged him to mention his visit to no one.
Now, I am curious to learn how Master Harry will
get over the fact that he passed the lodge at the hour
at which the murder was most probably committed;
or how he will get out of the dilemma of having re-
passed the lodge on his way back to the house, and
not noticed the wide-open window with the full
moon shining down on it?

"Another word! Keep out of the way when I arrive at the house, somewhere between two and three
in the afternoon, to serve the warrant. I do not wish
your professional capacity to get wind, for you will
most likely yet be of some use to us in the house.

"S.G."

Loveday read this note, seated at Mr. Craven's writing-table,
with the old gentleman himself reclining motionless beside her in
his easy-chair. A little smile played about the corners of her mouth
as she read over again the words—"for you will most likely yet be
of some use to us in the house."

Loveday's second day in Mr. Craven's study promised to be as
unfruitful as the first. For fully an hour after she had received
Griffiths' note, she sat at the writing-table with her pen in her hand,
ready to transcribe Mr. Craven's inspirations. Beyond, however,
the phrase, muttered with closed eyes—"It's all here, in my brain,
but I can't put it into words"—not a half-syllable escaped his lips.

At the end of that hour the sound of footsteps on the outside
gravel made her turn her head towards the window. It was Griffiths
approaching with two constables. She heard the hall door opened
to admit them, but, beyond that, not a sound reached her ear, and
she realized how fully she was cut off from communication with
the rest of the household at the farther end of this unoccupied wing.

Mr. Craven, still reclining in his semi-trance, evidently had not the faintest suspicion that so important an event as the arrest of his only son on a charge of murder was about to be enacted in the house.

Meantime, Griffiths and his constables had mounted the stairs leading to the north wing, and were being guided through the corridors to the sick-room by the flying figure of Moggie, the maid.

"Hoot, mistress!" cried the girl, "here are three men coming up the stairs—policemen, every one of them—will ye come and ask them what they be wanting?"

Outside the door of the sick-room stood Mrs. Craven—a tall, sharp-featured woman with sandy hair going rapidly grey.

"What is the meaning of this? What is your business here?" she said haughtily, addressing Griffiths, who headed the party.

Griffiths respectfully explained what his business was, and requested her to stand on one side that he might enter her son's room.

"This is my daughter's room; satisfy yourself of the fact," said the lady, throwing back the door as she spoke.

And Griffiths and his confrères entered, to find pretty Miss Craven, looking very white and scared, seated beside a fire in a long flowing *robe de chambre*.

Griffiths departed in haste and confusion, without the chance of a professional talk with Loveday. That afternoon saw him telegraphing wildly in all directions, and dispatching messengers in all quarters. Finally he spent over an hour drawing up an elaborate report to his chief at Newcastle, assuring him of the identity of one, Harold Cousins, who had sailed in the *Bonnie Dundee* for Natal, with Harry Craven, of Troyte's Hill, and advising that the police authorities in that far-away district should be immediately communicated with.

The ink had not dried on the pen with which this report was written before a note, in Loveday's writing, was put into his hand.

Loveday evidently had had some difficulty in finding a messenger for this note, for it was brought by a gardener's boy, who informed Griffiths that the lady had said he would receive a gold sovereign if he delivered the letter all right.

Griffiths paid the boy and dismissed him, and then proceeded to read Loveday's communication.

It was written hurriedly in pencil, and ran as follows:

"Things are getting critical here. Directly you receive this, come up to the house with two of your men, and post yourselves anywhere in the grounds where you can see and not be seen. There will be no difficulty in this, for it will be dark by the time you are able to get there. I am not sure whether I shall want your aid to-night, but you had better keep in the grounds until morning, in case of need; and above all, never once lose sight of the study windows." (This was underscored.) "If I put a lamp with a green shade in one of those windows, do not lose a moment in entering by that window, which I will contrive to keep unlocked."

Detective Griffiths rubbed his forehead—rubbed his eyes, as he finished reading this.

"Well, I daresay it's all right," he said, "but I'm bothered, that's all, and for the life of me I can't see one step of the way she is going."

He looked at his watch: the hands pointed to a quarter past six. The short September day was drawing rapidly to a close. A good five miles lay between him and Troyte's Hill—there was evidently not a moment to lose.

At the very moment that Griffiths, with his two constables, were once more starting along the Grenfell High Road behind the best horse they could procure, Mr. Craven was rousing himself from his long slumber, and beginning to look around him. That slumber, however, though long, had not been a peaceful one, and it was sundry of the old gentleman's muttered exclamations, as he had started uneasily in his sleep, that had caused Loveday to open, and then to creep out of the room to dispatch, her hurried note.

What effect the occurrence of the morning had had upon the household generally, Loveday, in her isolated corner of the house, had no means of ascertaining. She only noted that when Hales brought in her tea, as he did precisely at five o'clock, he wore a particularly ill-tempered expression of countenance, and she heard him mutter, as he set down the tea-tray with a clatter, something about being a respectable man, and not used to such "goings on."

It was not until nearly an hour and a half after this that Mr. Craven had awakened with a sudden start, and, looking wildly around him, had questioned Loveday who had entered the room.

Loveday explained that the butler had brought in lunch at one, and tea at five, but that since then no one had come in.

"Now that's false," said Mr. Craven, in a sharp, unnatural sort of voice; "I saw him sneaking round the room, the whining, canting hypocrite, and you must have seen him, too! Didn't you hear him say, in his squeaky old voice: 'Master, I knows your secret—'" He broke off abruptly, looking wildly round. "Eh, what's this?" he cried. "No, no, I'm all wrong—Sandy is dead and buried—they held an inquest on him, and we all praised him up as if he were a saint."

"He must have been a bad man, that old Sandy," said Loveday sympathetically.

"You're right! you're right!" cried Mr. Craven, springing up excitedly from his chair and seizing her by the hand. "If ever a man deserved his death, he did. For thirty years he held that rod over my head, and then—ah, where was I?"

He put his hand to his head and again sank, as if exhausted, into his chair.

"I suppose it was some early indiscretion of yours at college that he knew of?" said Loveday, eager to get at as much of the truth as possible while the mood for confidence held sway in the feeble brain.

"That was it! I was fool enough to marry a disreputable girl—a barmaid in the town—and Sandy was present at the wedding, and then—" Here his eyes closed again and his mutterings became incoherent.

For ten minutes he lay back in his chair, muttering thus; "A yelp—a groan," were the only words Loveday could distinguish among those mutterings, then suddenly, slowly and distinctly, he said, as if answering some plainly-put question: "A good blow with the hammer and the thing was done."

"I should like amazingly to see that hammer," said Loveday; "do you keep it anywhere at hand?"

His eyes opened with a wild, cunning look in them.

"Who's talking about a hammer? I did not say I had one. If anyone says I did it with a hammer, they're telling a lie."

"Oh, you've spoken to me about the hammer two or three times," said Loveday calmly; "the one that killed your dog, Captain, and I should like to see it, that's all."

The look of cunning died out of the old man's eye—"Ah, poor Captain! splendid dog that! Well, now, where were we? Where did we leave off? Ah, I remember, it was the elemental sounds of speech that bothered me so that night. Were you here then? Ah, no! I remember. I had been trying all day to assimilate a dog's yelp of pain to a human groan, and I couldn't do it. The idea haunted me—followed me about wherever I went. If they were both elemental sounds, they must have something in common, but the link between them I could not find; then it occurred to me, would a well-bred, well-trained dog like my Captain in the stables, there, at the moment of death give an unmitigated currish yelp; would there not be something of a human note in his death-cry? The thing was worth putting to the test. If I could hand down in my treatise a fragment of fact on the matter, it would be worth a dozen dogs' lives. so I went out into the moonlight—ah, but you know all about it—now, don't you?"

"Yes. Poor Captain! did he yelp or groan?"

"Why, he gave one loud, long, hideous yelp, just as if he had been a common cur. I might just as well have let him alone; it only set that other brute opening his window and spying out on me, and saying in his cracked old voice: 'Master, what are you doing out here at this time of night?'"

Again he sank back in his chair, muttering incoherently with half-closed eyes.

Loveday let him alone for a minute or so; then she had another question to ask.

"And that other brute—did he yelp or groan when you dealt him his blow?"

"What, old Sandy—the brute? he fell back— Ah, I remember, you said you would like to see the hammer that stopped his babbling old tongue—now didn't you?"

He rose a little unsteadily from his chair, and seemed to drag his long limbs with an effort across the room to a cabinet at the farther end. Opening a drawer in this cabinet, he produced, from amidst some specimens of strata and fossils, a large-sized geological hammer.

He brandished it for a moment over his head, then paused with his finger on his lip.

"Hush!" he said, "we shall have the fools creeping in to peep at us if we don't take care." And to Loveday's horror he suddenly made for the door, turned the key in the lock, withdrew it and put it into his pocket.

She looked at the clock; the hands pointed to half-past seven. Had Griffiths received her note at the proper time, and were the men now in the grounds? She could only pray that they were.

"The light is too strong for my eyes," she said, and rising from her chair, she lifted the green-shaded lamp and placed it on a table that stood at the window.

"No, no, that won't do," said Mr. Craven; "that would show everyone outside what we're doing in here." He crossed to the window as he spoke and removed the lamp thence to the mantelpiece.

Loveday could only hope that in the few seconds it had remained in the window it had caught the eye of the outside watchers.

The old man beckoned to Loveday to come near and examine his deadly weapon. "Give it a good swing round," he said, suiting the action to the word, "and down it comes with a splendid crash." He brought the hammer round within an inch of Loveday's forehead.

She started back.

"Ha, ha," he laughed harshly and unnaturally, with the light of madness dancing in his eyes now; "did I frighten you? I wonder what sort of sound you would make if I were to give you a little tap just there." Here he lightly touched her forehead with the hammer. "Elemental, of course, it would be, and—"

Loveday steadied her nerves with difficulty. Locked in with this lunatic, her only chance lay in gaining time for the detectives to reach the house and enter through the window.

"Wait a minute," she said, striving to divert his attention; "you have not yet told me what sort of an elemental sound old Sandy made when he fell. If you'll give me pen and ink, I'll write down a full account of it all, and you can incorporate it afterwards in your treatise."

For a moment a look of real pleasure flitted across the old man's face, then it faded. "The brute fell back dead without a sound," he answered; "it was all for nothing, that night's work; yet not altogether for nothing. No, I don't mind owning I would do it all over again to get the wild thrill of joy at my heart that I had when I looked down into that old man's dead face and felt myself free at last! Free at last!" his voice rang out excitedly—once more he brought his hammer round with an ugly swing.

"For a moment I was a young man again; I leaped into his room—the moon was shining full in through the window—I thought of my old college days, and the fun we used to have at Pembroke—topsy turvey I turned everything—" He broke off abruptly, and drew a step nearer to Loveday. "The pity of it all was," he said, suddenly dropping from his high, excited tone to a low, pathetic one, "that he fell without a sound of any sort." Here he drew another step nearer. "I wonder—" he said, then broke off again, and came close to Loveday's side. "It has only this moment occurred to me," he said, now with his lips close to Loveday's ear, "that a woman, in her death agony, would be much more likely to give utterance to an elemental sound than a man."

He raised his hammer, and Loveday fled to the window, and was lifted from the outside by three pairs of strong arms.

"I thought I was conducting my very last case—I never had such a narrow escape before!" said Loveday, as she stood talking with Mr. Griffiths on the Grenfell platform, awaiting the train to carry her back to London. "It seems strange that no one before suspected the old gentleman's sanity—I suppose, however, people were so used to his eccentricities that they did not notice how they had deepened into positive lunacy. His cunning evidently stood him in good stead at the inquest."

"It is possible," said Griffiths thoughtfully, "that he did not absolutely cross the very slender line that divided eccentricity from madness until after the murder. The excitement consequent upon the discovery of the crime may just have pushed him over the border. Now, Miss Brooke, we have exactly ten minutes before your train comes in. I should feel greatly obliged to you if you would explain one or two things that have a professional interest for me."

"With pleasure," said Loveday. "Put your questions in categorical order and I will answer them."

"Well, then, in the first place, what suggested to your mind the old man's guilt?"

"The relations that subsisted between him and Sandy seemed to me to savour too much of fear on the one side and power on the other. Also the income paid to Sandy during Mr. Craven's absence in Natal bore, to my mind, an unpleasant resemblance to hush-money."

"Poor wretched being! And I hear that, after all, the woman he married in his wild young days died soon afterwards of drink. I have no doubt, however, that Sandy sedulously kept up the fiction of her existence, even after his master's second marriage. Now for another question: how was it you knew that Miss Craven had taken her brother's place in the sick-room?"

"On the evening of my arrival I discovered a rather long lock of fair hair in the unswept fireplace of my room, which, as it happened, was usually occupied by Miss Craven. It at once occurred to me that the young lady had been cutting off her hair and that there must be some powerful motive to induce such a sacrifice. The suspicious circumstances attending her brother's illness soon supplied me with such a motive."

"Ah! that typhoid fever business was very cleverly done. Not a servant in the house, I verily believe, but who thought Master Harry was upstairs, ill in bed, and Miss Craven away at her friends' in Newcastle. The young fellow must have got a clear start off within an hour of the murder. His sister, sent away the next day to Newcastle, dismissed her maid there, I hear, on the plea of no accommodation at her friends' house—sent the girl to her own home for a holiday and herself returned to Troyte's Hill in the middle of the night, having walked the five miles from Grenfell. No doubt her mother admitted her through one of those easily-opened front windows, cut her hair and put her to bed to personate her brother without delay. With Miss Craven's strong likeness to Master Harry, and in a darkened room, it is easy to understand that the eyes of a doctor, personally unacquainted with the family, might easily be deceived. Now, Miss Brooke, you must admit that with all this elaborate chicanery and double dealing going on, it was only natural that my suspicions should set in strongly in that quarter."

"I read it all in another light, you see," said Loveday. "It seemed to me that the mother, knowing her son's evil proclivities, believed in his guilt, in spite, possibly, of his assertions of innocence. The son, most likely, on his way back to the house after pledging the family plate, had met old Mr. Craven with the hammer in his hand. Seeing, no doubt, how impossible it would be for him to clear himself without incriminating his father, he preferred flight to Natal to giving evidence at the inquest."

"Now about his alias?" said Mr. Griffiths briskly, for the train was at that moment steaming into the station. "How did you know that Harold Cousins was identical with Harry Craven, and had sailed in the *Bonnie Dundee*?"

"Oh, that was easy enough," said Loveday, as she stepped into the train; "a newspaper sent down to Mr. Craven by his wife, was folded so as to direct his attention to the shipping list. In it I saw that the *Bonnie Dundee* had sailed two days previously for Natal. Now it was only natural to connect Natal with Mrs. Craven, who had passed the greater part of her life there; and it was easy to understand her wish to get her scapegrace son among her early friends. The alias under which he sailed came readily enough to light. I found it scribbled all over one of Mr. Craven's writing pads in his study; evidently it had been drummed into his ears by his wife as his son's alias, and the old gentleman had taken this method of fixing it in his memory. We'll hope that the young fellow, under his new name, will make a new reputation for himself—at any rate, he'll have a better chance of doing so with the ocean between him and his evil companions. Now it's good-bye, I think."

"No," said Mr. Griffiths; "it's *au revoir*, for you'll have to come back again for the assizes, and give the evidence that will shut old Mr. Craven in an asylum for the rest of his life."

THE REDHILL SISTERHOOD

"They want you at Redhill, now," said Mr. Dyer, taking a packet of papers from one of his pigeon-holes. "The idea seems gaining ground in manly quarters that in cases of mere suspicion, women detectives are more satisfactory than men, for they are less likely to attract attention. And this Redhill affair, so far as I can make out, is one of suspicion only."

It was a dreary November morning; every gas jet in the Lynch Court office was alight, and a yellow curtain of outside fog draped its narrow windows.

"Nevertheless, I suppose one can't afford to leave it uninvestigated at this season of the year, with country-house robberies beginning in so many quarters," said Miss Brooke.

"No; and the circumstances in this case certainly seem to point in the direction of the country-house burglar. Two days ago a somewhat curious application was made privately, by a man giving the name of John Murray, to Inspector Gunning, of the Reigate police—Redhill, I must tell you is in the Reigate police district. Murray stated that he had been a greengrocer somewhere in South London, had sold his business there, and had, with the proceeds of the sale, bought two small houses in Redhill, intending to let the one and live in the other. These houses are situated in a blind alley, known as Paved Court, a narrow turning leading off the London and Brighton coach road. Paved Court has been known to the sanitary authorities for the past ten years as a regular fever nest, and as the houses which Murray bought—numbers 7 and 8—stand

at the very end of the blind alley, with no chance of thorough ventilation, I dare say the man got them for next to nothing. He told
the Inspector that he had had great difficulty in procuring a ten-
ant for the house he wished to let, number 8, and that consequently
when, about three weeks back, a lady, dressed as a nun, made him
an offer for it, he immediately closed with her. The lady gave her
name simply as 'Sister Monica,' and stated that she was a member
of an undenominational Sisterhood that had recently been founded
by a wealthy lady, who wished her name kept a secret. Sister Monica
gave no references, but, instead, paid a quarter's rent in advance,
saying that she wished to take possession of the house immediately, and open it as a home for crippled orphans."

"Gave no references—home for cripples," murmured Loveday,
scribbling hard and fast in her note-book.

"Murray made no objection to this," continued Mr. Dyer, "and,
accordingly, the next day, Sister Monica, accompanied by three
other Sisters and some sickly children, took possession of the
house, which they furnished with the barest possible necessaries
from cheap shops in the neighbourhood. For a time, Murray said,
he thought he had secured most desirable tenants, but during the
last ten days suspicions as to their real character have entered his
mind, and these suspicions he thought it his duty to communicate
to the police. Among their possessions, it seems, these Sisters
number an old donkey and a tiny cart, and this they start daily on
a sort of begging tour through the adjoining villages, bringing back
every evening a perfect hoard of broken victuals and bundles of
old garments. Now comes the extraordinary fact on which Murray
bases his suspicions. He says, and Gunning verifies his statement,
that in whatever direction those Sisters turn the wheels of their
donkey-cart, burglaries, or attempts at burglaries, are sure to follow. A week ago they went along towards Horley, where, at an out-
lying house, they received much kindness from a wealthy gentleman. That very night an attempt was made to break into that
gentleman's house—an attempt, however, that was happily frus-
trated by the barking of the house-dog. And so on in other instances

that I need not go into. Murray suggests that it might be as well to have the daily movements of these sisters closely watched, and that extra vigilance should be exercised by the police in the districts that have had the honour of a morning call from them. Gunning coincides with this idea, and so has sent to me to secure your services."

Loveday closed her note-book. "I suppose Gunning will meet me somewhere and tell me where I'm to take up my quarters?" she said.

"Yes; he will get into your carriage at Merstham—the station before Redhill—if you will put your hand out of window, with the morning paper in it. By-the-way, he takes it for granted that you will save the 11.5 train from Victoria. Murray, it seems has been good enough to place his little house at the disposal of the police, but Gunning does not think espionage could be so well carried on there as from other quarters. The presence of a stranger in an alley of that sort is bound to attract attention. So he has hired a room for you in a draper's shop that immediately faces the head of the court. There is a private door to this shop of which you will have the key, and can let yourself in and out as you please. You are supposed to be a nursery governess on the lookout for a situation, and Gunning will keep you supplied with letters to give colour to the idea. He suggests that you need only occupy the room during the day, at night you will find far more comfortable quarters at Laker's Hotel, just outside the town."

This was about the sum total of the instructions that Mr. Dyer had to give.

The 11.5 train from Victoria, that carried Loveday to her work among the Surrey Hills, did not get clear of the London fog till well away on the other side of Purley. When the train halted at Merstham, in response to her signal a tall, soldier-like individual made for her carriage, and, jumping in, took the seat facing her. He introduced himself to her as Inspector Gunning, recalled to her memory a former occasion on which they had met, and then, naturally enough, turned the talk upon the present suspicious circumstances they were bent upon investigating.

"It won't do for you and me to be seen together," he said; "of course I am known for miles round, and anyone seen in my company will be at once set down as my coadjutor, and spied upon accordingly. I walked from Redhill to Merstham on purpose to avoid recognition on the platform at Redhill, and half-way here, to my great annoyance, found that I was being followed by a man in a workman's dress and carrying a basket of tools. I doubled, however, and gave him the slip, taking a short cut down a lane which, if he had been living in the place, he would have known as well as I did. By Jove!" this was added with a sudden start, "there is the fellow, I declare; he has weathered me after all, and has no doubt taken good stock of us both, with the train going at this snail's pace. It was unfortunate that your face should have been turned towards that window, Miss Brooke."

"My veil is something of a disguise, and I will put on another cloak before he has a chance of seeing me again," said Loveday.

All she had seen in the brief glimpse that the train had allowed, was a tall, powerfully-built man walking along a siding of the line. His cap was drawn low over his eyes, and in his hand he carried a workman's basket.

Gunning seemed much annoyed at the circumstance. "Instead of landing at Redhill," he said, "we'll go on to Three Bridges and wait there for a Brighton train to bring us back, that will enable you to get to your room somewhere between the lights; I don't want to have you spotted before you've so much as started your work."

Then they went back to their discussion of the Redhill Sisterhood.

"They call themselves 'undenominational,' whatever that means," said Gunning "they say they are connected with no religious sect whatever, they attend sometimes one place of worship, sometimes another, sometimes none at all. They refuse to give up the name of the founder of their order, and really no one has any right to demand it of them, for, as no doubt you see, up to the present moment the case is one of mere suspicion, and it may be a pure coincidence that attempts at burglary have followed their footsteps in this neighbourhood. By-the-way, I have heard of a man's face being enough to hang him, but until I saw Sister Monica's, I never saw a woman's face that could perform the same kind office for her. Of all the lowest criminal types of faces I have ever seen, I think hers is about the lowest and most repulsive."

After the Sisters, they passed in review the chief families resident in the neighbourhood.

"This," said Gunning, unfolding a paper, "is a map I have specially drawn up for you—it takes in the district for ten miles round Redhill, and every country house of any importance is marked with it in red ink. Here, in addition, is an index to those houses, with special notes of my own to every house."

Loveday studied the map for a minute or so, then turned her attention to the index.

"Those four houses you've marked, I see, are those that have been already attempted. I don't think I'll run them through, but I'll mark them 'doubtful;' you see the gang—for, of course, it is a gang—might follow our reasoning on the matter, and look upon those houses as our weak point. Here's one I'll run through, 'house empty during winter months,' that means plate and jewellery sent to the bankers. Oh! and this one may as well be crossed off, 'father and four sons all athletes and sportsmen,' that means firearms always handy—I don't think burglars will be likely to trouble them. Ah! now we come to something! Here's a house to be marked 'tempting' in a burglar's list. 'Wootton Hall, lately changed hands and re-built, with complicated passages and corridors. Splendid family plate in daily use and left entirely to the care of the butler.' I wonder, does the master of that house trust to his 'complicated passages' to preserve his plate for him? A dismissed dishonest servant would supply a dozen maps of the place for half-a-sovereign. What do these initials, 'E.L.,' against the next house in the list, North Cape, stand for?"

"Electric lighted. I think you might almost cross that house off also. I consider electric lighting one of the greatest safeguards against burglars that a man can give his house."

"Yes, if he doesn't rely exclusively upon it; it might be a nasty trap under certain circumstances. I see this gentleman also has magnificent presentation and other plate."

"Yes. Mr. Jameson is a wealthy man and very popular in the neighbourhood; his cups and epergnes are worth looking at."

"Is it the only house in the district that is lighted with electricity?"

"Yes; and, begging your pardon, Miss Brooke, I only wish it were not so. If electric lighting were generally in vogue it would save the police a lot of trouble on these dark winter nights."

"The burglars would find some way of meeting such a condition of things, depend upon it; they have reached a very high development in these days. They no longer stalk about as they did fifty years ago with blunderbuss and bludgeon; they plot, plan, contrive and bring imagination and artistic resource to their aid. By-the-way, it often occurs to me that the popular detective stories, for which there seems to large a demand at the present day, must be, at times, uncommonly useful to the criminal classes."

At Three Bridges they had to wait so long for a return train that it was nearly dark when Loveday got back to Redhill. Mr. Gunning did not accompany her thither, having alighted at a previous station. Loveday had directed her portmanteau to be sent direct to Laker's Hotel, where she had engaged a room by telegram from Victoria Station. So, unburthened by luggage, she slipped quietly out of the Redhill Station and made her way straight for the draper's shop in the London Road. She had no difficulty in finding it, thanks to the minute directions given her by the Inspector.

Street lamps were being lighted in the sleepy little town as she went along, and as she turned into the London Road, shopkeepers were lighting up their windows on both sides of the way. A few yards down this road, a dark patch between the lighted shops showed her where Paved Court led off from the thoroughfare. A side-door of one of the shops that stood at the corner of the court seemed to offer a post of observation whence she could see without being seen, and here Loveday, shrinking into the shadows, ensconced herself in order to take stock of the little alley and its inhabitants. She found it much as it had been described to her—a collection of four-roomed houses of which more than half were unlet. Numbers 7 and 8 at the head of the court presented a slightly less neglected appearance than the other tenements. Number 7 stood in total darkness, but in the upper window of number 8 there showed what seemed to be a night-light burning, so Loveday conjectured that this possibly was the room set apart as a dormitory for the little cripples.

While she stood thus surveying the home of the suspected Sisterhood, the Sisters themselves—two, at least, of them—came into view, with their donkey-cart and their cripples, in the main road. It was an odd little cortège. One Sister, habited in a nun's dress of dark blue serge, led the donkey by the bridle; another Sister, similarly attired, walked alongside the low cart, in which were seated two sickly-looking children. They were evidently returning from one of their long country circuits, and unless they had lost their way and been belated—it certainly seemed a late hour for the sickly little cripples to be abroad.

As they passed under the gas lamp at the corner of the court, Loveday caught a glimpse of the faces of the Sisters. It was easy, with Inspector Gunning's description before her mind, to identify the older and taller woman as Sister Monica, and a more coarse-featured and generally repellant face Loveday admitted to herself she had never before seen. In striking contrast to this forbidding countenance, was that of the younger Sister. Loveday could only catch a brief passing view of it, but that one brief view was enough to impress it on her memory as of unusual sadness and beauty. As the donkey stopped at the corner of the court, Loveday heard this sad-looking young woman addressed as "Sister Anna" by one of the cripples, who asked plaintively when they were going to have something to eat.

"Now, at once," said Sister Anna, lifting the little one, as it seemed to Loveday, tenderly out of the cart, and carrying him on her shoulder down the court to the door of number 8, which opened to them at their approach. The other Sister did the same with the other child; then both Sisters returned, unloaded the cart of sundry bundles and baskets, and, this done, led off the old donkey and trap down the road, possibly to a neighbouring costermonger's stables.

A man, coming along on a bicycle, exchanged a word of greeting with the Sisters as they passed, then swung himself off his machine at the corner of the court, and walked it along the paved way to the door of number 7. This he opened with a key, and then, pushing the machine before him, entered the house.

Loveday took it for granted that this man must be the John Murray of whom she had heard. She had closely scrutinized him as he had passed her, and had seen that he was a dark, well-featured man of about fifty years of age.

She congratulated herself on her good fortune in having seen so much in such a brief space of time, and coming forth from her sheltered corner turned her steps in the direction of the draper's shop on the other side of the road.

It was easy to find it. "Golightly" was the singular name that figured above the shop-front, in which were displayed a variety of goods calculated to meet the wants of servants and the poorer classes generally. A tall, powerfully-built man appeared to be looking in at this window. Loveday's foot was on the doorstep of the draper's private entrance, her hand on the door-knocker, when this individual, suddenly turning, convinced her of his identity with the journeyman workman who had so disturbed Mr. Gunning's equanimity. It was true he wore a bowler instead of a journeyman's cap, and he no longer carried a basket of tools, but there was no possibility for anyone, with so good an eye for an outline as Loveday possessed, not to recognize the carriage of the head and shoulders as that of the man she had seen walking along the railway siding. He gave her no time to make minute observation of his appearance, but turned quickly away, and disappeared down a by-street.

Loveday's work seemed to bristle with difficulties now. Here was she, as it were, unearthed in her own ambush; for there could be but little doubt that during the whole time she had stood watching those Sisters, that man, from a safe vantage point, had been watching her.

She found Mrs. Golightly a civil and obliging person. She showed Loveday to her room above the shop, brought her the letters which Inspector Gunning had been careful to have posted to her during the day. Then she supplied her with pen and ink and, in response to Loveday's request, with some strong coffee that she said, with a little attempt at a joke, would "keep a dormouse awake all through the winter without winking."

While the obliging landlady busied herself about the room, Loveday had a few questions to ask about the Sisterhood who lived down the court opposite. On this head, however, Mrs. Golightly could tell her no more than she already knew, beyond the fact that they started every morning on their rounds at eleven o'clock punctually, and that before that hour they were never to be seen outside their door.

Loveday's watch that night was to be a fruitless one. Although she sat, with her lamp turned out and safely screened from observation, until close upon midnight, with eyes fixed upon numbers 7 and 8 Paved Court, not so much as a door opening or shutting at either house rewarded her vigil. The lights flitted from the lower to the upper floors in both houses, and then disappeared somewhere between nine and ten in the evening; and after that, not a sign of life did either tenement show.

And all through the long hours of that watch, backwards and forwards there seemed to flit before her mind's eye, as if in some sort it were fixed upon its retina, the sweet, sad face of Sister Anna.

Why it was this face should so haunt her, she found it hard to say.

"It has a mournful past and a mournful future written upon it as a hopeless whole," she said to herself. "It is the face of an Andromeda! 'here am I,' it seems to say, 'tied to my stake, helpless and hopeless.'"

The church clocks were sounding the midnight hour as Loveday made her way through the dark streets to her hotel outside the town. As she passed under the railway arch that ended in the open country road, the echo of not very distant footsteps caught her ear. When she stopped they stopped, when she went on they went on, and she knew that once more she was being followed and watched, although the darkness of the arch prevented her seeing even the shadow of the man who was thus dogging her steps.

The next morning broke keen and frosty. Loveday studied her map and her country-house index over a seven o'clock breakfast, and then set off for a brisk walk along the country road. No doubt in London the streets were walled in and roofed with yellow fog; here, however, bright sunshine played in and out of the bare tree-boughs and leafless hedges on to a thousand frost spangles, turning the prosaic macadamized road into a gangway fit for Queen Titania herself and her fairy train.

Loveday turned her back on the town and set herself to follow the road as it wound away over the hill in the direction of a village called Northfield. Early as she was, she was not to have that road to herself. A team of strong horses trudged by on their way to their work in the fuller's-earth pits. A young fellow on a bicycle flashed past at a tremendous pace, considering the upward slant of the road. He looked hard at her as he passed, then slackened pace, dismounted, and awaited her coming on the brow of the hill.

"Good morning, Miss Brooke," he said, lifting his cap as she came alongside of him. "May I have five minutes' talk with you?"

The young man who thus accosted her had not the appearance of a gentleman. He was a handsome, bright-faced young fellow of about two-and-twenty, and was dressed in ordinary cyclists' dress; his cap was pushed back from his brow over thick, curly, fair hair, and Loveday, as she looked at him, could not repress the thought how well he would look at the head of a troop of cavalry, giving the order to charge the enemy.

He led his machine to the side of the footpath.

"You have the advantage of me," said Loveday; "I haven't the remotest notion who you are."

"No," he said; "although I know you, you cannot possibly know me. I am a north country man, and I was present, about a month ago, at the trial of old Mr. Craven, of Troyte's Hill—in fact, I acted as reporter for one of the local papers. I watched your face so closely as you gave your evidence that I should know it anywhere, among a thousand."

"And your name is—?"

"George White, of Grenfell. My father is part proprietor of one of the Newcastle papers. I am a bit of a literary man myself, and sometimes figure as a reporter, sometimes as leader-writer, to that paper." Here he gave a glance towards his side pocket, from which protruded a small volume of Tennyson's poems.

The facts he had stated did not seem to invite comment, and Loveday ejaculated merely:

"Indeed!"

The young man went back to the subject that was evidently filling his thoughts. "I have special reasons for being glad to have met you this morning, Miss Brooke," he want on, making his footsteps keep pace with hers. "I am in great trouble, and I believe you are the only person in the whole world who can help me out of that trouble."

"I am rather doubtful as to my power of helping anyone out of trouble," said Loveday; "so far as my experience goes, our troubles are as much a part of ourselves as our skins are of our bodies."

"Ah, but not such trouble as mine," said White eagerly. He broke off for a moment, then, with a sudden rush of words, told her what that trouble was. For the past year he had been engaged to be married to a young girl, who, until quite recently had been fulfilling the duties of a nursery governess in a large house in the neighbourhood of Redhill.

"Will you kindly give me the name of that house?" interrupted Loveday.

"Certainly; Wootton Hall, the place is called, and Annie Lee is my sweetheart's name. I don't care who knows it!" He threw his head back as he said this, as if he would be delighted to announce the fact to the whole world. "Annie's mother," he went on, "died when she was a baby, and we both thought her father was dead also, when suddenly, about a fortnight ago, it came to her knowledge that instead of being dead, he was serving his time at Portland for some offence committed years ago."

"Do you know how this came to Annie's knowledge?"

"Not the least in the world; I only know that I suddenly got a letter from her announcing the fact, and at the same time, breaking off her engagement with me. I tore the letter into a thousand pieces, and wrote back saying I would not allow the engagement to be broken off, but would marry her to-morrow if she would have me. To this letter she did not reply; there came instead a few lines from Mrs. Copeland, the lady at Wootton Hall, saying that Annie had thrown up her engagement and joined some Sisterhood, and that she, Mrs. Copeland, had pledged her word to Annie to reveal to no one the name and whereabouts of that Sisterhood."

"And I suppose you imagine I am able to do what Mrs. Copeland is pledged not to do?"

"That's just it, Miss Brooke," cried the young man enthusiastically. "You do such wonderful things; everyone knows you do. It seems as if, when anything is wanted to be found out, you just walk into a place, look round you and, in a moment, everything becomes clear as noonday."

"I can't quite lay claim to such wonderful powers as that. As it happens, however, in the present instance, no particular skill is needed to find out what you wish to know, for I fancy I have already come upon the traces of Miss Annie Lee."

"Miss Brooke!"

"Of course, I cannot say for certain, but is a matter you can easily settle for yourself—settle, too, in a way that will confer a great obligation on me."

"I shall be only too delighted to be of any—the slightest service to you," cried White, enthusiastically as before.

"Thank you. I will explain. I came down here specially to watch the movements of a certain Sisterhood who have somehow aroused the suspicions of the police. Well, I find that instead of being able to do this, I am myself so closely watched—possibly by confederates of these Sisters—that unless I can do my work by deputy I may as well go back to town at once."

"Ah! I see—you want me to be that deputy."

"Precisely. I want you to go to the room in Redhill that I have hired, take your place at the window—screened, of course, from observation—at which I ought to be seated—watch as closely as possible the movements of these Sisters and report them to me at the hotel, where I shall remain shut in from morning till night—it is the only way in which I can throw my persistent spies off the scent. Now, in doing this for me, you will be also doing yourself a good turn, for I have little doubt but what under the blue serge hood of one of the sisters you will discover the pretty face of Miss Annie Lee."

As they had talked they had walked, and now stood on the top of the hill at the head of the one little street that constituted the whole of the village of Northfield.

On their left hand stood the village schools and the master's house; nearly facing these, on the opposite side of the road, beneath a clump of elms, stood the village pound. Beyond this pound, on either side of the way, were two rows of small cottages with tiny squares of garden in front, and in the midst of these small cottages a swinging sign beneath a lamp announced a "Postal and Telegraph Office."

"Now that we have come into the land of habitations again," said Loveday, "it will be best for us to part. It will not do for you and me to be seen together, or my spies will be transferring their attentions from me to you, and I shall have to find another deputy. You had better start on your bicycle for Redhill at once, and I will walk back at leisurely speed. Come to me at my hotel without fail at one o'clock and report proceedings. I do not say anything definite about remuneration, but I assure you, if you carry out my instructions to the letter, your services will be amply rewarded by me and by my employers."

There were yet a few more details to arrange. White had been, he said, only a day and night in the neighbourhood, and special directions as to the locality had to be given to him. Loveday advised him not to attract attention by going to the draper's private door, but to enter the shop as if he were a customer, and then explain matters to Mrs. Golightly, who, no doubt, would be in her place behind the counter; tell her he was the brother of the Miss Smith who had hired her room, and ask permission to go through the shop to that room, as he had been commissioned by his sister to read and answer any letters that might have arrived there for her.

"Show her the key of the side door—here it is," said Loveday; "it will be your credentials, and tell her you did not like to make use of it without acquainting her with the fact."

The young man took the key, endeavoured to put it in his waist-coat pocket, found the space there occupied and so transferred it to the keeping of a side pocket in his tunic.

All this time Loveday stood watching him.

"You have a capital machine there," she said, as the young man mounted his bicycle once more, "and I hope you will turn it to account in following the movements of these Sisters about the neighbourood. I feel confident you will have something definite to tell me when you bring me your first report at one o'clock."

White once more broke into a profusion of thanks, and then, lifting his cap to the lady, started his machine at a fairly good pace.

Loveday watched him out of sight down the slope of the hill, then, instead of following him as she had said she would "at a leisurely pace," she turned her steps in the opposite direction along the village street.

It was an altogether ideal country village. Neatly-dressed chubby-faced children, now on their way to the schools, dropped quaint little curtsies, or tugged at curly locks as Loveday passed; every cottage looked the picture of cleanliness and trimness, and although so late in the year, the gardens were full of late flowering chrysanthemums and early flowering Christmas roses.

At the end of the village, Loveday came suddenly into view of a large, handsome, red-brick mansion. It presented a wide frontage to the road, from which it lay back amid extensive pleasure grounds. On the right hand, and a little in the rear of the house, stood what seemed to be large and commodious stables, and immediately adjoining these stables was a low-built, red-brick shed, that had evidently been recently erected.

That low-build, red-brick shed excited Loveday's curiosity.

"Is this house called North Cape?" she asked of a man, who chanced at that moment to be passing with a pickaxe and shovel.

The man answered in the affirmative, and Loveday then asked another question: could he tell her what was that small shed so close to the house—it looked like a glorified cowhouse—now what could be its use?

The man's face lighted up as if it were a subject on which he liked to be questioned. He explained that that small shed was the engine-house where the electricity that lighted North Cape was made and stored. Then he dwelt with pride upon the fact, as if he held a personal interest in it, that North Cape was the only house, far or near, that was thus lighted.

"I suppose the wires are carried underground to the house," said Loveday, looking in vain for signs of them anywhere.

The man was delighted to go into details on the matter. He had helped to lay those wires, he said: they were two in number, one for supply and one for return, and were laid three feet below ground, in boxes filled with pitch. These wires were switched on to jars in the engine-house, where the electricity was stored, and, after passing underground, entered the family mansion under its flooring at its western end.

Loveday listened attentively to these details, and then took a minute and leisurely survey of the house and its surroundings. This done, she retraced her steps through the village, pausing, however, at the "Postal and Telegraph Office" to dispatch a telegram to Inspector Gunning.

It was one to send the Inspector to his cipher-book. It ran as follows:

"Rely solely on chemist and coal-merchant throughout the day.—L. B."

After this, she quickened her pace, and in something over three-quarters of an hour was back again at her hotel.

There she found more of life stirring than when she had quitted it in the early morning. There was to be a meeting of the "Surrey Stags," about a couple of miles off, and a good many hunting men were hanging about the entrance to the house, discussing the chances of sport after last night's frost. Loveday made her way through the throng in leisurely fashion, and not a man but what had keen scrutiny from her sharp eyes. No, there was no cause for suspicion there: they were evidently one and all just what they seemed to be—loud-voiced, hard-riding men, bent on a day's sport; but—and here Loveday's eyes traveled beyond the hotel court-yard to the other side of the road—who was that man with a bill-hook hacking at the hedge there—a thin-featured, round-shouldered old fellow, with a bent-about hat? It might be as well not to take it too rashly for granted that her spies had withdrawn, and had left her free to do her work in her own fashion.

She went upstairs to her room. It was situated on the first floor in the front of the house, and consequently commanded a good view of the high road. She stood well back from the window, and at an angle whence she could see and not be seen, took a long, steady survey of the hedger. And the longer she looked the more convinced she was that the man's real work was something other than the bill-hook seemed to imply. He worked, so to speak, with his head over his shoulder, and when Loveday supplemented her eyesight with a strong field-glass, she could see more than one stealthy glance shot from beneath his bent-about hat in the direction of her window.

There could be little doubt about it: her movements were to be as closely watched to-day as they had been yesterday. Now it was of first importance that she should communicate with Inspector Gunning in the course of the afternoon: the question to solve was how it was to be done?

To all appearance Loveday answered the question in extraordinary fashion. She pulled up her blind, she drew back her curtain, and seated herself, in full view, at a small table in the window recess. Then she took a pocket inkstand from her pocket, a packet of correspondence cards from her letter-case, and with rapid pen, set to work on them.

About an hour and a half afterwards, White, coming in, according to his promise, to report proceedings, found her still seated at the window, not, however, with writing materials before her, but with needle and thread in her hand with which she was mending her gloves.

"I return to town by the first train to-morrow morning," she said as he entered, "and I find these wretched things want no end of stitches. Now for your report."

White appeared to be in an elated frame of mind. "I've seen her!" he cried, "my Annie—they've got her, those confounded

Sisters; but they sha'n't keep her—no, not if I have to pull the house down about their ears to get her out."

"Well, now you know where she is, you can take your time about getting her out," said Loveday. "I hope, however, you haven't broken faith with me, and betrayed yourself by trying to speak with her, because, if so, I shall have to look out for another deputy."

"Honour, Miss Brooke!" answered White indignantly. "I stuck to my duty, though it cost me something to see her hanging over those kids and tucking them into the cart, and never say a word to her, never so much as wave my hand."

"Did she go out with the donkey-cart to-day?"

"No, she only tucked the kids into the cart with a blanket, and then went back to the house. Two old Sisters, ugly as sin, went out with them. I watched them from the window, jolt, jolt, jolt, round the corner, out of sight, and then I whipped down the stairs, and on to my machine, and was after them in a trice and managed to keep them well in sight for over an hour and a half."

"And their destination to-day was?"

"Wootton Hall."

"Ah, just as I expected."

"Just as you expected?" echoed White.

"I forgot. You do not know the nature of the suspicions that are attached to this Sisterhood, and the reasons I have for thinking that Wootton Hall, at this season of the year, might have an especial attraction for them."

White continued staring at her. "Miss Brooke," he said presently, in an altered tone, "whatever suspicions may attach to the Sisterhood, I'll stake my life on it, my Annie has had no share in any wickedness of any sort."

"Oh, quite so; it is most likely that your Annie has, in some way, been inveigled into joining these Sisters—has been taken possession of by them, in fact, just as they have taken possession of the little cripples."

"That's it!" he cried excitedly; "that was the idea that occurred to me when you spoke to me on the hill about them, otherwise you may be sure—"

"Did they get relief of any sort at the Hall?" interrupted
Loveday.

"Yes; one of the two ugly old women stopped outside the lodge
gates with the donkey-cart, and the other beauty went up to the
house alone. She stayed there, I should think, about a quarter of
an hour, and when she came back, was followed by a servant, carrying a bundle and a basket."

"Ah! I've no doubt they brought away with them something else
beside old garments and broken victuals."

White stood in front of her, fixing a hard, steady gaze upon her.

"Miss Brooke," he said presently, in a voice that matched the
look on his face, "what do you suppose was the real object of these
women in going to Wootton Hall this morning?"

"Mr. White, if I wished to help a gang of thieves break into
Wootton Hall tonight, don't you think I should be greatly interested in procuring from them the information that the master of
the house was away from home; that two of the men servants, who
slept in the house, had recently been dismissed and their places
had not yet been filled; also that the dogs were never unchained at
night, and that their kennels were at the side of the house at which
the butler's pantry is not situated? These are particulars I have
gathered in this house without stirring from my chair, and I am
satisfied that they are likely to be true. A the same time, if I were a
professed burglar, I should not be content with information that
was likely to be true, but would be careful to procure such that
was certain to be true, and so would set accomplices to work at the
fountain head. Now do you understand?"

White folded his arms and looked down on her.

"What are you going to do?" he asked, in short, brusque tones.

Loveday looked him full in the face. "Communicate with the
police immediately," she answered; "and I should feel greatly
obliged if you will at once take a note from me to Inspector Gunning at Reigate."

"And what becomes of Annie?"

"I don't think you need have any anxiety on that head. I've no
doubt that when the circumstances of her admission to the Sisterhood are investigated, it will be proved that she has been as much

deceived and imposed upon as the man, John Murray, who so foolishly let his house to these women. Remember, Annie has Mrs. Copeland's good word to support her integrity."

White stood silent for a while.

"What sort of a note do you wish me to take to the Inspector?" he presently asked.

"You shall read it as I write it, if you like," answered Loveday. She took a correspondence card from her letter case, and, with an indelible pencil, wrote as follows—

"Wooton Hall is threatened to-night—concentrate attention there.

"L. B."

White read the words as she wrote them with a curious expression passing over his handsome features.

"Yes," he said, curtly as before. "I'll deliver that, I give you my word, but I'll bring back no answer to you. I'll do no more spying for you—it's a trade that doesn't suit me. There's a straight-forward way of doing straight-forward work, and I'll take that way—no other—to get my Annie out of that den."

He took the note, which she sealed and handed to him, and strode out of the room.

Loveday, from the window, watched him mount his bicycle. Was it her fancy, or did there pass a swift, furtive glance of recognition between him and the hedger on the other side of the way as he rode out of the court-yard?

Loveday seemed determined to make that hedger's work easy for him. The short winter's day was closing in now, and her room must consequently have been growing dim to outside observation. She lighted the gas chandelier which hung from the ceiling and, still with blinds and curtains undrawn, took her old place at the window, spread writing materials before her and commenced a long and elaborate report to her chief at Lynch Court.

About half-an-hour afterwards, as she threw a casual glance across the road, she saw that the hedger had disappeared, but that two ill-looking tramps sat munching bread and cheese under the hedge to which his bill-hook had done so little service. Evidently the intention was, one way or another, not to lose sight of her so long as she remained in Redhill.

Meantime, White had delivered Loveday's note to the Inspector at Reigate, and had disappeared on his bicycle once more.

Gunning read it without a change of expression. Then he crossed the room to the fire-place and held the card as close to the bars as he could without scorching it.

"I had a telegram from her this morning," he explained to his confidential man, "telling me to rely upon chemicals and coals throughout the day, and that, of course, meant that she would write to me in invisible ink. No doubt this message about Wootton Hall means nothing—"

He broke off abruptly, exclaiming: "Eh! what's this!" as, having withdrawn the card from the fire, Loveday's real message stood out in bold, clear characters between the lines of the false one.

Thus it ran:

> "North Cape will be attacked to-night—a desperate gang—be prepared for a struggle. Above all, guard the electrical engine-house. On no account attempt to communicate with me; I am so closely watched that any endeavour to do so may frustrate your chance of trapping the scoundrels. L. B."

That night when the moon went down behind Reigate Hill an exciting scene was enacted at "North Cape." The *Surrey Gazette*, in its issue the following day, gave the subjoined account of it under the heading, "Desperate encounter with burglars."

> "Last night, 'North Cape,' the residence of Mr. Jameson, was the scene of an affray between the police and a desperate gang of burglars. 'North Cape' is lighted throughout with electricity, and the burglars, four in number, divided in half—two being told

off to enter and rob the house, and two to remain at the engine-shed, where the electricity is stored, so that, at a given signal, should need arise, the wires might be unswitched, the inmates of the house thrown into sudden darkness and confusion, and the escape of the marauders thereby facilitated. Mr. Jameson, however, had received timely warning from the police of the intended attack, and he, with his two sons, all well armed, sat in darkness in the inner hall awaiting the coming of the thieves. The police were stationed, some in the stables, some in out-buildings nearer to the house, and others in more distant parts of the grounds. The burglars effected their entrance by means of a ladder placed to a window of the servants' stair case which leads straight down to the butler's pantry and to the safe where the silver is kept. The fellows, however, had no sooner got into the house than the police issuing from their hiding-place outside, mounted the ladder after them and thus cut off their retreat. Mr. Jameson and his two sons, at the same moment, attacked them in front, and thus overwhelmed by numbers, the scoundrels were easily secured. It was at the engine-house outside that the sharpest struggle took place. The thieves had forced open the door of this engine-shed with their jimmies immediately on their arrival, under the very eyes of the police, who lay in ambush in the stables, and when one of the men, captured in the house, contrived to sound an alarm on his whistle, these outside watchers made a rush for the electrical jars, in order to unswitch the wires. Upon this the police closed upon them, and a hand-to-hand struggle followed, and if it had not been for the timely assistance of Mr. Jameson and his sons, who had fortunately conjectured that their presence here might be useful, it is more than likely that one of the burglars, a powerfully-built man, would have escaped.

"The names of the captured men are John Murray, Arthur and George Lee (father and son), and a man with so many aliases that it is difficult to know which is his real name. The whole thing had been most cunningly and carefully planned. The elder Lee, lately released from penal servitude for a similar offence, appears to have been prime mover in the affair. This man had, it seems, a son and a daughter, who, through the kindness of friends, had been fairly well placed in life: the son at an electrical engineers' in London, the daughter as nursery governess at Wootton Hall. Directly this man was released from Portland, he seems to have found out his children and done his best to ruin them both. He was constantly at Wootton Hall endeavouring to induce his daughter to act as an accomplice to a robbery of the house. This so worried the girl that she threw up her situation and joined a Sisterhood that had recently been established in the neighbourhood. Upon this, Lee's thoughts turned in another direction. He induced his son, who had saved a little money, to throw up his work in London, and join him in his disreputable career. The boy is a handsome young fellow, but appears to have in him the makings of a first-class criminal. In his work as an electrical engineer he had made the acquaintance of the man John Murray, who, it is said, has been rapidly going downhill of late. Murray was the owner of the house rented by the Sisterhood that Miss Lee had joined, and the idea evidently struck the brains of these three scoundrels that this Sisterhood, whose antecedents were a little mysterious, might be utilized to draw off the attention of the police from themselves and from the especial house in the neighbourhood that they had planned to attack. With this end in view, Murray made an application to the police to have the Sisters watched, and still further to give colour to the suspicions he had endeavoured to set afloat concerning them, he and his confederates made feeble attempts at burglary upon the houses at which the Sisters had called, begging for scraps. It is a matter for congratulation that the plot, from beginning to end, has been thus successfully unearthed, and it is felt on all sides that great credit is due to Inspector Gunning and his skilled coadjutors for the vigilance and promptitude they have displayed throughout the affair."

Loveday read aloud this report, with her feet on the fender of the Lynch Court office.

"Accurate, as far as it goes," she said, as she laid down the paper.

"But we want to know a little more," said Mr. Dyer. "In the first place, I would like to know what it was that diverted your suspicions from the unfortunate Sisters?"

"The way in which they handled the children," answered Loveday promptly. "I have seen female criminals of all kinds handling children, and I have noticed that although they may occasionally—even this is rare—treat them with a certain rough sort of kindness, of tenderness they are utterly incapable. Now Sister Monica, I must admit, is not pleasant to look at; at the same time, there was something absolutely beautiful in the way in which she lifted the little cripple out of the cart, put his tiny thin hand round her neck, and carried him into the house. By-the-way I would like to ask some rapid physiognomist how he would account for Sister Monica's repulsiveness of feature as contrasted with young Lee's undoubted good looks—heredity, in this case, throws no light on the matter."

"Another question," said Mr. Dyer, not paying much heed to Loveday's digression: "how was it you transferred your suspicions to John Murray?"

"I did not do so immediately, although at the very first it had struck me as odd that he should be so anxious to do the work of the police for them. The chief thing I noticed concerning Murray, on the first and only occasion on which I saw him, was that he had had an accident with his bicycle, for in the right-hand corner of his lamp-glass there was a tiny star, and the lamp itself had a dent on the same side, had also lost its hook, and was fastened to the machine by a bit of electric fuse. The next morning as I was walking up the hill towards Northfield, I was accosted by a young man mounted on that self-same bicycle—not a doubt of it—star in glass, dent, fuse, all three."

"Ah, that sounded an important keynote, and led you to connect Murray and the younger Lee immediately."

"It did, and, of course, also at once gave the lie to his statement that he was a stranger in the place, and confirmed my opinion that there was nothing of the north-countryman in his accent. Other details in his manner and appearance gave rise to other suspicions. For instance, he called himself a press reporter by profession, and his hands were coarse and grimy as only a mechanic's could be. He said he was a bit of a literary man, but the Tennyson that showed so obtrusively from his pocket was new, and in parts uncut, and totally unlike the well-thumbed volume of the literary student. Finally, when he tried and failed to put my latch-key into his waistcoat pocket, I saw the reason lay in the fact that the pocket was already occupied by a soft coil of electric fuse, the end of which protruded. Now, an electric fuse is what an electrical engineer might almost unconsciously carry about with him, it is so essential a part of his working tools, but it is a thing that a literary man or a press reporter could have no possible use for."

"Exactly, exactly. And it was no doubt, that bit of electric fuse that turned your thoughts to the one house in the neighbourhood lighted by electricity, and suggested to your mind the possibility of electrical engineers turning their talents to account in that direction. Now, will you tell me, what, at that stage of your day's work, induced you to wire to Gunning that you would bring your invisible-ink bottle into use?"

"That was simply a matter or precaution; it did not compel me to the use of invisible ink, if I saw other safe methods of communication. I felt myself being hemmed in on all sides with spies, and I could not tell what emergency might arise. I don't think I have ever had a more difficult game to play. As I walked and talked with the young fellow up the hill, it became clear to me that if I wished to do my work I must lull the suspicions of the gang, and seem to walk into their trap. I saw by the persistent way in which Wootton Hall was forced on my notice that it was wished to fix my suspicions there. I accordingly, to all appearance, did so, and allowed the fellows to think they were making a fool of me."

"Ha! ha! Capital that—the biter bit, with a vengeance! Splendid idea to make that young rascal himself deliver the letter that was to land him and his pals in jail. And he all the time laughing in his sleeve and thinking what a fool he was making of you! Ha, ha, ha!" And Mr. Dyer made the office ring again with his merriment.

"The only person one is at all sorry for in this affair is poor little Sister Anna," said Loveday pityingly; "and yet, perhaps, all things considered, after her sorry experience of life, she may not be so badly placed in a Sisterhood where practical Christianity— not religious hysterics—is the one and only rule of the order."

A PRINCESS'S VENGEANCE

"The girl is young, pretty, friendless and a foreigner, you say, and has disappeared as completely as if the earth had opened to receive her," said Miss Brooke, making a résumé of the facts that Mr. Dyer had been relating to her. "Now, will you tell me why two days were allowed to elapse before the police were communicated with?"

"Mrs. Druce, the lady to whom Lucie Cunier acted as amanuensis," answered Mr. Dyer, "took the matter very calmly at first and said she felt sure that the girl would write to her in a day or so, explaining her extraordinary conduct. Major Druce, her son, the gentleman who came to me this morning, was away from home, on a visit, when the girl took flight. Immediately on his return, however, he communicated the fullest particulars to the police."

"They do not seem to have taken up the case very heartily at Scotland Yard."

"No, they have as good as dropped it. They advised Major Druce to place the matter in my hands, saying that they considered it a case for private rather than police investigation."

"I wonder what made them come to that conclusion."

"I think I can tell you, although the Major seemed quite at a loss on the matter. It seems he had a photograph of the missing girl, which he kept in a drawer of his writing-table. (By-the-way, I think the young man is a good deal 'gone' on this Mdlle. Cunier, in spite of his engagement to another lady.) Well, this portrait he naturally thought would be most useful in helping to trace the girl, and he went to his drawer for it, intending to take it with him to Scotland Yard. To his astonishment, however, it was nowhere to be seen, and, although he at once instituted a rigorous search, and questioned his mother and the servants, one and all, on the matter, it was all to no purpose."

Loveday thought for a moment.

"Well, of course," she said presently "that photograph must have been stolen by someone in the house, and, equally of course, that someone must know more on the matter than he or she cares to avow, and, most probably, has some interest in throwing obstacles in the way of tracing the girl. At the same time, however, the fact in no way disproves the possibility that a crime, and a very black one, may underlie the girl's disappearance."

"The Major himself appears confident that a crime of some sort has been committed, and he grew very excited and a little mixed in his statements more than once just now."

"What sort of woman is the Major's mother?"

"Mrs. Druce? She is rather a well-known personage in certain sets. Her husband died about ten years ago, and since his death she has posed as promoter and propagandist of all sorts of benevolent, though occasionally somewhat visionary ideas; theatrical missions, magic-lantern and playing cards missions, societies for providing perpetual music for the sick poor, for supplying cabmen with comforters, and a hundred other similar schemes have in turn occupied her attention. Her house is a rendezvous for faddists of every description. The latest fad, however, seems to have put all others to flight; it is a scheme for alleviating the condition of 'our sisters in the East,' so she puts it in her prospectus; in other words a Harem Mission on somewhat similar, but I suppose broader lines than the old-fashioned Zenana Mission. This Harem Mission has gathered about her a number of Turkish and Egyptian potentates resident in or visiting London, and has thus incidentally brought about the engagement of her son, Major Druce, with the Princess Dullah-Veih. This Princess is a beauty and an heiress, and although of Turkish parentage, has been brought up under European influence in Cairo."

"Is anything known of the antecedents of Mdlle. Cunier?"

"Very little. She came to Mrs. Druce from a certain Lady Gwynne, who had brought her to England from an orphanage for the daughters of jewellers and watchmakers at Echallets, in Geneva. Lady Gwynne intended to make her governess to her young children, but when she saw that the girl's good looks had attracted her husband's attention, she thought better of it, and suggested to Mrs. Druce that Mademoiselle might be useful to her in conducting her foreign correspondence. Mrs. Druce accordingly engaged the young lady to act as her secretary and amanuensis, and appears, on the whole, to have taken to the girl, and to have been on a pleasant, friendly footing with her. I wonder if the Princess Dullah-Veih was on an equally pleasant footing with her when she saw, as no doubt she did, the attention she received at the Major's hands." (Mr. Dyer shrugged his shoulders.) "The Major's suspicions do not point in that direction, in spite of the fact which I elicited from him by judicious questioning, that the Princess has a violent and jealous temper, and has at times made his life a burden to him. His suspicions centre solely upon a certain Hafiz Cassimi, son of the Turkish-Egyptian banker of that name. It was at the house of these Cassimis that the Major first met the Princess, and he states that she and young Cassimi are like brother and sister to each other. He says that this young man has had the run of his mother's house and made himself very much at home in it for the past three weeks, ever since, in fact, the Princess came to stay with Mrs. Druce, in order to be initiated into the mysteries of English family life. Hafiz Cassimi, according to the Major's account, fell desperately in love with the little Swiss girl almost at first sight and pestered her with his attentions, and off and on there appear to have passed hot words between the two young men."

"One could scarcely expect a princess with Eastern blood in her veins to be a quiet and passive spectator to such a drama of cross-purposes."

"Scarcely. The Major, perhaps, hardly takes the Princess sufficiently into his reckoning. According to him, young Cassimi is a thorough-going Iago, and he begs me to concentrate attention entirely on him. Cassimi, he says, has stolen the photograph. Cassimi has inveigled the girl out of the house on some pretext—perhaps out of the country also, and he suggests that it might be as well to communicate with the police at Cairo, with as little delay as possible."

"And it hasn't so much as entered his mind that his Princess might have a hand in such a plot as that!"

"Apparently not. I think I told you that Mademoiselle had taken no luggage—not so much as a hand-bag—with her. Nothing, beyond her coat and hat, has disappeared from her wardrobe. Her writing-desk, and, in fact, all her boxes and drawers, have been opened and searched, but no letters or papers of any sort have been found that throw any light upon her movements."

"At what hour in the day is the girl supposed to have left the house?"

"No one can say for certain. It is conjectured that it was some time in the afternoon of the second of this month—a week ago to-day. It was one of Mrs. Druce's big reception days, and with a stream of people going and coming, a young lady, more or less, leaving the house would scarcely be noticed."

"I suppose," said Loveday, after a moment's pause, "this Princess Dullah-Veih has something of a history. One does not often get a Turkish princess in London."

"Yes, she has a history. She is only remotely connected with the present reigning dynasty in Turkey, and I dare say her princess-ship has been made the most of. All the same, however, she has had an altogether exceptional career for an Oriental lady. She was left an orphan at an early age, and was consigned to the guardianship of the elder Cassimi by her relatives. The Cassimis, both father and son, seem to be very advanced and European in their ideas, and by them she was taken to Cairo for her education. About a year ago they 'brought her out' in London, where she made the acquaintance of Major Druce. The young man, by-the-way, appears to be rather hot-headed in his love-making, for within six weeks of his introduction to her their engagement was announced. No doubt it had Mrs. Druce's fullest approval, for knowing her son's extravagant habits and his numerous debts, it must have been patent to her that a rich wife was a necessity to him. The marriage, I believe, was to have taken place this season; but taking into consideration the young man's ill-advised attentions to the little Swiss girl, and the fervour he is throwing into the search for her, I should say it was exceedingly doubtful whether—"

"Major Druce, sir, wishes to see you," said a clerk at that moment, opening the door leading from the outer office.

"Very good; show him in," said Mr. Dyer. Then he turned to Loveday.

"Of course I have spoken to him about you, and he is very anxious to take you to his mother's reception this afternoon, so that you may have a look round and—"

He broke off, having to rise and greet Major Druce, who at that moment entered the room.

He was a tall, handsome young fellow of about seven or eight and twenty, "well turned out" from head to foot, moustache waxed, orchid in button-hole, light kid gloves, and patent leather boots. There was assuredly nothing in his appearance to substantiate his statement to Mr. Dyer that he "hadn't slept a wink all night, that in fact another twenty-four hours of this terrible suspense would send him into his grave."

Mr. Dyer introduced Miss Brooke, and she expressed her sympathy with him on the painful matter that was filling his thoughts.

"It is very good of you, I'm sure," he replied, in a slow, soft drawl, not unpleasant to listen to. "My mother receives this afternoon from half past four to half past six, and I shall be very glad if you will allow me to introduce you to the inside of our house, and to the very ill-looking set that we have somehow managed to gather about us."

"The ill-looking set?"

"Yes; Jews, Turks, heretics and infidels—all there. And they're on the increase too, that's the worst of it. Every week a fresh importation from Cairo."

"Ah, Mrs. Druce is a large-hearted, benevolent woman," interposed Mr. Dyer; "all nationalities gather within her walls."

"Was your mother a large-hearted, benevolent woman?" said the young man, turning upon him. "No! well then, thank Providence that she wasn't; and admit that you know nothing at all on the matter. Miss Brooke," he continued, turning to Loveday, "I've brought round my hansom for you; it's nearly half past four now, and it's a good twenty minutes' drive from here to Portland Place. If you're ready, I'm at your service."

Major Druce's hansom was, like himself, in all respects "well turned out," and the India rubber tires round its wheels allowed an easy flow of conversation to be kept up during the twenty minutes' drive from Lynch Court to Portland Place.

The Major led off the talk in frank and easy fashion.

"My mother," he said, "prides herself on being cosmopolitan in her tastes, and just now we are very cosmopolitan indeed. Even our servants represent divers nationalities; the butler is French, the two footmen Italians, the maids, I believe, are some of them German, some Irish; and I've no doubt if you penetrated to the kitchen-quarters, you'd find the staff there composed in part of Scandinavians, in part of South Sea Islanders. The other quarters of the globe you will find fully represented in the drawing-room."

Loveday had a direct question to ask.

"Are you certain that Mdlle. Cunier had no friends in England?" she said.

"Positive. She hadn't a friend in the world outside my mother's four walls, poor child! She told me more than once that she was 'seule sur la terre.'" He broke off for a moment, as if overcome by a sad memory, then added: "But I'll put a bullet into him, take my word for it, if she isn't found within another twenty-four hours. Personally I should prefer settling the brute in that fashion to handing him over to the police."

His face flushed a deep red, there came a sudden flash to his eye, but for all that, his voice was as soft and slow and unemotional, as though he were talking of nothing more serious than bringing down a partridge.

There fell a brief pause; then Loveday asked another question.

"Is Mademoiselle Catholic or Protestant, can you tell me?"

The Major thought for a moment, then replied:

"'Pon my word, I don't know. She used sometimes to attend a little charge in South Savile Street—I've walked with her occasionally to the church door—but I couldn't for the life of me say whether it was a Catholic, Protestant, or Pagan place of worship. But—but you don't think those confounded priests have—"

"Here, we are in Portland Place," interrupted Loveday. "Mrs. Druce's rooms are already full, to judge from that long line of carriages!"

"Miss Brooke," said the Major suddenly, bethinking himself of his responsibilities, "how am I to introduce you? what rôle will you take up this afternoon? Pose as a faddist of some sort, if you want to win my mother's heart. What do you say to having started a grand scheme for supplying Hottentots and Kaffirs with eyeglasses? My mother would swear eternal friendship with you at once."

"Don't introduce me at all at first," answered Loveday. "Get me into some quiet corner, where I can see without being seen. Later on in the afternoon, when I have had time to look round a little, I'll tell you whether it will be necessary to introduce me or not."

"It will be a mob this afternoon, and no mistake," said Major Druce, as side by side, they entered the house. "Do you hear that fizzing and clucking just behind us? That's Arabic; you'll get it in whiffs between gusts of French and German all the afternoon. The Egyptian contingent seems to be in full force to-day. I don't see any Choctaw Indians, but no doubt they'll send their representatives later on. Come in at this side door, and we'll work our way round to that big palm. My mother is sure to be at the principal doorway."

The drawing rooms were packed from end to end, and Major Druce's progress, as he headed Loveday through the crowd, was impeded by hand-shaking and the interchange of civilities with his mother's guests.

Eventually the big palm standing in a Chinese cistern was reached, and there, half screened from view by its graceful branches, he placed a chair for Miss Brooke.

From this quiet nook, as now and again the crowd parted, Loveday could command a fair view of both drawing-rooms.

"Don't attract attention to me by standing at my elbow," she whispered to the Major.

He answered her whisper with another.

"There's the Beast—Iago, I mean," he said; "do you see him? He's standing talking to that fair, handsome woman in pale green, with a picture hat. She's Lady Gwynne. And there's my mother, and there's Dolly—the Princess I mean—alone on the sofa. Ah! you can't see her now for the crowd. Yes, I'll go, but if you want me, just nod to me and I shall understand."

If was easy to see what had brought such a fashionable crowd to Mrs. Druce's rooms that afternoon. Every caller, as soon as she had shaken hands with the hostess, passed on to the Princess's sofa, and there waited patiently till opportunity presented itself for an introduction to her Eastern Highness.

Loveday found it impossible to get more than the merest glimpse of her, and so transferred her attention to Mr. Hafiz Cassimi, who had been referred to in such unceremonious language by Major Druce.

He was a swarthy, well-featured man, with bold, black eyes, and lips that had the habit of parting now and again, not to smile, but as if for no other purpose than to show a double row of gleaming white teeth. The European dress he wore seemed to accord ill with the man; and Loveday could fancy that those black eyes and that double row of white teeth would have shown to better advantage beneath a turban or a fez cap. From Cassimi, her eye wandered to Mrs. Druce—a tall, stout woman, dressed in black velvet, and with hair mounted high on her head, that had the appearance of being either bleached or powdered. She gave Loveday the impression of being that essentially modern product of modern society—the woman who combines in one person the hard-working philanthropist with the hard-working woman of fashion. As arrivals began to slacken, she left her post near the door and began to make the round of the room. From snatches of talk that came to her where she sat, Loveday could gather that with one hand, as it were, this energetic lady was organizing a grand charity concert, and with the other pushing the interests of a big ball that was shortly to be given by the officers of her son's regiment.

It was a hot June day. In spite of closed blinds and open windows, the rooms were stifling to a degree. The butler, a small dark, slight Frenchman, made his way through the throng to a window at Loveday's right hand, to see if a little more air could be admitted.

Major Druce followed on his heels to Loveday's side.

"Will you come into the next room and have some tea?" he asked; "I'm sure you must feel nearly suffocated here." He broke off, then added in a lower tone: "I hope you have kept your eyes on the Beast. Did you ever in your life see a more repulsive-looking animal?"

Loveday took his questions in their order.

"No tea, thank you," she said, "but I shall be glad if you will tell your butler to bring me a glass of water—there he is, at your elbow. Yes, off and on I have been studying Mr. Cassimi, and I must admit I do not like his smileless smile."

The butler brought the water. The Major, much to his annoyance, was seized upon simultaneously by two ladies, one eager to know if any tidings had been received of Mdlle. Cunier, the other anxious to learn if a distinguished president to the Harem Mission had been decided upon.

Soon after six the rooms began to thin somewhat, and presentations to the Princess ceasing, Loveday was able to get a full view of her.

She presented a striking picture, seated, half-reclining, on a sofa, with two white-robed, dark-skinned Egyptian maidens standing behind it. A more unfortunate sobriquet than "Dolly" could scarcely have been found by the Major for this Oriental beauty, with her olive complexion, her flashing eyes and extravagant richness of attire.

"'Queen of Sheba' would be far more appropriate," thought Loveday. "She turns the commonplace sofa into a throne, and, I should say, makes every one of those ladies feel as if she ought to have donned court dress and plumes for the occasion."

It was difficult for her, from where she sat, to follow the details of the Princess's dress. She could only see that a quantity of soft orange-tinted silk was wound about the upper part of her arms and fell from her shoulders like drooping wings, and that here and there jewels flashed out from its folds. Her thick black hair was loosely knotted, and kept in its place by jeweled pins and a bandeau of pearls; and similar bandeaus adored her slender throat and wrists.

"Are you lost in admiration?" said the Major, once more at her elbow, in a slightly sarcastic tone. "That sort of thing is very taking and effective at first, but after a time—"

He did not finish his sentence, shrugged his shoulders and walked away. Half-past six chimed from a small clock on a bracket. Carriage after carriage was rolling away from the door now, and progress on the stairs was rendered difficult by a descending crowd.

A quarter to seven struck, the last hand-shaking had been gone through, and Mrs. Druce, looking hot and tired, had sunk into a chair at the Princess's right hand, bending slightly forward to render conversation with her easy.

On the Princess's left hand, Lady Gwynne had taken a chair, and sat in converse with Hafiz Cassimi, who stood beside her.

Evidently these four were on very easy and intimate terms with each other. Lady Gwynne had tossed her big picture hat on a chair at her left hand, and was fanning herself with a palm-leaf. Mrs. Druce, beckoning to the butler, desired him to bring them some claret-cup from the refreshment-room.

No one seemed to observe Loveday seated still in her nook beside the big palm.

She signaled to the Major, who stood looking discontentedly from one of the windows.

"That is a most interesting group," she said; "now, if you like, you may introduce me to your mother."

"Oh, with pleasure—under what name?" he asked.

"Under my own," she answered, "and please be very distinct in pronouncing it, raise your voice slightly so that every one of those persons may hear it. And then, please add my profession, and say I am here at your request to investigate the circumstances connected with Mdlle. Cunier's disappearance."

Major Druce looked astounded.

"But—but," he stammered, "have you seen anything—found out anything? If not, don't you think it will be better to preserve your incognita a little longer."

"Don't stop to ask questions," said Loveday sharply; "now, this very minute, do what I ask you, or the opportunity will be gone."

The Major without further demur, escorted Loveday across the room. The conversation between the four intimate friends had now become general and animated, and he had to wait for a minute or so before he could get an opportunity to speak to his mother.

During that minute Loveday stood a little in his rear, with Lady Gwynne and Cassimi at her right hand.

"I want to introduce this lady to you," said the Major, when a pause in the talk gave him his opportunity. "This is Miss Loveday Brooke, a lady detective, and she is here at my request to investigate the circumstances connected with the disappearance of Mdlle. Cunier."

He said the words slowly and distinctly.

"There!" he said to himself complacently, as he ended; "if I had been reading the lessons in church, I couldn't have been more emphatic."

A blank silence for a moment fell upon the group, and even the butler, just then entering with the claret-cup, came to a standstill at the door.

Then, simultaneously, a glance flashed from Mrs. Druce to Lady Gwynne, from Lady Gwynne to Mrs. Druce, and then, also simultaneously, the eyes of both ladies rested, though only for an instant, on the big picture hat lying on the chair.

Lady Gwynne started to her feet and seized her hat, adjusting it without so much as a glance at a mirror.

"I must go at once; this very minute," she said. "I promised Charlie I would back soon after six, and now it is past seven. Mr. Cassimi, will you take me down to my carriage?" And with the most hurried of leave-takings to the Princess and her hostess, the lady swept out of the room, followed by Mr. Cassimi.

The butler still standing at the door, drew back to allow the lady to pass, and then, claret-cup and all, followed her out of the room.

Mrs. Druce drew a long breath and bowed formally to Loveday.

"I was a little taken by surprise," she began—

But here the Princess rose suddenly from the sofa.

"Moi, je suis fatiguée," she said in excellent French to Mrs. Druce, and she too swept out of the room, throwing, as she passed, what seemed to Loveday a slightly scornful glance towards the Major.

Her two attendants, one carrying her fan, and the other her reclining cushions, followed.

Mrs. Druce again turned to Loveday.

"Yes, I confess I was taken a little by surprise," she said, her manner thawing slightly. "I am not accustomed to the presence of detectives in my house; but now tell me what do you propose doing: how do you mean to begin your investigations—by going over the house and looking in all the corners, or by cross-questioning the servants? Forgive my asking, but really I am quite at a loss; I haven't the remotest idea how such investigations are generally conducted."

"I do not propose to do much in the way of investigation to-night," answered Loveday as formally as she had been addressed, "for I have very important business to transact before eight o'clock this evening. I shall ask you to allow me to see Mdlle. Cunier's room—ten minutes there will be sufficient—after that, I do not think I need further trouble you."

"Certainly; by all means," answered Mrs. Druce; "you'll find the room exactly as Lucie left it, nothing has been disturbed."

She turned to the butler, who had by this time returned and stood presenting the claret-cup, and, in French, desired him to summon her maid, and tell her to show Miss Brooke to Mdlle. Cunier's room.

The ten minutes that Loveday had said would suffice for her survey of this room extended themselves to fifteen, but the extra five minutes assuredly were not expended by her in the investigation of drawers and boxes. The maid, a pleasant, well-spoken young woman, jingled her keys, and opened every lock, and seemed not at all disinclined to enter into the light gossip that Loveday contrived to set going.

She answered freely a variety of questions that Loveday put to her respecting Mademoiselle and her general habits, and from Mademoiselle, the talk drifted to other members of Mrs. Druce's household.

If Loveday had, as she had stated, important business to transact that evening, she certainly set about it in a strange fashion.

After she quitted Mademoiselle's room, she went straight out of the house, without leaving a message of any sort for either Mrs. or Major Druce. She walked the length of Portland Place in leisurely fashion, and then, having first ascertained that her movements were not being watched, she called a hansom, and desired the man to drive her to Madame Céline's, a fashionable milliner's in Old Bond Street.

At Madame Céline's she spent close upon half-an-hour, giving many and minute directions for the making of a hat, which assuredly, when finished, would compare with nothing in the way of millinery that she had ever before put upon her head.

From Madame Céline's the hansom conveyed her to an undertaker's shop, at the corner of South Savile Street, and here she spent a brief ten minutes in conversation with the undertaker himself in his little back parlour.

From the undertaker's she drove home to her rooms in Gower Street, and then, before she divested herself of hat and coat, she wrote a brief note to Major Druce, requesting him to meet her on the following morning at Eglacé's, the confectioner's, in South Savile Street, at nine o'clock punctually.

This note she committed to the charge of the cab-driver, desiring him to deliver it at Portland Place on his way back to his stand.

"They've queer ways of doing things—these people!" said the Major, as he opened and read the note. "Suppose I must keep the appointment though, confound it. I can't see that she can possibly have found out anything by just sitting still in a corner for a couple of hours! And I'm confident she didn't give that beast Cassimi one quarter the attention she bestowed on other people."

In spite of his grumbling, however, the Major kept his appointment, and nine o'clock the next morning saw him shaking hands with Miss Brooke on Eglacé's doorstep.

"Dismiss your hansom," she said to him. "I only want you to come a few doors down the street, to the French Protestant church, to which you have sometimes escorted Mdlle. Cunier."

At the church door Loveday paused a moment.

"Before we enter," she said, "I want you to promise that whatever you may see going on there—however greatly you may be surprised—you will make no disturbance, not so much as open your lips till we come out."

The Major, not a little bewildered, gave the required promise; and, side by side, the two entered the church.

It was little more than a big room; at the farther end, in the middle of the nave, stood the pulpit, and immediately behind this was a low platform, enclosed by a brass rail.

Behind this brass rail, in black Geneva gown, stood the pastor of the church, and before him, on cushions, kneeled two persons, a man and a woman.

These two persons and an old man, the verger, formed the whole of the congregation. The position of the church, amid shops and narrow back-yards, had necessitated the filling in of every one of its windows with stained glass; it was, consequently, so dim that, coming in from the outside glare of sunlight, the Major found it difficult to make out what was going on at the farther end.

The verger came forward and offered to show them to a seat. Loveday shook her head—they would be leaving in a minute, she said, and would prefer standing where they were.

The Major began to take in the situation.

"Why they're being married!" he said in a loud whisper. "What on earth have you brought me in here for?"

Loveday laid her finger on her lips and frowned severely at him.

The marriage service came to an end, the pastor extended his black-gowned arms like the wings of a bat and pronounced the benediction; the man and woman rose from their knees and proceeded to follow him into the vestry.

The woman was neatly dressed in a long dove-coloured travelling cloak. She wore a large hat, from which fell a white gossamer veil that completely hid her face from view. The man was small, dark and slight, and as he passed on to the vestry beside his bride, the Major at once identified him as his mother's butler.

"Why, that's Lebrun!" he said in a still louder whisper than before. "Why, in the name of all that's wonderful, have you brought me here to see that fellow married?"

"You'd better come outside if you can't keep quiet," said Loveday severely, and leading the way out of the church as she spoke.

Outside, South Savile Street was busy with early morning traffic.

"Let us go back to Eglacé's" said Loveday, "and have some coffee. I will explain to you there all you are wishing to know."

But before the coffee could be brought to them, the Major had asked at least a dozen questions.

Loveday put them all on one side.

"All in good time" she said. "You are leaving out the most important question of all. Have you no curiosity to know who was the bride that Lebrun has chosen?"

"I don't suppose it concerns me in the slightest degree," he answered indifferently; "but since you wish me to ask the question—Who was she?"

"Lucie Cunier, lately your mother's amanuensis."

"The —!" cried the Major, jumping to his feet and uttering an exclamation that must be indicated by a blank.

"Take it calmly," said Loveday; "don't rave. Sit down and I'll tell you all about it. No, it is not the doing of your friend Cassimi, so you need not threaten to put a bullet into him; the girl has married Lebrun of her own free will—no one has forced her into it."

"Lucie has married Lebrun of her own free will!" he echoed, growing very white and taking the chair which faced Loveday at the little table.

"Will you have sugar?" asked Loveday, stirring the coffee, which the waiter at that moment brought.

"Yes, I repeat," she presently resumed, "Lucie has married Lebrun of her own free will, although I conjecture she might not perhaps have been quite so willing to crown his happiness if the Princess Dullah-Veih had not made it greatly to her interest to do so."

"Dolly made it to her interest to do so?" again echoed the Major.

"Do not interrupt me with exclamations; let me tell the story my own fashion, and then you may ask as many questions as you please. Now, to begin at the beginning, Lucie became engaged to Lebrun within a month of her coming to your mother's house, but she carefully kept the secret from everyone, even from the servants, until about a month ago, when she mentioned the fact in confidence to Mrs. Druce in order to defend herself from the charge of having sought to attract your attention. There was nothing surprising in this engagement; they were both lonely and in a foreign land, spoke the same language, and no doubt had many things in common; and, although chance has lifted Lucie somewhat out of her station, she really belongs to the same class in life as Lebrun. Their love-making appears to have run along smoothly enough until you came home on leave, and the girl's pretty face attracted your attention. Your evident admiration for her disturbed the equanimity of the Princess, who saw your devotion to herself waning; of Lebrun, who fancied Lucie's manner to him had changed; of your mother, who was anxious that you should make a suitable marriage. Also additional complications arose from the fact that your attentions to the little Swiss girl had drawn Mr. Cassimi's notice to her numerous attractions, and there was the danger of you two young men posing as rivals. At this juncture Lady Gwynne, as an intimate friend, and one who had herself suffered a twinge of heartache on Mademoiselle's account, was taken into your mother's confidence, and the three ladies in council decided that Lucie, in some fashion, must be got out of the way before you and Mr. Cassimi came to an open breach, or you had spoilt your matrimonial prospects."

Here the Major made a slightly impatient movement.

Loveday went on: "It was the Princess who solved the question how this was to be done. Fair Rosamonds are no longer put out of the way by 'a cup of cold poison'—golden guineas do the thing far more easily and innocently. The Princess expressed her willingness to bestow a thousand pounds on Lucie on the day that she married Lebrun, and to set her up afterwards as a fashionable milliner in Paris. After this munificent offer, everything else became mere matter of detail. The main thing was to get the damsel out of the way without your being able to trace her—perhaps work on her feelings, and induce her, at the last moment, to throw over Lebrun. Your absence from home, on a three days' visit, gave them the wished-for opportunity. Lady Gwynne took her milliner into her confidence. Madame Céline consented to receive Lucie into her house, seclude her in a room on the upper floor, and at the same time give her an insight into the profession of a fashionable milliner. The rest I think you know. Lucie quietly walks out of the house one afternoon, taking no luggage, calling no cab, and thereby cutting off one very obvious means of being traced. Madame Céline receives and hides her—not a difficult feat to accomplish in London, more especially if the one to be hidden is a foreign amanuensis, who is seldom seen out of doors, and who leaves no photograph behind her."

"I suppose it was Lebrun who had the confounded cheek to go to my drawer and appropriate that photograph. I wish it had been Cassimi—I could have kicked him, but—but it makes one feel rather small to have posed as rival to one's mother's butler."

"I think you may congratulate yourself that Lebrun did nothing worse than go to your drawer and appropriate that photograph. I never saw a man bestow a more deadly look of hatred than he threw at you yesterday afternoon in your mother's drawing-room; it was that look of hatred that first drew my attention to the man and set me on the track that has ended in the Swiss Protestant church this morning."

"Ah! let me hear about that—let me have the links in the chain, one by one, as you came upon them," said the Major.

He was still pale—almost as the marble table at which they sat, but his voice had gone back to its normal slow, soft drawl.

"With pleasure. The look that Lebrun threw at you, as he crossed the room to open the window, was link number one. As I saw that look, I said to myself there is someone in that corner whom that man hates with a deadly hatred. Then you came forward to speak to me, and I saw that it was you that the man was ready to murder, if opportunity offered. After this, I scrutinized him closely—not a detail of his features or his dress escaped me, and I noticed, among other things, that on the fourth finger of his left hand, half hidden by a more pretentious ring, was an old fashioned curious looking silver one. That silver ring was link number two in the chain."

"Ah, I suppose you asked for that glass of water on purpose to get a closer view of the ring?"

"I did, I found it was a Genevese ring of ancient make, the like of which I had not seen since I was a child and played with one, that my old Swiss bonne used to wear. Now I must tell you a little bit of Genevese history before I can make you understand how important a link that silver ring was to me. Echallets, the town in which Lucie was born, and her father had kept a watchmaker's shop, has long been famous for its jewellery and watchmaking. The two trades, however, were not combined in one until about a hundred years ago, when the corporation of the town passed a law decreeing that they should unite in one guild for their common good. To celebrate this amalgamation of interests, the jewellers fabricated a certain number of silver rings, consisting of a plain band of silver, on which two hands, in relief, clasped each other. These rings were distributed among the members of the guild, and as time has gone on they have become scarce and valuable as relics of the past. In certain families, they have been handed down as heirlooms, and have frequently done duty as betrothal rings—the clasped hands no doubt suggesting their suitability for this purpose. Now, when I saw such a ring on Lebrun's finger, I naturally guessed from whom he had received it, and at once classed his interests with those of your mother and the Princess, and looked upon him as their possible coadjutor."

"What made you throw the brute Cassimi altogether out of your reckoning?"

"I did not do so at this stage of events; only, so to speak, marked him as 'doubtful' and kept my eye on him. I determined to try an experiment that I have never before attempted in my work. You know what that experiment was. I saw five persons, Mrs. Druce, the Princess, Lady Gwynne, Mr. Cassimi and Lebrun all in the room within a few yards of each other, and I asked you to take them by surprise and announce my name and profession, so that every one of those five persons could hear you."

"You did. I could not, for the life of me, make out what was your motive for so doing."

"My motive for so doing was simply, as it were, to raise the sudden cry, 'The enemy is upon you,' and to set every one of those five persons guarding their weak point—that is, if they had one. I'll draw your attention to what followed. Mr. Cassimi remained nonchalant and impassive; your mother and Lady Gwynne exchanged glances, and they both simultaneously threw a nervous look at Lady Gwynne's hat lying on the chair. Now as I had stood waiting to be introduced to Mrs. Druce, I had casually read the name of Madame Céline on the lining of the hat and I at once concluded that Madame Céline must be a very weak point indeed; a conclusion that was confirmed when Lady Gwynne hurriedly seized her hat and as hurriedly departed. Then the Princess scarcely less abruptly rose and left the room, and Lebrun on the point of entering, quitted it also. When he returned five minutes later, with the claret-cup, he had removed the ring from his finger, so I had now little doubt where his weak point lay."

"It's wonderful; it's like a fairy tale!" drawled the Major. "Pray, go on."

"After this," continued Loveday, "my work became very simple. I did not care two straws for seeing Mademoiselle's room, but I cared very much to have a talk with Mrs. Druce's maid. From her I elicited the important fact that Lebrun was leaving very unexpectedly on the following day, and that his boxes were packed and labeled for Paris. After I left your house, I drove to Madame Céline's, and there, as a sort of entrance fee, ordered an elaborate hat. I praised freely the hats they had on view, and while giving minute directions as to the one I required, I extracted the information that Madame Céline had recently taken on a new milliner who had very great artistic skill. Upon this, I asked permission to see this new milliner and give her special instructions concerning my hat. My request was referred to Madame Céline, who appeared much ruffled by it, and informed me that it would be quite useless for me to see this new milliner; she could execute no more orders, as she was leaving the next day for Paris, where she intended opening an establishment on her own account.

"Now you see the point at which I had arrived. There was Lebrun and there was this new milliner each leaving for Paris on the same day; it was not unreasonable to suppose that they might start in company, and that before so doing, a little ceremony might be gone through in the Swiss Protestant church that Mademoiselle occasionally attended. This conjecture sent me to the undertaker in South Savile Street, who combines with his undertaking the office of verger to the little church. From him I learned that a marriage was to take place at the church at a quarter to nine the next morning and that the names of the contracting parties were Pierre Lebrun and Lucie Cuénin."

"Cuénin!"

"Yes, that is the girl's real name; it seems Lady Gwynne re-christened her Cunier, because she said the English pronunciation of Cuénin grated on her ear—people would insist upon adding a *g* after the *n*. She introduced her to Mrs. Druce under the name of Cunier, forgetting, perhaps, the girl's real name, or else thinking it a matter of no importance. This fact, no doubt, considerably lessened Lebrun's fear of detection in procuring his licence and transmitting it to the

Swiss pastor. Perhaps you are a little surprised at my knowledge of the facts I related to you at the beginning of our conversation. I got at them through Lebrun this morning. At half-past eight I went down to the church and found him there, waiting for his bride. He grew terribly excited at seeing me, and thought I was going to bring you down on him and upset his wedding arrangements at the last moment. I assured him to the contrary, and his version of the facts I have handed on to you. Should, however, any details of the story seem to you to be lacking, I have no doubt that Mrs. Druce or the Princess will supply them, now that all necessity for secrecy has come to an end."

The Major drew on his gloves; his colour had come back to him; he had resumed his easy suavity of manner.

"I don't think," he said slowly, "I'll trouble my mother or the Princess; and I shall be glad, if you have the opportunity, if you will make people understand that I only moved in the matter at all out of—of mere kindness to a young and friendless foreigner."

DRAWN DAGGERS

"I admit that the dagger business is something of a puzzle to me, but as for the lost necklace—well, I should have thought a child would have understood that," said Mr. Dyer irritably. "When a young lady loses a valuable article of jewellery and wishes to hush the matter up, the explanation is obvious."

"Sometimes," answered Miss Brooke calmly, "the explanation that is obvious is the one to be rejected, not accepted."

Off and on these two had been, so to speak, "jangling" a good deal that morning. Perhaps the fact was in part to be attributed to the biting east wind which had set Loveday's eyes watering with the gritty dust, as she had made her way to Lynch Court, and which was, at the present moment, sending the smoke, in aggravating gusts, down the chimney into Mr. Dyer's face. Thus it was, however. On the various topics that had chanced to come up for discussion that morning between Mr. Dyer and his colleague, they had each taken up, as if by design, diametrically opposite points of view.

His temper altogether gave way now.

"If," he said, bringing his hand down with emphasis on his writing table, "you lay it down as a principle that the obvious is to be rejected in favour of the abstruse, you'll soon find yourself launched in the predicament of having to prove that two apples added to two other apples do not make four. But there, if you don't choose to see things from my point of view, that is no reason why you should lose your temper!"

"Mr. Hawke wishes to see you, sir," said a clerk, at that moment entering the room.

It was a fortunate diversion. Whatever might be the differences of opinion in which these two might indulge in private, they were careful never to parade those differences before their clients.

Mr. Dyer's irritability vanished in a moment.

"Show the gentleman in," he said to the clerk. Then he turned to Loveday. "This is the Rev. Anthony Hawke, the gentleman at whose house I told you that Miss Monroe is staying temporarily. He is a clergyman of the Church of England, but gave up his living some twenty years ago when he married a wealthy lady. Miss Monroe has been sent over to his guardianship from Pekin by her father, Sir George Monroe, in order to get her out of the way of a troublesome and undesirable suitor."

The last sentence was added in a low and hurried tone, for Mr. Hawke was at that moment entering the room.

He was a man close upon sixty years of age, white-haired, clean shaven, with a full, round face, to which a small nose imparted a somewhat infantine expression. His manner of greeting was urbane but slightly flurried and nervous. He gave Loveday the impression of being an easy-going, happy-tempered man who, for the moment, was unusually disturbed and perplexed.

He glanced uneasily at Loveday. Mr. Dyer hastened to explain that this was the lady by whose aid he hoped to get to the bottom of the matter now under consideration.

"In that case there can be no objection to my showing you this," said Mr. Hawke; "it came by post this morning. You see my enemy still pursues me."

As he spoke he took from his pocket a big, square envelope, from which he drew a large-sized sheet of paper.

On this sheet of paper were roughly drawn, in ink, two daggers, about six inches in length, with remarkably pointed blades.

Mr. Dyer looked at the sketch with interest.

"We will compare this drawing and its envelope with those you previously received," he said, opening a drawer of his writing-table and taking thence a precisely similar envelope. On the sheet of paper, however, that this envelope enclosed, there was drawn one dagger only.

He placed both envelopes and their enclosures side by side, and in silence compared them. Then, without a word, he handed them to Miss Brooke, who, taking a glass from her pocket, subjected them to a similar careful and minute scrutiny.

Both envelopes were of precisely the same make, and were each addressed to Mr. Hawke's London address in a round, school-boyish, copybook sort of hand—the hand so easy to write and so difficult to bring home to any writer on account of its want of individuality. Each envelope likewise bore a Cork and a London postmark.

The sheet of paper, however, that the first envelope enclosed bore the sketch of one dagger only.

Loveday laid down her glass.

"The envelopes," she said, "have, undoubtedly, been addressed by the same person, but these last two daggers have not been drawn by the hand that drew the first. Dagger number one was, evidently, drawn by a timid, uncertain and inartistic hand—see how the lines wave and how they have been patched here and there. The person who drew the other daggers, I should say, could do better work; the outline, though rugged, is bold and free. I should like to take these sketches home with me and compare them again at my leisure."

"Ah, I felt sure what your opinion would be!" said Mr. Dyer complacently.

Mr. Hawke seemed much disturbed.

"Good gracious!" he ejaculated; "you don't mean to say I have two enemies pursuing me in this fashion! What does it mean? Can it be—is it possible, do you think, that these things have been sent to me by the members of some Secret Society in Ireland—under error, of course—mistaking me for someone else? They can't be meant for me; I have never, in my whole life, been mixed up with any political agitation of any sort."

Mr. Dyer shook his head. "Members of secret societies generally make pretty sure of their ground before they send out missives of this kind," he said. "I have never heard of such an error being made. I think, too, we mustn't build any theories on the Irish postmark; the letters may have been posted in Cork for the whole and sole purpose of drawing off attention from some other quarter."

"Will you mind telling me a little about the loss of the necklace?" here said Loveday, bringing the conversation suddenly round from the daggers to the diamonds.

"I think," interposed Mr. Dyers, turning towards her, "that the episode of the drawn daggers—drawn in a double sense—should be treated entirely on its own merits, considered as a thing apart from the loss of the necklace. I am inclined to believe that when we have gone a little further into the matter we shall find that each circumstance belongs to a different group of facts. After all, it is possible that these daggers may have been sent by way of a joke—a rather foolish one, I admit—by some harum-scarum fellow bent on causing a sensation."

Mr. Hawke's face brightened.

"Ah! now, do you think so—really think so?" he ejaculated. "It would lift such a load from my mind if you could bring the thing home, in this way, to some practical joker. There are a lot of such fellows knocking about the world. Why, now I come to think of it, my nephew, Jack, who is a good deal with us just now, and is not quite so steady a fellow as I should like him to be, must have a good many such scamps among his acquaintances."

"A good many such scamps among his acquaintances," echoed Loveday; "that certainly gives plausibility to Mr. Dyer's supposition. At the same time, I think we are bound to look at the other side of the case, and admit the possibility of these daggers being sent in right-down sober earnest by persons concerned in the robbery, with the intention of intimidating you and preventing full investigation of the matter. If this be so, it will not signify which thread we take up and follow. If we find the sender of the daggers we are safe to come upon the thief; or, if we follow up and find the thief, the sender of the daggers will not be far off."

Mr. Hawke's face fell once more.

"It's an uncomfortable position to be in," he said slowly. "I suppose, whoever they are, they will do the regulation thing, and next time will send an instalment of three daggers, in which case I may consider myself a doomed man. It did not occur to me before, but I remember now that I did not receive the first dagger until after I had spoken very strongly to Mrs. Hawke, before the servants, about my wish to set the police to work. I told her I felt bound, in honour to Sir George, to do so, as the necklace had been lost under my roof."

"Did Mrs. Hawke object to your calling in the aid of the police?" asked Loveday.

"Yes, most strongly. She entirely supported Miss Monroe in her wish to take no steps in the matter. Indeed, I should not have come round as I did last night to Mr. Dyer, if my wife had not been suddenly summoned from home by the serious illness of her sister. At least," he corrected himself with a little attempt at self-assertion, "my coming to him might have been a little delayed. I hope you understand, Mr. Dyer; I do not mean to imply that I am not master in my own house."

"Oh, quite so, quite so," responded Mr. Dyer. "Did Mrs. Hawke or Miss Monroe give any reasons for not wishing you to move in the matter?"

"All told, I should think they gave about a hundred reasons—I can't remember them all. For one thing, Miss Monroe said it might necessitate her appearing in the police courts, a thing she would not consent to do; and she certainly did not consider the necklace was worth the fuss I was making over it. And that necklace, sir, has been valued at over nine hundred pounds, and has come down to the young lady from her mother."

"And Mrs. Hawke?"

"Mrs. Hawke supported Miss Monroe in her views in her presence. But privately to me afterwards, she gave other reasons for not wishing the police called in. Girls, she said, were always careless with their jewellery, she might have lost the necklace in Pekin, and never have brought it to England at all."

"Quite so," said Mr. Dyer. "I think I understood you to say that no one had seen the necklace since Miss Monroe's arrival in England. Also, I believe it was she who first discovered it to be missing?"

"Yes. Sir George, when he wrote apprising me of his daughter's visit, added a postscript to his letter, saying that his daughter was bringing her necklace with her and that he would feel greatly obliged if I would have it deposited with as little delay as possible at my bankers', where it could be easily got at if required. I spoke to Miss Monroe about doing this two or three times, but she did not seem at all inclined to comply with her father's wishes. Then my wife took the matter in hand—Mrs. Hawke, I must tell you, has a very firm, resolute manner—she told Miss Monroe plainly that she would not have the responsibility of those diamonds in the house, and insisted that there and then they should be sent off to the bankers. Upon this Miss Monroe went up to her room, and presently returned, saying that her necklace had disappeared. She herself, she said, had placed it in her jewel-case and the jewel-case in her wardrobe, when her boxes were unpacked. The jewel-case was in the wardrobe right enough, and no other article of jewellery appeared to have been disturbed, but the little padded niche in which the necklace had been deposited was empty. My wife and her maid went upstairs immediately, and searched every corner of the room, but, I'm sorry to say, without any result."

"Miss Monroe, I suppose, has her own maid?"

"No, she has not. The maid—an elderly native woman—who left Pekin with her, suffered so terribly from sea-sickness that, when they reached Malta, Miss Monroe allowed her to land and remain there in charge of an agent of the P. and O. Company till an outward bound packet could take her back to China. It seems the poor woman thought she was going to die, and was in a terrible state of mind because she hadn't brought her coffin with her. I dare say you know the terror these Chinese have of being buried in foreign soil. After her departure, Miss Monroe engaged one of the steerage passengers to act as her maid for the remainder of the voyage."

"Did Miss Monroe make the long journey from Pekin accompanied only by this native woman?"

"No; friends escorted her to Hong King—by far the roughest part of the journey. From Hong Kong she came on in *The Colombo*, accompanied only by her maid. I wrote and told her father I would meet her at the docks in London; the young lady, however, preferred landing at Plymouth, and telegraphed to me from there that she was coming on by rail to Waterloo, where, if I liked, I might meet her."

"She seems to be a young lady of independent habits. Was she brought up and educated in China?"

"Yes; by a succession of French and American governesses. After her mother's death, when she was little more than a baby, Sir George could not make up his mind to part with her, as she was his only child."

"I suppose you and Sir George Monroe are old friends?"

"Yes; he and I were great chums before he went out to China—now about twenty years ago—and it was only natural, when he wished to get his daughter out of the way of young Danvers's impertinent attentions, that he should ask me to take charge of her till he could claim his retiring pension and set up his tent in England."

"What was the chief objection to Mr. Danvers's attentions?"

"Well, he is only a boy of one-and-twenty, and has no money into the bargain. He has been sent out to Pekin by his father to study the language, in order to qualify for a billet in the customs, and it may be a dozen years before he is in a position to keep a wife. Now, Miss Monroe is an heiress—will come into her mother's large fortune when she is of age—and Sir George, naturally, would like her to make a good match."

"I suppose Miss Monroe came to England very reluctantly?"

"I imagine so. No doubt it was a great wrench for her to leave her home and friends in that sudden fashion and come to us, who are, one and all, utter strangers to her. She is very quiet, very shy and reserved. She goes nowhere, sees no one. When some old China friends of her father's called to see her the other day, she immediately found she had a headache, and went to bed. I think, on the whole, she gets on better with my nephew than with anyone else."

"Will you kindly tell me of how many persons your household consists at the present moment?

"At the present moment we are one more than usual, for my nephew, Jack, is home with his regiment from India, and is staying with us. As a rule, my household consists of my wife and myself, butler, cook, housemaid and my wife's maid, who just now is doing double duty as Miss Monroe's maid also."

Mr. Dyer looked at his watch.

"I have an important engagement in ten minutes' time," he said, "so I must leave you and Miss Brooke to arrange details as to how and when she is to begin her work inside your house, for, of course, in a case of this sort we must, in the first instance at any rate, concentrate attention within your four walls."

"The less delay the better," said Loveday. "I should like to attack the mystery at once—this afternoon."

Mr. Hawke thought for a moment.

"According to present arrangements," he said, with a little hesitation, "Mrs. Hawke will return next Friday, that is the day after to-morrow, so I can only ask you to remain in the house till the morning of that day. I'm sure you will understand that there might be some—some little awkwardness in—"

"Oh, quite so," interrupted Loveday. "I don't see at present that there will be any necessity for me to sleep in the house at all. How would it be for me to assume the part of a lady house decorator in the employment of a West-end firm, and sent by them to survey your house and advise upon its re-decoration? All I should have to do, would be to walk about your rooms with my head on one side, and a pencil and note-book in my hand. I should interfere with no one, your family life would go on as usual, and I could make my work as short or as long as necessity might dictate."

Mr. Hawke had no objection to offer to this. He had, however, a request to make as he rose to depart, and he made it a little nervously.

"If," he said, "by any chance there should come a telegram from Mrs. Hawke, saying she will return by an earlier train, I suppose—I hope, that is, you will make some excuse, and—and not get me into hot water, I mean."

To this, Loveday answered a little evasively that she trusted no such telegram would be forthcoming, but that, in any case, he might rely upon her discretion.

Four o'clock was striking from a neighbouring church clock as Loveday lifted the old-fashioned brass knocker of Mr. Hawke's house in Tavistock Square. An elderly butler admitted her and showed her into the drawing-room on the first floor. A single glance round showed Loveday that if her rôle had been real instead of assumed, she would have found plenty of scope for her talents. Although the house was in all respects comfortably furnished, it bore unmistakably the impress of those early Victorian days when aesthetic surroundings were not deemed a necessity of existence; an impress which people past middle age, and growing increasingly indifferent to the accessories of life, are frequently careless to remove.

"Young life here is evidently an excrescence, not part of the home; a troop of daughters turned into this room would speedily set going a different condition of things," thought Loveday, taking stock of the faded white and gold wall paper, the chairs covered with lilies and roses in cross-stitch, and the knick-knacks of a past generation that were scattered about on tables and mantelpiece.

A yellow damask curtain, half-festooned, divided the back drawing-room from the front in which she was seated. From the other side of this curtain there came to her the sound of voices—those of a man and a girl.

"Cut the cards again, please," said the man's voice. "Thank you. There you are again—the queen of hearts, surrounded with diamonds, and turning her back on a knave. Miss Monroe, you can't do better than make that fortune come true. Turn your back on the man who let you go without a word and—"

"Hush!" interrupted the girl with a little laugh: "I heard the next room door open—I'm sure someone came in."

The girl's laugh seemed to Loveday utterly destitute of that echo of heart-ache that in the circumstances might have been expected.

At this moment Mr. Hawke entered the room, and almost simultaneously the two young people came from the other side of the yellow curtain and crossed towards the door.

Loveday took a survey of them as they passed.

The young man—evidently "my nephew, Jack"—was a good-looking young fellow, with dark eyes and hair. The girl was small, slight and fair. She was perceptibly less at home with Jack's uncle than she was with Jack, for her manner changed and grew formal and reserved as she came face to face with him.

"We're going downstairs to have a game of billiards," said Jack, addressing Mr. Hawke, and throwing a look of curiosity at Loveday.

"Jack," said the old gentleman, "what would you say if I told you I was going to have the house re-decorated from top to bottom, and that this lady had come to advise on the matter."

This was the nearest (and most Anglicé) approach to a fabrication that Mr. Hawke would allow to pass his lips.

"Well," answered Jack promptly, "I should say, 'not before its time.' That would cover a good deal."

Then the two young people departed in company.

Loveday went straight to her work.

"I'll begin my surveying at the top of the house, and at once, if you please," she said. "Will you kindly tell one of your maids to show me through the bed-rooms? If it is possible, let that maid be the one who waits on Miss Monroe and Mrs. Hawke."

The maid who responded to Mr. Hawke's summons was in perfect harmony with the general appearance of the house. In addition, however, to being elderly and faded, she was also remarkably sour-visaged, and carried herself as if she thought that Mr. Hawke had taken a great liberty in thus commanding her attendance.

In dignified silence she showed Loveday over the topmost story, where the servants' bed-rooms were situated, and with a somewhat supercilious expression of countenance, watched her making various entries in her note-book.

In dignified silence, also, she led the way down to the second floor, where were the principal bed-rooms of the house.

"This is Miss Monroe's room," she said, as she threw back a door of one of these rooms, and then shut her lips with a snap, as if they were never going to open again.

The room that Loveday entered was, like the rest of the house, furnished in the style that prevailed in the early Victorian period. The bedstead was elaborately curtained with pink lined upholstery; the toilet-table was befrilled with muslin and tarlatan out of all likeness to a table. The one point, however, that chiefly attracted Loveday's attention was the extreme neatness that prevailed throughout the apartment—a neatness, however, that was carried out with so strict an eye to comfort and convenience that it seemed to proclaim the hand of a first-class maid. Everything in the room was, so to speak, squared to the quarter of an inch, and yet everything that a lady could require in dressing lay ready to hand. The dressing-gown lying on the back of a chair had footstool and slippers beside it. A chair stood in front of the toilet table, and on a small Japanese table to the right of the chair were placed hair-pin box, comb and brush, and hand mirror.

"This room will want money spent upon it," said Loveday, letting her eyes roam critically in all directions. "Nothing but Moorish wood-work will take off the squareness of those corners. But what a maid Miss Monroe must have. I never before saw a room so orderly and, at the same time, so comfortable."

This was so direct an appeal to conversation that the sour-visaged maid felt compelled to open her lips.

"I wait on Miss Monroe, for the present," she said snappishly; "but, to speak the truth, she scarcely requires a maid. I never before in my life had dealings with such a young lady."

"She does so much for herself, you mean—declines much assistance."

"She's like no one else I ever had to do with." (This was said even more snappishly than before.) "She not only won't be helped in dressing, but she arranges her room every day before leaving it, even to placing the chair in front of the looking glass."

"And to opening the lid of the hair-pin box, so that she may have the pins ready to her hand," added Loveday, for a moment bending over the Japanese table, with its toilet accessories.

Another five minutes were all that Loveday accorded to the inspection of this room. Then, a little to the surprise of the dignified maid, she announced her intention of completing her survey of the bed-rooms some other time, and dismissed her at the drawing-room door, to tell Mr. Hawke that she wished to see him before leaving.

Mr. Hawke, looking much disturbed and with a telegram in his hand, quickly made his appearance.

"From my wife, to say she'll be back to-night. She'll be at Waterloo in about half an hour from now," he said, holding up the brown envelope. "Now, Miss Brooke, what are we to do? I told you how much Mrs. Hawke objected to the investigation of this matter, and she is very—well—firm when she once says a thing, and—and—"

"Set your mind at rest," interrupted Loveday; "I have done all I wished to do within your walls, and the remainder of my investigation can be carried on just as well at Lynch Court or at my own private rooms."

"Done all you wished to do!" echoed Mr. Hawke in amazement; "why, you've not been an hour in the house, and do you mean to tell me you've found out anything about the necklace or the daggers?"

"Don't ask me any questions just yet; I want you to answer one or two instead. Now, can you tell me anything about any letters Miss Monroe may have written or received since she has been in your house?"

"Yes, certainly, Sir George wrote to me very strongly about her correspondence, and begged me to keep a sharp eye on it, so as to nip in the bud any attempt to communicate with Danvers. So far, however, she does not appear to have made any such attempt. She is frankness itself over her correspondence. Every letter that has come addressed to her, she has shown either to me or to my wife, and they have one and all been letters from old friends of her father's, wishing to make her acquaintance now that she is in England. With regard to letter-writing, I am sorry to say she has a marked and most peculiar objection to it. Every one of the letters she has received, my wife tells, me, remain unanswered still. She has never once been seen, since she came to the house, with a pen in her hand. And if she wrote on the sly, I don't know how she would get her letters posted—she never goes outside the door by herself, and she would have no opportunity of giving them to any of the servants to post except Mrs. Hawke's maid, and she is beyond suspicion in such a matter. She has been well cautioned, and, in addition, is not the sort of person who would assist a young lady in carrying on a clandestine correspondence."

"I should imagine not! I suppose Miss Monroe has been present at the breakfast table each time that you have received your daggers through the post—you told me, I think, that they had come by the first post in the morning?"

"Yes; Miss Monroe is very punctual at meals, and has been present each time. Naturally, when I received such unpleasant missives, I made some sort of exclamation and then handed the thing round the table for inspection, and Miss Monroe was very much concerned to know who my secret enemy could be."

"No doubt. Now, Mr. Hawke, I have a very special request to make to you, and I hope you will be most exact in carrying it out."

"You may rely upon my doing so to the very letter."

"Thank you. If, then, you should receive by post to-morrow morning one of those big envelopes you already know the look of, and find that it contains a sketch of three, not two, drawn daggers—"

"Good gracious! what makes you think such a thing likely?" exclaimed Mr. Hawke, greatly disturbed. "Why am I to be persecuted in this way? Am I to take it for granted that I am a doomed man?"

He began to pace the room in a state of great excitement.

"I don't think I would if I were you," answered Loveday calmly. "Pray let me finish. I want you to open the big envelope that may come to you by post to-morrow morning just you have opened the others—in full view of your family at the breakfast-table—and to hand round the sketch it may contain for inspection to your wife, your nephew and to Miss Monroe. Now, will you promise me to do this?"

"Oh, certainly; I should most likely have done so without any promising. But—but—I'm sure you'll understand that I feel myself to be in a peculiarly uncomfortable position, and I shall feel so very much obliged to you if you'll tell me—that is if you'll enter a little more fully into an explanation."

Loveday looked at her watch. "I should think Mrs. Hawke would be just at this moment arriving at Waterloo; I'm sure you'll be glad to see the last of me. Please come to me at my rooms in Gower Street to-morrow at twelve—here is my card. I shall then be able to enter into fuller explanations I hope. Good-bye."

The old gentleman showed her politely downstairs, and, as he shook hands with her at the front door, again asked, in a most emphatic manner, if she did not consider him to be placed in a "peculiarly unpleasant position."

Those last words at parting were to be the first with which he greeted her on the following morning when he presented himself at her rooms in Gower Street. They were, however, repeated in considerably more agitated a manner.

"Was there ever a man in a more miserable position!" he exclaimed, as he took the chair that Loveday indicated. "I not only received the three daggers for which you prepared me, but I got an additional worry, for which I was totally unprepared. This morning, immediately after breakfast, Miss Monroe walked out of the house all by herself, and no one knows where she has gone. And the girl has never before been outside the door alone. It seems the servants saw her go out, but did not think it necessary to tell either me or Mrs. Hawke, feeling sure we must have been aware of the fact."

"So Mrs. Hawke has returned," said Loveday. "Well, I suppose you will be greatly surprised if I inform you that the young lady, who has so unceremoniously left your house, is at the present moment to be found at the Charing Cross Hotel, where she has engaged a private room in her real name of Miss Mary O'Grady."

"Eh! What! Private room! Real name O'Grady! I'm all bewildered!"

"It is a little bewildering; let me explain. The young lady whom you received into your house as the daughter of your old friend, was in reality the person engaged by Miss Monroe to fulfill the duties of her maid on board ship, after her native attendant had been landed at Malta. Her real name, as I have told you, is Mary O'Grady, and she has proved herself a valuable coadjutor to Miss Monroe in assisting her to carry out a programme, which she must have arranged with her lover, Mr. Danvers, before she left Pekin."

"Eh! what!" again ejaculated Mr. Hawke; "how do you know all this? Tell me the whole story."

"I will tell you the whole story first, and then explain to you how I came to know it. From what has followed, it seems to me that Miss Monroe must have arranged with Mr. Danvers that he was to leave Pekin within ten days of her so doing, travel by the route by which she came, and land at Plymouth, where he was to receive a note from her, apprising him of her whereabouts. So soon as she was on board ship, Miss Monroe appears to have set her wits to work with great energy; every obstacle to the carrying-out of her programme she appears to have met and conquered. Step number one was to get rid of her native maid, who, perhaps, might have been faithful to her master's interests and have proved troublesome. I have no doubt the poor woman suffered terribly from sea-sickness, as it was her first voyage, and I have equally no doubt that Miss Monroe worked on her fears, and persuaded her to land at Malta, and return to China by the next packet. Step number two was to find a suitable person, who for a consideration, would be willing to play the part of the Pekin heiress among the heiress's friends in England, while the young lady herself arranged her private affairs to her own liking. That person was quickly found among the steerage passengers of the *Colombo* in Miss Mary O'Grady, who had come on board with her mother at Ceylon, and who, from the glimpse I had of her, must, I should conjecture, have been absent many years from the land of her birth. You know how cleverly this young lady has played her part in your house—how, without attracting attention to the matter, she has shunned the society of her father's old Chinese friends, who might be likely to involve her in embarrassing conversations; how she has avoided the use of pen and ink lest—"

"Yes, yes," interrupted Mr. Hawke; "but, my dear Miss Brooke, wouldn't it be as well for you and me to go at once to the Charing Cross Hotel, and get all the information we can out of her respecting Miss Monroe and her movements—she may be bolting, you know?"

"I do not think she will. She is waiting there patiently for an answer to a telegram she dispatched more than two hours ago to her mother, Mrs. O'Grady, at 14, Woburn Place, Cork."

"Dear me! dear me! How is it possible for you to know all this."

"Oh, that last little fact was simply a matter of astuteness on the part of the man whom I have deputed to watch the young lady's movements to-day. Other details, I assure you, in this somewhat intricate case, have been infinitely more difficult to get at. I think I have to thank those 'drawn daggers,' that caused you so much consternation, for having, in the first instance, put me on the right track."

"Ah—h," said Mr. Hawke, drawing a long breath; "now we come to the daggers! I feel sure you are going to set my mind at rest on that score."

"I hope so. Would it surprise you very much to be told that it was I who sent to you those three daggers this morning?"

"You! Is it possible?"

"Yes, they were sent by me, and for a reason that I will presently explain to you. But let me begin at the beginning. Those roughly-drawn sketches, that to you suggested terrifying ideas of blood-shedding and violence, to my mind were open to a more peaceful and commonplace explanation. They appeared to me to suggest the herald's office rather than the armoury; the cross fitchée of the knight's shield rather than the poniard with which the members of secret societies are supposed to render their recalcitrant brethren familiar. Now, if you will look at these sketches again, you will see what I mean." Here Loveday produced from her writing-table the missives which had so greatly disturbed Mr. Hawke's peace of mind. "To begin with, the blade of the dagger of common life is, as a rule, at least two-thirds of the weapon in length; in this sketch, what you would call the blade, does not exceed the hilt in length. Secondly, please note the absence of guard for the hand. Thirdly, let me draw your attention to the squareness of what you considered the hilt of the weapon, and what, to my mind, suggested the upper portion of a crusader's cross. No hand could grip such a hilt as the one outlined here. After your departure yesterday, I drove to the British Museum, and there consulted a certain valuable work on heraldry, which has more than once done me good service. There I found my surmise substantiated in a surprising manner. Among the illustrations of the various crosses borne on armorial shields, I found one that had been taken by Henri d'Anvers from his own armorial bearings, for his crest when he joined the Crusaders under Edward I., and which has since been handed down as the crest of the Danvers family. This was an important item of information to me. Here was someone in Cork sending to your house, on two several occasions, the crest of the Danvers family; with what object it would be difficult to say, unless it were in some sort a communication to someone in your house. With my mind full of this idea, I left the Museum and drove next to the office of the P. and O. Company, and requested to have given me the list of the passengers who arrived by the *Colombo*. I found this list to be a remarkably small one; I suppose people, if possible, avoid crossing the Bay of Biscay during the Equinoxes. The only passengers who landed at Plymouth besides Miss Monroe, I found, were a certain Mrs. and Miss O'Grady, steerage passengers who had gone on board at Ceylon on their way home from Australia. Their name, together with their landing at Plymouth, suggested the possibility that Cork might be their destination. After this I asked to see the list of the passengers who arrived by the packet following the *Colombo*, telling the clerk who attended to me that I was on the look-out for the arrival of a friend. In that second list of arrivals I quickly found my friend—William Wentworth Danvers by name."

"No! The effrontery! How dared he! In his own name, too!"

"Well, you see, a plausible pretext for leaving Pekin could easily be invented by him—the death of a relative, the illness of a father or mother. And Sir George, though he might dislike the idea of the young man going to England so soon after his daughter's departure, and may, perhaps, write to you by the next mail on the matter, was utterly powerless to prevent his so doing. This young man, like Miss Monroe and the O'Gradys, also landed at Plymouth. I had only arrived so far in my investigation when I went to your house yesterday afternoon. By chance, as I waited a few minutes in your drawing-room, another important item of information was acquired. A fragment of conversation between your nephew and the supposed Miss Monroe fell upon my ear, and one word spoken by the young lady convinced me of her nationality. That one word was the monosyllable 'Hush.'"

"No! You surprise me!"

"Have you never noted the difference between the 'hush' of an Englishman and that of an Irishman? The former begins his 'hush' with a distinct aspirate, the latter with as distinct a W. That W is a mark of his nationality which he never loses. The unmitigated 'whist' may lapse into a 'whish' when he is transplanted to another soil, and the 'whish' may in course of time pass into a 'whush,' but to the distinct aspirate of the English 'hush,' he never attains. Now Miss O'Grady's was as pronounced a 'whush' as it was possible for the lips of a Hibernian to utter."

"And from that you concluded that Mary O'Grady was playing the part of Miss Monroe in my house?"

"Not immediately. My suspicions were excited, certainly; and when I went up to her room, in company with Mrs. Hawke's maid, those suspicions were confirmed. The orderliness of that room was something remarkable. Now, there is the orderliness of a lady in the arrangement of her room, and the orderliness of a maid, and the two things, believe me, are widely different. A lady, who has no maid, and who has the gift of orderliness, will put things away when done with, and so leave her room a picture of neatness. I don't think, however, it would for a moment occur to her to pull things so as to be conveniently ready for her to use the next time she dresses in that room. This would be what a maid, accustomed to arrange a room for her mistress's use, would do mechanically. Miss Monroe's room was the neatness of a maid—not of a lady, and I was assured by Mrs. Hawke's maid that it was a neatness accomplished by her own hands. As I stood there, looking at that room, the whole conspiracy—if I may so call it—little by little pieced itself together, and became plain to me. Possibilities quickly grew into probabilities, and these probabilities once admitted, brought other suppositions in their train. Now, supposing that Miss Monroe and Mary O'Grady had agreed to change places, the Pekin heiress, for the time being, occupying Mary O'Grady's place in the humble home at Cork and vice versa, what means of communicating with each other had they arranged? How was Mary O'Grady to know when she might lay aside her assumed rôle and go back to her mother's house. There was no denying the necessity for such communication; the difficulties in its way must have been equally obvious to the two girls. Now, I think we must admit that we must credit these young women with having hit upon a very clever way of meeting those difficulties. An anonymous and startling missive sent to you would be bound to be mentioned in the house, and in this way a code of signals might be set up between them that could not direct suspicion to them. In this connection, the Danvers crest, which it is possible that they mistook for a dagger, suggested itself naturally, for no doubt Miss Monroe had many impressions of it on her lover's letters. As I thought over these things, it occurred to me that possibly dagger (or cross) number one was sent to notify the safe arrival of Miss Monroe and Mrs. O'Grady at Cork. The two daggers or crosses you subsequently received were sent on the day of Mr. Danvers's arrival at Plymouth, and were, I should say, sketched by his hand. Now, was it not within the bounds of likelihood that Miss Monroe's marriage to this young man, and the consequent release of Mary O'Grady from the onerous part she was playing, might be notified to her by the sending of three such crosses or daggers to you. The idea no sooner occurred to me than I determined to act upon it, forestall the sending of this latest communication, and watch the result. Accordingly, after I left your house yesterday, I had a sketch made of three daggers of crosses exactly similar to those you had already received, and had it posted to you so that you would get it by the first post. I told off one of our staff at Lynch Court to watch your house, and gave him special directions to follow and report on Miss O'Grady's movements throughout the day. The results I anticipated quickly came to pass. About half-past nine this morning the man sent a telegram to me from your house to the Charing Cross Hotel, and furthermore had ascertained that she had since despatched a telegram, which (possibly by following the hotel servant who carried it to the telegraph office), he had overheard was addressed to Mrs. O'Grady, at

Woburn Place, Cork. Since I received this information an altogether remarkable cross-firing of telegrams has been going backwards and forwards along the wires to Cork."

"A cross-firing of telegrams! I do not understand."

"In this way. So soon as I knew Mrs. O'Grady's address I telegraphed to her, in her daughter's name, desiring her to address her reply to 1154 Gower Street, not to Charing Cross Hotel. About three-quarters of an hour afterwards I received in reply this telegram, which I am sure you will read with interest."

Here Loveday handed a telegram—one of several that lay on her writing-table—to Mr. Hawke.

He opened it and read aloud as follows:

> "Am puzzled. Why such hurry? Wedding took place this morning. You will receive signal as agreed to-morrow. Better return to Tavistock Square for the night."

"The wedding took place this morning," repeated Mr. Hawke blankly. "My poor old friend! It will break his heart."

"Now that the thing is done past recall we must hope he will make the best of it," said Loveday. "In reply to this telegram," she went on, "I sent another, asking as to the movements of the bride and bridegroom, and got in reply this:"

Here she read aloud as follows:

> "They will be at Plymouth to-morrow night; at Charing Cross Hotel and next day, as agreed."

"So, Mr. Hawke," she added, "if you wish to see your old friend's daughter and tell her what you think of the part she has played, all you will have to do will be to watch the arrival of the Plymouth trains."

"Miss O'Grady has called to see a lady and gentleman," said a maid at that moment entering.

"Miss O'Grady!" repeated Mr. Hawke in astonishment.

"Ah, yes, I telegraphed to her, just before you came in, to come here to meet a lady and gentlemen, and she, no doubt thinking that she would find here the newly-married pair, has, you see, lost no time in complying with my request. Show the lady in."

"It's all so intricate—so bewildering," said Mr. Hawke, as he lay back in his chair. "I can scarcely get it all into my head."

His bewilderment, however, was nothing compared with that of Miss O'Grady, when she entered the room and found herself face to face with her late guardian, instead of the radiant bride and bridegroom whom she had expected to meet.

She stood silent in the middle of the room, looking the picture of astonishment and distress.

Mr. Hawke also seemed a little at a loss for words, so Loveday took the initiative.

"Please sit down," she said, placing a chair for the girl. "Mr. Hawke and I have sent to you in order to ask you a few questions. Before doing so, however, let me tell you that the whole of your conspiracy with Miss Monroe has been brought to light, and the best thing you can do, if you want your share in it treated leniently, will be to answer our questions as fully and truthfully as possible."

The girl burst into tears. "It was all Miss Monroe's fault from beginning to end," she sobbed. "Mother didn't want to do it—I didn't want to—to go into a gentleman's house and pretend to be what I was not. And we didn't want her hundred pounds—"

Here sobs checked her speech.

"Oh," said Loveday contemptuously, "so you were to have a hundred pounds for your share in this fraud, were you?"

"We didn't want to take it," said the girl, between hysterical bursts of tears; "but Miss Monroe said if we didn't help her some-one else would, and so I agreed to—"

"I think," interrupted Loveday, "that you can tell us very little that we do not already know about what you agreed to do. What we want you to tell us is what has been done with Miss Monroe's diamond necklace—who has possession of it now?"

The girl's sobs and tears redoubled. "I've had nothing to do with the necklace—it has never been in my possession," she sobbed.

"Miss Monroe gave it to Mr. Danvers two or three months before she left Pekin, and he sent it on to some people he knew in Hong Kong, diamond merchants, who lent him money on it. Decastro, Miss Monroe said, was the name of these people."

"Decastro, diamond merchant, Hong Kong. I should think that would be sufficient address," said Loveday, entering it in a ledger; "and I suppose Mr. Danvers retained part of that money for his own use and travelling expenses, and handed the remainder to Miss Monroe to enable her to bribe such creatures as you and your mother, to practice a fraud that ought to land both of you in jail."

The girl grew deadly white. "Oh, don't do that—don't send us to prison!" she implored, clasping her hands together. "We haven't touched a penny of Miss Monroe's money yet, and we don't want to touch a penny, if you'll only let us off! Oh, pray, pray, pray be merciful!"

Loveday looked at Mr. Hawke.

He rose from his chair. "I think the best thing you can do," he said, "will be to get back home to your mother at Cork as quickly as possible, and advise her never to play such a risky game again. Have you any money in your purse? No—well then here's some for you, and lose no time in getting home. It will be best for Miss Monroe—Mrs. Danvers I mean—to come to my house and claim her own property there. At any rate, there it will remain until she does so."

As the girl, with incoherent expressions of gratitude, left the room, he turned to Loveday.

"I should like to have consulted Mrs. Hawke before arranging matters in this way," he said a little hesitatingly; "but still, I don't see that I could have done otherwise."

"I feel sure Mrs. Hawke will approve what you have done when she hears all the circumstance of the case," said Loveday.

"And," continued the old clergyman, "when I write to Sir George, as, of course, I must immediately, I shall advise him to make the best of a bad bargain, now that the thing is done. 'Past cure should be past care;' eh, Miss Brooke? And, think! what a narrow escape my nephew, Jack, has had!"

THE GHOST OF FOUNTAIN LANE

"Will you be good enough to tell me how you procured my address?" said Miss Brooke, a little irritably. "I left strict orders that it was to be given to no one."

"I only obtained it with great difficulty from Mr. Dyer; had, in fact, to telegraph three times before I could get it," answered Mr. Clampe, the individual thus addressed. "I'm sure I'm awfully sorry to break into your holiday in this fashion, but—but pardon me if I say that it seems to be one in little more than name." Here he glanced meaningly at the newspapers, memoranda and books of reference with which the table at which Loveday sat was strewn.

She gave a little sigh.

"I suppose you are right," she answered; "it is a holiday in little more than name. I verily believe that we hard workers, after a time, lose our capacity for holiday-keeping. I thought I was pining for a week of perfect laziness and sea-breezes, and so I locked up my desk and fled. No sooner, however, do I find myself in full view of that magnificent sea-and-sky picture than I shut my eyes to it, fasten them instead on the daily papers and set my brains to work, *con amore*, on a ridiculous case that is never likely to come into my hands."

That "magnificent sea-and-sky picture" was one framed by the windows of a room on the fifth floor of the Métropole, at Brighton, whither Loveday, overtaxed in mind and body, had fled for a brief respite from hard work. Here Inspector Clampe, of the Local District Constabulary, had found her out, in order to press the claims of what seemed to him an important case upon her. He was a neat, dapper-looking man, of about fifty, with a manner less brusque and business-like than that of most men in his profession.

"Oh pray drop the ridiculous case," he said earnestly, "and set to work, 'con amore,' upon another far from ridiculous, and most interesting."

"I'm not sure that it would interest me one quarter so much as the ridiculous one."

"Don't be sure till you've heard the particulars. Listen to this." Here the inspector took a newspaper-cutting from his pocket-book and read aloud as follows:

> "'A cheque, the property of the Rev. Charles Turner, Vicar of East Downes, has been stolen under somewhat peculiar circumstances. It appears that the Rev. gentleman was suddenly called from home by the death of a relative, and thinking he might possibly be away some little time, he left with his wife four blank cheques, signed, for her to fill in as required. They were made payable to self or bearer, and were drawn on the West Sussex Bank. Mrs. Turner, when first questioned on the matter, stated that as soon as her husband had departed, she locked up these cheques in her writing desk. She subsequently, however, corrected this statement, and admitted having left them on the table while she went into the garden to cut some flowers. In all, she was absent, she says, about ten minutes. When she came in from cutting her flowers, she immediately put the cheques away. She had not counted them on receiving them from her husband, and when, as she put them into her Davenport, she saw there were only three, she concluded that that was the number he had left with her. The loss of the cheque was not discovered until her husband's return, about a week later on. As soon as he was aware of the fact, he telegraphed to the West Sussex Bank to stop payment,

only, however, to make the unpleasant discovery that the cheque, filled in to the amount of six hundred pounds, had been presented and cashed (in gold) two days previously. The clerk who cashed it took no particular notice of the person presenting it, except that he was of gentlemanly appearance, and declares himself to be quite incapable of identifying him. The largeness of the amount raised no suspicion in the mind of the clerk, as Mr. Turner is a man of good means, and since his marriage, about six months back, has been refurnishing the Vicarage, and paying away large sums for old oak furniture and for pictures.'"

"There, Miss Brooke," said the inspector as he finished reading, "if, in addition to these particulars, I tell you that one or two circumstances that have arisen seem to point suspicion in the direction of the young wife, I feel sure you will admit that a more interesting case, and one more worthy of your talents, is not to be found."

Loveday's answer was to take up a newspaper that lay beside her on the table. "So much for your interesting case," she said; "now listen to my ridiculous one." Then she read aloud as follows:—

"'AUTHENTIC GHOST STORY.—The inhabitants of Fountain Lane, a small turning leading off Ship Street, have been greatly disturbed by the sudden appearance of a ghost in their midst. Last Tuesday night, between ten and eleven o'clock, a little girl named Martha Watts, who lives as a help to a shoemaker and his wife at No. 5 in the lane, ran out into the streets in her night-clothes in a great state of terror, saying that a ghost had come to her bedside. The child refused to return to the house to sleep, and was accordingly taken in by some neighbours. The shoemaker and his wife, Freer by name, when questioned by the neighbours on the matter, admitted, with great reluctance, that they, too, had seen the apparition, which they described as being a soldier-like individual, with a broad, white forehead and having his arms folded on his breast. This description is, in all respects confirmed by the child, Martha Watts, who asserts that the ghost she saw reminded her of pictures she had seen of the great Napoleon. The Freers state that it first appeared in the course of a prayer-meeting held at their house on the previous night, when it was distinctly seen by Mr. Freer. Subsequently, the wife, awakening suddenly in the middle of the night, saw the apparition standing at the foot of the bed. They are quite at a loss for an explanation of the matter. The affair has caused quite a sensation in the district, and at the time of going to press, the lane is so thronged and crowded by would-be ghost-seers that the inhabitants have great difficulty in going to and from their houses.'"

"A scare—a vulgar scare, nothing more," said the inspector as Loveday laid aside the paper. "Now, Miss Brooke, I ask you seriously, supposing you get to the bottom of such a stupid, commonplace fraud as that, will you in any way add to your reputation?"

"And supposing I get to the bottom of such a stupid, commonplace fraud as a stolen cheque, how much, I should like to know, do I add to my reputation?"

"Well, put it on other grounds and allow Christian charity to have some claims. Think of the misery in that gentleman's house unless suspicion can be lifted from the young wife and directed to the proper quarter."

"Think of the misery of the landlord of the Fountain Lane houses if all his tenants decamp in a body, as they no doubt will, unless the ghost mystery is solved."

The inspector sighed. "Well, I suppose I must take it for granted that you will have nothing to do with the case," he said. "I brought the cheque with me, thinking you might like to see it."

"I suppose it's very much like other cheques?" said Loveday indifferently, and turning over her memoranda as if she meant to go back to her ghost again.

"Ye—es," said Mr. Clampe, taking the cheque from his pocket-book and glancing down at it. "I suppose the cheque is very much like other cheques. This little scribble of figures in pencil at the back—144,000—can scarcely be called a distinguishing mark."

"What's that, Mr. Clampe?" asked Loveday, pushing her memoranda on one side. "144,000 did you say?"

Her whole manner had suddenly changed from apathy to that of keenest interest.

Mr. Clampe, delighted, rose and spread the cheque before her on the table.

"The writing of the words 'six hundred pounds,'" he said, "bears so close a resemblance to Mr. Turner's signature, that the gentleman himself told me he would have thought it was his own writing if he had not known that he had not drawn a cheque for that amount on the given date. You see it is that round, school-boy's hand, so easy to imitate, I could write it myself with half-an-hour's practice; no flourishes, nothing distinctive about it."

Loveday made no reply. She had turned the cheque, and was now closely scrutinizing the pencilled figures at the back.

"Of course," continued the inspector, "those figures were not written by the person who wrote the figures on the face of the cheque. That, however, matters but little. I really do not think they are of the slightest importance in the case. They might have been scribbled by some one making a calculation as to the number of pennies in six hundred pounds—there are, as no doubt you know, exactly 144,000."

"Who has engaged your services in this case, the Bank or Mr. Turner?"

"Mr. Turner. When the loss of the cheque was first discovered, he was very excited and irate, and when he came to me the day before yesterday, I had much difficulty in persuading him that there was no need to telegraph to London for half-a-dozen detectives, as we could do the work quite as well as the London men. When, however, I went over to East Downes yesterday to look round and ask a few questions; I found things had altogether changed. He was exceedingly reluctant to answer any questions, lost his temper when I pressed them, and as good as told me that he wished he had not moved in the matter at all. It was this sudden change of demeanour that turned my thoughts in the direction of Mrs. Turner. A man must have a very strong reason for wishing to sit idle under a loss of six hundred pounds, for, of course, under the circumstances, the Bank will not bear the brunt of it."

"Some other motives may be at work in his mind, consideration for old servants, the wish to avoid a scandal in the house."

"Quite so. The fact, taken by itself, would give no ground for suspicion, but certainly looks ugly if taken in connection with another fact which I have since ascertained, namely, that during her husband's absence from home, Mrs. Turner paid off certain debts contracted by her in Brighton before the marriage, and amounting to nearly £500. Paid them off, too, in gold. I think I mentioned to you that the gentleman who presented the stolen cheque at the Bank preferred payment in gold."

"You are supposing not only a confederate, but also a vast amount of cunning as well as of simplicity on the lady's part."

"Quite so. Three parts cunning to one of simplicity is precisely what lady criminals are composed of. And it is, as a rule, that one part of simplicity that betrays them and leads to their detection."

"What sort of woman is Mrs. Turner in other respects?"

"She is young, handsome and of good birth, but is scarcely suited for the position of vicar's wife in a country parish. She has lived a good deal in society and is fond of gaiety, and, in addition, is a Roman Catholic, and, I am told, utterly ignores her husband's church and drives every Sunday to Brighton to attend mass."

"What about the servants in the house? Do they seem steady-going and respectable?"

"There was nothing on the surface to excite suspicion against any one of them. But it is precisely in that quarter than your services would be invaluable. It will, however, be impossible to get you inside the vicarage walls. Mr. Turner, I am confident, would never open his doors to you."

"What do you suggest?"

"I can suggest nothing better than the house of the village schoolmistress, or, rather, of the village schoolmistress's mother, Mrs. Brown. It is only a stone's throw from the vicarage; in fact, its windows overlook the vicarage grounds. It is a four-roomed cottage, and Mrs. Brown, who is a very respectable person, turns over a little money in the summer by receiving lady lodgers desirous of a breath of country air. There would be no difficulty in getting you in there; her spare bedroom is empty now."

"I should have preferred being at the vicarage, but if it cannot be, I must make the most of my stay at Mrs. Brown's. How do we get there?'"

"I drove from East Downes here in a trap I hired at the village inn where I put up last night, and where I shall stay to-night. I will drive you, if you will allow me; it is only seven miles off. It's a lovely day for a drive; breezy and not too much dust. Could you be ready in about half an hour's time, say?"

But this, Loveday said, would be an impossibility. She had a special engagement that afternoon; there was a religious service in the town that she particularly wished to attend. It would not be over until three o'clock, and, consequently, not until half-past three would she be ready for the drive to East Downes.

Although Mr. Clampe looked unutterable astonishment at the claims of a religious service being set before those of professional duty, he made no demur to the arrangement, and accordingly half-past three saw Loveday and the inspector in a high-wheeled dog-cart rattling along the Marina in the direction of East Downes.

Loveday made no further allusion to her ghost story, so Mr. Clampe, out of politeness, felt compelled to refer to it.

"I heard all about the Fountain Lane ghost yesterday, before I started for East Downes," he said; "and it seemed to me, with all deference to you, Miss Brooke, an every-day sort of affair, the sort of thing to be explained by a heavy supper or an extra glass of beer."

"There are a few points in this ghost story that separate it from the every-day ghost story," answered Loveday. "For instance, you would expect that such emotionally religious people, as I have since found the Freers to be, would have seen a vision of angels, or at least a solitary saint. Instead, they see a soldier! A soldier, too, in the likeness of a man who is anathema maranatha to every religious mind—the great Napoleon."

"To what denomination do the Freers belong?"

"To the Wesleyan. Their fathers and mothers before them were Wesleyans; their relatives and friends are Wesleyans, one and all, they say; and, most important item of all, the man's boot and shoe connection lies exclusively among Wesleyan ministers. This, he told me, is the most paying connection that a small boot-maker can have. Half-a-dozen Wesleyan ministers pay better than three times the number of Church clergy, for whereas the Wesleyan minister is always on the tramp among his people, the clergyman generally contrives in the country to keep a horse, or else turns student, and shuts himself up in his study."

"Ha, ha! Capital," laughed Mr. Clampe; "tell that to the Church Defence Society in Wales. Isn't this a first-rate little horse? In another ten minutes we shall be in sight of East Downes."

The long, dusty road down which they had driven, was ending now in a narrow, sloping lane, hedged in on either side with hawthorns and wild plum trees. Through these, the August sunshine was beginning to slant now, and from a distant wood there came a faint sound of fluting and piping, as if the blackbirds were thinking of tuning up for their evening carols.

A sudden, sharp curve in this lane brought them in sight of East Downes, a tiny hamlet of about thirty cottages, dominated by the steeple of a church of early English architecture. Adjoining the church was the vicarage, a goodly-sized house, with extensive grounds, and in a lane running alongside these grounds were situated the village schools and the schoolmistress's house. The latter was simply a four-roomed cottage, standing in a pretty garden, with cluster roses and honeysuckle, now in the fullness of their August glory, climbing upwards to its very roof.

Outside this cottage Mr. Clampe drew rein.

"If you'll give me five minutes' grace," he said, "I'll go in and tell the good woman that I have brought her, as a lodger, a friend of mine, who is anxious to get away for a time from the noise and glare of Brighton. Of course, the story of the stolen cheque is all over the place, but I don't think anyone has, at present, connected me with the affair. I am supposed to be a gentleman from Brighton, who is anxious to buy a horse the Vicar wishes to sell, and who can't quite arrange terms with him."

While Loveday waited outside in the cart, an open carriage drove past and then in through the vicarage gates. In the carriage were seated a gentleman and lady whom, from the respectful greetings they received from the village children, she conjectured to be the Rev. Charles and Mrs. Turner. Mr. Turner was sanguine-complexioned, red-haired, and wore a distinctly troubled expression of countenance. With Mrs. Turner's appearance Loveday was not favourably impressed. Although a decidedly handsome woman, she was hard-featured and had a scornful curl to her upper lip. She was dressed in the extreme of London fashion.

They threw a look of enquiry at Loveday as they passed, and she felt sure that enquiries as to the latest addition to Mrs. Brown's ménage would soon be afloat in the village.

Mr. Clampe speedily returned, saying that Mrs. Brown was only too delighted to get her spare-room occupied. He whispered a hint as they made their way up to the cottage door between borders thickly planted with stocks and mignonette.

It was:

"Don't ask her any questions, or she'll draw herself up as straight as a ramrod, and say she never listens to gossip of any sort. But just let her alone, and she'll run on like a mill-stream, and tell you as much as you'll want to know about everyone and everything. She and the village postmistress are great friends, and between them they contrive to know pretty much what goes on inside every house in the place."

Mrs. Brown was a stout, rosy-cheeked woman of about fifty, neatly dressed in a dark stuff gown with a big white cap and apron.

She welcomed Loveday respectfully, and introduced, evidently with a little pride, her daughter, the village schoolmistress, a well-spoken young woman of about eight-and-twenty.

Mr. Clampe departed with his dog-cart to the village inn, announcing his intention of calling on Loveday at the cottage on the following morning before he returned to Brighton.

Miss Brown also departed, saying she would prepare tea. Left alone with Loveday, Mrs. Brown speedily unloosed her tongue. She had a dozen questions to ask respecting Mr. Clampe and his business in the village. Now, was it true that he had come to East Downes for the whole and sole purpose of buying one of the Vicar's horses? She had heard it whispered that he had been sent by the police to watch the servants at the vicarage. She hoped it was not true, for a more respectable set of servants were not to be met with in any house, far or near. Had Miss Brooke heard about that lost cheque? Such a terrible affair! She had been told that the story of it had reached London. Now, had Miss Brooke seen an account of it in any of the London papers?

Here a reply from Loveday in the negative formed a sufficient excuse for relating with elaborate detail the story of the stolen cheque. Except in its elaborateness of detail, it differed but little from the one Loveday had already heard.

She listened patiently, bearing in mind Mr. Clampe's hint, and asking no questions. And when, in about a quarter of an hour's time, Miss Brown came in with the tea-tray in her hand, Loveday could have passed an examination in the events of the daily family life at the vicarage. She could have answered questions as to the ill-assortedness of the newly-married couple; she knew that they wrangled from morning till night; that the chief subjects of their disagreement were religion and money matters; that the Vicar was hot-tempered, and said whatever came to the tip of his tongue; that the beautiful young wife, though slower of speech, was scathing and sarcastic, and that, in addition, she was wildly extravagant and threw money away in all directions.

In addition to these interesting facts, Loveday could have undertaken to supply information respecting the number of servants at the vicarage, together with their names, ages and respective duties.

During tea, conversation flagged somewhat; Miss Brown's presence evidently acted repressively on her mother, and it was not until the meal was over and Loveday was being shown to her room by Mrs. Brown that opportunity to continue the talk was found.

Loveday opened the ball by remarking on the fact that no Dissenting chapel was to be found in the village.

"Generally, wherever there is a handful of cottages, we find a church at one end and a chapel at the other," she said; "but here, willy-nilly, one must go to church."

"Do you belong to chapel, ma'am?" was Mrs. Brown's reply. "Old Mrs. Turner, the Vicar's mother, who died over a year ago, was so 'low' she was almost chapel, and used often to drive over to Brighton to attend the Countess of Huntingdon's church. People used to say that was bad enough in the Vicar's mother; but what was it compared with what goes on now—the Vicar's wife driving regularly every Sunday into Brighton to a Catholic Church to say her prayers to candles and images? I'm glad you like the room, ma'am. Feather bolster, feather pillows, do you see, ma'am? I've nothing in the way of flock or wool on either of my beds to make people's head ache." Here Mrs. Brown, by way of emphasis, patted and pinched the fat pillows and bolster showing above the spotless white counterpane.

Loveday stood at the cottage window drinking in the sweetness of the country air, laden now with the heavy evening scents of carnation and jessamine. Across the road, from the vicarage, came the loud clanging of a dinner-gong, and almost simultaneously the church clock chimed the hour—seven o'clock.

"Who is that person coming up the lane?" asked Loveday, her attention suddenly attracted by a tall, thin figure, dressed in shabby black, with a large, dowdyish bonnet, and carrying a basket in her hand as if she were returning from some errand. Mrs. Brown peeped over Loveday's shoulder.

"Ah, that's the peculiar young woman I was telling you about, ma'am—Maria Lisle, who used to be old Mrs. Turner's maid. Not that she is over young now; she's five-and-thirty if she's a day. The Vicar kept her on to be his wife's maid after the old lady died, but young Mrs. Turner will have nothing to do with her, she's not good enough for her; so Mr. Turner is just paying her £30 a year for doing nothing. And what Maria does with all that money it would be hard to say. She doesn't spend it on dress, that's certain, and she hasn't kith nor kin, not a soul belonging to her to give a penny to."

"Perhaps she gives it to charities in Brighton. There are plenty of outlets for money there."

"She may," said Mrs. Brown dubiously; "she is always going to Brighton whenever she gets a chance. She used to be a Wesleyan in old Mrs. Turner's time, and went regularly to all the revival meetings for miles round; what she is now, it would be hard to say. Where she goes to church in Brighton, no one knows. She drives over with Mrs. Turner every Sunday, but everyone knows nothing would induce her to go near the candles and images. Thomas—that's the coachman—says he puts her down at the corner of a dirty little street in mid-Brighton, and there he picks her up again after he has fetched Mrs. Turner from her church. No, there's something very queer in her ways."

Maria passed in through the lodge gates of the vicarage. She walked with her head bent, her eyes cast down to the ground.

"Something very queer in her ways," repeated Mrs. Brown. "She never speaks to a soul unless they speak first to her, and gets by herself on every possible opportunity. Do you see that old summer-house over there in the vicarage grounds—it stands between the orchard and kitchen garden—well, every evening at sunset, out comes Maria and disappears into it, and there she stays for over an hour at a time. And what she does there goodness only knows!"

"Perhaps she keeps books there, and studies."

"Studies! My daughter showed her some new books that had come down for the fifth standard the other day, and Maria turned upon her and said quite sharply that there was only one book in the whole world that people ought to study, and that book was the Bible."

"How pretty those vicarage gardens are," said Loveday, a little abruptly. "Does the Vicar ever allow people to see them?"

"Oh, yes, miss; he doesn't at all mind people taking a walk round them. Only yesterday he said to me, 'Mrs. Brown, if ever you feel yourself circumscribed'—yes, 'circumscribed' was the word—'just walk out of your garden-gate and in at mine and enjoy yourself at your leisure among my fruit-trees.' Not that I would like to take advantage of his kindness and make too free; but if you'd care, ma'am, to go for a walk through the grounds, I'll go with you with pleasure. There's a wonderful old cedar hard by the pond people have come ever so far to see."

"It's that old summer-house and little bit of orchard that fascinate me," said Loveday, putting on her hat.

"We shall frighten Maria to death if she sees us so near her haunt," said Mrs. Brown as she led the way downstairs. "This way, if you please, ma'am, the kitchen-garden leads straight into the orchard."

Twilight was deepening rapidly into night now. Bird notes had ceased, the whirr of insects, the croaking of a distant frog were the only sounds that broke the evening stillness.

As Mrs. Brown swung back the gate that divided the kitchen-garden from the orchard, the gaunt, black figure of Maria Lisle was seen approaching in an opposite direction.

"Well, really, I don't see why she should expect to have the orchard all to herself every evening," said Mrs. Brown, with a little toss of her head. "Mind the gooseberry bushes, ma'am, they do catch at your clothes so. My word! what a fine show of fruit the Vicar has this year! I never saw pear trees more laden!"

They were now in the "bit of orchard" to be seen from the cottage windows. As they rounded the corner of the path in which the old summer-house stood, Maria Lisle turned its corner at the farther end, and suddenly found herself almost face to face with them. If her eyes and not been so persistently fastened on the ground, she would have noted the approach of the intruders as quickly as they had noted hers. Now, as she saw them for the first time, she gave a sudden start, paused for a moment irresolutely, and then turned sharply and walked rapidly away in an opposite direction.

"Maria, Maria!" called Mrs. Brown, "don't run away; we sha'n't stay here for more than a minute or so."

Her words met with no response. The woman did not so much as turn her head.

Loveday stood at the entrance of the old summer-house. It was considerably out of repair, and most probably was never entered by anyone save Maria Lisle, its unswept, undusted condition suggesting colonies of spiders and other creeping things within.

Loveday braved them all and took her seat on the bench that ran round the little place in a semi-circle.

"Do try and overtake the girl, and tell her we shall be gone in a minute," she said, addressing Mrs. Brown. "I will wait here meanwhile. I am so sorry to have frightened her away in that fashion."

Mrs. Brown, under protest, and with a little grumble at the ridiculousness of "people who couldn't look other people in the face," set off in pursuit of Maria.

It was getting dim inside the summer-house now. There was, however, sufficient light to enable Loveday to discover a small packet of books lying in a corner of the bench on which she sat.

One by one she took them in her hand and closely scrutinized them. The first was a much read and pencil-marked Bible; the others were respectively, a "congregational hymn-book," a book in a paper cover, on which was printed a flaming picture of a red and yellow angel, pouring blood and fire from out a big black bottle, and entitled "The End of the Age," and a smaller book, also in a paper cover, on which was depicted a huge black horse, snorting fire and brimstone into ochre-coloured clouds. This book was entitled "The Year Book of the Saints," and was simply a ruled diary with sensational mottoes for every day in the year. In parts, this diary was filled in with large and very untidy handwriting.

In these books seemed to lie the explanation of Maria Lisle's love of evening solitude and the lonely old summer-house.

Mrs. Brown pursued Maria to the servants' entrance to the house, but could not overtake her, the girl making good her retreat there.

She returned to Loveday a little hot, a little breathless and a little out of temper. It was all so absurd, she said; why couldn't the woman have stayed and had a chat with them? It wasn't as if she would get any harm out of the talk; she knew as well as everyone else in the village that she (Mrs. Brown) was no idle gossip, tittle-tattling over other people's affairs.

But here Loveday, a little sharply, cut short her meanderings.

"Mrs. Brown," she said, and to Mrs. Brown's fancy her voice and manner had entirely changed from that of the pleasant, chatty lady of half-an-hour ago, "I'm sorry to say it will be impossible for me to stay even one night in your pleasant home, I have just recollected some important business that I must transact in Brighton to-night. I haven't unpacked my portmanteau, so if you'll kindly have it taken to your garden-gate, I'll call for it as we drive past— I am going now, at once, to the inn, to see if Mr. Clampe can drive me back into Brighton to-night."

Mrs. Brown had no words ready wherewith to express her astonishment, and Loveday assuredly gave her no time to hunt for them. Ten minutes later saw her rousing Mr. Clampe from a comfortable supper, to which he had just settled himself, with the surprising announcement that she must get back to Brighton with as little delay as possible; now, would he be good enough to drive her there?

"We'll have a pair if they are to be had," she added. "The road is good; it will be moonlight in a quarter of an hour; we ought to do it in less than half the time we took coming."

While a phaeton and pair were being got ready, Loveday had time for a few words of explanation.

Maria Lisle's diary in the old summer-house had given her the last of the links in her chain of evidence that was to bring the theft of the cheque home to the criminal.

"It will be best to drive straight to the police station," she said; "they must take out three warrants, one for Maria Lisle, and two others respectively for Richard Steele, late Wesleyan minister of a chapel in Gordon Street, Brighton, and John Rogers, formerly elder of the same chapel. And let me tell you," she added with a little smile, "that these three worthies would most likely have been left at large to carry on their depredations for some little time to come if it had not been for that ridiculous ghost in Fountain Lane."

More than this there was not time to add, and when, a few minutes later, the two were rattling along the road to Brighton, the presence of the man, whom they were forced to take with them in order to bring back the horses to East Downes, prevented any but the most jerky and fragmentary of additions to this brief explanation.

"I very much fear that John Rogers has bolted," once Loveday whispered under her breath.

And again, a little later, when a smooth bit of road admitted of low-voiced talk, she said:

"We can't wait for the warrant for Steele; they must follow us with it to 15, Draycott Street."

"But I want to know about the ghost," said Mr. Clampe; "I am deeply interested in that 'ridiculous ghost.'"

"Wait till we get to 15, Draycott Street," was Loveday's reply; "when you've been there, I feel sure you will understand everything."

Church clocks were chiming a quarter to nine as they drove through Kemp Town at a pace that made the passers-by imagine they must be bound on an errand of life and death.

Loveday did not alight at the police station, and five minutes' talk with the inspector in charge there was all that Mr. Clampe required to put things *en train* for the arrest of the three criminals.

It had evidently been an "excursionists' day" at Brighton. The streets leading to the railway station were thronged, and their progress along the bye streets was impeded by the overflow of traffic from the main road.

"We shall get along better on foot; Draycott Street is only a stone's throw from here," said Loveday; "there's a turning on the north side of Western Road that will bring us straight into it."

So they dismissed their trap, and Loveday, acting as cicerone still, led the way through narrow turnings into the district, half town, half country, that skirts the road leading to the Dyke.

Draycott Street was not difficult to find. It consisted of two rows of newly-built houses of the eight-roomed, lodging-letting order. A dim light shone from the first-floor windows of number fifteen, but the lower window was dark and uncurtained, and a board hanging from its balcony rails proclaimed that it was "to let unfurnished." The door of the house stood slightly ajar, and pushing it open, Loveday led the way up a flight of stairs—lighted halfway up with a paraffin lamp—to the first floor.

"I know the way. I was here this afternoon," she whispered to her companion. "This is the last lecture he will give before he starts for Judaea; or, in other words, bolts with the money he has managed to conjure from other people's purses into his own."

The door of the room for which they were making, on the first floor, stood open, possibly on account of the heat. It laid bare to view a double row of forms, on which were seated some eight or ten persons in the attitude of all-absorbed listeners. Their faces were upturned, as if fixed on a preacher at the farther end of the room, and wore that expression of rapt, painful interest that is sometimes seen on the faces of a congregation of revivalists before the smouldering excitement bursts into flame.

As Loveday and her companion mounted the last of the flight of stairs, the voice of the preacher—full, arrestive, resonant—fell upon their ear; and, standing on the small outside landing, it was possible to catch a glimpse of that preacher through the crack of the half-opened door.

He was a tall, dignified-looking man, of about five-and-forty, with a close crop of white hair, black eye-brows and remarkably luminous and expressive eyes. Altogether his appearance matched his voice: it was emphatically that of a man born to sway, lead, govern the multitude.

A boy came out of an adjoining room and asked Loveday respectfully if she would not like to go in and hear the lecture. She shook her head.

"I could not stand the heat," she said. "Kindly bring us chairs here."

The lecture was evidently drawing to a close now, and Loveday and Mr. Clampe, as they sat outside listening, could not resist an occasional thrill of admiration at the skilful manner in which the preacher led his hearers from one figure of rhetoric to another, until the oratorical climax was reached.

"That man is a born orator," whispered Loveday; "and in addition to the power of the voice has the power of the eye. That audience is as completely hypnotized by him as if they had surrendered themselves to a professional mesmerist."

To judge from the portion of the discourse that fell upon their ear, the preacher was a member of one of the many sects known under the generic name, "Millenarian." His topic was Apollyon and the great battle of Armageddon. This he described as vividly as if it were being fought out under his very eye, and it would scarcely be an exaggeration to say that he made the cannon roar in the ears of his listeners and the tortured cries of the wounded wail in them. He drew an appalling picture of the carnage of that battlefield, of the blood flowing like a river across the plain, of the mangled men and horses, with the birds of prey swooping down from all quarters, and the stealthy tigers and leopards creeping out from their mountain lairs. "And all this time," he said, suddenly raising his voice from a whisper to a full, thrilling tone, "gazing calmly down upon the field of slaughter, with bent brows and folded arms, stands the imperial Apollyon. Apollyon did I say? No, I will give him his right name, the name in which he will stand revealed in that dread day, Napoleon! A Napoleon it will be who, in that day, will stand as the embodiment of Satanic majesty. Out of the mists suddenly he will walk, a tall, dark figure, with frowning brows and firm-set lips. A man to rule, a man to drive, a man to kill! Apollyon the mighty, Napoleon the imperial, they are one and the same—"

Here a sob and a choking cry from one of the women in the front seats interrupted the discourse and sent the small boy who acted as verger into the room with a glass of water.

"That sermon has been preached before," said Loveday. "Now can you not understand the origin of the ghost in Fountain Lane?"

"Hysterics are catching, there's another woman off now," said Mr. Clampe; "it's high time this sort of thing was put a stop to. Pearson ought to be here in another minute with his warrant."

The words had scarcely passed his lips before heavy steps mounting the stairs announced that Pearson and his warrant were at hand.

"I don't think I can be of any further use," said Loveday, rising to depart. "If you like to come to me to-morrow morning at my hotel at ten o'clock I will tell you, step by step, how I came to connect a stolen cheque with a 'ridiculous ghost.'"

"We had a tussle—he showed fight at first," said Mr. Clampe, when, precisely at ten o'clock the next morning, he called upon Miss Brooke at the Métropole. "If he had had time to get his wits together and had called some of the men in that room to the rescue, I verily believe we should have been roughly handled and he might have slipped through our fingers after all. It's wonderful what power these 'born orators,' as you call them, have over minds of a certain order."

"Ah, yes," answered Loveday thoughtfully; "we talk glibly enough about 'magnetic influence,' but scarcely realize how literally true the phrase is. It is my firm opinion that the 'leaders of men,' as they are called, have as absolute and genuine hypnotic power as any modern French expert, although perhaps it may be less consciously exercised. Now tell me about Rogers and Maria Lisle."

"Rogers had bolted, as you expected he would have done, with the six hundred pounds he had been good enough to cash for his reverend colleague. Ostensibly he had started for Judea to collect the elect, as he phrased it, under one banner. In reality, he has sailed for New York, where, thanks to the cable, he will be arrested on his arrival and sent back by return packet. Maria Lisle was arrested this morning on a charge of having stolen the cheque from Mrs. Turner. By the way, Miss Brooke, I think it is almost a pity you didn't take possession of her diary when you had the chance. It would have been invaluable evidence against her and her rascally colleagues."

"I did not see the slightest necessity for so doing. Remember, she is not one of the criminal classes, but a religious enthusiast, and when put upon her defence will at once confess and plead religious conviction as an extenuating circumstance—at least, if she is well advised she will do so. I never read anything that laid bare more frankly than did this diary the mischief that the sensational teaching of these millenarians is doing at the present moment. But I must not take up your time with moralizing. I know you are anxious to learn what, in the first instance, led me to identify a millenarian preacher with a receiver of stolen property."

"Yes, that's it; I want to know about the ghost; that's the point that interests me."

"Very well. As I told you yesterday afternoon, the first thing that struck me as remarkable in this ghost story was the soldierly character of the ghost. One expects emotionally religious people like Freer and his wife to see visions, but one also expects those visions to partake of the nature of those emotions, and to be somewhat shadowy and ecstatic. It seemed to me certain that this Napoleonic ghost must have some sort of religious significance to these people. This conviction it was that set my thoughts running in the direction of the millenarians, who have attached a religious significance (although not a polite one) to the name of Napoleon by embodying the evil Apollyon in the person of a descendant of the great Emperor, and endowing him with all the qualities of his illustrious ancestor. I called upon the Freers, ordered a pair of boots, and while the man was taking my measure, I asked him a few very pointed questions on these millenarian notions. The man prevaricated a good deal at first, but at length was driven to admit that he and his wife were millenarians at heart, that, in fact, the prayer meeting at which the Napoleonic ghost had made its first appearance was a millenarian one, held by a man who had at one time been a Wesleyan preacher in the chapel in Gordon Street, but who had been dismissed from his charge there because his teaching had been held to be unsound. Freer further stated that this man had been so much liked that many members of the congregation seized every opportunity that presented itself of attending his ministrations, some openly, others, like himself and his wife, secretly, lest they might give offence to the elders and ministers of their chapel."

"And the bootmaking connection suffer proportionately," laughed Mr. Clampe.

"Precisely. A visit to the Wesleyan chapel in Gordon Street and a talk with the chapel attendant enabled me to complete the history of this inhibited preacher, the Rev. Richard Steele. From this attendant I ascertained that a certain elder of their chapel, John Rogers by name, had seceded from their communion, thrown in his lot with Richard Steele, and that the two together were now going about the country preaching that the world would come to an end on Thursday, April 11th, 1901, and that five years before this event, viz., on the 5th of March, 1896 one hundred and forty-four thousand living saints would be caught up to heaven. They furthermore announced that this translation would take place in the land of Judaea, that, shortly, saints from all parts of the world would be hastening thither, and that in view of this event a society had been formed to provide homes—a series, I suppose—for the multitudes who would otherwise be homeless. Also (a very vital point this), that subscriptions for this society would be gladly received by either gentleman. I had arrived so far in my ghost enquiry when you came to me, bringing the stolen cheque with its pencilled figures, 144,000."

"Ah, I begin to see!" murmured Mr. Clampe.

"It immediately occurred to me that the man who could make persons see an embodiment of his thought at will, would have very little difficulty in influencing other equally receptive minds to a breach of the ten commandments. The world, it seems to me, abounds in people who are little more than blank sheets of paper, on which a strong hand may transcribe what it will—hysteric subjects, the doctors would call them; hypnotic subjects others would say; really the line that divides the hysteric condition from the hypnotic is a very hazy one. So now, when I saw your stolen cheque, I said to myself, 'there is a sheet of blank paper somewhere in that country vicarage, the thing is to find it out.'"

"Ah, good Mrs. Brown's gossip made your work easy to you there."

"It did. She not only gave me a complete summary of the history of the people within the vicarage walls, but she put so many graphic touches to that history that they lived and moved before me. For instance, she told me that Maria Lisle was in the habit of speaking of Mrs. Turner as a 'Child of the Scarlet Woman,' a 'Daughter of Babylon,' and gave me various other minute particulars, which enabled me, so to speak, to see Maria Lisle going about her daily duties, rendering her mistress reluctant service, hating her in her heart as a member of a corrupt faith, and thinking she was doing God service by despoiling her of some of her wealth, in order to devote it to what seemed to her a holy cause. I would like here to read to you two entries which I copied from her diary under dates respectively, August 3rd (the day the cheque was lost), and August 7th (the following Sunday), when Maria no doubt found opportunity to meet Steele at some prayer-meeting in Brighton."

Here Loveday produced her note-book and read from it as follows:

"'To-day I have spoiled the Egyptians! Taken from a Daughter of Babylon that which would go to increase the power of the Beast!'

"And again, under date August 7th, she writes:

"'I have handed to-day to my beloved pastor that of which I despoiled at Daughter of Babylon. It was blank, but he told me he would fill it in so that 144,000 of the elect would be each the richer by one penny. Blessed thought! this is the doing of my most unworthy hand.'

"A wonderful farrago, that diary of distorted Scriptural phraseology—wild eulogies on the beloved pastor, and morbid ecstatics, such as one would think could be the outcome only of a diseased brain. It seems to me that Portland or Broadmoor, and the ministrations of a sober-minded chaplain, may be about the happiest thing that could befall Maria Lisle at this period of her career. I think I ought to mention in this connection that when at the religious service yesterday afternoon (to attend which I slightly postponed my drive to East Downes), I heard Steele pronounce a fervid eulogy on those who had strengthened his hands for the fight which he knew it would shortly fall to his lot to wage against Apollyon, I did not wonder at weak-minded persons like Maria Lisle, swayed by such eloquence, setting up new standards of right and wrong for themselves."

"Miss Brooke, another question or two. Can you in any way account for the sudden payment of Mrs. Turner's debts—a circumstance that led me a little astray in the first instance?"

"Mrs. Brown explained the matter easily enough. She said that a day or two back, when she was walking on the other side of the vicarage hedge, and the husband and wife in the garden were squabbling as usual over money-matters, she heard Mr. Turner say indignantly, 'only a week or two ago I gave you nearly £500 to pay your debts in Brighton, and now there comes another bill.'"

"Ah, that makes it plain enough. One more question and I have done. I have no doubt there's something in your theory of the hypnotic power (unconsciously exercised) of such men as Richard Steele, although, at the same time, it seems to me a trifle far-fetched and fanciful. But even admitting it, I don't see how you account for the girl, Martha Watts, seeing the ghost. She was not present at the prayer-meeting which called the ghost into being, nor does she appear in any way to have come into contact with the Rev. Richard Steele."

"Don't you think that ghost-seeing is quite as catching as scarlet-fever or measles?" answered Loveday, with a little smile. "Let one member of a family see a much individualized and easily described ghost, such as the one these good people saw, and ten to one others in the same house will see it before the week is over. We are all in the habit of asserting that 'seeing is believing.' Don't you think the converse of the saying is true also, and that 'believing is seeing?'"

MISSING!

"Now, Miss Brooke, if this doesn't inspire you I don't know what will," said Mr. Dyer. And, taking up a handbill that lay upon his writing-table, he read aloud as follows:

"Five hundred pounds reward.—Missing, since Monday, September 20th, Irené, only daughter of Richard Golding, of Langford Hall, Langford Cross, Leicestershire. Age 18, height five feet seven; dark hair and eyes, olive complexion, small features; was dressed when she left home in dark blue serge walking costume, with white straw sailor hat trimmed with cream ribbon. Jewellery worn; plain gold brooch, leather strap bracelet holding small watch, and on the third finger of left hand a marquise ring consisting of one large diamond, surrounded with twelve rubies. Was last seen about ten o'clock on the morning of the 20th leaving Langford Hall Park for the high road leading to Langford Cross. The above reward will be paid to any one giving such information as will lead to the young lady's restoration to her home; or portions of the reward, according to the value of the information received. All communications to be addressed to the Chief Inspector, Police Station, Langford Cross."

"Was last seen on the 20th of September!" exclaimed Loveday, as Mr. Dyer finished reading. "Why, that is ten days ago! Do you mean to say that reward has not stimulated the energies of the local police and long ago put them on the traces of the missing girl?"

"It has stimulated their energies, not a doubt, for the local papers teem with accounts of the way in which the whole country about Langford has been turned upside down generally. Every river, far and near has been dragged; every wood scoured; every railway official at every station for miles round has been driven nearly mad with persistent cross-questioning. But all to no purpose. The affair remains as great a mystery as ever. The girl, as the handbill says, was seen leaving the Park for the high road by some children who chanced to be passing, but after that she seems to have disappeared as completely as if the earth had opened to receive her."

"Cannot her own people suggest any possible motive for her thus suddenly leaving home?"

"It appears not; they seem absolutely incapable of assigning any reason whatever for her extraordinary conduct. This morning I received a letter from Inspector Ramsay, asking me to get you to take up the case. Mr. Golding will not have the slightest objection to your staying at the Hall and thoroughly investigating the matter. Ramsay says it is just possible that they have concentrated too much attention on the search outside the house, and that a promising field for investigation may lie within."

"They should have thought of that before," said Loveday sharply. "I hope you declined the case. Here's the country inspector to the backbone! He'll keep a case in his own hands so long as there's a chance of success; then, when it becomes practically hopeless, hand it over to you just to keep his own failure in countenance by yours."

"Ye-es," said Mr. Dyer, slowly. "I suppose that's about it. But still, business has been slack of late—expenses are heavy—if you thought there was a ghost of a chance—"

"After ten days!" interrupted Miss Brooke, "when the house has settled down into routine, and every one has his story cut and dried, and all sorts of small details have been falsified or smudged over! Criminal cases are like fevers; they should be taken in hand within twenty-four hours."

"Yes, I know," said Mr. Dyer irritably, "but still, as I said before, business is slack—"

"Oh, well, if I'm to go, I'm to go, and there's an end of it," said Loveday resignedly. "I only say it would have been better, for the credit of the office, if you had declined such a hopeless affair. Tell me a little about this Mr. Richard Golding, who and what he is."

Mr. Dyer's temper grew serene again.

"He is a very wealthy man," he answered, "an Australian merchant; came over to England about a dozen years ago, and settled down at Langford Hall. He had, however, been living in Italy for some six or seven years previously. On his way home from Australia he did Italy, as so many Australians do, fell in love with a pretty girl, whom he met at Naples, and married her, and by her had this one child, Irené, who is causing such a sensation at the present moment."

"Is this Italian wife living?"

"No, she died just before Mr. Golding came to England. He has not yet married again, but I hear is on the point of so doing. The lady he contemplates making the second Mrs. Golding is a certain Mrs. Greenhow, a widow, who for the past year or so has acted as chaperon to his daughter and housekeeper to himself."

"It is possible that Miss Irené was not too well pleased at the idea of having a stepmother."

"Such is the fact. From all accounts she and her future stepmother did not get on at all well together. Miss Irené has a very hasty, imperious temper, and Mrs. Greenhow seems to have been quite incapable of holding her own with her. She was to have left the hall this month to make her preparations for the approaching wedding; the young lady's disappearance, however, has naturally brought matters to a standstill."

"Did Miss Golding take any money away with her, do you know?"

"Ah, nobody seems sure on that head. Mr. Golding gave her a liberal allowance and exacted no accounts. Sometimes she had her purse full at the end of the quarter, sometimes it was empty before her quarterly cheque had been cashed a week. I fear you will have to do without exact information on that most important point.

"She had lovers, of course?"

"Yes; in spite of her quick temper she seems to have been a lovable and most attractive young woman, with her half-Australian half-Italian parentage, and to have turned the heads of all the men in the neighbourhood. Only two, however, appear to have found the slightest favour in her eyes—a certain Lord Guilleroy, who owns nearly all the land for miles round Langford, and a young fellow called Gordon Cleeve, the only son of Sir Gordon Cleeve, a wealthy baronet. The girl seems to have coquetted pretty equally with these two; then suddenly, for some reason or other, she gives Mr. Cleeve to understand that his attentions are distasteful to her, and gives unequivocal encouragement to Lord Guilleroy. Gordon Cleeve does not sit down quietly under this treatment. He threatens to shoot first his rival, then himself, then Miss Golding; finally, does none of these three things, but starts off on a three years' journey round the world."

"Threatens to shoot her; starts off on a journey round the world," summed up Loveday. "Do you know the date of the day on which he left Langford?"

"Yes, it was on the 19th; the day before Miss Golding disappeared. But Ramsay has already traced him down to Brindisi; ascertained that he went on board the *Buckingham, en route* for Alexandria, and has beaten out the theory that he can, by any possibility, be connected with the affair. So I wouldn't advise you to look in that quarter for your clue."

"I am not at all sanguine about finding a clue in any quarter," said Loveday, as she rose to take leave.

She did not feel in the best of tempers, and was a little disposed to resent having a case, so to speak, forced upon her under such disadvantageous conditions.

Her last words to Mr. Dyer were almost the first she addressed to Inspector Ramsay when, towards the close of the day, she was met by him at Langford Cross Station. Ramsay was a lanky, bony Scotchman, sandy-haired and slow of speech.

"Our hopes centre on you; we trust you'll not disappoint us," he said, by way of a greeting.

His use of the plural number made Loveday turn in the direction of a tall, good-looking man, with a remarkably frank expression of countenance, who stood at the inspector's elbow.

"I am Lord Guilleroy," said this gentleman, coming forward. "Will you allow me to drive you to Langford Hall? My cab is waiting outside."

"Thank you; one moment," answered Loveday, again turning to Ramsay. "Now, do you wish," she said, addressing him, "to tell me anything beyond the facts you have already communicated to Mr. Dyer?"

"No-o," answered the inspector, slowly and sententiously. "I would rather not bias your mind in any direction by any theory of mine." ("It would be rather a waste of time to attempt such a thing," thought Loveday.) "The only additional fact I have to mention is one you would see for yourself so soon as you arrived at the Hall, namely, that Mr. Golding is keeping up with great difficulty—in fact, is on the verge of a break-down. He has not had half an hour's sleep since his daughter left home—a serious thing that for a man at his age."

Loveday was favourably impressed with Lord Guilleroy. He gave her the idea of being a man of strong common-sense and great energy. His conversation was marked by a certain reserve. Although, however, he evidently declined to wear his heart upon his sleeve, it was easy to see, from a few words that escaped him, that if the search for Miss Golding proved fruitless his whole life would be wrecked.

He did not share Inspector Ramsay's wish not to bias Loveday's mind by any theory of his own.

"If I had a theory you should have it in a minute," he said, as he whipped up his horse and drove rapidly along the country road; "but I confess at the present moment my mind is a perfect blank on the matter. I have had a dozen theories, and have been compelled, one by one, to let them all go. I have suspected every one in turn, Cleeve, her own father (God forgive me!), her intended stepmother, the very servants in the house, and, one by one, circumstances have seemed to exonerate them all. It's bewildering—it's maddening! And most maddening of all it is to have to sit here with idle hands, when I would scour the earth from end to end to find her!"

The country around Langford Hall, like most of the hunting districts in Leicestershire, was as flat as if a gigantic stream-roller had passed over it. The Hall itself was a somewhat imposing Gothic structure, of rough grey stone. Very grey and drear it showed in the autumn landscape as Loveday drove in through the park gates and caught her first glimpse of it between the all but leafless elms that flanked the drive. The equinoctial gales had set in early this year, and heavy rains had helped forward their work of wreckage and destruction. The green sward of the park was near akin to a swamp; and the trout stream that flowed across it at an angle showed swollen to its very banks. The sky was leaden with gathering masses of clouds; a flight of rooks, wheeling low and flapping their black wings, with their mournful cawing, completed the dreariness of the scene.

"A companion picture, this," Loveday thought, "to the desolation that must reign within the house with the fate of its only daughter unknown—unguessed at even."

As she alighted at the hall door, a magnificent Newfoundland dog came bounding forth. Lord Guilleroy caressed it heartily.

"It was her dog," he explained. "We have tried in vain to make him track down his mistress—these dogs haven't the scent of hounds."

He excused himself from entering the house with Loveday.

"It's like a vault—a catacomb; I can't stand it," he said. "No, I'll take back my horse;" this was said to the man who stood waiting. "Tell Mr. Golding he'll see me round in the morning without fail."

Loveday was shown into the library, where Mr. Golding was waiting to receive her. In the circumstances no disguise as to her name and profession had been deemed necessary, and she was announced simply as Miss Brooke from Lynch Court.

Mr. Golding greeted her warmly. One glance at him convinced her that Inspector Ramsay had given no exaggerated account of the bereaved father. His face was wan and haggard; his head was bowed; his voice sounded strained and weak. He seemed incapable of speaking on any save the one topic that filled his thoughts.

"We pin our faith on you, Miss Brooke," he said; "you are our last hope. Now, tell me you do not despair of being able to end this awful suspense one way or another. A day or two more of it will put me into my coffin!"

"Miss Brooke will perhaps like to have some tea, and to rest a little, after her long journey before she begins to talk?" said a lady, at that moment entering the room and advancing towards her. Loveday could only conjecture that this was Mrs. Greenhow, for Mr. Golding was too preoccupied to make any attempt to an introduction.

Mrs. Greenhow was a small, slight woman, with fluffy hair and green-grey eyes. Her voice suggested a purr; her eyes, a scratch.

"Cat-tribe!" thought Loveday; "the velvet paw and the hidden claw—the exact antithesis, I should say, to one of Miss Golding's temperament."

Mr. Golding went back to the one subject he had at heart.

"You have had my daughter's photograph given to you, I've no doubt," he said; "but this I consider a far better likeness." Here he pointed to a portrait in pastels that hung above his writing-table. It was that of a large-eyed, handsome girl of eighteen, with a remarkably sweet expression about the mouth.

Mrs. Greenhow again interposed. "I think, if you don't mind my saying so," she said, "you would slightly mislead Miss Brooke if you led her to think that that was a perfect likeness of dear René. Much as I love the dear girl," here she turned to Loveday, "I'm bound to admit that one seldom or never saw her wearing such a sweet expression of countenance."

Mr. Golding frowned, and sharply changed the subject.

"Tell me, Miss Brooke," he said, "what was your first impression when the facts of the case were submitted to you? I have been told that first impressions with you are generally infallible."

Loveday parried the question.

"I am not at present sure that I am in possession of all the facts," she answered. "There are one or two questions I particularly want to ask—you must forgive me if they seem to you a little irrelevant to the matter in hand. First and foremost, I want to know if any formal good-bye took place between your daughter and Mr. Gordon Cleeve?"

"I think not. A sudden coolness arose between them, and the young fellow went away without so much as shaking hands with me."

"I fear an irreparable breach has occurred between the Cleeves and yourself on account of dear René's extraordinary treatment of Gordon," said Mrs. Greenhow sweetly.

"There was no extraordinary treatment," said Mr. Golding, now almost in anger. "My daughter and Mr. Cleeve were good friends—nothing more, I assure you—until one day René saw him cruelly thrashing one of his setters, and after that she cut him dead—would have nothing whatever to do with him."

"Maddalena told Inspector Ramsay," said Mrs. Greenhow, sweetly still, "that on the evening before Gordon Cleeve left Langford dear René received a note from him—"

"Which she tossed unopened into the fire," finished Mr. Golding.

"Who is Maddalena?" interrupted Loveday.

"My daughter's maid. I brought her over from Naples twelve years ago as nurse, and as René grew older she naturally enough fell into her duties as René's maid. She is a dear, faithful creature; her aunt was nurse to René's mother."

"Is it possible for Maddalena to be told off to wait upon me while I am in the house?" asked Loveday, turning to Mrs. Greenhow.

"Certainly, if you wish it. At the same time, I warn you that she is not in a particularly amiable frame of mind just now, and will be very likely to be sullen and disobliging," answered the lady.

"Maddalena is not generally either one or the other," said Mr. Golding deprecatingly; "but just now she is a little unlike herself. The truth is, all the servants have been a little too rigorously cross-examined by the police on matters of which they could have absolutely no knowledge, and Ramsay made such a dead set at Lena that the girl felt herself insulted, grew sullen, and refused to open her lips."

"She must be handled judiciously. I suppose she was broken-hearted when Miss Golding did not return from her morning's walk?"

A reply was prevented by the entrance of a servant with a telegram in his hand.

Mr. Golding tore it open, and, in a trembling voice, read aloud as follows:

> "Some one answering to the description of your daughter was seen yesterday in the Champs Elysées, but disappeared before she could be detained. Watch arrivals at Folkestone and Dover."

The telegram was dated from Paris, and was from M. Dulau, of the Paris police. Mr. Golding's agitation was pitiable.

"Great heavens! is it possible?" he cried, putting his hand to his forehead as if stunned. "I'll start for Dover—no, Paris, I think, at once." He staggered to his feet, looking around him in a dazed and bewildered fashion. He might as well have talked of starting for the moon or the north star.

"Pardon me," said Loveday, "Inspector Ramsay is the right person to deal with that telegram. It should be sent to him at once."

Mr. Golding sank back in his chair, trembling from head to foot.

"I think you are right," he said faintly. "I might break down and lose a possible chance."

Then he turned once more to the man, who stood waiting for orders, and desired him to take the fastest horse to the stables and ride at once with the telegram to the Inspector.

"And," he added, "on your way back call at the Castle, see Lord Guilleroy, and give him the news." He turned a pleading face towards Loveday. "This is good news—you consider it good news, do you not?" he asked piteously.

"It won't do to depend too much on it, will it?" said Mrs. Greenhow. "You see, there have been so many false alarms—if I may use the word."—This was said to Loveday.—"Three times last week we had telegrams from different parts of the country saying dear René had been seen—now here, now there, I think there must be a good many girls like her wandering about the world."

"The dress has something to do with it, no doubt," answered Loveday; "it is not a very distinctive one. Still, we must hope for the best. It is possible, of course, that at this very moment the young lady may be on her way home with a full explanation of what has seemed extraordinary conduct on her part. Now, if you will allow me, I will go to my room. And will you please give the order that Maddalena shall follow me there as quickly as possible?"

Loveday's thoughts were very busy when, in the quietude of her own room, she sank into an easy chair beside the fire. The case to which she had so unwillingly devoted her attention was beginning to present some interesting intricacies. She passed in view the *dramatis personae* of the little drama which she could only hope might not end in a tragedy. The broken-hearted father; the would-be-step-mother, with her feline affinities; the faithful maid; the cruel-tempered lover; the open-faced, energetic one; each in turn received their meed of attention.

"That man would be one to depend on in an emergency," she said to herself, allowing her thoughts to dwell a little longer upon Lord Guilleroy than upon the others. "He has, I should say, a good head on his shoulders and—"

But here a tap-tap at the door brought her thinking to a standstill, and in response to her "come in" the door opened and the maid Lena entered.

She was a tall, black-eyed, dark-skinned woman of about thirty, dressed in a neat black stuff gown. Twelve years of English domestic life had considerably modified the outer tokens of her nationality; a gold dagger that kept a thick coil of hair in its place, and a massive Roman-cut cameo ring on the third finger of her right hand, were about the only things that differentiated her appearance from that of the ordinary English lady's maid. Possibly as a rule she wore a pleasant, smiling expression of countenance. For the moment, however, her face was shadowed by a sullen scowl, that said plainly as words could: "I am here very much against my will, and intend to render you the most unwilling of services."

Loveday felt that she must be taken in hand at once.

"You are Miss Golding's maid, I believe?" she said in a short, sharp tone.

"Yes, madame." This in a slow, sullen one.

"Very well, Kindly unstrap that portmanteau and open my dressing-bag. I am glad you are to wait upon me while I am here. I don't suppose you ever before in your life acted maid to a lady detective?"

"Never, madame." This in a still more sullen tone than before.

"Ah, it will be a new experience to you, and I hope that it may be made a profitable one also. Tell me, are you saving up money to get married?"

Lena, on her knees unstrapping the portmanteau, started and looked up.

"How does madame know that?" she asked, Loveday pointed to the cameo ring on her third finger. "I only guessed at such a possibility," she answered. "Well, now, Lena, I am going to make you an offer. I will give you fifty pounds—fifty, remember, in English gold—if you will procure for me certain information that I require in the prosecution of my work here."

The sullen look on Lena's face deepened.

"I am a servant of the house," she answered, bending lower over the portmanteau; "I do not sell its secrets even for English gold."

"But it is not the secrets of your master's house I am wanting to buy—no, nor anybody else's secrets; I only want you to procure for me certain information that I could easily have procured for myself if I had been a little sooner on the scene. And the information I want relates to no one inside the house, but some one outside of it—Mr. Gordon Cleeve."

The sullen look on Lena's face gave place to one of intense, unutterable relief.

"Mr. Gordon Cleeve!" she repeated. "Oh-h, for fifty pounds, I will undertake to bring madame a good deal of information about him; I know some of the servants in Sir Gordon's house. I know, too, the mother of Mr. Cleeve's valet who has started with him on his journey round the world."

"Good. So, then, it is a bargain. Now, Lena, tell me truly, is this Mr. Cleeve a great favourite with you?"

"With me! Ah, the good God forbid, madame! I never liked him; I used to say to Miss René when I brought her his flowers and his notes: 'Have nothing to do with him, he is cruel—bad at heart.'"

"Ah, yes; I read all that in your face when I mentioned his name. Now what I want you first and foremost to do for me is to find out how this young man spent the last day that he was at Langford. I want you to bring me a report of his doings—as exact a report as possible—on the 18th of this month."

"I will do my best, madame."

"Very good. Now, there is something else. Would you be greatly surprised if I told you that the young man did not sail in the *Buckingham* from Brindisi as is generally supposed?"

"Madame! Inspector Ramsay said he had ascertained beyond a doubt that Mr. Cleeve went on board the *Buckingham* at Brindisi!"

"Ah, to go on board is one thing; to sail is another! Now, listen, Lena, very carefully to what I am going to say. I am expecting daily to receive some most important information respecting this gentleman's movements, and I may want some one to set off at a minute's notice for Paris, perhaps; or, perhaps, Florence or Naples, to verify that information: would you do this for me?—of course, I would supply you with money and full details as to your journey."

A flush of pleasure passed over Lena's face.

"Yes, madame," she answered; "if you could get my master's permission for me to go."

"I will undertake to do so." She pondered a moment, then added a little tentatively, and closely watching Lena's face as she asked the question, "I suppose Miss Golding resembled her mother in appearance—I do not see any likeness between her portrait and her father."

Lena's sullenness and stateliness had vanished together now, and once upon the topic of her nursling she was the warm-hearted, enthusiastic Italian woman once more. She became voluble in her description of her dear Miss René, her beauty, her fascinating ways, which she traced entirely to the Italian blood that flowed in her veins; and anecdote after anecdote she related of the happy time when they lived among the lakes and mountains of her native land.

The room grew dark and darker, while she gossiped apace, and presently the dressing-bell clanged through the house.

"Light the candles now," said Loveday, rising from her seat beside the fire; "draw down the blinds and shut out that dreary autumn scene, it sets me shivering!"

It might well do so. The black clouds had fulfilled their threat, and rain was now dashing in torrents against the panes. A tall sycamore, immediately outside the window, creaked and groaned dismally in response to the wind that came whistling round the corner of the house, and between the swaying and all but leafless elms Loveday could catch a glimpse of the grey, winding trout stream, swollen now to its limits and threatening to overflow its banks.

Dinner that night was in keeping with the gloom that overhung the house within and without; although the telegram from Paris had seemed to let in a ray of hope, Mr. Golding was evidently afraid to put much trust in it.

"As Mrs. Greenhow says, 'we have had so many disappointments,'" he said sadly, as he took his place at table. "So many false clues—false scents started. Ramsay has at once put himself in communication with the police at Boulogne and Calais, as well as at Dover and Folkestone. We can only pray that something may come of it!"

"And dear Lord Guilleroy," chimed in Mrs. Greenhow, in her soft, purring voice, "has started for Paris immediately. The young man has such a vast amount of energy, and thinks he can do the work of the police better than they can do it for themselves."

"That's hardly a fair way of putting it, Clare," interrupted Mr. Golding irritably; "he is working heart and soul with the police, and thinks it advisable that some one representing me should be in Paris, in case an emergency should arise; also he wants himself to question Dulau respecting my daughter's sudden appearance and disappearance in the Paris streets. Guilleroy," here he turned to Loveday, "is devotedly attached to my daughter, and—why, Dryad, what's the matter, old man? down, down! Don't growl and whine in that miserable fashion."

He had broken off to address these words to the Newfoundland, who, until that moment, had been comfortably stretched on the hearth-rug before the fire, but who now had suddenly started to his feet with ears erect, and given a prolonged growl, that ended in something akin to a whine.

"It may be a fox trotting past the window," said Mrs. Greenhow, whipping at the dog with her lace handkerchief. But Dryad was not to be so easily subdued. With his nose to the ground now he was sniffing uneasily at and around the heavy curtains that half draped the long French windows of the room.

"Something has evidently disturbed him. Why not let him out into the garden?" said Loveday. And Mr. Golding, with a "Hey, Dryad, go find!" unfastened the window and let the dog out into the windy darkness.

Dinner was a short meal that night. It was easy to see that it was only by a strong effort of will that Mr. Golding kept his place at table, and made even a pretence of eating.

At the close of the meal Loveday asked for a quiet corner, in which to write some business letters, and was shown into the library by Mr. Golding.

"You'll find all you require here, I think," he said, with something of a sigh, as he placed a chair for her at a lady's davenport. "This was René's favourite corner, and here are the last flowers she gathered—dead, all dead, but I will not have them touched!" He broke off abruptly, set down the vase of dead asters which he had taken in his hand, and quitted the room, leaving Loveday to the use of René's pen, ink, paper, and blotting-pad.

Loveday soon became absorbed in her business letters. Time flew swiftly, and it was not until a clock on the mantelpiece chimed the hour—ten o'clock—that she gave a thought as to what might be the hour for retiring at the Hall.

Something else beside the striking of the clock almost simultaneously caught her ear—the whining and scratching of a dog at one of the windows. These, like those of the dining-room, opened as doors into an outside verandah. They were, however, closely shuttered, and Loveday had to ring for a servant to undo the patent fastener.

So soon as the window was opened Dryad rushed into the room, plastered with mud, and dripping with water from every hair.

"He must have been in the stream," said the footman, trying to collar the dog and lead him out of the room.

"Stop! one moment!" cried Loveday, for her eye had caught sight of something hanging in shreds between the dog's teeth. She bent over him, patting and soothing him, and contrived to disentangle those shreds, which a closer examination proved to be a few tattered fragments of dark blue serge.

"Is your letter-writing nearly ended, Miss Brooke?" asked Mr. Golding, at that moment entering the room.

For reply, Loveday held up the shreds of blue serge. His face grew ashen white; he needed no explanation; those shreds and the dripping dog seemed to tell their own tale.

"Great heavens!" he cried, "why did I not follow the dog out! There must be a search at once. Get men, lanterns, ropes, a ladder—the dog, too, will be of use."

A terrible energy took possession of him. "Find, Dryad, find!" he shouted to the dog, and then, hatless and thin-shoed as he was, he rushed out into the darkness with Dryad at his heels.

In less than five minutes afterwards the whole of the men-servants of the house, with lanterns, ropes, and a ladder long enough to span the stream, had followed him. The wind had fallen, the rain had ceased now, and a watery half-moon was struggling through the thin, flying clouds. Loveday and Mrs. Greenhow, standing beneath the verandah, watched the men disappear in the direction of the trout stream, whither Dryad had led the way. From time to time shouts came to them, through the night stillness, of "This way!" "No, here!" together with Dryad's sharp bark and the occasional distant flash of a bull's-eye lantern. It was not until nearly half an hour afterwards that one of the men came running back to the house with a solemn white face and a pitiful tale. He wanted something that would serve for a stretcher, he said in a subdued tone—the two-fold oak screen in the hall would do—and please, into which room was "it" to be brought?—

On the following evening Mr. Dyer received a lengthy dispatch from Miss Brooke, which ran as follows:—

> "Langford Hall.
>
> "This is to supplement my telegram of an hour back, telling you of the finding of Miss Golding's body in the stream that runs through her father's grounds. Mr. Golding has himself identified the body, and has now utterly collapsed. At the present moment it seems rather doubtful whether he will be in a fit state to give evidence at the inquest, which will be held to-morrow. Miss Golding appears to be dressed as she was when she left home, with this notable exception—the marquise ring has disappeared from the third finger of her left hand, and in its stead she wears a plain gold wedding-ring. Now this is a remarkable circumstance, and strikes a strange keynote to my mind. I am writing hurriedly, and can only give you the most important points in this very singular case. The maid, Lena, a reserved, self-contained woman, gave way to a passion of grief when the young lady's body was brought in and laid upon her own bed. She insisted on performing all the last sad offices for the dead, however, in spite of her grief, and is now, I am glad to say, calmer and

capable of a little quiet conversation with me. I keep
her continually in attendance on me, as I am rather
anxious to keep my eye on her just now. I have telegraphed to Lord Guilleroy, asking him, in spite of
the terrible news which will in due course reach him,
to be good enough to remain in Paris awaiting directions from me, which may have to be carried out
at a minute's notice. I hope to have further news to
send a little later on."

Mr. Dyer laid aside the letter with a grunt of dissatisfaction.

"Well," he said to himself, "I suppose she expects me to be able
to read between the lines, but I'm bothered if I can make head or
tail of it all. She seems to me to be going a little wide of the mark
just now; it might be as well to give her a hint." So he dashed off a
few brief lines as follows:—

"I suppose you are concentrating now on finding out what were Miss Golding's movements while
absent from her home. It seems to me this could be
better done in Paris than at Langford Hall. The ring
on her finger necessarily implies that she has gone
through a marriage service somewhere, and as she
was seen in Paris a day or two ago, it is as likely as
not that the ceremony took place there. The Paris
police could give you 'yea or nay' on this matter
within twenty-four hours. As to the maid, Lena, I
think you are laying too much stress upon her possible knowledge of her mistress's movements.

"If she had been tied down to secrecy by promise of reward, she would naturally, now that all such
promises are rendered futile, reveal all she knows
on the matter—she has nothing to gain by keeping
the secrets of the dead."

This letter crossed on its road a telegram from Loveday running thus:—

> "Inquest over. Verdict, 'Found drowned, but how deceased got into the water there is no evidence to show.' Funeral takes place to-morrow; Mr. Golding delirious with brain fever."

On the day following Mr. Dyer received a second letter from Loveday. Thus it ran:—

> "The funeral is over; Mr. Golding is much worse, I have dispatched Lena to Paris, telling her I require her services there to follow up a clue I hold respecting Mr. Gordon Cleeve, and promising her rewards commensurate with the manner in which she carries out my orders. I have also written to Lord Guilleroy, telling him the sort of assistance I require from him. If he is the man I take him for he will be more useful to me than all the Paris police put together. I will answer your letter in detail in a day or two. The neighbourhood is still in a state of great excitement, and all sorts of wild reports are flying about. Ramsay and Dulau have traced a lady, dressed in dark blue serge, and answering in other respects to Miss Golding's description, from the Gare du Midi, Paris, step by step to her arrival at Langford Cross, whence, poor thing, she must have walked through the pouring rain to the Hall. I do not see, however, that this information helps us forward one step towards the solution of the mystery of the girl's disappearance. Ramsay is a little inclined to criticize what he calls my 'leisurely handling' of the case. Mrs. Greenhow, who is a terribly empty-headed, but at the same time essentially hard-natured little

woman, appears disposed to follow suit, and has more than once thrown out hints that my stay in the house is being unnecessarily prolonged. As there is practically no further necessity for my remaining at the Hall, I have told her that I shall to-day take up my quarters at the Roebuck Inn (by courtesy hotel), at Langford Cross. I believe she is unfeignedly glad at what she considers the ending of the affair. The imperious yet fascinating young lady no doubt ruled her and the household generally with a rod of iron, and the little woman, I feel sure, if she had dared, would have ordered bonfires and a general rejoicing on the day of the funeral. Well, I have not much sympathy with her, and am preparing for her a shock to her not too-sensitive nerves which she little suspects. My chief anxiety at the present moment is Mr. Golding, who still remains unconscious. I have requested the doctors to send me two bulletins daily of his condition, which I fear is a most serious one."

There could be little doubt on this head. The doctors' verdict on the day that Loveday left Langford Hall for "The Roebuck" was: "Absolutely no hope." The bulletin brought to her on the following morning was "Condition remains unchanged." On the third day, however, the report was "Slight improvement." Then followed the welcome bulletins of "Improvement maintained," and "Out of danger," to be followed by the most welcome report of all: "Is making steady progress towards recovery."

"It is Mr. Golding's illness that has kept me here so long," said Loveday to Inspector Ramsay, as if by way of apology for her continued presence on the scene. "I think, however, I can see my way to departure now. Going to Paris? Oh, dear me, no. I have telegraphed to Mr. Dyer to expect me back the day after to-morrow; if you will like to come to me here, or will meet me at Langford Cross Station, I will give you a full report of all I have done since I took the case in hand. Now I am going to the Hall to ascertain at what hour to-morrow it will be convenient for me to say good-bye to Mr. Golding."

More than this Ramsay was unable to extract from Miss Brooke. His open strictures upon what he called her "leisurely handling of the case" had put her upon her mettle, and she had decided that Ramsay and his colleagues should be taught that Lynch Court had a special way of doing things, and could hold its own with the best.

On her way to the Hall Loveday called at the post-office, and there had a letter with a London postmark handed to her. This she at once opened and read, and then dispatched a reply to it by telegram. The reply was an enigmatic one to the village postmaster, for Loveday, after a few casual questions as to his knowledge of Continental languages, chose German as her medium of communication. The address, however, "to Lord Guilleroy, at Charing Cross Hotel," was plain reading enough.

At the Hall Loveday found Mrs. Greenhow in an active state of mind. Mr. Golding, she informed her with a sweet effusiveness, would come downstairs for a short time on the following day, and she was doing all that lay in her power to put out of sight anything that might awaken painful recollections. "I have had dear René's harp removed to a lumber room, her portrait taken down from the library wall," she said, in her usual purring tones; "and her davenport is being wheeled into my own sitting-room. Poor dear René! If only she could have been taught to govern her willful temper a happier fate might have befallen her. What that fate was I suppose we shall never know now."

Loveday's only reply to this was to ask for an exact report of the doctor's opinion of Mr. Golding's condition. Mrs. Greenhow put her handkerchief to her eyes as she answered that Doctor Godwin's opinion was that, so far as bodily strength was concerned, he was considerably better, but that his mental condition was a serious one. His brain appeared to be in a state of semi-stupefaction, which it was possible might be indicative of the softening of its tissues.

Loveday expressed a wish to see this doctor—to time her farewell visit to Mr. Golding on the following day with Dr. Godwin's daily call. In fact, she would like a little private talk with him before she went in to see his patient.

To all this Mrs. Greenhow offered no objection. Lady detectives, she said to herself, were a race apart, and had a curious way of doing things; but, thank Heaven, she would soon see the last of this one!

The stormy autumnal weather had given place now to a brief spell of late summer sunshine, and on the last day of her visit to Langford, Miss Brooke had a cheerier view of the Hall and its surroundings than she had had on the day of her arrival there. The trout stream had retreated to its natural proportions, and showed like a streak of molten silver—not a grey, turbid flood—in the bright sunlight that played at hide-and-seek between the branches of the stript elms. Even the old rooks seemed to have a cheery undernote to their "caw, caw" as they wheeled about the old house; and Dryad himself, as he once more came bounding forth to greet her, appeared to her fancy to have a less dolorous ring in his noisy bark.

"That dog is a perfect nuisance—has been utterly spoilt. I must have him chained up," said Mrs. Greenhow, as she led the way into a room where Dr. Godwin sat awaiting Loveday. She introduced them one to the other. "Shall I remain, or do you wish to converse alone?" she asked.

And as Loveday answered with decision "Alone," the little woman had no choice but to withdraw, wondering once more over the vagaries of lady detectives.

Half an hour afterwards the doctor, a clever-looking, active little man, led the way into the library where Mr. Golding was seated.

Loveday was greatly shocked at the change which a few days' illness had wrought in him. His chair was drawn close to the window, and the autumn sunshine that filled the room threw into pitiful relief his shrunken frame and pallid face, aged now by about a dozen years. His eyes were closed, his head was bent low on his breast, and he did not lift it as the door opened.

"You need not remain," said Dr. Godwin to the nurse, who rose as they entered; and Loveday and the doctor were left alone with the patient.

Loveday drew near softly. "I am going back to town this evening, and have come to say good-bye," she said, extending her hand.

Mr. Golding opened his eyes, staring vaguely at the extended hand. "To say good-bye!" he repeated, in a dreamy, far-away tone.

"I am Miss Brooke," Loveday explained. "I came down from London to investigate the strange circumstances connected with your daughter's disappearance."

"My daughter's disappearance!" He started and began to tremble violently.

The doctor had his hand on his patient's pulse now.

"I have conducted my investigations under somewhat disadvantageous circumstances," Loveday went on quietly, "and, for a time, with but little result. A few days back, however, I received important information from Lord Guilleroy, and to-day I have seen and communicated with him. In fact, it was his carriage that brought me to your house this afternoon."

"Lord Guilleroy!" repeated Mr. Golding slowly. His voice had a more natural ring in it; recollection, although, perhaps, a painful one, seemed to sound in it.

"Yes. He said he would wander about the park until I had seen and prepared you for his visit. Ah! there he is coming up the drive."

Here she drew back the curtain that half draped the open window.

This window commanded a good view of the drive, with its overarching elms, that led from the lodge gates to the house. Along that drive two persons were advancing at that moment in leisurely fashion; one of those two was undoubtedly Lord Guilleroy, the other was a tall, graceful girl, dressed in deep mourning.

Mr. Golding's eyes followed Loveday's at first with a blank, expressionless stare. Then, little by little, that stare changed into a look of intelligence and recognition. His face grew ashen white, then a wave of colour swept over it.

"Lord Guilleroy, yes," he said, panting and struggling for breath. "But—but who is that walking with him? Tell me, tell me quickly, for the love of Heaven!"

He tried to rise to his feet, but his limbs failed him. The doctor poured out a cordial, and put it to his lips.

"Drink this, please," he said. "Now tell him quickly," he whispered to Loveday.

"That young lady," she resumed calmly, "is your daughter René. She drove up with me and Lord Guilleroy from Langford Cross. Shall I ask her to come in and see you? She is only waiting for Dr. Godwin's permission to do so."

Time to grant or refuse that permission, however, was not accorded to Dr. Godwin. René—a sadder, sweeter-faced René than the one who had so impetuously discarded home and father—now stood outside in the "half-sun, half-shade" of the verandah, and had caught the sound of Loveday's last words.

She swept impetuously past her into the room.

"Father, father!" she said, as she knelt down beside his chair, "I have come back at last! Are you not glad to see me?"

"I daresay it all seems very mysterious to you," said Loveday to Inspector Ramsay, as together they paced the platform of Langford Cross Station, waiting for the incoming of the London train, "but, I assure you, it all admits of the easiest and simplest of explanations—Who on earth was it that the inquest was held over, and who was buried about a week ago, do you say? Oh, that was Mr. Golding's wife, Irené, daughter of Count Mascagni, of Alguida, in South Italy, whom every one believed to be dead. It is her history that holds the key to the whole affair from first to last. I will begin at the beginning, and tell you her story as nearly as possible as it was told to me. To be quite frank with you, I would have admitted you long ago into my confidence, and told you, step by step, how things were working themselves out, if you had not offended me by criticizing my method of doing my work."

"I'm sure I'm very sorry," here broke in Ramsay in a deprecating tone.

"Oh, pray don't mention it. Let me see, where was I? Ah, I must go back some nineteen or twenty years in Mr. Golding's life in order to make things clear to you. The particulars which I had from Mr. Dyer, and which I fancy you supplied him with, respecting Mr. Golding's early life were so meager that directly I arrived at the

Hall I set to work to supplement them; this I contrived to do in a before-dinner chat with Lena, Miss Golding's maid. I found out through her that Irené Mascagni was a typical Italian woman of the half-educated, passionate, beautiful, animal kind, and that Mr. Golding's early married life was anything but a happy one. Irené was motherless, and had been so spoilt from babyhood upwards by her old nurse, Lena's aunt, that she could not brook the slightest opposition to her whims and wishes. She was a great coquette also; lovers were an absolute necessity to her. Remonstrance on Mr. Golding's part was useless; Irené met it by appeals to her father for protection against what she considered her husband's brutality; in consequence, a serious quarrel ensued between the Count and Mr. Golding, and when the latter announced his intention of breaking up his Italian home and buying an estate in England, Irené, accompanied by her nurse, Antonia, left her husband and little daughter and went back to her father's house, vowing that nothing would induce her to leave her beloved Italy. At this crisis in his affairs, Mr. Golding was suddenly compelled to undertake a journey to Australia to adjust certain complicated matters of business. He took with him on this voyage his little girl, René, and her nurse—now her maid, Lena. The visit to Australia in all occupied about six months. During that time no communication of any sort passed between him and his wife or her father. He resolved, however, to make one more effort to induce Irené to return to her home and her duty; and, with this object, he went to Naples on his return to Europe and wrote to his wife from there, asking her to appoint a day for a meeting. In reply to this letter he received a visit from Antonia, who, with a great show of sorrow, informed him that Irené had caught a fever during his absence, and had died, and now lay buried in the family vault at Alguida. Mr. Golding's grief at the tidings was no doubt mitigated by the recollection of the unfortunate married life he had led. He made no attempt to communicate with Count Mascagni, started at once for England, and set up his establishment at Langford Hall. All this, with the exception of the name of Irené's father and that of his estate, was told me by Lena, who, I may mention in passing, laid great stress upon the wonderful likeness that existed between Miss Golding and her mother. She was, she said, the exact counterpart of what her mother had been at her age."

"It is marvelous to me how you contrived to get anything out of that woman Lena," said Ramsay; "she was most obstinately taciturn with me."

"Pardon me if I say that was because she had been most injudiciously handled. In the circumstances it would never have occurred to me to put a single direct question to her, although I like you, felt convinced that she was the one and only person likely to be in her young mistress's confidence. So fully imbued was I with this idea that I felt certain that, if she could be sent out of the house on any pretext, by closely following her movements we should, sooner or later, come upon the traces of Miss Golding. To attain this end, I feigned suspicion of Mr. Gordon Cleeve, and promised her rewards if she would bring me tidings of his doings. This was to pave the way to dismissing her on a journey to Italy. It also had the most welcome effect of calming her mind and convincing her of my belief in her innocence. With her fears thus allayed, I found her no longer sullen but communicative to a degree."

"Pardon my interrupting you at this point, but will you kindly tell me what, in the first instance, aroused your suspicious as to the identity of the person 'found drowned' by the coroner's jury?"

"Lena's conduct when the body was brought into the house. I should, however, tell you that a keynote of suspicion as to the possibility of Mrs. Golding being still alive had been struck when, as I sat writing at Miss Golding's davenport, I found the words "Mia Madre" scribbled here and there on her blotting-pad. Now what, I said to myself, could, after all these years, have turned her thoughts to her mother and her early Italian home? The wedding-ring on the lady's finger, coupled with Lena's statement as to Miss Golding's marvelous likeness to her mother, together with an exclamation of Mr. Golding's, after identifying the body, that his daughter had 'aged by a dozen years,' made these suspicions grow stronger. It was, however, Lena's own conduct that resolved them into positive certainty. I watched her narrowly after the body had been brought into the house. At first her grief was passionate and intense, and in it she let fall—in Italian—the extraordinary exclamation that a woman should break her heart for her lover, not for her mother. Then she, too, went into the room where the body lay— went in weeping, came out dry-eyed, and in the most methodical manner set to work to perform the last sad offices for the dead."

"Ah, yes, I see. Pray go on."

"It was on the day of the funeral, if you remember, that I dispatched Lena to Paris. I had previously written to Lord Guilleroy, hinting my suspicions, and begging him, in spite of everything, to remain at Paris, and to carry out any directions I might send him to the very letter. On dispatching Lena, I again wrote to him, telling him when she would arrive, where she would put up, and bidding him keep his eye on her, and follow her movements step by step. From Paris, I sent Lena on to Naples, bidding her await further orders there, and, all unknown to her, the train that carried her thither, carried also Lord Guilleroy. Naples had been the only place she had mentioned to me by name in her gossip about her life in Italy, but I felt confident, from some casual remarks she had let fall, that Irené Mascagni's early home, as well, also, as the home of her own lover, was within easy reach of the city. It was only natural to conjecture that if I kept her waiting there for orders she would utilize the opportunity for paying a visit to her friends and relatives, and also to her young mistress, if she were, as I supposed, in that neighbourhood. The result proved my conjecture correct."

"And Lord Guilleroy, thus following her movements, step by step, came upon her and Miss Golding in company?"

"He did. I think Lord Guilleroy deserves high encomium for the way in which he performed his share in this somewhat intricate case. No trained detective could have done better. He tracked Lena home to Alguida, a small hamlet within fifteen miles of Naples, and came upon her talking to Miss Golding, who stood at the gate of her grandfather's chateau dressed in her mother's Neapolitan dress. Miss Golding was unfeignedly glad to be taken possession of, so to speak, by one of her father's English friends, for she was becoming nervous and distressed at the position in which she found herself. Her mother was dead; her grandfather, a man of a violent temper, refused to allow her to leave his chateau, as he alleged he required, in his old age, the attendance of one who was his own kith and kin. Also there was in her mind a natural shrinking from the story she would have to tell her father, and the fear lest he might not be willing to forgive her for the part she had played. Nothing could have been more opportune than Lord Guilleroy's arrival. Miss Golding accorded to him her full confidence, and from this point the story ceases to be mine and becomes Lord Guilleroy's as communicated to him by Miss Golding."

"It is, in fact, the other half of the story that was told you by Lena?"

"It is; it starts from the period, twelve years back, when Mrs. Golding was supposed by her husband and child to be dead. Instead of dying, however, she had, after a month's stay at her father's lonely country house, joined a company of actors, then passing through Alguida. Her great personal beauty ensured her ready admission to the corps; and in her new life, no doubt, her vanity and innate love of coquetry found ample gratification. The faithful old nurse had followed her in her new career; the dramatic corps was actually in Naples when Mr. Golding arrived there, and the two women, neither of whom was disposed to enter upon the dull routine of English domestic life, had fabricated the lie in order the more effectually to retain their liberty. It is most probable that Count Mascagni knew nothing whatever of his daughter's movements at this period of her career. It is possible that, after a time, he may have believed her to be dead, for eleven years passed without his receiving any communication from her."

"Eleven years! Was she on the stage the whole of that time?"

"I have not been able to ascertain—in fact, I have not been very keen in making inquiries on this point, for it really is of little or no importance to the case. So far as we are concerned, her career is of importance only after her return to her father's house, now about a year ago. She came back one day, attended by Antonia, evidently out of health and in great poverty. Her father received her back conditionally; she had disgraced him and his ancient name, he said; dead she was supposed to be by her friends, dead she must remain—she must go nowhere, she must see no one."

"Ah, a sad story! And I suppose after a time the poor woman's thoughts flew to her husband and little daughter?"

"Yes. Antonia wrote to Lena that the mother was dying for the sight of her child, and implored her to tell René that her mother lived—a mother who had been cruelly treated alike by husband and father—and beg her, at all hazards, to come to her, that she might clasp her in her arms before the shadows of death closed in around her. This part of the story I had from René herself as we drove together to the Hall. The girl told me that when she read that letter all her blood was stirred within her. She was seized with a burning desire there and then to kiss that mother and to right her wrongs. For the moment she hated her father, felt that she must at once confront him and denounce him for his cruelty. Second thoughts suggested another course. Her father might forbid her all intercourse with her mother; she had plenty of money, why not start for Italy at once, and from her mother's lips dictate to her father the terms on which she would return to her English home? So the journey was planned, and Lena was promised by the young lady a pair of her handsome diamond earrings if she kept her secret till she herself gave her permission to speak. Not so much as a hand-bag was packed, for fear of exciting attention in the house; the undistinctive blue serge and sailor hat—supplemented subsequently by a thick veil—were selected as a travelling dress. Market-day at Langford, with a crowded railway station, was chosen for the day of departure, and the young lady walked the two miles that lay between it and her father's house in easy, leisurely fashion, as if she contemplated nothing more serious than a morning walk."

"Of course, so soon as she reached London all was plain sailing to her?"

"Yes. Lena, no doubt, supplied her with all necessary details respecting her journey. When she arrived at the Chateau Mascagni, she appears to have at once thoroughly succumbed to her mother's influence. Out of health although that mother was, René described her to me as the most fascinating woman she had ever met. I suppose the likeness between the two must have been something remarkable, for René said, after she had been a few days in the house and the mother had rallied a little in strength, the servants declared it was only by their dress that they could distinguish one from the other. On the fourth day after Miss Golding's arrival at the Chateau, her mother met her with a plan which, for fear of the effect that a refusal might have upon her health, she at once fell in with. It was to the effect that, instead of attempting negotiations with Mr. Golding through lawyers or by letter, she should herself go to him at his country house, throw herself upon his generosity, plead for forgiveness, and beg to be taken back to his heart once more."

"But why did not Miss René accompany her mother on this journey?"

"René was a force to be held in reserve. If her father refused her mother's request, she in her turn would refuse to return to her home, but would live on with her mother and grandfather at Alguida. The girl appears to have entertained bitter feelings against her father at this juncture—feelings possibly intensified by the thought of the sort of step-mother he intended to bestow upon her."

"Well, anyhow, so far as I can make out, Miss René's own mother hadn't much to boast of—in the way of common sense, at any rate. In fact, the two together appear to me to have acted more like a couple of school-girls than anything else. What made Mrs. Golding dress up in her daughter's clothes?"

"That, I believe, was a matter of convenience merely. Mrs. Golding had no money, and her father was not over-burdened with riches, and what little he had he held tightly. She had, for some reason or other, returned home with next to no wardrobe; René's dress was suitable for travelling, and not likely to attract attention. They neither of them seem to have given a thought to the possibility of rewards being offered for tidings of René; and thus, no doubt, while waiting for her train in Paris, Mrs. Golding did not hesitate to show herself in Paris streets. I need not go into the details of her journey to Langford; they are already known to you. The poor woman, not seeing any conveyance at the country station, must have walked in the drenching rain to the Hall. At the hall door, possibly, her courage suddenly failed her, and, instead of ringing for admission, she creeps to a window to get a glimpse of the home-life within. That glimpse is fatal. She sees her husband and the woman he intends to marry seated together at table. She takes in at a glance the refinement of the home, together with the rigid conventionality of English domestic life. A wave of memory, perhaps, brings before her episodes in her past career altogether out of tune with this home picture. She feels the impracticability of the mission on which she is bent; a fit of her old impetuosity seizes her; she rushes away in the darkness, takes a wrong turning, perhaps—who knows—?"

"Ah, yes; and the stream was there waiting for her, and she thought she would end it all. Poor soul!"

"Or it may be," said Loveday pityingly, "that some sweet story of sainthood and martyrdom that she had heard in her childish days came floating dimly into her brain as she made her way through the darkness, and she thought she would do her best to make atonement to the one whom she had so deeply injured by not standing in the way of his future happiness. Here is my train! Ah, yes; it is a sad, sad story!"

"Yes; for the present things are a trifle gloomy for the family at the Hall, I'll admit," said Ramsay, as he shut the carriage-door on Loveday; "but they'll turn over a new leaf there before long. There'll be a couple of weddings in the house before the year comes to an end, I'll be bound."

"No," said Loveday, as she steeled herself comfortably in a corner; "Mrs. Greenhow has shown herself in her true colours at this time of distress, and, from what I hear, will stand but little chance of becoming the second Mrs. Golding. Lord Guilleroy and the runaway René are the only two who will have to be congratulated as bride and bridegroom."

LADY MOLLY
OF SCOTLAND YARD

THE NINESCORE MYSTERY

Well, you know, some say she is the daughter of a duke, others that she was born in the gutter, and that the handle has been soldered on to her name in order to give her style and influence.

I could say a lot, of course, but "my lips are sealed," as the poets say. All through her successful career at the Yard she honoured me with her friendship and confidence, but when she took me in partnership, as it were, she made me promise that I would never breathe a word of her private life, and this I swore on my Bible oath— "wish I may die," and all the rest of it.

Yes, we always called her "my lady," from the moment that she was put at the head of our section; and the chief called her "Lady Molly" in our presence. We of the Female Department are dreadfully snubbed by the men, though don't tell me that women have not ten times as much intuition as the blundering and sterner sex; my firm belief is that we shouldn't have half so many undetected crimes if some of the so-called mysteries were put to the test of feminine investigation.

Do you suppose for a moment, for instance, that the truth about that extraordinary case at Ninescore would ever have come to light if the men alone had had the handling of it? Would any man have taken so bold a risk as Lady Molly did when— But I am anticipating.

Let me go back to that memorable morning when she came into my room in a wild state of agitation.

"The chief says I may go down to Ninescore if I like, Mary," she said in a voice all a-quiver with excitement.

"You!" I ejaculated. "What for?"

"What for—what for?" she repeated eagerly. "Mary, don't you understand? It is the chance I have been waiting for—the chance of a lifetime? They are all desperate about the case up at the Yard; the public is furious, and columns of sarcastic letters appear in the daily press. None of our men know what to do; they are at their wits' end, and so this morning I went to the chief—"

"Yes?" I queried eagerly, for she had suddenly ceased speaking.

"Well, never mind now how I did it—I will tell you all about it on the way, for we have just got time to catch the 11 a.m. down to Canterbury. The chief says I may go, and that I may take whom I like with me. He suggested one of the men, but somehow I feel that this is woman's work, and I'd rather have you, Mary, than anyone. We will go over the preliminaries of the case together in the train, as I don't suppose that you have got them at your fingers' ends yet, and you have only just got time to put a few things together and meet me at Charing Cross booking-office in time for that 11.0 sharp."

She was off before I could ask her any more questions, and anyhow I was too flabbergasted to say much. A murder case in the hands of the Female Department! Such a thing had been unheard of until now. But I was all excitement, too, and you may be sure I was at the station in good time.

Fortunately Lady Molly and I had a carriage to ourselves. It was a non-stop run to Canterbury, so we had plenty of time before us, and I was longing to know all about this case, you bet, since I was to have the honour of helping Lady Molly in it.

The murder of Mary Nicholls had actually been committed at Ash Court, a fine old mansion which stands in the village of Ninescore. The Court is surrounded by magnificently timbered grounds, the most fascinating portion of which is an island in the midst of a small pond, which is spanned by a tiny rustic bridge. The island is called "The Wilderness," and is at the furthermost end of the grounds, out of sight and earshot of the mansion itself. It was in this charming spot, on the edge of the pond, that the body of a girl was found on the 5th of February last.

I will spare you the horrible details of this gruesome discovery. Suffice it to say for the present that the unfortunate woman was lying on her face, with the lower portion of her body on the small grass-covered embankment, and her head, arms, and shoulders sunk in the slime of the stagnant water just below.

It was Timothy Coleman, one of the under-gardeners at Ash Court, who first made this appalling discovery. He had crossed the rustic bridge and traversed the little island in its entirety, when he noticed something blue lying half in and half out of the water beyond. Timothy is a stolid, unemotional kind of yokel, and, once having ascertained that the object was a woman's body in a blue dress with white facings, he quietly stooped and tried to lift it out of the mud.

But here even his stolidity gave way at the terrible sight which was revealed before him. That the woman—whoever she might be— had been brutally murdered was obvious, her dress in front being stained with blood; but what was so awful that it even turned old Timothy sick with horror, was that, owing to the head, arms and shoulders having apparently been in the slime for some time, they were in an advanced state of decomposition.

Well, whatever was necessary was immediately done, of course. Coleman went to get assistance from the lodge, and soon the police were on the scene and had removed the unfortunate victim's remains to the small local police-station.

Ninescore is a sleepy, out-of-the-way village, situated some seven miles from Canterbury and four from Sandwich. Soon everyone in the place had heard that a terrible murder had been committed in the village, and all the details were already freely discussed at the Green Man.

To begin with, everyone said that though the body itself might be practically unrecognisable, the bright blue serge dress with the white facings was unmistakable, as were the pearl and ruby ring and the red leather purse found by Inspector Meisures close to the murdered woman's hand.

Within two hours of Timothy Coleman's gruesome find the identity of the unfortunate victim was firmly established as that of

Mary Nicholls, who lived with her sister Susan at 2, Elm Cottages, in Ninescore Lane, almost opposite Ash Court. It was also known that when the police called at that address they found the place locked and apparently uninhabited.

Mrs. Hooker, who lived at No. 1 next door, explained to Inspector Meisures that Susan and Mary Nicholls had left home about a fortnight ago, and that she had not seen them since.

"It'll be a fortnight to-morrow," she said. "I was just inside my own front door a-calling to the cat to come in. It was past seven o'clock, and as dark a night as ever you did see. You could hardly see your 'and afore your eyes, and there was a nasty damp drizzle comin' from everywhere. Susan and Mary come out of their cottage; I couldn't rightly see Susan, but I 'eard Mary's voice quite distinck. She says: 'We'll have to 'urry,' says she. I, thinkin' they might be goin' to do some shoppin' in the village, calls out to them that I'd just 'eard the church clock strike seven, and that bein' Thursday, and early closin', they'd find all the shops shut at Ninescore. But they took no notice, and walked off towards the village, and that's the last I ever seed o' them two."

Further questioning among the village folk brought forth many curious details. It seems that Mary Nicholls was a very flighty young woman, about whom there had already been quite a good deal of scandal, whilst Susan, on the other hand—who was very sober and steady in her conduct—had chafed considerably under her younger sister's questionable reputation, and, according to Mrs. Hooker, many were the bitter quarrels which occurred between the two girls. These quarrels, it seems, had been especially violent within the last year whenever Mr. Lionel Lydgate called at the cottage. He was a London gentleman, it appears—a young man about town, it afterwards transpired—but he frequently stayed at Canterbury, where he had some friends, and on those occasions he would come over to Ninescore in his smart dogcart and take Mary out for drives.

Mr. Lydgate is brother to Lord Edbrooke, the multi-millionaire, who was the recipient of birthday honours last year. His lordship resides at Edbrooke Castle, but he and his brother Lionel had rented Ash Court once or twice, as both were keen golfers and

Sandwich Links are very close by. Lord Edbrooke, I may add, is a married man. Mr. Lionel Lydgate, on the other hand, is just engaged to Miss Marbury, daughter of one of the canons of Canterbury.

No wonder, therefore, that Susan Nicholls strongly objected to her sister's name being still coupled with that of a young man far above her in station, who, moreover, was about to marry a young lady in his own rank of life.

But Mary seemed not to care. She was a young woman who only liked fun and pleasure, and she shrugged her shoulders at public opinion, even though there were ugly rumours anent the parentage of a little baby girl whom she herself had placed under the care of Mrs. Williams, a widow who lived in a somewhat isolated cottage on the Canterbury road. Mary had told Mrs. Williams that the father of the child, who was her own brother, had died very suddenly, leaving the little one on her and Susan's hands; and, as they couldn't look after it properly, they wished Mrs. Williams to have charge of it. To this the latter readily agreed.

The sum for the keep of the infant was decided upon, and thereafter Mary Nicholls had come every week to see the little girl, and always brought the money with her.

Inspector Meisures called on Mrs. Williams, and certainly the worthy widow had a very startling sequel to relate to the above story.

"A fortnight to-morrow," explained Mrs. Williams to the inspector, "a little after seven o'clock, Mary Nicholls come runnin' into my cottage. It was an awful night, pitch dark and a nasty drizzle. Mary says to me she's in a great hurry; she is goin' up to London by a train from Canterbury and wants to say good-bye to the child. She seemed terribly excited, and her clothes were very wet. I brings baby to her, and she kisses it rather wild-like and says to me: 'You'll take great care of her, Mrs. Williams,' she says; 'I may be gone some time.' Then she puts baby down and gives me £2, the child's keep for eight weeks."

After which, it appears, Mary once more said "good-bye" and ran out of the cottage, Mrs. Williams going as far as the front door with her. The night was very dark, and she couldn't see if Mary was alone or not, until presently she heard her voice saying tearfully: "I had to kiss baby—" then the voice died out in the distance "on the way to Canterbury," Mrs. Williams said most emphatically.

So far, you see, Inspector Meisures was able to fix the departure of the two sisters Nicholls from Ninescore on the night of January 23rd. Obviously they left their cottage about seven, went to Mrs. Williams, where Susan remained outside while Mary went in to say good-bye to the child.

After that all traces of them seem to have vanished. Whether they did go to Canterbury, and caught the last up train, at what station they alighted, or when poor Mary came back, could not at present be discovered.

According to the medical officer, the unfortunate girl must have been dead twelve or thirteen days at the very least, as, though the stagnant water may have accelerated decomposition, the head could not have got into such an advanced state much under a fortnight.

At Canterbury station neither the booking-clerk nor the porters could throw any light upon the subject. Canterbury West is a busy station, and scores of passengers buy tickets and go through the barriers every day. It was impossible, therefore, to give any positive information about two young women who may or may not have travelled by the last up train on Saturday, January 23rd—that is, a fortnight before.

One thing only was certain—whether Susan went to Canterbury and travelled by that up train or not, alone or with her sister—Mary had undoubtedly come back to Ninescore either the same night or the following day, since Timothy Coleman found her half-decomposed remains in the grounds of Ash Court a fortnight later.

Had she come back to meet her lover, or what? And where was Susan now?

From the first, therefore, you see, there was a great element of mystery about the whole case, and it was only natural that the local police should feel that, unless something more definite came out at the inquest, they would like to have the assistance of some of the fellows at the Yard.

So the preliminary notes were sent up to London, and some of them drifted into our hands. Lady Molly was deeply interested in it from the first, and my firm belief is that she simply worried the chief into allowing her to go down to Ninescore and see what she could do.

2

At first it was understood that Lady Molly should only go down to Canterbury after the inquest, if the local police still felt that they were in want of assistance from London. But nothing was further from my lady's intentions than to wait until then.

"I was not going to miss the first act of a romantic drama," she said to me just as our train steamed into Canterbury station. "Pick up your bag, Mary. We're going to tramp it to Ninescore—two lady artists on a sketching tour, remember—and we'll find lodgings in the village, I dare say."

We had some lunch in Canterbury, and then we started to walk the six and a half miles to Ninescore, carrying our bags. We put up at one of the cottages, where the legend "Apartments for single respectable lady or gentleman" had hospitably invited us to enter, and at eight o'clock the next morning we found our way to the local police-station, where the inquest was to take place. Such a funny little place, you know—just a cottage converted for official use— and the small room packed to its utmost holding capacity. The entire able-bodied population of the neighbourhood had, I verily believe, congregated in these ten cubic yards of stuffy atmosphere.

Inspector Meisures, apprised by the chief of our arrival, had reserved two good places for us well in sight of witnesses, coroner and jury. The room was insupportably close, but I assure you that neither Lady Molly nor I thought much about our comfort then. We were terribly interested.

From the outset the case seemed, as it were, to wrap itself more and more in its mantle of impenetrable mystery. There was precious little in the way of clues, only that awful intuition, that dark unspoken suspicion with regard to one particular man's guilt, which one could feel hovering in the minds of all those present.

Neither the police nor Timothy Coleman had anything to add
to what was already known. The ring and purse were produced,
also the dress worn by the murdered woman. All were sworn to by
several witnesses as having been the property of Mary Nicholls.

Timothy, on being closely questioned, said that, in his opinion, the girl's body had been pushed into the mud, as the head was
absolutely embedded in it, and he didn't see how she could have
fallen like that.

Medical evidence was repeated; it was as uncertain—as vague—
as before. Owing to the state of the head and neck it was impossible to ascertain by what means the death blow had been dealt.
The doctor repeated his statement that the unfortunate girl must
have been dead quite a fortnight. The body was discovered on February 5th—a fortnight before that would have been on or about
January 23rd.

The caretaker who lived at the lodge at Ash Court could also
throw but little light on the mysterious event. Neither he nor any
member of his family had seen or heard anything to arouse their
suspicions. Against that he explained that "The Wilderness," where
the murder was committed, is situated some 200 yards from the
lodge, with the mansion and flower garden lying between. Replying to a question put to him by a juryman, he said that that portion of the grounds is only divided off from Ninescore Lane by a
low, brick wall, which has a door in it, opening into the lane almost opposite Elm Cottages. He added that the mansion had been
empty for over a year, and that he succeeded the last man, who
died, about twelve months ago. Mr. Lydgate had not been down
for golf since witness had been in charge.

It would be useless to recapitulate all that the various witnesses
had already told the police, and were now prepared to swear to.
The private life of the two sisters Nicholls was gone into at full
length, as much, at least, as was publicly known. But you know
what village folk are; except when there is a bit of scandal and gossip, they know precious little of one another's inner lives.

The two girls appeared to be very comfortably off. Mary was
always smartly dressed; and the baby girl, whom she had placed in

Mrs. Williams's charge, had plenty of good and expensive clothes, whilst her keep, 5s. a week, was paid with unfailing regularity. What seemed certain, however, was that they did not get on well together, that Susan violently objected to Mary's association with Mr. Lydgate, and that recently she had spoken to the vicar asking him to try to persuade her sister to go away from Ninescore altogether, so as to break entirely with the past. The Reverend Octavius Ludlow, Vicar of Ninescore, seems thereupon to have had a little talk with Mary on the subject, suggesting that she should accept a good situation in London.

"But," continued the reverend gentleman, "I didn't make much impression on her. All she replied to me was that she certainly need never go into service, as she had a good income of her own, and could obtain £5,000 or more quite easily at any time if she chose."

"Did you mention Mr. Lydgate's name to her at all?" asked the coroner.

"Yes, I did," said the vicar, after a slight hesitation.

"Well, what was her attitude then?"

"I am afraid she laughed," replied the Reverend Octavius, primly, "and said very picturesquely, if somewhat ungrammatically, that 'some folks didn't know what they was talkin' about.'"

All very indefinite, you see. Nothing to get hold of, no motive suggested—beyond a very vague suspicion, perhaps, of blackmail—to account for a brutal crime. I must not, however, forget to tell you the two other facts which came to light in the course of this extraordinary inquest. Though, at the time, these facts seemed of wonderful moment for the elucidation of the mystery, they only helped ultimately to plunge the whole case into darkness still more impenetrable than before.

I am alluding, firstly, to the deposition of James Franklin, a carter in the employ of one of the local farmers. He stated that about half-past six on that same Saturday night, January 23rd, he was walking along Ninescore Lane leading his horse and cart, as the night was indeed pitch dark. Just as he came somewhere near Elm Cottages he heard a man's voice saying in a kind of hoarse whisper:

"Open the door, can't you? It's as dark as blazes!"

Then a pause, after which the same voice added:

"Mary, where the dickens are you?"

Whereupon a girl's voice replied: "All right, I'm coming."

James Franklin heard nothing more after that, nor did he see anyone in the gloom.

With the stolidity peculiar to the Kentish peasantry, he thought no more of this until the day when he heard that Mary Nicholls had been murdered; then he voluntarily came forward and told his story to the police. Now, when he was closely questioned, he was quite unable to say whether these voices proceeded from that side of the lane where stand Elm Cottages or from the other side, which is edged by the low, brick wall.

Finally, Inspector Meisures, who really showed an extraordinary sense of what was dramatic, here produced a document which he had reserved for the last. This was a piece of paper which he had found in the red leather purse already mentioned, and which at first had not been thought very important, as the writing was identified by several people as that of the deceased, and consisted merely of a series of dates and hours scribbled in pencil on a scrap of notepaper. But suddenly these dates had assumed a weird and terrible significance: two of them, at least—December 26th and January 1st followed by "10 a.m."—were days on which Mr. Lydgate came over to Ninescore and took Mary for drives. One or two witnesses swore to this positively. Both dates had been local meets of the harriers, to which other folk from the village had gone, and Mary had openly said afterwards how much she had enjoyed these.

The other dates (there were six altogether) were more or less vague. One Mrs. Hooker remembered as being coincident with a day Mary Nicholls had spent away from home; but the last date, scribbled in the same handwriting, was January 23rd, and below it the hour—6 p.m.

The coroner now adjourned the inquest. An explanation from Mr. Lionel Lydgate had become imperative.

3

Public excitement had by now reached a very high pitch; it was no longer a case of mere local interest. The country inns all round the immediate neighbourhood were packed with visitors from London, artists, journalists, dramatists, and actor-managers, whilst the hotels and fly-proprietors of Canterbury were doing a roaring trade.

Certain facts and one vivid picture stood out clearly before the thoughtful mind in the midst of a chaos of conflicting and irrelevant evidence: the picture was that of the two women tramping in the wet and pitch dark night towards Canterbury. Beyond that everything was a blur.

When did Mary Nicholls come back to Ninescore, and why?

To keep an appointment made with Lionel Lydgate, it was openly whispered; but that appointment—if the rough notes were interpreted rightly—was for the very day on which she and her sister went away from home. A man's voice called to her at half-past six certainly, and she replied to it. Franklin, the carter, heard her; but half an hour afterwards Mrs. Hooker heard her voice when she left home with her sister, and she visited Mrs. Williams after that.

The only theory compatible with all this was, of course, that Mary merely accompanied Susan part of the way to Canterbury, then went back to meet her lover, who enticed her into the deserted grounds of Ash Court, and there murdered her.

The motive was not far to seek. Mr. Lionel Lydgate, about to marry, wished to silence for ever a voice that threatened to be unpleasantly persistent in its demands for money and in its threats of scandal.

But there was one great argument against that theory—the disappearance of Susan Nicholls. She had been extensively advertised for. The murder of her sister was published broadcast in every newspaper in the United Kingdom—she could not be ignorant of it. And, above all, she hated Mr. Lydgate. Why did she not come and add the weight of her testimony against him if, indeed, he was guilty?

And if Mr. Lydgate was innocent, then where was the criminal? And why had Susan Nicholls disappeared?

Why? Why? Why?

Well, the next day would show. Mr. Lionel Lydgate had been cited by the police to give evidence at the adjourned inquest.

Good-looking, very athletic, and obviously frightfully upset and nervous, he entered the little courtroom, accompanied by his solicitor, just before the coroner and jury took their seats.

He looked keenly at Lady Molly as he sat down, and from the expression on his face I guessed that he was much puzzled to know who she was.

He was the first witness called. Manfully and clearly he gave a concise account of his association with the deceased.

"She was pretty and amusing," he said. "I liked to take her out when I was in the neighborhood; it was no trouble to me. There was no harm in her, whatever the village gossips might say. I know she had been in trouble, as they say, but that had nothing to do with me. It wasn't for me to be hard on a girl, and I fancy that she has been very badly treated by some scoundrel."

Here he was hard pressed by the coroner, who wished him to explain what he meant. But Mr. Lydgate turned obstinate, and to every leading question he replied stolidly and very emphatically:

"I don't know who it was. It had nothing to do with me, but I was sorry for the girl because of everyone turning against her, including her sister, and I tried to give her a little pleasure when I could."

That was all right. Very sympathetically told. The public quite liked this pleasing specimen of English cricket-, golf- and football-loving manhood. Subsequently Mr. Lydgate admitted meeting Mary on December 26th and January 1st, but he swore most emphatically that that was the last he ever saw of her.

"But the 23rd of January," here insinuated the coroner; "you made an appointment with the deceased then?"

"Certainly not," he replied.

"But you met her on that day?"

"Most emphatically no," he replied quietly. "I went down to Edbrooke Castle, my brother's place in Lincolnshire, on the 20th of last month, and only got back to town about three days ago."

"You swear to that, Mr. Lydgate?" asked the coroner.

"I do, indeed, and there are a score of witnesses to bear me out. The family, the house-party, the servants."

He tried to dominate his own excitement. I suppose, poor man, he had only just realised that certain horrible suspicions had been resting upon him. His solicitor pacified him, and presently he sat down, whilst I must say that everyone there present was relieved at the thought that the handsome young athlete was not a murderer, after all. To look at him it certainly seemed preposterous.

But then, of course, there was the deadlock, and as there were no more witnesses to be heard, no new facts to elucidate, the jury returned the usual verdict against some person or persons unknown; and we, the keenly interested spectators, were left to face the problem— Who murdered Mary Nicholls, and where was her sister Susan?

4

After the verdict we found our way back to our lodgings. Lady Molly tramped along silently, with that deep furrow between her brows which I knew meant that she was deep in thought.

"Now we'll have some tea," I said, with a sigh of relief, as soon as we entered the cottage door.

"No, you won't," replied my lady, dryly. "I am going to write out a telegram, and we'll go straight on to Canterbury and send it from there."

"To Canterbury!" I gasped. "Two hours' walk at least, for I don't suppose we can get a trap, and it is past three o'clock. Why not send your telegram from Ninescore?"

"Mary, you are stupid," was all the reply I got.

She wrote out two telegrams—one of which was at least three dozen words long—and, once more calling to me to come along, we set out for Canterbury.

I was tea-less, cross, and puzzled. Lady Molly was alert, cheerful, and irritatingly active.

We reached the first telegraph office a little before five. My lady sent the telegram without condescending to tell me anything of its destination or contents; then she took me to the Castle Hotel and graciously offered me tea.

"May I be allowed to inquire whether you propose tramping back to Ninescore to-night?" I asked with a slight touch of sarcasm, as I really felt put out.

"No, Mary," she replied, quietly munching a bit of Sally Lunn; "I have engaged a couple of rooms at this hotel and wired the chief that any message will find us here to-morrow morning."

After that there was nothing for it but quietude, patience, and finally supper and bed.

The next morning my lady walked into my room before I had finished dressing. She had a newspaper in her hand, and threw it down on the bed as she said calmly:

"It was in the evening paper all right last night. I think we shall be in time."

No use asking her what "it" meant. It was easier to pick up the paper, which I did. It was a late edition of one of the leading London evening shockers, and at once the front page, with its startling headline, attracted my attention:

THE NINESCORE MYSTERY
MARY NICHOLL'S BABY DYING

Then, below that, a short paragraph:—

"We regret to learn that the little baby daughter of the unfortunate girl who was murdered recently at Ash Court, Ninescore, Kent, under such terrible and mysterious circumstances, is very seriously ill at the cottage of Mrs. Williams, in whose charge she is. The local doctor who visited her to-day declares that she cannot last more than a few hours. At the time of going to press the nature of the child's complaint was not known to our special representative at Ninescore."

"What does this mean?" I gasped.

But before she could reply there was a knock at the door.

"A telegram for Miss Granard," said the voice of the hall-porter.

"Quick, Mary," said Lady Molly, eagerly. "I told the chief and also Meisures to wire here and to you."

The telegram turned out to have come from Ninescore, and was signed "Meisures." Lady Molly read it aloud:

> "Mary Nicholls arrived here this morning. De-tained her at station. Come at once."

"Mary Nicholls! I don't understand," was all I could contrive to say.

But she only replied:

"I knew it! I knew it! Oh, Mary, what a wonderful thing is human nature, and how I thank Heaven that gave me a knowledge of it!"

She made me get dressed all in a hurry, and then we swallowed some breakfast hastily whilst a fly was being got for us. I had, per-force, to satisfy my curiosity from my own inner consciousness. Lady Molly was too absorbed to take any notice of me. Evidently the chief knew what she had done and approved of it: the telegram from Meisures pointed to that.

My lady had suddenly become a personality. Dressed very qui-etly, and in a smart close-fitting hat, she looked years older than her age, owing also to the seriousness of her mien.

The fly took us to Ninescore fairly quickly. At the little police-station we found Meisures awaiting us. He had Elliot and Pegram from the Yard with him. They had obviously got their orders, for all three of them were mighty deferential.

"The woman is Mary Nicholls, right enough," said Meisures, as Lady Molly brushed quickly past him, "the woman who was sup-posed to have been murdered. It's that silly bogus paragraph about the infant brought her out of her hiding-place. I wonder how it got in," he added blandly; "the child is well enough."

"I wonder," said Lady Molly, whilst a smile—the first I had seen that morning—lit up her pretty face.

"I suppose the other sister will turn up too, presently," rejoined Elliot. "Pretty lot of trouble we shall have now. If Mary Nicholls is alive and kickin', who was murdered at Ash Court, say I?"

"I wonder," said Lady Molly, with the same charming smile.

Then she went in to see Mary Nicholls.

The Reverend Octavius Ludlow was sitting beside the girl, who seemed in great distress, for she was crying bitterly.

Lady Molly asked Elliott and the others to remain in the passage whilst she herself went into the room, I following behind her.

When the door was shut, she went up to Mary Nicholls, and assuming a hard and severe manner, she said:

"Well, you have at last made up your mind, have you, Nicholls? I suppose you know that we have applied for a warrant for your arrest?"

The woman gave a shriek which unmistakably was one of fear.

"My arrest?" she gasped. "What for?"

"The murder of your sister Susan."

"'Twasn't me!" she said quickly.

"Then Susan *is* dead?" retorted Lady Molly, quietly.

Mary saw that she had betrayed herself. She gave Lady Molly a look of agonised horror, then turned as white as a sheet and would have fallen had not the Reverend Octavius Ludlow gently led her to a chair.

"It wasn't me," she repeated, with a heart-broken sob.

"That will be for you to prove," said Lady Molly dryly. "The child cannot now, of course remain with Mrs. Williams; she will be removed to the workhouse, and—"

"No, that shan't be," said the mother excitedly. "She shan't be, I tell you. The workhouse, indeed," she added in a paroxysm of hysterical tears, "and her father a lord!"

The reverend gentleman and I gasped in astonishment; but Lady Molly had worked up to this climax so ingeniously that it was obvious she had guessed it all along, and had merely led Mary Nicholls on in order to get this admission from her.

How well she had known human nature in pitting the child against the sweetheart! Mary Nicholls was ready enough to hide herself, to part from her child even for a while, in order to save the man she had once loved from the consequences of his crime; but when she heard that her child was dying, she no longer could bear to leave it among strangers, and when Lady Molly taunted her with the workhouse, she exclaimed in her maternal pride:

"The workhouse! And her father a lord!"

Driven into a corner, she confessed the whole truth.

Lord Edbrooke, then Mr. Lydgate, was the father of her child. Knowing this, her sister Susan had, for over a year now, systematically blackmailed the unfortunate man—not altogether, it seems, without Mary's connivance. In January last she got him to come down to Ninescore under the distinct promise that Mary would meet him and hand over to him the letters she had received from him, as well as the ring he had given her, in exchange for the sum of £5,000.

The meeting-place was arranged, but at the last moment Mary was afraid to go in the dark. Susan, nothing daunted, but anxious about her own reputation in case she should be seen talking to a man so late at night, put on Mary's dress, took the ring and the letters, also her sister's purse, and went to meet Lord Edbrooke.

What happened at that interview no one will ever know. It ended with the murder of the blackmailer. I suppose the fact that Susan had, in measure, begun by impersonating her sister, gave the murderer the first thought of confusing the identity of his victim by the horrible device of burying the body in the slimy mud. Anyway, he almost did succeed in hoodwinking the police, and would have done so entirely but for Lady Molly's strange intuition in the matter.

After his crime he ran instinctively to Mary's cottage. He had to make a clean breast of it to her, as, without her help, he was a doomed man.

So he persuaded her to go away from home and to leave no clue or trace of herself or her sister in Ninescore. With the help of money which he would give her, she could begin life anew somewhere else, and no doubt he deluded the unfortunate girl with promises that her child would be restored to her very soon.

Thus he enticed Mary Nicholls away, who would have been the great and all-important witness against him the moment his crime was discovered. A girl of Mary's type and class instinctively obeys the man she has once loved, the man who is the father of her child. She consented to disappear and to allow all the world to believe that she had been murdered by some unknown miscreant.

Then the murderer quietly returned to his luxurious home at Edbrooke Castle, unsuspected. No one had thought of mentioning his name in connection with that of Mary Nicholls. In the days when he used to come down to Ash Court he was Mr. Lydgate, and, when he became a peer, sleepy, out-of-the-way Ninescore ceased to think of him.

Perhaps Mr. Lionel Lydgate knew all about his brother's association with the village girl. From his attitude at the inquest I should say he did, but of course he would not betray his own brother unless forced to do so.

Now, of course, the whole aspect of the case was changed: the veil of mystery had been torn asunder owing to the insight, the marvelous intuition, of a woman who, in my opinion, is the most wonderful psychologist of her time.

You know the sequel. Our fellows at the Yard, aided by the local police, took their lead from Lady Molly, and began their investigations of Lord Edbrooke's movements on or about the 23rd of January.

Even their preliminary inquiries revealed the fact that his lordship had left Edbrooke Castle on the 21st. He went up to town, saying to his wife and household that he was called away on business, and not even taking his valet with him. He put up at the Langham Hotel.

But here police investigations came to an abrupt ending. Lord Edbrooke evidently got wind of them. Anyway, the day after Lady Molly so cleverly enticed Mary Nicholls out of her hiding-place, and surprised her into an admission of the truth, the unfortunate man threw himself in front of the express train at Grantham railway station, and was instantly killed. Human justice cannot reach him now!

But don't tell me that a man would have thought of that bogus paragraph, or of the taunt which stung the motherly pride of the village girl to the quick, and thus wrung from her an admission which no amount of male ingenuity would ever have obtained.

THE FREWIN MINIATURES

1

Although, mind you, Lady Molly's methods in connection with the Ninescore mystery were not altogether approved of at the Yard, nevertheless, her shrewdness and ingenuity in the matter were so undoubted that they earned for her a reputation, then and there, which placed her in the foremost rank of the force. And presently, when everyone—public and police alike—were set by the ears over the Frewin miniatures, and a reward of 1,000 guineas was offered for information that would lead to the apprehension of the thief, the chief, of his own accord and without any hesitation, offered the job to her.

I don't know much about so-called works of art myself, but you can't be in the detective force, female or otherwise, without knowing something of the value of most things, and I don't think that Mr. Frewin put an excessive value on his Englehearts when he stated that they were worth £10,000. There were eight of them, all on ivory, about three to four inches high, and they were said to be the most perfect specimens of their kind. Mr. Frewin himself had had an offer for them, less than two years ago, of 200,000 francs from the trustees of the Louvre, which offer, mind you, he had refused. I dare say you know that he was an immensely wealthy man, a great collector himself, as well as dealer, and that several of the most unique and most highly priced works of art found their way into his private collection. Among them, of course, the Engleheart miniatures were the most noteworthy.

For some time before his death Mr. Frewin had been a great invalid, and for over two years he had not been able to go beyond the boundary of his charming property, Blatchley House, near Brighton.

There is a sad story in connection with the serious illness of Mr. Frewin—an illness which, if you remember, has since resulted in the poor old gentleman's death. He had an only son, a young man on whom the old art-dealer had lavished all the education and, subsequently, all the social advantages which money could give. The boy was exceptionally good-looking, and had inherited from his mother a great charm of manner which made him very popular. The Honourable Mrs. Frewin is the daughter of an English peer, more endowed with physical attributes than with worldly goods. Besides that, she is an exceptionally beautiful woman, has a glorious voice, is a fine violinist, and is no mean water-colour artist, having more than once exhibited at the Royal Academy.

Unfortunately, at one time, young Frewin had got into very bad company, made many debts, some of which were quite unavowable, and there were rumours current at the time to the effect that had the police got wind of certain transactions in connection with a brother officer's cheque, a very unpleasant prosecution would have followed. Be that as it may, young Lionel Frewin had to quit his regiment, and presently he went off to Canada, where he is supposed to have gone in for farming. According to the story related by some of the servants at Blatchley House, there were violent scenes between father and son before the former consented to pay some of the young spendthrift's most pressing debts, and then find the further sum of money which was to enable young Frewin to commence a new life in the colonies.

Mrs. Frewin, of course, took the matter very much to heart. She was a dainty, refined, artistic creature, who idolised her only son, but she had evidently no influence whatever over her husband, who, in common with certain English families of Jewish extraction, had an extraordinary hardness of character where the integrity of his own business fame was concerned. He absolutely never forgave his son what he considered a slur cast upon his name by the young spendthrift; he packed him off to Canada, and openly told him that he was to expect nothing further from him. All the Frewin money and the priceless art collection would be left by will to a nephew, James Hyam, whose honour and general conduct had always been beyond reproach.

That Mr. Frewin really took his hereto idolised son's defalcations very much to heart was shown by the fact that the poor old man's health completely broke down after that. He had an apoplectic fit, and, although he somewhat recovered, he always remained an invalid.

His eyesight and brain power were distinctly enfeebled, and about nine months ago he had a renewed seizure, which resulted in paralysis first, and subsequently in his death. The greatest, if not the only, joy the poor old man had during the two years which he spent pinned to an invalid chair was his art collection. Blatchley House was a perfect art museum, and the invalid would have his chair wheeled up and down the great hall and along the rooms where his pictures and china and, above all, where his priceless miniatures were stored. He took an enormous pride in these, and it was, I think, with a view to brightening him up a little that Mrs. Frewin invited Monsieur de Colinville—who had always been a great friend of her husband—to come and stay at Blatchley. Of course, there is no greater connoisseur of art anywhere than that distinguished Frenchman, and it was through him that the celebrated offer of £8,000 was made by the Louvre for the Engleheart miniatures.

Though, of course, the invalid declined the offer, he took a great pleasure and pride in the fact that it had been made, as, in addition to Monsieur de Colinville himself, several members of the committee of art advisers to the Louvre came over from Paris in order to try and persuade Mr. Frewin to sell his unique treasures.

However, the invalid was obdurate about that. He was not in want of money, and the celebrated Frewin art collection would go intact to his widow for her life, and then to his heir, Mr. James Hyam, a great connoisseur himself and art dealer of St. Petersburg and London.

It was really a merciful dispensation of Providence that the old man never knew of the disappearance of his valued miniatures. By the time that extraordinary mystery had come to light he was dead.

On the evening of January the 14th, at half-past eight, Mr. Frewin had a third paralytic seizure, from which he never recovered. His valet, Kennet, and his two nurses were with him at the time, and Mrs. Frewin, quickly apprised of the terrible event, flew to his bedside, whilst the motor was at once despatched for the doctor. About an hour or two later the dying man seemed to rally somewhat, but he appeared very restless and agitated, and his eyes were roaming anxiously about the room.

"I expect it is his precious miniatures he wants," said Nurse Dawson. "He is always quiet when he can play with them."

She reached for the large, leather case which contained the priceless art treasures, and, opening it, placed it on the bed beside the patient. Mr. Frewin, however, was obviously too near death to care even for his favourite toy. He fingered the miniatures with trembling hands for a few moments, and then sank back exhausted on the pillows.

"He is dying," said the doctor quietly, turning to Mrs. Frewin.

"I have something to say to him," she then said. "Can I remain alone with him for a few minutes?"

"Certainly," said the doctor, as he himself discreetly retired; "but I think one of the nurses had better remain within earshot."

Nurse Dawson, it appeared, remained within earshot to some purpose, for she overheard what Mrs. Frewin was saying to her dying husband.

"It is about Lionel—your only son," she said. "Can you understand what I say?"

The sick man nodded.

"You remember that he is in Brighton, staying with Alicia. I can go and fetch him in the motor if you will consent to see him."

Again the dying man nodded. I suppose Mrs. Frewin took this to mean acquiescence, for the next moment she rang for John Chipps, the butler, and gave him instructions to order her motor at once. She then kissed the patient on the forehead and prepared to leave the room; but just before she did so, her eyes lighted on the case of miniatures, and she said to Kennet, the valet:

"Give these to Chipps, and tell him to put them in the library."

She then went to put on her furs preparatory to going out. When she was quite ready she met Chipps on the landing, who had just come up to tell her that the motor was at the door. He had in his hand the case of miniatures which Kennet had given him.

"Put the case on the library table, Chipps, when you go down," she said.

"Yes, madam," he replied.

He followed her downstairs, then slipped into the library, put the case on the table as he had been directed, after which he saw his mistress into the motor, and finally closed the front door.

2

About an hour later Mrs. Frewin came back, but without her son. It transpired afterwards that the young man was more vindictive than his father; he refused to go to the latter's bedside in order to be reconciled at the eleventh hour to a man who then had no longer either his wits or his physical senses about him. However, the dying man was spared the knowledge of his son's irreconcilable conduct, for, after a long and wearisome night passed in a state of coma, he died at about 6.0 a.m.

It was quite late the following afternoon when Mrs. Frewin suddenly recollected the case of miniatures, which should have been locked in their accustomed cabinet. She strolled leisurely into the library—she was very fatigued and worn out with the long vigil and the sorrow and anxiety she had just gone through. A quarter of an hour later John Chipps found her in the same room, sitting dazed and almost fainting in an arm-chair. In response to the old butler's anxious query, she murmured:

"The miniatures—where are they?"

Scared at the abruptness of the query and at his mistress's changed tone of voice, Chipps gazed quickly around him.

"You told me to put them on the table, ma'am," he murmured, "and I did so. They certainly don't seem to be in the room now—" he added, with a sudden feeling of terror.

"Run and ask one of the nurses at once if the case was taken up to Mr. Frewin's room during the night?"

Chipps, needless to say, did not wait to be told twice. He was beginning to feel very anxious. He spoke to Kennet and also to the two nurses, and asked them if, by any chance, the miniatures were in the late master's room. To this Kennet and the nurses replied in the negative. The last they had seen of the miniatures was when Chipps took them from the valet and followed his mistress downstairs with the case in his hands.

The poor old butler was in despair; the cook was in hysterics, and consternation reigned throughout the house. The disappearance of the miniatures caused almost a greater excitement than the death of the master, who had been a dying man so long that he was almost a stranger to the servants at Blatchley.

Mrs. Frewin was the first to recover her presence of mind.

"Send a motor at once to the police-station at Brighton," she said very calmly, as soon as she completely realised that the miniatures were nowhere to be found. "It is my duty to see that this matter is thoroughly gone into at once."

Within half an hour of the discovery of the theft, Detective Inspector Hankin and Police Constable McLeod had both arrived from Brighton, having availed themselves of Mrs. Frewin's motor. They are shrewd men, both of them, and it did not take them many minutes before they had made up their minds how the robbery had taken place. By whom it was done was quite another matter, and would take some time and some ingenuity to find out.

What Detective Inspector Hankin had gathered was this: While John Chipps saw his mistress into the motor, the front door of the house had, of necessity, been left wide open. The motor then made a start, but after a few paces it stopped, and Mrs. Frewin put her head out of the window and shouted to Chipps some instructions with regard to the nurses' evening collation, which, in view of Mr.

Frewin's state, she feared might be forgotten. Chipps, being an elderly man and a little deaf, did not hear her voice distinctly, so he
ran up to the motor, and she repeated her instructions to him. In
Inspector Hankin's mind there was no doubt that the thief, who
must have been hanging about the shrubbery that evening, took
that opportunity to sneak into the house, then to hide himself in a
convenient spot until he could find an opportunity for the robbery
which he had in view.

The butler declared that, when he returned, he saw nothing
unusual. He had only been gone a little over a minute; he then
fastened and bolted the front door, and, according to his usual
custom, he put up all the shutters of the ground-floor windows,
including, of course, those in the library. He had no light with him
when he did this accustomed round, for, of course, he knew his
way well enough in the dark, and the electric chandelier in the hall
gave him what light he wanted.

While he was putting up the shutters, Chipps was giving no
particular thought to the miniatures, but, strangely enough, he
seems to have thought of them about an hour later, when most of
the servants had gone to bed and he was waiting up for his mistress. He then, quite casually and almost absent-mindedly, when
crossing the hall, turned the key of the library door, thus locking it
from the outside.

Of course, throughout all this we must remember that Blatchley
House was not in its normal state that night, since its master was
actually dying in a room on the floor above the library. The two
nurses and Kennet, the valet, were all awake, and with him during
the whole of that night. Kennet certainly was in and out of the room
several times, having to run down and fetch various things required
by the doctor or the nurses. In order to do this he did not use the
principal staircase, nor did he have to cross the hall, but, as far as
the upper landing and the secondary stairs were concerned, he
certainly had not noticed anything unusual or suspicious; whilst
when Mrs. Frewin came home, she went straight up to the first
floor, and certainly noticed nothing in any way to arouse her

suspicions. But, of course, this meant very little, as she certainly must have been too upset and agitated to see anything.

The servants were not apprised of the death of their master until after their breakfast. In the meanwhile Emily, the housemaid, had been in, as usual, to "do" the library. She distinctly noticed, when she first went in, that none of the shutters were up and that one of the windows was open. She thought at the time that some-one must have been in the room before her, and meant to ask Chipps about it, when the news of the master's death drove all thoughts of open windows from her mind. Strangely enough, when Hankin questioned her more closely about it, and she had had time to recollect everything more clearly, she made the extraordinary statement that she certainly had noticed that the door of the lib-rary was locked on the outside when she first went into the room, the key being in the lock.

"Then, didn't it strike you as very funny," asked Hankin, "that the door was locked on the outside, and yet that the shutters were unbarred and one of the windows was open?"

"Yes, I did seem to think of that," replied Emily, with that pleas-ant vagueness peculiar to her class; "but then, the room did not look like burglars—it was quite tidy, just as it had been left last night, and burglars always seem to leave a great mess behind, else I should have noticed," she added, with offended dignity.

"But did you not see that the miniatures were not in their usual place?"

"Oh they often wasn't in the cabinet, as the master used to ask for them sometimes to be brought to his room."

That was, of course, indisputable. It was clearly evident that the burglar had had plenty of chances to make good his escape. You see, the actual time when the miscreant must have sneaked into the room had now been narrowed down to about an hour and a half, between the time when Mrs. Frewin finally left in her mo-tor to about an hour later, when Chipps turned the key in the door of the library and thus undoubtedly locked the thief in. At what precise time of the night he effected his escape could not anyhow be ascertained. It must have been after Mrs. Frewin came back again, as Hankin held that she or her chauffeur would have noticed that one of the library windows was open. This opinion was not shared by Elliott from the Yard, who helped in the investigation of this mysterious crime, as Mrs. Frewin was certainly very agitated and upset that evening, and her powers of perception would necessarily be blunted. As for the chauffeur: we all know that the strong headlights on a motor are so dazzling that nothing can be seen outside their blinding circle of light.

Be that as it may, it remained doubtful when the thief made good his escape. It was easy enough to effect, and, as there is a square of flagstones in front of the main door and just below the library windows, the thief left not the slightest trace of footprints, whilst the drop from the window is less than eight feet.

What was strange in the whole case, and struck Detective Hankin immediately, was the fact that the burglar, whoever he was, must have known a great deal about the house and its ways. He also must have had a definite purpose in his mind not usually to be found in the brain of a common housebreaker. He must have meant to steal the miniatures and nothing else, since he made his way straight to the library, and, having secured the booty, at once made good his escape without trying to get any other article which could more easily be disposed of than works of art.

You may imagine, therefore, how delicate a task now confronted Inspector Hankin. You see, he had questioned everyone in the house, including Mr. Frewin's valet and nurses, and from them he casually heard of Mrs. Frewin's parting words to her dying husband and of her mention of the scapegrace son, who was evidently in the immediate neighbourhood, and whom she wished to come and see his father. Mrs. Frewin, closely questioned by the detective, admitted that her son was staying in Brighton, and that she saw him that very evening.

"Mr. Lionel Frewin is staying at the Metropole Hotel," she said coldly, "and he was dining with my sister, Lady Steyne, last night. He was in the house at Sussex Square when I arrived in my motor," she added hastily, guessing, perhaps, the unavowed suspicion which had arisen in Hankin's mind, "and he was still there when I left. I drove home very fast, naturally, as my husband's condition was known to me to be quite hopeless, and that he was not expected to live more than perhaps a few hours. We covered the seven miles between this house and that of my sister in less than a quarter of an hour."

This statement of Mrs. Frewin's was, if you remember, fully confirmed both by her sister and her brother-in-law, Lady Steyne and Sir Michael. There was no doubt that young Lionel Frewin was staying at the Hotel Metropole in Brighton, that he was that evening dining with the Steynes at Sussex Square when his mother arrived in her motor. Mrs. Frewin stayed about an hour, during which time she, presumably, tried to influence her son to go back to Blatchley with her in order to see his dying father. Of course, what exactly happened at that family interview none of the four people present was inclined to reveal. Against that both Sir Michael and Lady Steyne were prepared to swear that Mr. Lionel Frewin was in the house when his mother arrived, and that he did not leave them until long after she had driven away.

There lay the hitch, you see, for already the public jumped to conclusions, and, terribly prejudiced as it is in a case of this sort, it had made up its mind that Mr. Lionel Frewin, once more pressed for money, had stolen his father's precious miniatures in order to sell them in America for a high sum. Everyone's sympathy was dead against the young son who refused to be reconciled to his father, although the latter was dying.

According to one of the footmen in Lady Steyne's employ, who had taken whiskies and sodas in while the interview between Mrs. Frewin and her son was taking place, Mr. Lionel had said very testily:

"It's all very well, mother, but that is sheer sentimentality. The guv'nor threw me on my beam ends when a little kindness and help would have meant a different future to me; he chose to break my life because of some early peccadilloes—and I am not going to fawn round him and play the hypocrite when he has no intention of altering his will and has cut me off with a shilling. He must be half imbecile by now, and won't know me anyway."

But with all this, and with public opinion so dead against him, it was quite impossible to bring the crime home to the young man. The burglar, whoever he was, must have sneaked into the library some time before Chipps closed the door on the outside, since it was still so found by Emily the following morning. Thereupon the public, determined that Lionel Frewin should in some way be implicated in the theft, made up its mind that the doting mother, hearing of her son's woeful want of money, stole the miniatures herself that night and gave them to him.

3

When Lady Molly heard this theory she laughed, and shrugged her pretty shoulders.

"Old Mr. Frewin was dying, was he not, at the time of the burglary?" she said. "Why should his wife, soon to become his widow, take the trouble to go through a laboured and daring comedy of a burglary in order to possess herself of things which would become hers within the next few hours? Even if, after Mr. Frewin's death, she could not actually dispose of the miniatures, the old man left her a large sum of money and a big income by his will, with which she could help her spendthrift son as much as she pleased."

This was, of course, why the mystery in this strange case was so deep. At the Yard they did all that they could. Within forty-eight hours they had notices printed in almost every European language, which contained rough sketches of the stolen miniatures hastily supplied by Mrs. Frewin herself. These were sent to as many of the great museums and art collectors abroad as possible, and of course to the principal American cities and to American millionaires. There is no doubt that the thief would find it very difficult to dispose of the miniatures, and until he could sell them his booty would, of course, not benefit him in any way. Works of art cannot be tampered with, or melted down or taken to pieces, like silver or jewellery, and, so far as could be ascertained, the thief did not appear to make the slightest attempt to dispose of the booty, and the mystery became more dark, more impenetrable than ever.

"Will you undertake the job?" said the chief one day to Lady Molly.

"Yes," she replied, "on two distinct conditions."

"What are they?"

"That you will not bother me with useless questions, and that you will send out fresh notices to all the museums and art collectors you can think of, and request them to let you know of any art purchases they may have made within the last two years."

"The last two years!" ejaculated the chief, "why, the miniatures were only stolen three months ago."

"Did I not say that you were not to ask me useless questions?"

This to the chief, mind you; and he only smiled, whilst I nearly fell backwards at her daring. But he did send out the notices, and it was generally understood that Lady Molly now had charge of the case.

4

It was about seven weeks later when, one morning, I found her at breakfast looking wonderfully bright and excited.

"The Yard has had sheaves of replies, Mary," she said gaily, "and the chief still thinks I am a complete fool."

"Why, what has happened?"

"Only this, that the art museum at Budapest has now in its possession a set of eight miniatures by Engleheart; but the authorities did not think that the first notices from Scotland Yard could possibly refer to these, as they had been purchased from a private source a little over two years ago."

"But two years ago the Frewin miniatures were still at Blatchley House, and Mr. Frewin was fingering them daily," I said, not understanding, and wondering what she was driving at.

"I know that," she said gaily, "so does the chief. That is why he thinks that I am a first-class idiot."

"But what do you wish to do now?"

"Go to Brighton, Mary, take you with me and try to elucidate the mystery of the Frewin miniatures."

"I don't understand," I gasped, bewildered.

"No, and you won't until we get there," she replied, running up to me and kissing me in her pretty, engaging way.

That same afternoon we went to Brighton and took up our abode at the Hotel Metropole. Now you know I always believed from the very first that she was a born lady and all the rest of it, but even I was taken aback at the number of acquaintances and smart friends she had all over the place. It was "Hello, Lady Molly! whoever would have thought of meeting you here?" and "Upon my word! this is good luck," all the time.

She smiled and chatted gaily with all the folk as if she had known them all her life, but I could easily see that none of these people knew that she had anything to do with the Yard.

Brighton is not such a very big place as one would suppose, and most of the fashionable residents of the gay city find their way sooner or later to the luxurious dining-room of the Hotel Metropole, if only for a quiet little dinner given when the cook is out. Therefore I was not a little surprised when, one evening, about a week after our arrival and just as we were sitting down to the *table d'hôte* dinner, Lady Molly suddenly placed one of her delicate hands on my arm.

"Look behind you, a little to your left, Mary, but not just this minute. When you do you will see two ladies and two gentlemen sitting at a small table quite close to us. They are Sir Michael and Lady Steyne, the Honourable Mrs. Frewin in deep black, and her son, Mr. Lionel Frewin."

I looked round as soon as I could, and gazed with some interest at the hero and heroine of the Blatchley House drama. We had a quiet little dinner, and Lady Molly having all of a sudden become very silent and self-possessed, altogether different from her gay, excited self of the past few days, I scented that something important was in the air, and tried to look as unconcerned as my lady herself. After dinner we ordered coffee, and as Lady Molly strolled through into the lounge, I noticed that she ordered our tray to be placed at a table which was in very close proximity to one already occupied by Lady Steyne and her party.

Lady Steyne, I noticed, gave Lady Molly a pleasant nod when we first came in, and Sir Michael got up and bowed, saying, "How d'ye do?" We sat down and began a desultory conversation together. Soon, as usual, we were joined by various friends and acquaintances who all congregated round our table and set themselves to entertaining us right pleasantly. Presently the conversation drifted to art matter, Sir Anthony Truscott being there, who is, as you know, one of the keepers of the Art Department at South Kensington Museum.

"I am crazy about miniatures just now," said Lady Molly in response to a remark from Sir Anthony.

I tried not to look astonished.

"And Miss Granard and I," continued my lady, quite unblushingly, "have been travelling all over the Continent in order to try and secure some rare specimens."

"Indeed," said Sir Anthony. "Have you found anything very wonderful?"

"We certainly have discovered some rare works of art," replied Lady Molly, "have we not, Mary? Now the two Englehearts we bought at Budapest are undoubtedly quite unique."

"Engleheart—and at Budapest!" remarked Sir Anthony. "I thought I knew the collections at most of the great Continental cities, but I certainly have no recollection of such treasures in the Hungarian capital."

"Oh, they were only purchased two years ago, and have only been shown to the public recently," remarked Lady Molly. "There was originally a set of eight, so the comptroller, Mr. Pulszky, informed me. He bought them from an English collector whose name I have now forgotten, and he is very proud of them, but they cost the country a great deal more money than it could afford, and in order somewhat to recoup himself Mr. Pulszky sold two out of the eight at, I must say, a very stiff price."

While she was talking I could not help noticing the strange glitter in her eyes. Then a curious smothered sound broke upon my ear. I turned and saw Mrs. Frewin looking with glowing and dilated eyes at the charming picture presented by Lady Molly.

"I should like to show you my purchases," said the latter to Sir Anthony. "One or two foreign connoisseurs have seen the two miniatures and declare them to be the finest in existence. Mary," she added, turning to me, "would you be so kind as to run up to my room and get me the small sealed packet which is at the bottom of my dressing-case? Here are the keys."

A little bewildered, yet guessing by her manner that I had a part to play, I took the keys from her and went up to her room. In her dressing-case I certainly found a small, square, flat packet, and with that in my hand I prepared to go downstairs again. I had just locked the bedroom door when I was suddenly confronted by a tall, graceful woman dressed in deep black, whom I at once recognised as the Honourable Mrs. Frewin.

"You are Miss Granard?" she said quickly and excitedly; her voice was tremulous and she seemed a prey to the greatest possible excitement. Without waiting for my reply she continued eagerly:

"Miss Granard, there is no time to be more explicit, but I give you my word, the word of a very wretched, heart-broken woman, that my very life depends upon my catching a glimpse of the contents of the parcel that you now have in your hand."

"But—" I murmured, hopelessly bewildered.

"There is no 'but,'" she replied. "It is a matter of life and death. Here are £200, Miss Granard, if you will let me handle that packet," and with trembling hands she drew a bundle of bank-notes from her reticule.

I hesitated, not because I had any notion of acceding to Mrs. Frewin's request, but because I did not quite know how I ought to act at this strange juncture, when a pleasant, mellow voice broke in suddenly:

"You may take the money, Mary, if you wish. You have my permission to hand the packet over to this lady," and Lady Molly, charming, graceful and elegant in her beautiful directoire gown, stood smiling some few feet away, with Hankin just visible in the gloom of the corridor.

She advanced towards us, took the small packet from my hands, and held it out towards Mrs. Frewin.

"Will you open it?" she said, "or shall I?"

Mrs. Frewin did not move. She stood as if turned to stone. Then with dexterous fingers my lady broke the seals of the packet and drew from it a few sheets of plain white cardboard and a thin piece of match-boarding.

"There!" said Lady Molly, fingering the bits of cardboard while she kept her fine large eyes fixed on Mrs. Frewin; "£200 is a big price to pay for a sight of these worthless things."

"Then this was a vulgar trick," said Mrs. Frewin, drawing herself up with an air which did not affect Lady Molly in the least.

"A trick, certainly," she replied with her winning smile, "vulgar, if you will call it so—pleasant to us all, Mrs. Frewin, since you so readily fell into it."

"Well, and what are you going to do next?"

"Report the matter to my chief," said Lady Molly, quietly. "We have all been very severely blamed for not discovering sooner the truth about the disappearance of the Frewin miniatures."

"You don't know the truth now," retorted Mrs. Frewin.

"Oh, yes, I do," replied Lady Molly, still smiling. "I know that two years ago your son, Mr. Lionel Frewin, was in terrible monetary difficulties. There was something unavowable, which he dared not tell his father. You had to set to work to find money somehow. You had no capital at your own disposal, and you wished to save your son from the terrible consequences of his own folly. It was soon after M. de Colinville's visit. Your husband had had his first apoplectic seizure; his mind and eyesight were somewhat impaired. You are a clever artist yourself, and you schemed out a plan whereby you carefully copied the priceless miniatures and then entrusted them to your son for sale to the Art Museum at Budapest, where there was but little likelihood of their being seen by anyone who knew they had belonged to your husband. English people do not stay more than one night there, at the Hotel Hungaria. Your copies were works of art in themselves, and you had no difficulty in deceiving your husband in the state of mind he then was, but when he lay dying you realised that his will would inevitably be proved, wherein he bequeathed the miniatures to Mr. James Hyam, and that these would have to be valued for probate. Frightened now that the substitution would be discovered, you devised the clever comedy of the burglary at Blatchley, which, in the circumstances, could never be brought home to you or your son. I don't know where you subsequently concealed the spurious Engleheart miniatures which you calmly took out of the library and hid away during the night of your husband's death, but no doubt our men will find that out," she added quietly, "now that they are on the track."

With a frightened shriek Mrs. Frewin turned as if she would fly, but Lady Molly was too quick for her, and barred the way. Then, with that wonderful charm of manner and that innate kindliness which always characterised her, she took hold of the unfortunate woman's wrist.

"Let me give you a word of advice," she said gently. "We at the Yard will be quite content with a confession from you, which will clear us of negligence and satisfy us that the crime has been brought home to its perpetrator. After that try and enter into an arrangement with your husband's legatee, Mr. James Hyam. Make a clean breast of the whole thing to him and offer him full monetary compensation. For the sake of the family he won't refuse. He would have nothing to gain by bruiting the whole thing abroad; and for his own sake and that of his late uncle, who was so good to him, I don't think you would find him hard to deal with."

Mrs. Frewin paused awhile, undecided and still defiant. Then her attitude softened; she turned and looked full at the beautiful, kind eyes turned eagerly up to hers, and pressing Lady Molly's tiny hand in both her own she whispered:

"I will take your advice. God bless you."

She was gone, and Lady Molly called Hankin to her side.

"Until we have that confession, Hankin," she said, with the quiet manner she always adopted where matters connected with her work were concerned, "Mum's the word."

"Ay, and after that, too, my lady," replied Hankin, earnestly.

You see, she could do anything she liked with the men, and I, of course, was her slave.

Now we have got the confession, Mrs. Frewin is on the best of terms with Mr. James Hyam, who has behaved very well about the whole thing, and the public has forgotten all about the mystery of the Frewin miniatures.

THE IRISH-TWEED COAT

It all began with the murder of Mr. Andrew Carrthwaite, at Palermo.

He had been found dead in the garden of his villa just outside the town, with a stiletto between his shoulder blades and a piece of rough Irish tweed, obviously torn from his assailant's coat, clutched tightly in his hand.

All that was known of Mr. Carrthwaite over here was that he was a Yorkshireman, owner of some marble works in Sicily, a man who employed a great many hands; and that, unlike most employers of labour over there, he had a perfect horror of the many secret societies and Socialist clubs which abound in that part of the world. He would not become a slave to the ever-growing tyranny of the Mafia and its kindred associations, and therefore he made it a hard and fast rule that no workman employed by him, from the foremost to the meanest hand, should belong to any society, club, or trade union of any sort or kind.

At first, robbery was thought to have been the sole object of the crime, for Mr. Carrthwaite's gold watch, marked with his initials "A. C.," and his chain were missing, but the Sicilian police were soon inclined to the belief that this was merely a blind, and that personal spite and revenge were at the bottom of that dastardly outrage.

One clue, remember, had remained in the possession of the authorities. This was the piece of rough Irish tweed, found in the murdered man's hand.

Within twenty-four hours a dozen witnesses were prepared to swear that that fragment of cloth was part of a coat habitually worn by Mr. Carrthwaite's English overseer, Mr. Cecil Shuttleworth. It appears that this young man had lately, in defiance of the rigid rules prescribed by his employer, joined a local society—semi-social, semi-religious—which came under the ban of the old Yorkshireman's prejudices.

Apparently there had been several bitter quarrels between Mr. Carrthwaite and young Shuttleworth, culminating in one tempestuous scene, witnessed by the former's servants at his villa; and although these people did not understand the actual words that passed between the two Englishmen, it was pretty clear that they amounted to an ultimatum on the one side and defiance on the other. The dismissal of the overseer followed immediately, and that same evening Mr. Carrthwaite was found murdered in his garden.

Mind you—according to English ideas—the preliminary investigations in that mysterious crime were hurried through in a manner which we should think unfair to the accused. It seemed from the first as if the Sicilian police had willfully made up their minds that Shuttleworth was guilty. For instance, although so many people were prepared to swear that the young English overseer had often worn a coat of which the piece found in the murdered man's hand was undoubtedly a torn fragment, yet the coat itself was not found among his effects, neither were his late master's watch and chain.

Nevertheless, the young man was arrested within a few hours of the murder, and—after the formalities of the preliminary "instruction"—was duly committed to stand his trial on the capital charge.

It was about this time that I severed my official connection with the Yard. Lady Molly now employed me as her private secretary, and I was working with her one day in the study of our snug little flat in Maida Vale, when our trim servant came in to us with a card and a letter on a salver.

Lady Molly glanced at the card, then handed it across to me. It bore the name: Mr. Jeremiah Shuttleworth.

The letter was from the chief.

"Not much in it," she commented, glancing rapidly at its contents. "The chief only says, 'This is the father of the man who is charged with the Palermo murder. As obstinate as a mule, but you have my permission to do what he wants.' Emily, show the gentleman in," she added.

The next moment a short, thick-set man entered our little study. He had sandy hair and a freckled skin; there was a great look of determination in the square face and a fund of dogged obstinacy in the broad, somewhat heavy jaw. In response to Lady Molly's invitation he sat down and began with extraordinary abruptness:

"I suppose you know what I have come about—er—miss?" he suggested.

"Well!" she replied, holding up his own card, "I can guess."

"My son, miss—I mean ma'am," he said in a husky voice. "He is innocent. I swear it by the living—"

He checked himself, obviously ashamed of this outburst; then he resumed more calmly.

"Of course, there's the business about the coat, and that coat did belong to my son, but—"

"Well, yes?" asked Lady Molly, for he had paused again, as if waiting to be encouraged in his narrative, "what about that coat?"

"It has been found in London, miss," he replied quietly. "The fiendish brutes who committed the crime thought out this monstrous way of diverting attention from themselves by getting hold of my son's coat and making the actual assassin wear it, in case he was espied in the gloom."

There was silence in the little study for awhile. I was amazed, aghast at the suggestion put forward by that rough north-countryman, that sorely stricken father who spoke with curious intensity of language and of feeling. Lady Molly was the first to break the solemn silence.

"What makes you think, Mr. Shuttleworth, that the assassination of Mr. Carrthwaite was the work of a gang of murderers?" she asked.

"I know Sicily," he replied simply. "My boy's mother was a native of Messina. The place is riddled with secret societies, murdering, anarchical clubs: organisations against which Mr. Carrthwaite waged deadly warfare. It is one of these—the Mafia, probably—that decreed that Mr. Carrthwaite should be done away with. They could not do with such a powerful and hard-headed enemy."

"You may be right, Mr. Shuttleworth, but tell me more about the coat."

"Well, that'll be damning proof against the blackguards, anyway. I am on the eve of a second marriage, miss—ma'am," continued the man with seeming irrelevance. "The lady is a widow. Mrs. Tadworth is her name—but her father was an Italian named Badeni, a connection of my first wife's, and that's how I came to know him and his daughter. You know Leather Lane, don't you? It might be in Italy, for Italian's the only language one hears about there. Badeni owned a house in Bread Street, Leather Lane, and let lodgings to his fellow-countrymen there; this business my future wife still carries on. About a week ago two men arrived at the house, father and son, so they said, who wanted a cheap bedroom; all their meals, including breakfast, they would take outside, and would be out, moreover, most of the day.

"It seems that they had often lodged at Badeni's before—the old reprobate no doubt was one of their gang—and when they understood that Mrs. Tadworth was their former friend's daughter they were quite satisfied.

"They gave their name as Piatti, and told Mrs. Tadworth that they came from Turin. But I happened to hear them talking on the stairs, and I knew that they were Sicilians, both of them.

"You may well imagine that just now everything hailing from Sicily is of vital importance to me, and somehow I suspected those two men from the very first. Mrs. Tadworth is quite at one with me in wanting to move heaven and earth to prove the innocence of my boy. She watched those people for me as a cat would watch a mouse. The older man professed to be very fond of gardening, and presently he obtained Mrs. Tadworth's permission to busy himself in the little strip of barren ground at the back of the house. This she told me last night whilst we were having supper together in her little parlour. Somehow I seemed to get an inspiration like. The

Piattis had gone out together as usual for their evening meal. I got a spade and went out into the strip of garden, I worked for about an hour, and then my heart gave one big leap—my spade had met a certain curious, soft resistance—the next moment I was working away with hands and nails, and soon unearthed a coat—*the* coat, miss," he continued, unable now to control his excitement, "with the bit torn out of the back, and in the pocket the watch and chain belonging to the murdered man, for they bear the initials 'A. C.' The fiendish brutes! I knew it—I knew it, and now I can prove the innocence of my boy!"

Again there was a pause. I was too much absorbed in the palpitating narrative to attempt to breathe a word, and I knew that Lady Molly was placidly waiting until the man had somewhat recovered from his vehement outburst.

"Of course, you can prove your boy's innocence now," she said, smiling encouragingly into his flushed face. "But what have you done with the coat?"

"Left it buried where I found it," he replied more calmly. "They must not suspect that I am on their track."

She nodded approvingly.

"No doubt, then, my chief has told you that the best course to pursue now will be to place the whole matter in the hands of the English police. Our people at Scotland Yard will then immediately communicate with the Sicilian authorities, and in the meanwhile we can keep the two men in Leather Lane well under surveillance."

"Yes, he told me all that," said Mr. Shuttleworth, quietly.

"Well?"

"And I told him that his 'communicating with the Sicilian police authorities' would result in my boy's trial being summarily concluded, in his being sent to the gallows, whilst every proof of his innocence would be destroyed, or, at any rate, kept back until too late."

"You are mad, Mr. Shuttleworth!" she ejaculated.

"Maybe I am," he rejoined quietly. "You see, you do not know Sicily, and I do. You do not know its many clubs and bands of assassins, beside whom the so-called Russian Nihilists are simple, blundering children. The Mafia, which is the parent of all such murderous organisations, has members and agents in every town, village, and hamlet in Italy, in every post-office and barracks, in every trade and profession from the highest to the lowest in the land. The Sicilian police force is infested with it, so are the Italian customs. I would not trust either with what means my boy's life and more to me."

"But—"

"The police would suppress the evidence connected with the proofs which I hold. At the frontier the coat, the watch and chain would disappear; of that I am as convinced as that I am a living man—"

Lady Molly made no comment. She was meditating. That there was truth in what the man said, no one could deny.

The few details which we had gleaned over here of the hurried investigations, the summary commitment for trial of the accused, the hasty dismissal of all evidence in his favour, proved that, at any rate, the father's anxiety was well founded.

"But, then, what in the world do you propose to do?" said Lady Molly after a while. "Do you want to take the proofs over yourself to your boy's advocate? Is that it?"

"No, that would be no good," he replied simply. "I am known in Sicily. I should be watched, probably murdered, too, and my death would not benefit my boy."

"But what then?"

"My boy's uncle is chief officer of police at Cividale, on the Austro-Italian frontier. I know that I can rely on his devotion. Mrs. Tadworth, whose interest in my boy is almost equal to my own, and whose connection with me cannot possibly be known out there, will take the proofs of my boy's innocence to him. He will know what to do and how to reach my son's advocate safely, which no one else could guarantee to do."

"Well," said Lady Molly, "that being so, what is it that you want us to do in the matter?"

"I want a lady's help, miss—er—ma'am," he replied, "someone who is able, willing, strong, and, if possible, enthusiastic, to ac-company Mrs. Tadworth—perhaps in the capacity of a maid—just to avert the usual suspicious glances thrown at a lady traveling

alone. Also the question of foreign languages comes in. The gentleman I saw at Scotland Yard said that if you cared to go he would
give you a fortnight's leave of absence."

"Yes, I'll go!" rejoined Lady Molly, simply.

2

We sat in the study a long while after that—Mr. Shuttleworth,
Lady Molly and I—discussing the plans of the exciting journey; for
I, too, as you will see, was destined to play my small part in this
drama which had the life or death of an innocent man for its
dénouement.

I don't think I need bore you with an account of our discussion; all, I think, that will interest you is the plan of campaign we
finally decided upon.

There seemed to be no doubt that Mr. Shuttleworth had succeeded so far in not arousing the suspicions of the Piattis. Therefore, that night, when they were safely out of the way, Mr. Shuttleworth would once more unearth the coat, and watch and chain,
and then bury a coat similar in colour and texture in that same
hole in the ground; this might perhaps serve to put the miscreants
off their guard, if by any chance one of them should busy himself
again in the garden.

After that Mrs. Tadworth would hide about her the proofs of
young Shuttleworth's innocence and join Lady Molly at our flat in
Maida Vale, where she would spend the night preparatory to the
two ladies leaving London for abroad, the following morning, by
the 9.0 a.m. train from Charing Cross *en route* for Vienna, Budapest, and finally Cividale.

But our scheme was even more comprehensive than that and
herein lay my own little share in it, of which I tell you presently.

The same evening at half-past nine Mrs. Tadworth arrived at
the flat with the coat, and watch and chain, which were to be placed
in the hands of Colonel Grassi, the chief police officer at Cividale.

I took a keen look at the lady, you may be sure of that. It was a
pretty little face enough, and she herself could not have been much

more than seven or eight and twenty, but to me the whole appearance and manner of the woman suggested weakness of character, rather than that devotion on which poor Mr. Shuttleworth so implicitly relied.

I suppose that it was on that account that I felt unaccountably down-hearted and anxious when I bade farewell to my own dear lady—a feeling in which she obviously did not share. Then I began to enact the *rôle* which had been assigned to me.

I dressed up in Mrs. Tadworth's clothes—we were about the same height—and putting on her hat and closely fitting veil, I set out for Leather Lane. For as many hours as I could possibly contrive to keep up the deception, I was to impersonate Mrs. Tadworth in her own house.

As I dare say you have guessed by now, that lady was not in affluent circumstances, and the house in a small by-street off Leather Lane did not boast of a staff of servants. In fact, Mrs. Tadworth did all the domestic work herself, with the help of a charwoman for a couple of hours in the mornings.

That charwoman had, in accordance with Lady Molly's plan, been given a week's wages in lieu of notice. I—as Mrs. Tadworth—would be supposed the next day to be confined to my room with a cold, and Emily—our own little maid, a bright girl, who would go through fire and water for Lady Molly or for me—would represent a new charwoman.

As soon as anything occurred to arouse my suspicions that our secret had been discovered, I was to wire to Lady Molly at the various points which she gave me.

Thus provided with an important and comprehensive part, I duly installed myself at Bread Street, Leather Lane. Emily—who had been told just enough of the story, and no more, to make her eager, excited and satisfied—entered into the spirit of her *rôle* as eagerly as I did myself.

That first night was quite uneventful. The Piattis came home some time after eleven and went straight up to their room.

Emily, looking as like a bedraggled charwoman as her trim figure would allow, was in the hall the next morning when the two men started off for breakfast. She told me afterwards that the younger one looked at her very keenly, and asked her why the other servant had gone. Emily replied with due and proper vagueness, whereupon the Sicilians said no more and went out together.

That was a long and wearisome day which I spent cooped up in the tiny, stuffy parlour, ceaselessly watching the tiny patch of ground at the back, devoured with anxiety, following the travellers in my mind on their way across Europe.

Towards midday one of the Piattis came home and presently strolled out into the garden. Evidently the change of servants had aroused his suspicions, for I could see him feeling about the earth with his spade and looking up now and again towards the window of the parlour, whereat I contrived to show him the form of a pseudo Mrs. Tadworth moving about the room.

Mr. Shuttleworth and I were having supper in that same back parlour at about nine o'clock on that memorable evening, when we suddenly heard the front door being opened with a latchkey, and then very cautiously shut again.

One of the two men had returned at an hour most unusual for their otherwise very regular habits. The way, too, in which the door had been opened and shut suggested a desire for secrecy and silence. Instinctively I turned off the gas in the parlour, and with a quick gesture pointed to the front room, the door of which stood open, and I whispered hurriedly to Mr. Shuttleworth.

"Speak to him!"

Fortunately, the great aim which he had in view had rendered his perceptions very keen.

He went into the front room, in which the gas, fortunately, was alight at the time, and opening the door which gave thence on to the passage, he said pleasantly:

"Oh, Mr. Piatti! is that you? Can I do any thing for you?"

"Ah, yes! zank you," replied the Sicilian, whose voice I could hear was husky and unsteady, "if you would be so kind—I—I feel so fainting and queer to-night—ze warm weazer, I zink. Would you—would you be so kind to fetch me a little—er—ammoniac—

er—sal volatile you call it, I zink—from ze apothecary? I would go lie on my bed—if you would be so kind—"

"Why, of course I will, Mr. Piatti," said Mr. Shuttleworth, who somehow got an intuition of what I wanted to do, and literally played into my hands. "I'll go at once."

He went to get his hat from the rack in the hall whilst the Sicilian murmured profuse "Zank you's," and then I heard the front door bang to.

From where I was I could not see Piatti, but I imagined him standing in the dimly-lighted passage listening to Mr. Shuttleworth's retreating footsteps.

Presently I heard him walking along towards the back door, and soon I perceived something moving about in the little bit of ground beyond. He had gone to get his spade. He meant to unearth the coat and the watch and chain which, for some reason or another, he must have thought were no longer safe in their original hiding-place. Had the gang of murderers heard that the man who frequently visited their landlady was the father of Cecil Shuttleworth over at Palermo?

At that moment I paused neither to speculate nor yet to plan. I ran down to the kitchen, for I no longer wanted to watch Piatti. I knew what he was doing.

I didn't want to frighten Emily, and she had been made to understand all along that she might have to leave the house with me again at any time, at a moment's notice; she and I had kept our small handbag ready packed in the kitchen, whence we could reach the area steps quickly and easily.

Now I quietly beckoned to her that the time had come. She took the bag and followed me. Just as we shut the area gate behind us, we heard the garden door violently slammed. Piatti had got the coat, and by now was examining the pockets in order to find the watch and chain. Within the next ten seconds he would realise that the coat which he held was not the one which he had buried in the garden, and that the real proofs of his guilt—or his complicity in the guilt of another—had disappeared.

We did not wait for those ten seconds, but flew down Bread Street, in the direction of Leather Lane, where I knew Mr. Shuttleworth would be on the lookout for me.

"Yes," I said hurriedly, directly I spied him at the angle of the street; "it's all up. I am off to Budapest by the early Continental to-morrow morning. I shall catch them at the Hungaria. See Emily safely to the flat."

Obviously there was no time to lose, and before either Mr. Shuttleworth or Emily could make a remark I had left them standing, and had quickly mixed my insignificant personality with the passers-by.

I strolled down Leather Lane quite leisurely; you see, my face was unknown to the Piattis. They had only seen dim outlines of me behind very dirty window-panes.

I did not go to the flat. I knew Mr. Shuttleworth would take care of Emily, so that night I slept at the Grand Hotel, Charing Cross, leaving the next morning by the 9.0 a.m., having booked my berth on the Orient Express as far as Budapest.

3

Well, you know the saying: It is easy to be wise after the event.

Of course, when I saw the older Piatti standing in the hall of the Hotel Hungaria at Budapest I realised that I had been followed from the moment that Emily and I ran out of the house at Bread Street. The son had obviously kept me in view whilst I was still in London, and the father had travelled across Europe, unperceived by me, in the same train as myself, had seen me step into the fiacre at Budapest, and heard me tell the smart coachman to drive to the Hungaria.

I made hasty arrangements for my room, and then asked if "Mrs. Carey," from London, was still at the hotel with her maid—for that was the name under which Mrs. Tadworth was to travel—and was answered in the affirmative. "Mrs. Carey" was even then supping in the dining-room, whence the strains of beautiful Hungarian melodies played by Berkes' inimitable band seemed to mock my anxiety.

"Mrs. Carey's maid," they told me, was having her meal in the steward's room.

I tried to prosecute my hasty inquiries as quietly as I could, but Piatti's eyes and sarcastic smile seemed to follow me everywhere, whilst he went about calmly ordering his room and seeing to the disposal of his luggage.

Almost every official at the Hungaria speaks English, and I had no difficulty in finding my way to the steward's room. To my chagrin Lady Molly was not there. Someone told me that no doubt "Mrs. Carey's maid" had gone back to her mistress's room, which they told me was No. 118 on the first floor.

A few precious moments were thus wasted whilst I ran back towards the hall; you know the long, seemingly interminable, corridors and passages of the Hungaria! Fortunately, in one of these I presently beheld my dear lady walking towards me. At sight of her all my anxieties seemed to fall from me like a discarded mantle.

She looked quite serene and placid, but with her own quick perception she at once guessed what had brought me to Budapest.

"They have found out about the coat," she said, quickly drawing me aside into one of the smaller passages, which fortunately at the moment was dark and deserted, "and, of course, he has followed you—"

I nodded affirmatively.

"That Mrs. Tadworth is a vapid, weak-kneed little fool," she said, with angry vehemence. "We ought to be at Cividale by now—and she declared herself too ill and too fatigued to continue the journey. How that poor Shuttleworth could be so blind as to trust her passes belief."

"Mary," she added more calmly, "go down into the hall at once. Watch that idiot of a woman for all you're worth. She is terrified of the Sicilians, and I firmly believe that Piatti can force her to give up the proofs of the crime to him."

"Where are they—the proofs, I mean?" I asked anxiously.

"Locked up in her trunk—she won't entrust them to me. Obstinate little fool."

I had never seen my dear lady so angry; however, she said nothing more then, and presently I took leave of her and worked my way back towards the hall. One glance round the brilliantly-lighted place assured me that neither Piatti nor Mrs. Tadworth was there. I could not tell you what it was that suddenly filled my heart with foreboding.

I ran up to the first floor and reached room No. 118. The outer door was open, and without a moment's hesitation I applied my eye to the keyhole of the inner one.

The room was brilliantly lighted from within, and exactly opposite, but with his back to me, stood Piatti, whilst squatting on a low stool beside him was Mrs. Tadworth.

A trunk stood open close to her hand, and she was obviously busy turning over its contents. My very heart stood still with horror. Was I about to witness—thus powerless to interfere—one of the most hideous acts of cowardly treachery it was possible to conceive?

Something, however, must at that moment have attracted Piatti's attention, for he suddenly turned and strode towards the door. Needless to say that I beat a hasty retreat.

My one idea was, of course, to find Lady Molly and tell her what I had seen. Unfortunately, the Hungaria is a veritable maze of corridors, stairs and passages, and I did not know the number of her room. At first I did not wish to attract further attention by again asking about "Mrs. Carey's maid" at the office, and my stupid ignorance of foreign languages precluded my talking to the female servants.

I had been up and down the stairs half a dozen times, tired, miserable, and anxious, when at last, in the far distance, I espied my dear lady's graceful silhouette. Eagerly I ran to her, and was promptly admonished for my careless impetuosity.

"Mrs. Tadworth is genuinely frightened," added Lady Molly in response to my look of painful suspense, "but so far she has been able to hoodwink Piatti by opening *my* trunk before him instead of hers, and telling him that the proofs were not in her own keeping. But she is too stupid to keep that deception up, and, of course, he won't allow himself to be put off a second time. We must start for Cividale as soon as possible. Unfortunately, the earliest train is not till 9.15 to-morrow morning. The danger to that unfortunate young man over at Palermo, brought about by this woman's cowardly idiocy and the father's misguided trust, is already incalculable."

It was, of course, useless for me to express fear now for my dear lady's safety. I smothered my anxiety as best I could, and, full of deadly forebodings, I bade her anon a fond good-night.

Needless to say that I scarcely slept, and at eight o'clock the next morning I was fully dressed and out of my room.

The first glance down the corridor on which gave No. 118 at once confirmed my worst fears. Unusual bustle reigned there at this early hour. Officials came and went, maids stood about gossiping, and the next moment, to my literally agonised horror, I beheld two gendarmes, with an officer, being escorted by the hotel manager to the rooms occupied by Mrs. Tadworth and Lady Molly.

Oh, how I cursed then our British ignorance of foreign tongues. The officials were too busy to bother about me, and the maids only knew that portion of the English language which refers to baths and to hot water. Finally, to my intense relief, I discovered a willing porter, ready and able to give me information in my own tongue of the events which had disturbed the serene quietude of the Hotel Hungaria.

Great heavens! Shall I ever forget what I endured when I grasped the full meaning of what he told me with a placid smile and a shrug of the shoulders!

"The affair is most mysterious," he explained, "not robbery— oh, no! no!—for it is Mrs. Carey, who has gone—disappeared! And it is Mrs. Carey's maid who was found, stunned, gagged and unconscious, tied to one of the bedposts in room No. 118."

4

Well, why should I bore you by recounting the agonised suspense, the mortal anxiety, which I endured for all those subsequent weary days which at the time seemed like so many centuries?

My own dear lady, the woman for whom I would have gone through fire and water with a cheerful smile, had been brutally assaulted, almost murdered, so the smiling porter assured me, and my very existence was ignored by the stolid officials, who looked down upon me with a frown of impassive disapproval whilst I entreated, raged and stormed alternately, begging to be allowed to go and nurse the sick lady, who was my own dearest friend, dearer than any child could be to its mother.

Oh, that awful red tapeism that besets one at every turn, paralyses and disheartens one! What I suffered I really could not describe.

But if I was not allowed to see Lady Molly, at least I was able to wreak vengeance upon her cowardly assailants. Mrs. Tadworth, by her disappearance, had tacitly confessed her participation in the outrage, of that I had no doubt, but I was equally certain that she was both too stupid and too weak to commit such a crime unaided.

Piatti was at the bottom of it all. Without a moment's hesitation I laid information against him through the medium of an interpreter. I accused him boldly of being an accessory to the assault for purposes of robbery. Unswervingly I repeated my story of how I had seen him in close conversation the day before with Mrs. Carey, whose real name I declared to be Mrs. Tadworth.

The chief object of the robbery I suggested to be a valuable gold watch and chain, with initials "A. C.," belonging to my friend, who had travelled with Mrs. Carey to Budapest as her companion, not her maid. This was a bold move on my part, and I felt reckless, I can tell you. Fortunately, my story was corroborated by the fact that the floor valet had seen Piatti hanging about the corridor outside No. 118 at an extraordinarily early hour of the morning. My firm belief was that the wretch had been admitted into the room by that horrid Mrs. Tadworth. He had terrorised her, probably had threatened her life. She had then agreed out of sheer cowardice to deliver to him the proofs of his own guilt in the Palermo murder case, and when Lady Molly, hearing the voices, came out of her own room, Piatti knocked her down lest she should intervene. Mrs. Tadworth thereupon—weak and silly little fool!—was seized with panic, and succeeded, no doubt with his help, in leaving the hotel, and probably Budapest, before the outrage was discovered.

Why Piatti had not done likewise, I could not conjecture. He seems to have gone back quietly to his own room after that; and it was not till an hour later that the chambermaid, surprised at seeing the door of No. 118 slightly ajar, had peeped in, and there was greeted by the awful sight of "the maid," gagged, bound and unconscious.

Well, I gained my wish, and had the satisfaction presently of knowing that Piatti—although, mind you, he emphatically denied my story from beginning to end—had been placed under arrest pending further inquiries.

The British Consul was very kind to me; though I was not allowed to see my dear lady, who had been removed to the hospital. I heard that the Hungarian police were moving heaven and earth to find "Mrs. Carey" and bring her to justice.

Her disappearance told severely against her, and after three days of such intense anxiety as I never wish to live through again, I received a message from the Consulate informing me that "Mrs. Carey" had been arrested at Alsórév, on the Austro-Hungarian frontier, and was even now on her way to Budapest under escort.

You may imagine how I quivered with anxiety and with rage when, on the morning after that welcome news, I was told that "Mrs. Carey" was detained at the gendarmerie, and had asked to see Miss Mary Granard from London, at present residing at the Hotel Hungaria.

The impudent wretch! Wanting to see me, indeed! Well, I, too, wanted to see her; the woman whom I despised as a coward and a traitor; who had betrayed the fond and foolish trust of a stricken father; who had dashed the last hopes of an innocent man in danger of his life; and who, finally, had been the cause of an assault that had all but killed, perhaps, the woman I loved best in the world.

I felt like the embodiment of hate and contempt. I loathed the woman, and I hied me in a fiacre to the gendarmerie, escorted by one of the clerks from the Consulate, simply thirsting with the desire to tell an ignoble female exactly what I thought of her.

I had to wait some two or three minutes in the bare, barrack-like room of the gendarmerie; then the door opened, there was a rustle of silk, followed by the sound of measured footsteps of soldiery, and the next moment Lady Molly, serene and placid and, as usual, exquisitely dressed, stood smiling before me.

"You have got me into this plight, Mary," she said, with her merry laugh; "you'll have to get me out of it again."

"But—I don't understand," was all that I could gasp.

"It is very simple, and I'll explain it all fully when we are on our way home to Maida Vale," she said. "For the moment you and Mrs. Tadworth will have to make sundry affidavits that I did not assault my maid nor rob her of a watch and chain. The British Consul will help you, and it is only a question of days, and in the meanwhile I may tell you that Budapest prison life is quite interesting, and not so uncomfortable as one would imagine."

Of course, the moment she spoke I got an intuition of what had really occurred, and I can assure you that I was heartily ashamed that I should ever have doubted Lady Molly's cleverness in carrying through successfully so important, so vital a business as the righting of an innocent man.

Mrs. Tadworth was pusillanimous and stupid. At Budapest she cried a halt, for she really felt unstrung and ill after the hurried journey, the change of air and food, and what not. Lady Molly, however, had no difficulty in persuading her that during the enforced stay of twenty-four hours at the Hungaria their two *rôles* should be reversed. Lady Molly would be "Mrs. Carey," coming from England, whilst Mrs. Tadworth would be the maid.

My dear lady—not thinking at the time that my knowledge of this fact would be of any importance to her own plans—had not mentioned it to me during the brief interview which I had with her. Then, when Piatti arrived upon the scene, Mrs. Tadworth got into a real panic. Fortunately, she had the good sense, or the cowardice, then and there to entrust the coat and watch and chain to Lady Molly, and when Piatti followed her into her room she was able to show him that the proofs were not then in her possession. This was the scene which I had witnessed through the keyhole.

But, of course, the Sicilian would return to the charge, and equally, of course, Mrs. Tadworth would sacrifice the Shuttleworths, father and son, to save her own skin. Lady Molly knew that.

She is strong, active and determined; she had a brief hand-to-hand struggle with Mrs. Tadworth that night, and finally succeeded in tying her, half unconscious, to the bedpost, thus assuring herself that for at least twenty-four hours that vapid little fool would be unable to either act for herself or to betray my dear, intrepid lady's plans.

When, the following morning, Piatti opened the door of No. 118, which had purposely been left on the latch, he was greeted with the sight of Mrs. Tadworth pinioned and half dead with fear, whilst the valuable proofs of his own guilt and young Shuttleworth's innocence had completely disappeared.

For remember that Lady Molly's face was not known to him or to his gang, and she had caught the first train to Cividale even whilst Piatti still believed that he held that silly Mrs. Tadworth in the hollow of his hand. I may as well tell you here that she reached the frontier safely, and was quite sharp enough to seek out Colonel Grassi and, with the necessary words of explanation, to hand over to him the proofs of young Shuttleworth's innocence.

My action in the matter helped her. At the hotel she was supposed to be the mistress and Mrs. Tadworth the maid, and everyone was told that "Mrs. Carey's maid" had been assaulted, and removed to the hospital. But I denounced Piatti then and there, thinking he had attacked my dear lady, and I got him put under lock and key so quickly that he had not the time to communicate with his associates.

Thanks to Colonel Grassi's exertions, young Shuttleworth was acquitted of the charge of murder; but I may as well tell you here that neither Piatti nor his son, nor any of that gang, were arrested for the crime. The proofs of their guilt—the Irish-tweed coat and the murdered man's watch and chain—were most mysteriously suppressed, after young Shuttleworth's advocate had obtained the verdict of "not guilty" for him.

Such is the Sicilian police. Mr. Shuttleworth, senior, evidently knew what he was talking about.

Of course, we had no difficulty in obtaining Lady Molly's release. The British Consul saw to that. But in Budapest they still call the assault on "Mrs. Carey" at the Hotel Hungaria a mystery, for she exonerated Lady Molly fully, but she refused to accuse Piatti. She was afraid of him, of course, and so they had to set him free.

I wonder where he is now, the wicked old wretch!

THE FORDWYCH CASTLE MYSTERY

Can you wonder that, when some of the ablest of our fellows at the Yard were at their wits' ends to know what to do, the chief instinctively turned to Lady Molly?

Surely the Fordwych Castle Mystery, as it was universally called, was a case which more than any other required feminine tact, intuition, and all those qualities of which my dear lady possessed more than her usual share.

With the exception of Mr. McKinley, the lawyer, and young Jack d'Alboukirk, there were only women connected with the case.

If you have studied Debrett at all, you know as well as I do that the peerage is one of those old English ones which date back some six hundred years, and that the present Lady d'Alboukirk is a baroness in her own right, the title and estates descending to heirs-general. If you have perused that same interesting volume carefully, you will also have discovered that the late Lord d'Alboukirk had two daughters, the eldest, Clementina Cecilia—the present Baroness, who succeeded him—the other, Margaret Florence, who married in 1884 Jean Laurent Duplessis, a Frenchman whom Debrett vaguely describes as "of Pondicherry, India," and of whom she had issue two daughters, Henriette Marie, heir now to the ancient barony of d'Alboukirk of Fordwych, and Joan, born two years later.

There seems to have been some mystery or romance attached to this marriage of the Honourable Margaret Florence d'Alboukirk to the dashing young officer of the Foreign Legion. Old Lord d'Alboukirk at the time was British Ambassador in Paris, and he seems to have had grave objections to the union, but Miss Margaret, openly flouting her father's displeasure, and throwing prudence to the winds, ran away from home one fine day with Captain Duplessis, and from Pondicherry wrote a curt letter to her relatives telling them of her marriage with the man she loved best in all the world. Old Lord d'Alboukirk never got over his daughter's willfulness. She had been his favourite, it appears, and her secret marriage and deceit practically broke his heart. He was kind to her, however, to the end, and when the first baby girl was born and the young pair seemed to be in straitened circumstances, he made them an allowance until the day of his daughter's death, which occurred three years after her elopement, on the birth of her second child.

When, on the death of her father, the Honourable Clementina Cecilia came into the title and fortune, she seemed to have thought it her duty to take some interest in her late sister's eldest child, who, failing her own marriage, and issue, was heir to the barony of d'Alboukirk. Thus it was that Miss Henriette Marie Duplessis came, with her father's consent, to live with her aunt at Fordwych Castle. Debrett will tell you, moreover, that in 1901 she assumed the name of d'Alboukirk, in lieu of her own, by royal licence. Failing her, the title and estate would devolve firstly on her sister Joan, and subsequently on a fairly distant cousin, Captain John d'Alboukirk, at present a young officer in the Guards.

According to her servants, the present Baroness d'Alboukirk is very self-willed, but otherwise neither more nor less eccentric than any north-country old maid would be who had such an exceptional position to keep up in the social world. The one soft trait in her otherwise not very lovable character is her great affection for her late sister's child. Miss Henriette Duplessis d'Alboukirk has inherited from her French father dark eyes and hair and a somewhat swarthy complexion, but no doubt it is from her English ancestry that she has derived a somewhat masculine frame and a very great fondness for all outdoor pursuits. She is very athletic, knows how to fence and to box, rides to hounds, and is a remarkably good shot.

From all accounts, the first hint of trouble in that gorgeous home was coincident with the arrival at Fordwych of a young, very pretty girl visitor, who was attended by her maid, a half-caste woman, dark-complexioned and surly of temper, but obviously of dog-like devotion towards her young mistress. This visit seems to have come as a surprise to the entire household at Fordwych Castle, her ladyship having said nothing about it until the very morning that the guests were expected. She then briefly ordered one of the housemaids to get a bedroom ready for a young lady, and to put up a small camp-bedstead in an adjoining dressing-room. Even Miss Henriette seems to have been taken by surprise at the announcement of this visit, for, according to Jane Taylor, the housemaid in question, there was a violent word-passage between the old lady and her niece, the latter winding up an excited speech with the words:

"At any rate, aunt, there won't be room for both of us in this house!" After which she flounced out of the room, banging the door behind her.

Very soon the household was made to understand that the newcomer was none other than Miss Joan Duplessis, Miss Henriette's younger sister. It appears that Captain Duplessis had recently died in Pondicherry, and that the young girl then wrote to her aunt, Lady d'Alboukirk, claiming her help and protection, which the old lady naturally considered it her duty to extend to her.

It appears that Miss Joan was very unlike her sister, as she was *petite* and fair, more English-looking than foreign, and had pretty, dainty ways which soon endeared her to the household. The devotion existing between her and the half-caste woman she had brought from India was, moreover, unique.

It seems, however, that from the moment these newcomers came into the house, dissensions, often degenerating into violent quarrels, became the order of the day. Henriette seemed to have taken a strong dislike to her younger sister, and most particularly to the latter's dark attendant, who was vaguely known in the house as Roonah.

That some events of serious import were looming ahead, the servants at Fordwych were pretty sure. The butler and footmen at dinner heard scraps of conversation which sounded very ominous. There was talk of "lawyers," of "proofs," of "marriage and birth certificates," quickly suppressed when the servants happened to be about. Her ladyship looked terribly anxious and worried, and she and Miss Henriette spent long hours closeted together in a small boudoir, whence proceeded ominous sounds of heartrending weeping on her ladyship's part, and angry and violent words from Miss Henriette.

Mr. McKinley, the eminent lawyer from London, came down two or three times to Fordwych, and held long conversations with her ladyship, after which the latter's eyes were very swollen and red. The household thought it more than strange that Roonah, the Indian servant, was almost invariably present at these interviews between Mr. McKinley, her ladyship, and Miss Joan. Otherwise the woman kept herself very much aloof; she spoke very little, hardly took any notice of anyone save of her ladyship and her young mistress, and the outbursts of Miss Henriette's temper seemed to leave her quite unmoved. A strange fact was that she had taken a sudden and great fancy for frequenting a small Roman Catholic convent chapel which was distant about half a mile from the Castle, and presently it was understood that Roonah, who had been a Parsee, had been converted by the attendant priest to the Roman Catholic faith.

All this happened, mind you, within the last two or three months; in fact, Miss Joan had been in the Castle exactly twelve weeks when Captain Jack d'Alboukirk came to pay his cousin one of his periodical visits. From the first he seems to have taken a great fancy to his cousin Joan, and soon everyone noticed that this fancy was rapidly ripening into love. It was equally certain that from that moment dissensions between the two sisters became more frequent and more violent; the generally accepted opinion being that Miss Henriette was jealous of Joan, whilst Lady d'Alboukirk herself, for some unexplainable reason, seems to have regarded this love-making with marked disfavour.

Then came the tragedy.

One morning Joan ran downstairs, pale, and trembling from head to foot, moaning and sobbing as she ran:

"Roonah!—my poor old Roonah!—I knew it—I knew it!"

Captain Jack happened to meet her at the foot of the stairs. He pressed her with questions, but the girl was unable to speak. She merely pointed mutely to the floor above. The young man, genuinely alarmed, ran quickly upstairs; he threw open the door leading to Roonah's room, and there, to his horror, he saw the unfortunate woman lying across the small camp-bedstead, with a handkerchief over her nose and mouth, her throat cut.

The sight was horrible.

Poor Roonah was obviously dead.

Without losing his presence of mind, Captain Jack quietly shut the door again, after urgently begging Joan to compose herself, and try to keep up, at any rate until the local doctor could be sent for and the terrible news gently broken to Lady d'Alboukirk.

The doctor, hastily summoned, arrived some twenty minutes later. He could but confirm Joan's and Captain Jack's fears. Roonah was indeed dead—in fact, she had been dead some hours.

2

From the very first, mind you, the public took a more than usually keen interest in this mysterious occurrence. The evening papers on the very day of the murder were ablaze with flaming headlines such as:

THE TRAGEDY AT FORDWYCH CASTLE
MYSTERIOUS MURDER OF AN IMPORTANT WITNESS
GRAVE CHARGES AGAINST PERSONS IN HIGH LIFE

and so forth.

As time went on, the mystery deepened more and more, and I suppose Lady Molly must have had an inkling that sooner or later the chief would have to rely on her help and advice, for she sent me down to attend the inquest, and gave me strict orders to keep eyes and ears open for every detail in connection with the crime—however trivial it might seem. She herself remained in town, awaiting a summons from the chief.

The inquest was held in the dining-room of Fordwych Castle, and the noble hall was crowded to its utmost when the coroner and jury finally took their seats, after having viewed the body of the poor murdered woman upstairs.

The scene was dramatic enough to please any novelist, and an awed hush descended over the crowd when, just before the proceedings began, a door was thrown open, and in walked—stiff and erect—the Baroness d'Alboukirk, escorted by her niece, Miss Henriette, and closely followed by her cousin, Captain Jack, of the Guards.

The old lady's face was as indifferent and haughty as usual, and so was that of her athletic niece. Captain Jack, on the other hand, looked troubled and flushed. Everyone noted that, directly he entered the room, his eyes sought a small, dark figure that sat silent and immovable beside the portly figure of the great lawyer, Mr. Hubert McKinley. This was Miss Joan Duplessis, in a plain black stuff gown, her young face pale and tear-stained.

Dr. Walker, the local practitioner, was, of course, the first witness called. His evidence was purely medical. He deposed to having made an examination of the body, and stated that he found that a handkerchief saturated with chloroform had been pressed to the woman's nostrils, probably while she was asleep, her throat having subsequently been cut with a sharp knife; death must have been instantaneous, as the poor thing did not appear to have struggled at all.

In answer to a question from the coroner, the doctor said that no great force or violence would be required for the gruesome deed, since the victim was undeniably unconscious when it was done. At the same time it argued unusual coolness and determination.

The handkerchief was produced, also the knife. The former was a bright-coloured one, stated to be the property of the deceased. The latter was a foreign, old-fashioned hunting-knife, one of a panoply of small arms and other weapons which adorned a corner of the hall. It had been found by Detective Elliott in a clump of gorse on the adjoining golf links. There could be no question that it had been used by the murderer for his fell purpose, since at the time it was found it still bore traces of blood.

Captain Jack was the next witness called. He had very little to say, as he merely saw the body from across the room, and immediately closed the door again and, having begged his cousin to compose herself, called his own valet and sent him off for the doctor.

Some of the staff of Fordwych Castle were called, all of whom testified to the Indian woman's curious taciturnity, which left her quite isolated among her fellow-servants. Miss Henriette's maid, however, Jane Partlett, had one or two more interesting facts to record. She seems to have been more intimate with the deceased woman than anyone else, and on one occasion, at least, had quite a confidential talk with her.

"She talked chiefly about her mistress," said Jane, in answer to a question from the coroner, "to whom she was most devoted. She told me that she loved her so, she would readily die for her. Of course, I thought that silly like, and just mad, foreign talk, but Roonah was very angry when I laughed at her, and then she undid her dress in front, and showed me some papers which were sown in the lining of her dress. 'All these papers my little missee's fortune,' she said to me. 'Roonah guard these with her life. Someone must kill Roonah before taking them from her!'

"This was about six weeks ago," continued Jane, whilst a strange feeling of awe seemed to descend upon all those present whilst the girl spoke. "Lately she became much more silent, and, on my once referring to the papers, she turned on me savage like and told me to hold my tongue."

Asked if she had mentioned the incident of the papers to anyone, Jane replied in the negative.

"Except to Miss Henriette, of course," she added, after a slight moment of hesitation.

Throughout all these preliminary examinations Lady d'Alboukirk, sitting between her cousin Captain Jack and her niece Henriette, had remained quite silent in an erect attitude expressive of haughty indifference. Henriette, on the other hand, looked distinctly bored. Once or twice she had yawned audibly, which caused quite a feeling of anger against her among the spectators. Such callousness in the midst of so mysterious a tragedy, and when her own sister was obviously in such deep sorrow, impressed everyone very unfavourably. It was well known that the young lady had had a fencing lesson just before the inquest in the room immediately below that where Roonah lay dead, and that within an hour of the discovery of the tragedy she was calmly playing golf.

Then Miss Joan Duplessis was called.

When the young girl stepped forward there was that awed hush in the room which usually falls upon an attentive audience when the curtain is about to rise on the crucial act of a dramatic play. But she was calm and self-possessed, and wonderfully pathetic-looking in her deep black and with the obvious lines of sorrow which the sad death of a faithful friend had traced on her young face.

In answer to the coroner, she gave her name as Joan Clarissa Duplessis, and briefly stated that until the day of her servant's death she had been a resident at Fordwych Castle, but that since then she had left that temporary home, and had taken up her abode at the d'Alboukirk Arms, a quiet little hostelry on the outskirts of the town.

There was a distinct feeling of astonishment on the part of those who were not aware of this fact, and then the coroner said kindly:

"You were born, I think, in Pondicherry, in India, and are the younger daughter of Captain and Mrs. Duplessis, who was own sister to her ladyship?"

"I was born in Pondicherry," replied the young girl, quietly, "and I am the only legitimate child of the late Captain and Mrs. Duplessis, own sister to her ladyship."

A wave of sensation, quickly suppressed by the coroner, went through the crowd at these words. The emphasis which the witness had put on the word "legitimate" could not be mistaken, and everyone felt that here must lie the clue to the, so far impenetrable, mystery of the Indian woman's death.

All eyes were now turned on old Lady d'Alboukirk and on her niece Henriette, but the two ladies were carrying on a whispered conversation together, and had apparently ceased to take any further interest in the proceedings.

"The deceased was your confidential maid, was she not?" asked the coroner, after a slight pause.

"Yes."

"She came over to England with you recently?"

"Yes; she had to accompany me in order to help me to make good my claim to being my late mother's only legitimate child, and therefore the heir to the barony of d'Alboukirk."

Her voice had trembled a little as she said this, but now, as breathless silence reigned in the room, she seemed to make a visible effort to control herself, and, replying to the coroner's question, she gave a clear and satisfactory account of her terrible discovery of her faithful servant's death. Her evidence had lasted about a quarter of an hour or so, when suddenly the coroner put the momentous question to her:

"Do you know anything about the papers which the deceased woman carried about her person, and reference to which has already been made?"

"Yes," she replied quietly; "they were the proofs relating to my claim. My father, Captain Duplessis, had in early youth, and before he met my mother, contracted a secret union with a half-caste woman, who was Roonah's own sister. Being tired of her, he chose to repudiate her—she had no children—but the legality of the marriage was never for a moment in question. After that, he married my mother, and his first wife subsequently died, chiefly of a broken heart; but her death only occurred two months *after* the birth of my sister Henriette. My father, I think, had been led to believe that his first wife had died some two years previously, and he was no doubt very much shocked when he realised what a grievous wrong he had done our mother. In order to mend matters somewhat, he and she went through a new form of marriage—a legal one this time—and my father paid a lot of money to Roonah's relatives to have the matter hushed up. Less than a year after this second—and only legal—marriage, I was born and my mother died."

"Then these papers of which so much has been said—what did they consist of?"

"There were the marriage certificates of my father's first wife—and two sworn statements as to her death, two months *after* the birth of my sister Henriette; one by Dr. Rénaud, who was at the time a well-known medical man in Pondicherry, and the other by Roonah herself, who had held her dying sister in her arms. Dr. Rénaud is dead, and now Roonah has been murdered, and all the proofs have gone with her—"

Her voice broke in a passion of sobs, which, with manifest self-control, she quickly suppressed. In that crowded court you could have heard a pin drop, so great was the tension of intense excitement and attention.

"Then those papers remained in your maid's possession? Why was that?" asked the coroner.

"I did not dare to carry the papers about with me," said the witness, while a curious look of terror crept into her young face as she looked across at her aunt and sister. "Roonah would not part with them. She carried them in the lining of her dress, and at night they were all under her pillow. After her—her death, and when Dr. Walker had left, I thought it my duty to take possession of the papers which meant my whole future to me, and which I desired then to place in Mr. McKinley's charge. But, though I carefully searched the bed and all the clothing by my poor Roonah's side, I did not find the papers. They were gone."

I won't attempt to describe to you the sensation caused by the deposition of this witness. All eyes wandered from her pale young face to that of her sister, who sat almost opposite to her, shrugging her athletic shoulders and gazing at the pathetic young figure before her with callous and haughty indifference.

"Now, putting aside the question of the papers for the moment," said the coroner, after a pause, "do you happen to know anything of your late servant's private life? Had she an enemy, or perhaps a lover?"

"No," replied the girl; "Roonah's whole life was centred in me and in my claim. I had often begged her to place our papers in Mr. McKinley's charge, but she would trust no one. I wish she had obeyed me," here moaned the poor girl involuntarily, "and I should not have lost what means my whole future to me, and the being who loved me best in all the world would not have been so foully murdered."

Of course, it was terrible to see this young girl thus instinctively, and surely unintentionally, proffering so awful an accusation against those who stood so near to her. That the whole case had become hopelessly involved and mysterious, nobody could deny. Can you imagine the mental picture formed in the mind of all present by the story, so pathetically told, of this girl who had come over to England in order to make good her claim which she felt to be just, and who, in one fell swoop, saw that claim rendered very difficult to prove through the dastardly murder of her principal witness?

That the claim was seriously jeopardised by the death of Roonah and the disappearance of the papers, was made very clear, mind you, through the statements of Mr. McKinley, the lawyer. He could not say very much, of course, and his statements could never have been taken as actual proof, because Roonah and Joan had never fully trusted him and had never actually placed the proofs of the claim in his hands. He certainly had seen the marriage certificate of Captain Duplessis's wife, and a copy of this, as he very properly stated, could easily be obtained. The woman seems to have died during the great cholera epidemic of 1881, when, owing to the great number of deaths which occurred, the deceit and concealment practiced by the natives at Pondicherry, and the supineness of the French Government, death certificates were very casually and often incorrectly made out.

Roonah had come over to England ready to swear that her sister had died in her arms two months after the birth of Captain Duplessis's eldest child, and there was the sworn testimony of Dr. Rénaud, since dead. These affidavits Mr. McKinley had seen and read.

Against that, the only proof which now remained of the justice of Joan Duplessis's claim was the fact that her mother and father went through a second form of marriage some time *after* the birth of their first child, Henriette. This fact was not denied, and, of course, it could be easily proved, if necessary, but even then it would in no way be conclusive. It implied the presence of a doubt in Captain Duplessis's mind, a doubt which the second marriage ceremony may have served to set at rest; but it in no way established the illegitimacy of his eldest daughter.

In fact, the more Mr. McKinley spoke, the more convinced did everyone become that the theft of the papers had everything to do with the murder of the unfortunate Roonah. She would not part with the proofs which meant her mistress's fortune, and she paid for her devotion with her life.

Several more witnesses were called after that. The servants were closely questioned, the doctor was recalled, but, in spite of long and arduous efforts, the coroner and jury could not bring a single real fact to light beyond those already stated.

The Indian woman had been murdered!

The papers which she always carried about her body had disappeared.

Beyond that, nothing! An impenetrable wall of silence and mystery!

The butler at Fordwych Castle had certainly missed the knife with which Roonah had been killed from its accustomed place on the morning after the murder had been committed, but not before, and the mystery further gained in intensity from the fact that the only purchase of chloroform in the district had been traced to the murdered woman herself.

She had gone down to the local chemist one day some two or three weeks previously, and shown him a prescription for cleansing the hair which required some chloroform in it. He gave her a very small quantity in a tiny bottle, which was subsequently found empty on her own dressing-table. No one at Fordwych Castle could

swear to having heard any unaccustomed noise during that memorable night. Even Joan, who slept in the room adjoining that where
the unfortunate Roonah lay, said she had heard nothing unusual.
But then, the door of communication between the two rooms was
shut, and the murderer had been quick and silent.

Thus this extraordinary inquest drew to a close, leaving in its
train an air of dark suspicion and of unexplainable horror.

The jury returned a verdict of "Willful murder against some
person or persons unknown," and the next moment Lady d'Alboukirk rose, and, leaning on her niece's arm, quietly walked out of
the room.

3

Two of our best men from the Yard, Pegram and Elliott, were
left in charge of the case. They remained at Fordwych (the little
town close by), as did Miss Joan, who had taken up her permanent
abode at the d'Alboukirk Arms, whilst I returned to town immediately after the inquest. Captain Jack had rejoined his regiment,
and apparently the ladies of the Castle had resumed their quiet,
luxurious life just the same as heretofore. The old lady led her own
somewhat isolated, semi-regal life; Miss Henriette fenced and
boxed, played hockey and golf, and over the fine Castle and its
haughty inmates there hovered like an ugly bird of prey the threatening presence of a nameless suspicion.

The two ladies might choose to flout public opinion, but public
opinion was dead against them. No one dared formulate a charge,
but everyone remembered that Miss Henriette had, on the very
morning of the murder, been playing golf in the field where the
knife was discovered, and that if Miss Joan Duplessis ever failed
to make good her claim to the barony of d'Alboukirk, Miss
Henriette would remain in undisputed possession. So now, when
the ladies drove past in the village street, no one doffed a cap to
salute them, and when at church the parson read out the sixth com-
mandment, "Thou shalt do no murder," all eyes gazed with fear-
some awe at the old Baroness and her niece.

Splendid isolation reigned at Fordwych Castle. The daily papers grew more and more sarcastic at the expense of the Scotland Yard authorities, and the public more and more impatient.

Then it was that the chief grew desperate and sent for Lady Molly, the result of the interview being that I once more made the journey down to Fordwych, but this time in the company of my dear lady, who had received *carte blanche* from headquarters to do whatever she thought right in the investigation of the mysterious crime.

She and I arrived at Fordwych at 8.0 p.m., after the usual long wait at Newcastle. We put up at the d'Alboukirk Arms, and, over a hasty and very bad supper, Lady Molly allowed me a brief insight into her plans.

"I can see every detail of that murder, Mary," she said earnestly, "just as if I had lived at the Castle all the time. I know exactly where our fellows are wrong, and why they cannot get on. But, although the chief has given me a free hand, what I am going to do is so irregular that if I fail I shall probably get my immediate *congé*, whilst some of the disgrace is bound to stick to you. It is not too late—you may yet draw back, and leave me to act alone."

I looked her straight in the face. Her dark eyes were gleaming; there was the power of second sight in them, or of marvelous intuition of "men and things."

"I'll follow your lead, my Lady Molly," I said quietly.

"Then go to bed now," she replied, with that strange transition of manner which to me was so attractive and to everyone else so unaccountable.

In spite of my protest, she refused to listen to any more talk or to answer any more questions, and, perforce, I had to go to my room. The next morning I saw her graceful figure, immaculately dressed in a perfect tailor-made gown, standing beside my bed at a very early hour.

"Why, what is the time?" I ejaculated, suddenly wide awake.

"Too early for you to get up," she replied quietly. "I am going to early Mass at the Roman Catholic convent close by."

"To Mass at the Roman Catholic convent?"

"Yes. Don't repeat all my words, Mary; it is silly, and wastes time. I have introduced myself in the neighbourhood as the American, Mrs. Silas A. Ogen, whose motor has broken down and is being repaired at Newcastle, while I, its owner, amuse myself by viewing the beauties of the neighbourhood. Being a Roman Catholic, I go to Mass first, and, having met Lady d'Alboukirk once in London, I go to pay her a respectful visit afterwards. When I come back we will have breakfast together. You might try in the meantime to scrape up an acquaintance with Miss Joan Duplessis, who is still staying here, and ask her to join us at breakfast."

She was gone before I could make another remark, and I could but obey her instantly to the letter.

An hour later I saw Miss Joan Duplessis strolling in the hotel garden. It was not difficult to pass the time of day with the young girl, who seemed quite to brighten up at having someone to talk to. We spoke of the weather and so forth, and I steadily avoided the topic of the Fordwych Castle tragedy until the return of Lady Molly at about ten o'clock. She came back looking just as smart, just as self-possessed, as when she had started three hours earlier. Only I, who knew her so well, noted the glitter of triumph in her eyes, and knew that she had not failed. She was accompanied by Pegram, who, however, immediately left her side and went straight into the hotel, whilst she joined us in the garden, and, after a few graceful words, introduced herself to Miss Joan Duplessis and asked her to join us in the coffee-room upstairs.

The room was empty and we sat down to table, I quivering with excitement and awaiting events. Through the open window I saw Elliott walking rapidly down the village street. Presently the waitress went off, and I being too excited to eat or speak, Lady Molly carried on a running conversation with Miss Joan, asking her about her life in India and her father, Captain Duplessis. Joan admitted that she had always been her father's favourite.

"He never liked Henriette, somehow," she explained.

Lady Molly asked her when she had first known Roonah.

"She came to the house when my mother died," replied Joan, "and she had charge of me as a baby." At Pondicherry no one had thought it strange that she came as a servant into an officer's house where her own sister had reigned as mistress. Pondicherry is a French settlement, and manners and customs there are often very peculiar.

I ventured to ask her what were her future plans.

"Well," she said, with a great touch of sadness, "I can, of course, do nothing whilst my aunt is alive. I cannot force her to let me live at Fordwych or to acknowledge me as her heir. After her death, if my sister does assume the title and fortune of d'Alboukirk," she added, whilst suddenly a strange look of vengefulness—almost of hatred and cruelty—marred the child-like expression of her face, "then I shall revive the story of the tragedy of Roonah's death, and I hope that public opinion—"

She paused here in her speech, and I, who had been gazing out of the window, turned my eyes on her. She was ashy-pale, staring straight before her; her hands dropped the knife and fork which she had held. Then I saw the Pegram had come into the room, that he had come up to the table and placed a packet of papers in Lady Molly's hand.

I saw it all as in a flash!

There was a loud cry of despair like an animal at bay, a shrill cry, followed by a deep one from Pegram of "No, you don't," and before anyone could prevent her, Joan's graceful young figure stood outlined for a short moment at the open window.

The next moment she had disappeared into the depth below, and we heard a dull thud which nearly froze the blood in my veins.

Pegram ran out of the room, but Lady Molly sat quite still.

"I have succeeded in clearing the innocent," she said quietly; "but the guilty has meted out to herself her own punishment."

"Then it was she?" I murmured, horror-struck.

"Yes. I suspected it from the first," replied Lady Molly calmly. "It was this conversion of Roonah to Roman Catholicism and her consequent change of manner which gave me the first clue."

"But why—why?" I muttered.

"A simple reason, Mary," she rejoined, tapping the packet of papers with her delicate hand; and, breaking open the string that held the letters, she laid them out upon the table. "The whole thing was a fraud from beginning to end. The woman's marriage certificate was all right, of course, but I mistrusted the genuineness of the other papers from the moment that I heard that Roonah would not part with them and would not allow Mr. McKinley to have charge of them. I am sure that the idea at first was merely one of blackmail. The papers were only to be the means of extorting money from the old lady, and there was no thought of taking them into court.

"Roonah's part was, of course, the important thing in the whole case, since she was here prepared to swear to the actual date of the first Madame Duplessis's death. The initiative, of course, may have come either from Joan or from Captain Duplessis himself, out of hatred for the family who would have nothing to do with him and his favourite younger daughter. That, of course, we shall never know. At first Roonah was a Parsee, with a dog-like devotion to the girl whom she had nursed as a baby, and who no doubt had drilled her well into the part she was to play. But presently she became a Roman Catholic—an ardent convert, remember, with all a Roman Catholic's fear of hell-fire. I went to the convent this morning. I heard the priest's sermon there, and I realised what an influence his eloquence must have had over poor, ignorant, superstitious Roonah. She was still ready to die for her young mistress, but she was no longer prepared to swear to a lie for her sake. After Mass I called at Fordwych Castle. I explained my position to old Lady d'Alboukirk, who took me into the room where Roonah had slept and died. There I found two things," continued Lady Molly, as she opened the elegant reticule which still hung upon her arm, and placed a big key and a prayer-book before me.

"The key I found in a drawer of an old cupboard in the dressing-room where Roonah slept, with all sorts of odds and ends belonging to the unfortunate woman, and going to the door which led into what had been Joan's bedroom, I found that it was locked, and that this key fitted into the lock. Roonah had locked that door herself on her own side—*she was afraid of her mistress.* I knew now that I was right in my surmise. The prayer-book is a Roman

Catholic one. It is heavily thumbmarked there, where false oaths and lying are denounced as being deadly sins for which hell-fire would be the punishment. Roonah, terrorised by fear of the supernatural, a new convert to the faith, was afraid of committing a deadly sin.

"Who knows what passed between the two women, both of whom have come to so violent and terrible an end? Who can tell what prayers, tears, persuasions Joan Duplessis employed from the time she realised that Roonah did not mean to swear to the lie which would have brought her mistress wealth and glamour until the awful day when she finally understood that Roonah would no longer even hold her tongue, and devised a terrible means of silencing her for ever?

"With this certainty before me, I ventured on my big *coup*. I was so sure, you see. I kept Joan talking in here whilst I sent Pegram to her room with orders to break open the locks of her hand-bag and dressing-case. There!—I told you that if I was wrong I would probably be dismissed the force for irregularity, as of course I had no right to do that; but if Pegram found the papers there where I felt sure they would be, we could bring the murderer to justice. I know my own sex pretty well, don't I, Mary? I knew that Joan Duplessis had not destroyed—never would destroy—those papers."

Even as Lady Molly spoke we could hear heavy tramping outside the passage. I ran to the door, and there was met by Pegram.

"She is quite dead, miss," he said. "It was a drop of forty feet, and a stone pavement down below."

The guilty had indeed meted out her own punishment to herself!

Lady d'Alboukirk sent Lady Molly a cheque for £5,000 the day the whole affair was made known to the public.

I think you will say that it had been well earned. With her own dainty hands my dear lady had lifted the veil which hung over the tragedy of Fordwych Castle, and with the finding of the papers in Joan Duplessis's dressing-bag, and the unfortunate girl's suicide, the murder of the Indian woman was no longer a mystery.

A DAY'S FOLLY

1

I don't think that anyone ever knew that the real elucidation of the extraordinary mystery known to the newspaper-reading public as the "Somersetshire Outrage" was evolved in my own dear lady's quick, intuitive brain.

As a matter of fact, to this day—as far as the public is concerned—the Somersetshire outrage never was properly explained; and it is a very usual thing for those busybodies who are so fond of criticising the police to point to that case as an instance of remarkable incompetence on the part of our detective department.

A young woman named Jane Turner, a visitor at Weston-super-Mare, had been discovered one afternoon in a helpless condition, bound and gagged, and suffering from terror and inanition, in the bedroom which she occupied in a well-known apartment-house of that town. The police had been immediately sent for, and as soon as Miss Turner had recovered she gave what explanation she could of the mysterious occurrence.

She was employed in one of the large drapery shops in Bristol, and was spending her annual holiday at Weston-super-Mare. Her father was the local butcher at Banwell—a village distant about four miles from Weston—and it appears that somewhere near one o'clock in the afternoon of Friday, the 3rd of September, she was busy in her bedroom putting a few things together in a handbag, preparatory to driving out to Banwell, meaning to pay her parents a week-end visit.

There was a knock at her door, and a voice said, "It's me, Jane—may I come in?"

She did not recognise the voice, but somehow thought that it must be that of a friend, so she shouted, "Come in!"

This was all that the poor thing recollected definitely, for the next moment the door was thrown open, someone rushed at her with amazing violence, she heard the crash of a falling table and felt a blow on the side of her head, whilst a damp handkerchief was pressed to her nose and mouth.

Then she remembered nothing more.

When she gradually came to her senses she found herself in the terrible plight in which Mrs. Skeward—her landlady—discovered her twenty-four hours later.

When pressed to try and describe her assailant, she said that when the door was thrown open she thought that she saw an elderly woman in a wide mantle and wearing bonnet and veil, but that, at the same time, she was quite sure, from the strength and brutality of the onslaught, that she was attacked by a man. She had no enemies, and no possessions worth stealing; but her hand-bag, which, however, only contained a few worthless trifles, had certainly disappeared.

The people of the house, on the other hand, could throw but little light on the mystery which surrounded this very extraordinary and seemingly purposeless assault.

Mrs. Skeward only remembered that on Friday Miss Turner told her that she was just off to Banwell, and would be away for the week-end; but that she wished to keep her room on, against her return on the Monday following.

That was somewhere about half-past twelve o'clock, at the hour when luncheons were being got ready for the various lodgers; small wonder, therefore, that no one in the busy apartment-house took much count of the fact that Miss Turner was not seen to leave the house after that, and no doubt the wretched girl would have been left for several days in the pitiable condition in which she was ultimately found but for the fact that Mrs. Skeward happened to be of the usual grasping type common to those of her kind.

Weston-super-Mare was over-full that week-end, and Mrs. Skeward, beset by applicants for accommodation, did not see why she should not let her absent lodger's room for the night or two that the latter happened to be away, and thus get money twice over for it.

She conducted a visitor up to Miss Turner's room on the Saturday afternoon, and, throwing open the door—which, by the way, was not locked—was horrified to see the poor girl half-sitting, half-slipping off the chair to which she had been tied with a rope, whilst a woolen shawl was wound round the lower part of her face.

As soon as she had released the unfortunate victim, Mrs. Skeward sent for the police, and it was through the intelligent efforts of Detective Parsons—a local man—that a few scraps of very hazy evidence were then and there collected.

First, there was the question of the elderly female in the wide mantle, spoken of by Jane Turner as her assailant. It seems that someone answering to that description had called on the Friday at about one o'clock, and asked to see Miss Turner. The maid who answered the door replied that she thought Miss Turner had gone to Banwell.

"Oh!" said the old dame, "she won't have started yet. I am Miss Turner's mother, and I was to call for her so that we might drive out together."

"Then p'r'aps Miss Turner is still in her room," suggested the maid. "Shall I go and see?"

"Don't trouble," replied the woman; "I know my way. I'll go myself."

Whereupon the old dame walked past the servant, crossed the hall and went upstairs. No one saw her come down again, but one of the lodgers seems to have heard a knock at Jane Turner's door, and the female voice saying, "It's me, Jane—may I come in?"

What happened subsequently, who the mysterious old female was, and how and for what purpose she assaulted Jane Turner and robbed her of a few valueless articles, was the puzzle which faced the police then, and which—so far as the public is concerned—has never been solved. Jane Turner's mother was in bed at the time suffering from a broken ankle and unable to move. The elderly woman was, therefore, an impostor, and the search after her—though keen and hot enough at the time, I assure you—has remained, in the eyes of the public, absolutely fruitless. But of this more anon.

On the actual scene of the crime there was but little to guide subsequent investigation. The rope with which Jane Turner had been pinioned supplied no clue; the wool shawl was Miss Turner's own, snatched up by the miscreant to smother the girl's screams; on the floor was a handkerchief, without initial or laundry mark, which obviously had been saturated with chloroform; and close by a bottle which had contained the anæsthetic. A small table was overturned, and the articles which had been resting upon it were lying all around—such as a vase which had held a few flowers, a box of biscuits, and several issues of the *West of England Times*.

And nothing more. The miscreant, having accomplished his fell purpose, succeeded evidently in walking straight out of the house unobserved; his exit being undoubtedly easily managed owing to it being the busy luncheon hour.

Various theories were, of course, put forward by some of our ablest fellows at the Yard; the most likely solution being the guilt or, at least, the complicity of the girl's sweetheart, Arthur Cutbush—a ne'er-do-well, who spent the greater part of his time on race-courses. Inspector Danvers, whom the chief had sent down to assist the local police, declared that Jane Turner herself suspected her sweetheart, and was trying to shield him by stating she possessed nothing of any value; whereas, no doubt, the young blackguard knew that she had some money, and had planned this amazing *coup* in order to rob her of it.

Danvers was quite chagrined when, on investigation, it was proved that Arthur Cutbush had gone to the York races three days before the assault, and never left that city until the Saturday evening, when a telegram from Miss Turner summoned him to Weston.

Moreover, the girl did not break off her engagement with young Cutbush, and thus the total absence of motive was a serious bar to the likelihood of the theory.

Then it was the Chief sent for Lady Molly. No doubt he began to feel that here, too, was a case where feminine tact and my lady's own marvellous intuition might prove more useful than the more approved methods of the sterner sex.

2

"Of course, there is a woman in the case, Mary," said Lady Molly to me, when she came home from the interview with the chief, "although they all pooh-pooh that theory at the Yard, and declare that the female voice—to which the only two witnesses we have are prepared to swear—was a disguised one."

"You think, then, that a woman assaulted Jane Turner?"

"Well," she replied somewhat evasively, "if a man assumes a feminine voice, the result is a high-pitched, unnatural treble; and that, I feel convinced, would have struck either the maid or the lodger, or both, as peculiar."

This was the train of thought which my dear lady and I were following up, when, with that sudden transition of manner so characteristic of her, she said abruptly to me:

"Mary, look out a train for Weston-super-Mare. We must try to get down there to-night."

"Chief's orders?" I asked.

"No—mine," she replied laconically. "Where's the A B C?"

Well, we got off that self-same afternoon, and in the evening we were having dinner at the Grand Hotel, Weston-super-Mare.

My dear lady had been pondering all through the journey, and even now she was singularly silent and absorbed. There was a deep frown between her eyes, and every now and then the luminous, dark orbs would suddenly narrow, and the pupils contract as if smitten with a sudden light.

I was not a little puzzled as to what was going on in that active brain of hers, but my experience was that silence on my part was the surest card to play.

Lady Molly had entered our names in the hotel book as Mrs. Walter Bell and Miss Granard from London; and the day after our arrival there came two heavy parcels for her under that name. She had them taken upstairs to our private sitting-room, and there we undid them together.

To my astonishment they contained stacks of newspapers: as far as I could see at a glance, back numbers of the *West of England Times* covering a whole year.

"Find and cut out the 'Personal' column of every number, Mary," said Lady Molly to me. "I'll look through them on my return. I am going for a walk, and will be home by lunch time."

I knew, of course, that she was intent on her business and on that only, and as soon as she had gone out I set myself to the wearisome task which she had allotted me. My dear lady was evidently working out a problem in her mind, the solution of which she expected to find in a back number of the *West of England Times*.

By the time she returned I had the "Personal" column of some three hundred numbers of the paper neatly filed and docketed for her perusal. She thanked me for my promptitude with one of her charming looks, but said little, if anything, all through luncheon. After that meal she set to work. I could see her studying each scrap of paper minutely, comparing one with the other, arranging them in sets in front of her, and making marginal notes on them all the while.

With but a brief interval for tea, she sat at her table for close on four hours, at the end of which she swept all the scraps of paper on one side, with the exception of a few which she kept in her hand. Then she looked up at me, and I sighed with relief.

My dear lady was positively beaming.

"You have found what you wanted?" I asked eagerly.

"What I expected," she replied.

"May I know?"

She spread out the bits of paper before me. There were six altogether, and each of these columns had one paragraph specially marked with a cross.

"Only look at the paragraphs which I have marked," she said.

I did what I was told. But if in my heart I had vaguely hoped that I should then and there be confronted with the solution of the mystery which surrounded the Somersetshire outrage, I was doomed to disappointment.

Each of the marked paragraphs in the "Personal" columns bore the initials H. S. H., and their purport was invariably an assignation at one of the small railway stations on the line between Bristol and Weston.

I suppose that my bewilderment must have been supremely comical, for my lady's rippling laugh went echoing through the bare, dull hotel sitting-room.

"You don't see it, Mary?" she asked gaily.

"I confess I don't," I replied. "It completely baffles me."

"And yet," she said more gravely, "those few silly paragraphs have given me the clue to the mysterious assault on Jane Turner, which has been puzzling our fellows at the Yard for over three weeks."

"But how? I don't understand."

"You will, Mary, directly we get back to town. During my morning walk I have learnt all that I want to know, and now these paragraphs have set my mind at rest."

3

The next day we were back in town.

Already, at Bristol, we had bought a London morning paper, which contained in its centre page a short notice under the following startling headlines:

THE SOMERSETSHIRE OUTRAGE
Amazing Discovery by the Police
An Unexpected Clue

The article went on to say:

"We are officially informed that the police have recently obtained knowledge of certain facts which establish beyond a doubt the motive of the brutal

assault committed on the person of Miss Jane
Turner. We are not authorised to say more at present
than that certain startling developments are immi-
nent."

On the way up my dear lady had initiated me into some of her
views with regard to the case itself, which at the chief's desire she
had now taken entirely in hand, and also into her immediate plans,
of which the above article was merely the preface.

She it was who had "officially informed" the Press Association,
and, needless to say, the news duly appeared in most of the London and provincial dailies.

How unerring was her intuition, and how well thought out her
scheme, was proved within the next four-and-twenty hours in our
own little flat, when our Emily, looking somewhat important and
awed, announced Her Serene Highness the Countess of Hohengebirg.

H. S. H.—the conspicuous initials in the "Personal" columns of
the *West of England Times*! You may imagine how I stared at the
exquisite apparition—all lace and chiffon and roses—which the next
moment literally swept into our office, past poor, open-mouthed
Emily.

Had my dear lady taken leave of her senses when she suggested
that this beautiful young woman with the soft, fair hair, with the
pleading blue eyes and childlike mouth, had anything to do with a
brutal assault on a shop girl?

The young Countess shook hands with Lady Molly and with me,
and then, with a deep sigh, she sank into the comfortable chair
which I was offering her.

Speaking throughout with great diffidence, but always in the
gentle tones of a child that knows it has been naughty, she began
by explaining that she had been to Scotland Yard, where a very
charming man—the chief, I presume—had been most kind and sent
her hither, where he promised her she would find help and conso-
lation in her dreadful, dreadful trouble.

Encouraged by Lady Molly, she soon plunged into her narrative: a pathetic tale of her own frivolity and foolishness.

She was originally Lady Muriel Wolfe-Strongham, daughter of the Duke of Weston, and when scarce out of the schoolroom had met the Grand Duke of Starkburg-Nauheim, who fell in love with her and married her. The union was a morganatic one, the Grand Duke conferring on his English wife the title of the Countess of Hohengebirg and the rank of Serene Highness.

It seems that, at first, the marriage was a fairly happy one, in spite of the bitter animosity of the mother and sister of the Grand Duke: the Dowager Grand Duchess holding that all English girls were loud and unwomanly, and the Princess Amalie, seeing in her brother's marriage a serious bar to the fulfilment of her own highly ambitious matrimonial hopes.

"They can't bear me, because I don't knit socks and don't know how to bake almond cakes," said her dear little Serene Highness, looking up with tender appeal at Lady Molly's grave and beautiful face; "and they will be so happy to see a real estrangement between my husband and myself."

It appears that last year, while the Grand Duke was doing his annual cure at Marienbad, the Countess of Hohengebirg went to Folkestone for the benefit of her little boy's health. She stayed at one of the Hotels there merely as any English lady of wealth might do—with nurses and her own maid, of course, but without the paraphernalia and nuisance of her usual German retinue.

Whilst there she met an old acquaintance of her father's, a Mr. Rumboldt, who is a rich financier, it seems, and who at one time moved in the best society, but whose reputation had greatly suffered recently, owing to a much talked of divorce case which brought his name into unenviable notoriety.

Her Serene Highness, with more mopping of her blue eyes, assured Lady Molly that over at Schloss Starkburg she did not read the English papers, and was therefore quite unaware that Mr. Rumboldt, who used to be a *persona grata* in her father's house, was no longer a fit and proper acquaintance for her.

"It was a very fine morning," she continued with gentle pathos, "and I was deadly dull at Folkestone. Mr. Rumboldt persuaded me to go with him on a short trip on his yacht. We were to cross over to Boulogne, have luncheon there, and come home in the cool of the evening."

"And, of course, something occurred to disable the yacht," concluded Lady Molly gravely, as the lady herself had paused in her narrative.

"Of course," whispered the little Countess through her tears.

"And, of course, it was too late to get back by the ordinary afternoon mail boat?"

"That boat had gone an hour before, and the next did not leave until the middle of the night."

"So you had perforce to wait until then, and in the meanwhile you were seen by a girl named Jane Turner, who knew you by sight, and who has been blackmailing you ever since."

"How did you guess that?" ejaculated Her Highness, with a look of such comical bewilderment in her large, blue eyes that Lady Molly and I had perforce to laugh.

"Well," replied my dear lady after awhile, resuming her gravity, "we have a way in our profession of putting two and two together, haven't we? And in this case it was not very difficult. The assignations for secret meetings at out-of-the-way railway stations which were addressed to H. S. H. in the columns of the *West of England Times* recently, gave me one clue, shall we say? The mysterious assault on a young woman, whose home was close to those very railway stations as well as to Bristol Castle—your parents' residence, where you have frequently been staying of late, was another piece that fitted in the puzzle; whilst the number of copies of the *West of England Times* that were found in that same young woman's room helped to draw my thoughts to her. Then your visit to me to-day—it is very simple, you see."

"I suppose so," said H. S. H. with a sigh. "Only it is worse even than you suggest, for that horrid Jane Turner, to whom I had been ever so kind when I was a girl, took a snapshot of me and Mr. Rumboldt standing on the steps of Hôtel des Bains at Boulogne. I saw her doing it and rushed down the steps to stop her. She talked quite nicely then—hypocritical wretch!—and said that perhaps the plate would be no good when it was developed, and if it were she would destroy it. I was not to worry; she would contrive to let me know through the agony column of the *West of England Times*, which—as I was going home to Bristol Castle to stay with my parents—I could see every day, but she had no idea I should have minded, and all that sort of rigmarole. Oh! she is a wicked girl, isn't she, to worry me so?"

And once again the lace handkerchief found its way to the most beautiful pair of blue eyes I think I have ever seen. I could not help smiling, though I was really very sorry for the silly, emotional, dear little thing.

"And instead of reassurance in the *West of England Times*, you found a demand for a secret meeting at a country railway station?"

"Yes! And when I went there—terrified lest I should be seen—Jane Turner did not meet me herself. Her mother came and at once talked of selling the photograph to my husband or to my mother-in-law. She said it was worth four thousand pounds to Jane, and that she had advised her daughter not to sell it to me for less."

"What did you reply?"

"That I hadn't got four thousand pounds," said the Countess ruefully; "so after a lot of argument it was agreed that I was to pay Jane two hundred and fifty pounds a year out of my dress allowance. She would keep the negative as security, but promised never to let anyone see it so long as she got her money regularly. It was also arranged that whenever I stayed with my parents at Bristol Castle, Jane would make appointments to meet me through the columns of the *West of England Times*, and I was to pay up the installments then just as she directed."

I could have laughed, if the whole thing had not been so tragic, for truly the way this silly, harmless little woman had allowed herself to be bullied and blackmailed by a pair of grasping females was beyond belief.

"And this has been going on for over a year," commented Lady Molly gravely.

"Yes, but I never met Jane Turner again: it was always her mother who came."

"You knew her mother before that, I presume?"

"Oh, no. I only knew Jane because she had been sewing-maid at the Castle some few years ago."

"I see," said Lady Molly slowly. "What was the woman like whom you used to meet at the railway stations, and to whom you paid over Miss Turner's money?"

"Oh, I couldn't tell you what she was like. I never saw her properly."

"Never saw her properly?" ejaculated Lady Molly, and it seemed to my well-trained ears as if there was a ring of exultation in my dear lady's voice.

"No," replied the little Countess ruefully. "She always appointed a late hour of the evening, and those little stations on that line are very badly lighted. I had such difficulties getting away from home without exciting comment, and used to beg her to let me meet her at a more convenient hour. But she always refused."

Lady Molly remained thoughtful for a while; then she asked abruptly:

"Why don't you prosecute Jane Turner for blackmail?"

"Oh, I dare not—I dare not!" ejaculated the little Countess, in genuine terror. "My husband would never forgive me, and his female relations would do their best afterwards to widen the breach between us. It was because of the article in the London newspaper about the assault on Jane Turner—the talk of a clue and of startling developments—that I got terrified, and went to Scotland Yard. Oh, no! no! no! Promise me that my name won't be dragged into this case. It would ruin me for ever!"

She was sobbing now; her grief and fear were very pathetic to witness, and she moaned through her sobs:

"Those wicked people know that I daren't risk an exposure, and simply prey on me like vampires because of that. The last time I saw the old woman I told her that I would confess everything to my husband—I couldn't bear to go on like this. But she only laughed; she knew I should never dare."

"When was this?" asked Lady Molly.

"About three weeks ago—just before Jane Turner was assaulted and robbed of the photographs."

"How do you know she was robbed of the photographs?"

"She wrote and told me so," replied the young Countess, who seemed strangely awed now by my dear lady's earnest question. And from a dainty reticule she took a piece of paper, which bore traces of many bitter tears on its crumpled surface. This she handed to Lady Molly, who took it from her. It was a type-written letter, which bore no signature. Lady Molly perused it in silence first, then read its contents out aloud to me:—

> "To H. S. H. the Countess of Hohengebirg.
>
> "You think I have been worrying you the past twelve months about your adventure with Mr. Rumboldt in Boulogne. But it was not me; it was one who has power over me, and who knew about the photograph. He made me act as I did. But whilst I kept the photo you were safe. Now he has assaulted me and nearly killed me, and taken the negative away. I can, and will, get it out of him again, but it will mean a large sum down. Can you manage one thousand pounds?"

"When did you get this?" asked Lady Molly.

"Only a few days ago," replied the Countess. "And oh! I have been enduring agonies of doubt and fear for the past three weeks, for I had heard nothing from Jane since the assault, and I wondered what had happened."

"You have not sent a reply, I hope."

"No. I was going to, when I saw the article in the London paper, and the fear that all had been discovered threw me into such a state of agony that I came straight up to town and saw the gentleman at Scotland Yard, who sent me on to you. Oh!" she entreated again and again, "you won't do anything that will cause a scandal! Promise me—promise me! I believe I should commit suicide rather than face it—and I could find a thousand pounds."

"I don't think you need do either," said Lady Molly. "Now, may I think over the whole matter quietly to myself," she added, "and talk it over with my friend here? I may be able to let you have some good news shortly."

She rose, intimating kindly that the interview was over. But it was by no means that yet, for there was still a good deal of entreaty and a great many tears on the one part, and reiterated kind assurances on the other. However when, some ten minutes later, the dainty clouds of lace and chiffon were finally wafted out of our office, we both felt that the poor, harmless, unutterably foolish little lady looked distinctly consoled and more happy than she had been for the past twelve months.

4

"Yes! she has been an utter little goose," Lady Molly was saying to me an hour later when we were having luncheon; "but that Jane Turner is a remarkably clever girl."

"I suppose you think, as I do, that the mysterious elderly female, who seems to have impersonated the mother all through, was an accomplice of Jane Turner's, and that the assault was a put-up job between them," I said. "Inspector Danvers will be delighted—for this theory is a near approach to his own."

"H'm!" was all the comment vouchsafed on my remark.

"I am sure it was Arthur Cutbush, the girl's sweetheart, after all," I retorted hotly, "and you'll see that, put to the test of sworn evidence, his alibi at the time of the assault itself won't hold good. Moreover, now," I added triumphantly, "we have knowledge which has been lacking all along—the motive."

"Ah!" said my lady, smiling at my enthusiasm, "that's how you argue, Mary, is it?"

"Yes, and in my opinion the only question in doubt is whether Arthur Cutbush acted in collusion with Jane Turner or against her."

"Well, suppose we go and elucidate that point—and some others— at once," concluded Lady Molly as she rose from the table.

She decided to return to Bristol that same evening. We were going by the 8.50 p.m., and I was just getting ready—the cab being already at the door—when I was somewhat startled by the sudden appearance into my room of an old lady, very beautifully dressed, with snow-white hair dressed high above a severe, interesting face.

A merry, rippling laugh issuing from the wrinkled mouth, and a closer scrutiny on my part, soon revealed the identity of my dear lady, dressed up to look like an extremely dignified *grande dame* of the old school, whilst a pair of long, old-fashioned earrings gave a curious, foreign look to her whole appearance.

I didn't quite see why she chose to arrive at the Grand Hotel, Bristol, in that particular disguise, nor why she entered our names in the hotel book as Grand Duchess and Princess Amalie von Starkburg, from Germany; nor did she tell me anything that evening.

But by the next afternoon, when we drove out together in a fly, I was well up in the *rôle* which I had to play. My lady had made me dress in a very rich black silk dress of her own, and ordered me to do my hair in a somewhat frumpish fashion, with a parting, and a "bun" at the back. She herself looked more like Royalty travelling incognito than ever, and no wonder small children and tradesmen's boys stared open-mouthed when we alighted from our fly outside one of the mean-looking little houses in Bread Street.

In answer to our ring, a smutty little servant opened the door, and my lady asked her if Miss Jane Turner lived here and if she were in.

"Yes, Miss Turner lives here, and it bein' Thursday and early closin' she's home from business."

"Then please tell her," said Lady Molly in her grandest manner, "that the Dowager Grand Duchess of Starkburg-Nauheim and the Princess Amalie desire to see her."

The poor little maid nearly fell backwards with astonishment. She gasped an agitated "Lor!" and then flew down the narrow passage and up the steep staircase, closely followed by my dear lady and myself.

On the first-floor landing the girl, with nervous haste, knocked at a door, opened it and muttered half audibly:

"Ladies to see you, miss!"

Then she fled incontinently upstairs. I have never been able to decide whether that little girl thought that we were lunatics, ghosts, or criminals.

But already Lady Molly had sailed into the room, where Miss Jane Turner apparently had been sitting reading a novel. She jumped up when we entered, and stared open-eyed at the gorgeous apparitions. She was not a bad-looking girl but for the provoking, bold look in her black eyes, and the general slatternly appearance of her person.

"Pray do not disturb yourself, Miss Turner," said Lady Molly in broken English, as she sank into a chair, and beckoned me to do likewise. "Pray sit down—I vill be brief. You have a compromising photograph—is it not?—of my daughter-in-law ze Countess of Hohengebirg. I am ze Grand Duchess of Starkburg-Nauheim—zis is my daughter, ze Princess Amalie. We are here incognito. You understand? Not?"

And, with inimitable elegance of gesture, my dear lady raised a pair of "starers" to her eyes and fixed them on Jane Turner's quaking figure.

Never had I seen suspicion, nay terror, depicted so plainly on a young face, but I will do the girl the justice to state that she pulled herself together with marvellous strength of will.

She fought down her awed respect of this great lady; or rather shall I say that the British middle-class want of respect for social superiority, especially if it be foreign, now stood her in good stead?

"I don't know what you are talking about," she said with an arrogant toss of the head.

"Zat is a lie, is it not?" rejoined Lady Molly calmly, as she drew from her reticule the typewritten letter which Jane Turner had sent to the Countess of Hohengebirg. "Zis you wrote to my daughter-in-law; ze letter reached me instead of her. It interests me much. I vill give you two tousend pounds for ze photograph of her and Mr.—er—Rumboldt. You vill sell it to me for zat, is it not?"

The production of the letter had somewhat cowed Jane's bold spirit. But she was still defiant.

"I haven't got the photograph here," she said.

"Ah, no! but you vill get it—yes?" said my lady, quietly replacing the letter in her reticule. "In ze letter you offer to get it for tousend pound. I vill give you two tousend. To-day is a holiday for you. You vill get ze photograph from ze gentleman—not? And I vill vait here till you come back."

Whereupon she rearranged her skirts round her and folded her hands placidly, like one prepared to wait.

"I haven't got the photograph," said Jane Turner, doggedly, "and I can't get it to-day. The—the person who has it doesn't live in Bristol."

"No? Ah! but quite close, isn't it?" rejoined my lady, placidly. "I can vait all ze day."

"No, you shan't!" retorted Jane Turner, whose voice now shook with obvious rage or fear—I knew not which. "I can't get the photograph to-day—so there! And I won't sell it to you—I won't. I don't want your two thousand pounds. How do I know you are not an imposter?"

"From zis, my good girl," said Lady Molly, quietly; "that if I leave zis room wizout ze photograph, I go straight to ze police with zis letter, and you shall be prosecuted by ze Grand Duke, my son, for blackmailing his wife. You see, I am not like my daughter-in-law; I am not afraid of a scandal. So you vill fetch ze photograph—isn't it? I and ze Princess Amalie vill vait for it here. Zat is your bedroom—not?" she added, pointing to a door which obviously gave on an inner room. "Vill you put on your hat and go at once, please? Two tousend pound or two years in prison—you have ze choice—isn't it?"

Jane Turner tried to keep up her air of defiance, looking Lady Molly full in the face; but I who watched her could see the boldness in her eyes gradually giving place to fear, and then to terror and even despair; the girl's face seemed literally to grow old as I looked at it—pale, haggard, and drawn—whilst Lady Molly kept her stern, luminous eyes fixed steadily upon her.

Then, with a curious, wild gesture, which somehow filled me with a nameless fear, Jane Turner turned on her heel and ran into the inner room.

There followed a moment of silence. To me it was tense and agonising. I was straining my ears to hear what was going on in that inner room. That my dear lady was not as callous as she wished to appear was shown by the strange look of expectancy in her beautiful eyes.

The minutes sped on—how many I could not afterwards have said. I was conscious of a clock ticking monotonously over the shabby mantelpiece, of an errand boy outside shouting at the top of his voice, of the measured step of the cab horse which had brought us hither being walked up and down the street.

Then suddenly there was a violent crash, as of heavy furniture being thrown down. I could not suppress a scream, for my nerves by now were terribly on the jar.

"Quick, Mary—the inner room!" said Lady Molly. "I thought the girl might do that."

I dared not pause in order to ask what "that" meant, but flew to the door.

It was locked.

"Downstairs—quick!" commanded my lady. "I ordered Danvers to be on the watch outside."

You may imagine how I flew, and how I blessed my dear lady's forethought in the midst of her daring plan, when, having literally torn open the front door, I saw Inspector Danvers in plain clothes, calmly patrolling the street. I beckoned to him—he was keeping a sharp look-out—and together we ran back into the house.

Fortunately, the landlady and the servant were busy in the basement, and had neither heard the crash nor seen me run in search of Danvers. My dear lady was still alone in the dingy parlour, stooping against the door of the inner room, her ear glued to the keyhole.

"Not too late, I think," she whispered hurriedly. "Break it open, Danvers."

Danvers, who is a great, strong man, soon put his shoulder to the rickety door, which yielded to the first blow.

The sight which greeted us filled me with horror, for I had never seen such a tragedy before. The wretched girl, Jane Turner, had tied a rope to a ring in the ceiling, which I suppose at one time held a hanging lamp; the other end of that rope she had formed into a slip-noose, and passed round her neck.

She had apparently climbed on to a table, and then used her best efforts to end her life by kicking the table away from under her. This was the crash which we had heard, and which had caused us to come to her rescue. Fortunately, her feet had caught in the back of a chair close by; the slip-noose was strangling her, and her face was awful to behold, but she was not dead.

Danvers soon got her down. He is a first-aid man, and has done these terrible jobs before. As soon as the girl had partially recovered, Lady Molly sent him and me out of the room. In the dark and dusty parlour, where but a few moments ago I had played my small part in a grim comedy, I now waited to hear what the sequel to it would be.

Danvers had been gone some time, and the shades of evening were drawing in; outside, the mean-looking street looked particularly dreary. It was close on six o'clock when at last I heard the welcome rustle of silks, the opening of a door, and at last my dear lady—looking grave but serene—came out of the inner room, and, beckoning to me, without a word led the way out of the house and into the fly, which was still waiting at the door.

"We'll send a doctor to her," were her first words as soon as we were clear of Bread Street. "But she is quite all right now, save that she wants a sleeping draught. Well, she has been punished enough, I think. She won't try her hand at blackmailing again."

"Then the photograph never existed?" I asked amazed.

"No; the plate was a failure, but Jane Turner would not thus readily give up the idea of getting money out of the poor, pusillanimous Countess. We know how she succeeded in terrorizing that silly little woman. It is wonderful how cleverly a girl like that worked out such a complicated scheme, all alone."

"All alone?"

"Yes; there was no one else. She was the elderly woman who used to meet the Countess, and who rang at the front door of the

Weston apartment-house. She arranged the whole of the *mise en scène* of the assault on herself, all alone, and took everybody in with it—it was so perfectly done. She planned and executed it because she was afraid that the little Countess would be goaded into confessing her folly to her husband, or to her own parents, when a prosecution for blackmail would inevitably follow. So she risked everything on a big *coup*, and almost succeeded in getting a thousand pounds from Her Serene Highness, meaning to reassure her, as soon as she had the money, by the statement that the negative and prints had been destroyed. But the appearance of the Grand Duchess of Starkburg-Nauheim this afternoon frightened her into an act of despair. Confronted with the prosecution she dreaded and with the prison she dared not face, she, in a mad moment, attempted to take her life."

"I suppose now the whole matter will be hushed up."

"Yes," replied Lady Molly with a wistful sigh. "The public will never know who assaulted Jane Turner."

She was naturally a little regretful at that. But it was a joy to see her the day when she was able to assure Her Serene Highness the Countess of Hohengebirg that she need never again fear the consequences of that fatal day's folly.

A CASTLE IN BRITTANY

1

Yes! we are just back from our holiday, my dear lady and I—a well-earned holiday, I can tell you that.

We went to Porhoët, you know—a dear little village in the hinterland of Brittany, not very far from the coast; an enchanting spot, hidden away in a valley, bordered by a mountain stream, wild, romantic, picturesque—Brittany, in fact.

We had discovered the little place quite accidentally last year, in the course of our wanderings, and stayed there then about three weeks, laying the foundations of that strange adventure which reached its culminating point just a month ago.

I don't know if the story will interest you, for Lady Molly's share in the adventure was purely a private one and had nothing whatever to do with her professional work. At the same time it illustrates in a very marked manner that extraordinary faculty which she possesses of divining her fellow-creatures' motives and intentions.

We had rooms and *pension* in the dear little convent on the outskirts of the village, close to the quaint church and the picturesque presbytery, and soon we made the acquaintance of the Curé, a simple-minded, kindly old man, whose sorrow at the thought that two such charming English ladies as Lady Molly and myself should be heretics was more than counter-balanced by his delight in having someone of the "great outside world"—as he called it—to talk to, whilst he told us quite ingenuously something of his own

simple life, of this village which he loved, and also of his parishio-
ners.

One personality among the latter occupied his thoughts and
conversation a great deal, and I must say interested us keenly. It
was that of Miss Angela de Genneville, who owned the magnificent château of Porhoët, one of the seven wonders of architectural
France. She was an Englishwoman by birth—being of a Jersey family—and was immensely wealthy, her uncle, who was also her god-
father, having bequeathed to her the largest cigar factory in St.
Heliers, besides three-quarters of a million sterling.

To say that Miss de Genneville was eccentric was but to put it
mildly; in the village she was generally thought to be quite mad.
The Curé vaguely hinted that a tragic love story was at the bottom
of all her eccentricities. Certain it is that, for no apparent reason,
and when she was still a youngish woman, she had sold the Jersey
business and realised the whole of her fortune. After two years of
continuous travelling, she came to Brittany on a visit to her sister—the widowed Marquise de Terhoven, who owned a small property close to Porhoët, and lived there in retirement and poverty
with her only son, Amédé.

Miss Angela de Genneville was agreeably taken with the beauty
and quietude of this remote little village. The beautiful château of
Porhoët being for sale at the time, she bought it, took out letters of
naturalization, became a French subject, and from that moment
never went outside the precincts of her newly acquired domain.

She never returned to England, and, with the exception of the
Curé and her own sister and nephew, saw no one beyond her small
retinue of servants.

But the dear old Curé thought all the world of her, for she was
supremely charitable to him and to the poor, and scarcely a day
passed but he told us something either of her kindness or of her
eccentric ways. One day he arrived at the convent at an unaccustomed hour; we had just finished our simple *déjeuner* of steaming
coffee and rolls when we saw him coming towards us across the
garden.

That he was excited and perturbed was at once apparent by his hurried gait and by the flush on his kindly face. He bade us a very hasty "Good morning, my daughters!" and plunged abruptly into his subject. He explained with great volubility, which was intended to mask his agitation, that he was the bearer of an invitation to the charming English lady—a curious invitation, ah, yes! perhaps!—Mademoiselle de Genneville—very eccentric—but she is in great trouble—in very serious trouble—and very ill too, now—poor lady—half paralysed and feeble—yes, feeble in the brain—and then her nephew, the Marquis Amédé de Terhoven—such a misguided young man—has got into bad company in that den of wickedness called Paris—since then it has been debts—always debts—his mother is so indulgent!—too indulgent! but an only son!—the charming English ladies would understand. It was very sad—very, very sad—and no wonder Mademoiselle de Genneville was very angry. She had paid Monsieur le Marquis' debts once, twice, three times—but now she will not pay any more—but she is in great trouble and wants a friend—a female friend, one of her own country, she declares—for he himself, alas! was only a poor *curé de village*, and did not understand great ladies and their curious ways. It would be true Christian charity if the charming English lady would come and see Mademoiselle.

"But her own sister, the Marquise?" suggested Lady Molly, breaking in on the old man's volubility.

"Ah! her sister, of course," he replied with a sigh. "Madame la Marquise—but then she is Monsieur le Marquis' mother, and the charming English lady would understand—a mother's heart, of course—"

"But I am a complete stranger to Miss de Genneville," protested Lady Molly.

"Ah, but Mademoiselle has always remained an Englishwoman at heart," replied the Curé. "She said to me to-day: 'I seem to long for an Englishwoman's handshake, a sober-minded, sensible Englishwoman, to help me in this difficulty. Bring your English friend to me, Monsieur le Curé, if she will come to the assistance of an old woman who has no one to turn to in her distress.'"

Of course, after that I knew that my dear lady would yield. Moreover, she was keenly interested in Miss de Genneville, and without further discussion she told Monsieur le Curé that she was quite ready to accompany him to the château of Porhoët.

2

Of course, I was not present at the interview, but Lady Molly has so often told me all that happened and how it happened, and with such a wealth of picturesque and minute detail, that sometimes I find it difficult to realise that I myself was not there in person.

It seems that Monsieur le Curé himself ushered my lady into the presence of Miss Angela de Genneville. The old lady was not alone when they entered; Madame la Marquise de Terhoven, an elderly, somewhat florid woman, whose features, though distinctly coarse, recalled those of her sister, sat on a high-backed chair close to a table, on which her fingers were nervously drumming a tattoo, whilst in the window embrasure stood a young man whose resemblance to both the ladies at once proclaimed him to Lady Molly's quick perception as the son of the one and nephew of the other—the Marquis de Terhoven, in fact.

Miss de Genneville sat erect in a huge armchair; her face was the hue of yellow wax, the flesh literally shrivelled on the bones, the eyes of a curious, unnatural brilliance; one hand clutched feverishly the arm of her chair, the other, totally paralysed, lay limp and inert on her lap.

"Ah! the Englishwoman at last, thank God!" she said in a high-pitched, strident voice as soon as Lady Molly entered the room. "Come here, my dear, for I have wanted one of your kind badly. A true-hearted Englishwoman is the finest product of God's earth, after all's said and done. *Pardieu!* but I breathe again," she added, as my dear lady advanced somewhat diffidently to greet her, and took the trembling hand which Miss Angela extended to her.

"Sit down close to me," commanded the eccentric old lady, whilst Lady Molly, confused, and not a little angered at finding herself in the very midst of what was obviously a family conclave, was vaguely wondering how soon she could slip away again. But the trembling hand of the paralytic clutched her own slender wrist so tightly, forcing her to sink into a low chair close by, and holding her there as with a grip of steel, that it would have been useless and perhaps cruel to resist.

Satisfied now that her newly found friend, as well as Monsieur le Curé, were prepared to remain by her and to listen to what she had to say, the sick woman turned with a look of violent wrath towards the window embrasure.

"I was just telling that fine nephew of mine that he is counting his chickens before they are hatched. I am not yet dead, as Monsieur my nephew can see; and I have made a will—aye, and placed it where his thievish fingers can never reach it."

The young man, who up to now had been gazing stolidly out of the window, now suddenly turned on his heel, confronting the old woman, with a look of hate gleaming in his eyes.

"We can fight the will," here interposed Madame la Marquise, icily.

"On what grounds?" queried the other.

"That you were paralysed and imbecile when you made it," replied the Marquise, dryly.

Monsieur le Curé, who up to now had been fidgeting nervously with his hat, now raised his hands and eyes up to the ceiling to emphasise the horror which he felt at this callous suggestion. Lady Molly no longer desired to go; the half-paralysed grip on her wrist had relaxed, but she sat there quietly, interested with every fibre of her quick intelligence in the moving drama which was being unfolded before her.

There was a pause now, a silence broken only by the monotonous ticking of a monumental, curious-looking clock which stood in an angle of the room. Miss de Genneville had made no reply to her sister's cruel taunt, but a look, furtive, maniacal, almost dangerous, now crept into her eyes.

Then she addressed the Curé.

"I pray you pen, ink and paper—here, on this table," she requested. Then as he complied with alacrity, she once more turned to her nephew, and pointing to the writing materials:

"Sit down and write, Amédé," she commanded.

"Write what?" he queried.

"A confession, my nephew," said the old woman, with a shrill laugh. "A confession of those little pecaddilloes of yours, which, unless I come to your rescue now, will land you for seven years in a penal settlement, if I mistake not. Eh, my fine nephew?"

"A confession?" retorted Amédé de Terhoven savagely. "Do you take me for a fool?"

"No, my nephew, I take you for a wise man—who understands that his dear aunt will not buy those interesting forgeries, perpetrated by Monsieur le Marquis Amédé de Terhoven, and offered to her by Rubinstein the money-lender, unless that confession is written and signed by you. Write Amédé, write that confession, my dear nephew, if you do not wish to see yourself in the dock on a charge of forging your aunt's name to a bill for one hundred thousand francs."

Amédé muttered a curse between his teeth. Obviously the old woman's shaft had struck home. He knew himself to be in a hopeless plight. It appears that a money-lender had threatened to send the forged bills to Monsieur le Procureur de la République unless they were paid within twenty-four hours, and no one could pay them but Miss de Genneville, who had refused to do it except at the price of this humiliating confession.

A look of intelligence passed between mother and son. Intercepted by Lady Molly and interpreted by her, it seemed to suggest the idea of humouring the old aunt, for the moment, until the forgeries were safely out of the money-lender's hands, then of mollifying her later on, when perhaps she would have forgotten, or sunk deeper into helplessness and imbecility.

As if in answer to his mother's look the young man now said curtly:

"I must know what use you mean to make of the confession if I do write it."

"That will depend on yourself," replied Mademoiselle, dryly. "You may be sure that I will not willingly send my own nephew to penal servitude."

For another moment the young man hesitated, then he sat down, sullen and wrathful, and said:

"I'll write—you may dictate—"

The old woman laughed a short, dry, sarcastic laugh. Then, at her dictation, Amédé wrote:

> "I, Amédé, Marquis de Terhoven, hereby make confession to having forged Mademoiselle Angela de Genneville's name to the annexed bills, thereby obtaining the sum of one hundred thousand francs from Abraham Rubinstein, of Brest."

"Now, Monsieur le Curé, will you kindly witness le Marquis' signature?" said the irascible old lady when Amédé had finished writing; "and you, too, my dear?" she added, turning to Lady Molly.

My dear lady hesitated for a moment. Naturally she did not desire to be thus mixed up in this family feud, but a strange impulse had drawn her sympathy to this eccentric old lady, who, in the midst of her semi-regal splendour seemed so forlorn, between her nephew, who was a criminal and a blackguard, and her sister, who was but little less contemptible.

Obeying this impulse, and also a look of entreaty from the Curé, she affixed her own signature as witness to the document, and this despite the fact that both the Marquise and her son threw her a look of hate which might have made a weaker spirit tremble with foreboding.

Not so Lady Molly. Those very same threatening looks served but to decide her. Then, at Mademoiselle's command, she folded up the document, slipped it into an envelope, sealed it, and finally addressed it to M. le Procureur de la République, resident at Caen.

Amédé watched all these proceedings with eyes that were burning with impotent wrath.

"This letter," now resumed the old lady, more calmly, "will be sent under cover to my lawyer Maître Vendôme, of Paris, who drew up my will, with orders only to post it in case of certain eventualities, which I will explain later on. In the meanwhile, my dear nephew, you may apprise your friend, Abraham Rubinstein, that I will buy back those interesting forgeries of yours on the day on which I hear from Maître Vendôme that he has safely received my letter with this enclosure."

"This is infamous—" here broke in the Marquise, rising in full wrath, unable to control herself any longer. "I'll have you put under restraint as a dangerous lunatic. I—"

"Then, of course, I could not buy back the bills from Rubinstein," rejoined Mademoiselle, calmly.

Then, as the Marquise subsided—cowed, terrified, realising the hopelessness of her son's position—the old lady turned placidly to my dear lady, whilst her trembling fingers once more clutched the slender hand of her newly found English friend.

"I have asked you, my dear, and Monsieur le Curé, to come to me to-day," she said, "because I wish you both to be of assistance to me in the carrying out of my dying wishes. You must promise me most solemnly, both of you, that when I am dead you will carry out these wishes to the letter. Promise!" she added with passionate earnestness.

The promise was duly given by Lady Molly and the old Curé, then Mademoiselle resumed more calmly:

"And now I want you to look at that clock," she said abruptly, with seeming irrelevance. "It is an old heirloom which belonged to the former owners of Porhoët, and which I bought along with the house. You will notice that it is one of the most remarkable pieces of mechanism which brain of man has ever devised, for it has this great peculiarity, that it goes for three hundred and sixty-six days consecutively, keeping most perfect time. When the works have all but run down, the weights—which are enormous—release a certain spring, and the great doors of the case open of themselves, thus allowing the clock to be wound up. After that is done, and the doors pushed to again, no one can open them until another three hundred and sixty-six days have gone by—that is to say, not without breaking the case to pieces."

Lady Molly examined the curious old clock with great attention. Vaguely she guessed already what the drift of the old lady's curious explanations would be.

"Two days ago," continued Mademoiselle, "the clock was open, and Monsieur le Curé wound it up, but before I pushed the doors to again I slipped certain papers into the case—you remember, Monsieur?"

"Yes, Mademoiselle, I remember," responded the old man.

"Those papers were my last will and testament, bequeathing all I possess to the parish of Porhoët," said Miss de Genneville, dryly, "and now the doors of the massive case are closed. No one can get at my will for another three hundred and sixty-four days— no one," she added with a shrill laugh, "not even my nephew, Amédé de Terhoven."

A silence ensued, only broken by the rustle of Madame la Marquise's silk dress as she shrugged her shoulders and gave a short, sarcastic chuckle.

"My dear," resumed Mademoiselle, looking straight into Lady Molly's eager, glowing face, "you must promise me that, three hundred and sixty-four days hence, that is to say on the 20th September next year, you and Monsieur le Curé—or one of you if the other be incapacitated—will be present in this room at this hour when the door of the clock will open. You will then wind up the family heirloom, take out the papers which you will find buried beneath the weights, and hand them over to Maître Vendôme for probate at the earliest opportunity. Monseigneur the Bishop of Caen, the Mayor of this Commune, and the Souspréfet of this Department have all been informed of the contents of my will, and also that it is practically in the keeping of le Curé de Porhoët, who, no doubt, realises what the serious consequences to himself would be if he failed to produce the will at the necessary time."

The poor Curé gasped with terror.

"But—but—but—" he stammered meekly, "I may be forcibly prevented from entering the house—I might be ill or—"

He shuddered with an unavowable fear, then added more calmly:

"I might be unjustly accused then of stealing the will—of defrauding the poor of Porhoët in favour of—Mademoiselle's direct heirs."

"Have no fear, my good friend," said Mademoiselle, dryly; "though I have one foot in the grave I am not quite so imbecile as

my dear sister and nephew here would suggest, and I have provided for every eventuality. If you are ill or otherwise prevented
by outside causes from being present here on the day and hour
named, this charming English lady will be able to replace you. But
if either of you is forcibly prevented from entering this house, or
if, having entered this room, the slightest violence or even pres-
sure is put upon you, or if you should find the clock broken, damaged and—stripped of its contents, all you need do is to apprise
Maître Vendôme of the fact. He will know how to act."

"What would he do?"

"Send a certain confession we all know of to Monsieur le
Procureur de la République," replied the old lady, fixing the young
Marquis Amédé with her irascible eye. "That same confession," she
continued lightly, "Maître Vendôme is instructed to destroy if you,
Monsieur, and my English friend here, and the clock, are all un-
damaged on the eventful day."

There was silence in the great, dark room for awhile, broken
only by the sarcastic chuckle of the enfeebled invalid, tired out
after this harrowing scene, wherein she had pitted her half-
maniacal ingenuity against the greed and rapacity of a conscience-
less roué.

That she had hemmed her nephew and sister in on every side
could not be denied. Lady Molly herself felt somewhat awed at this
weird revenge conceived by the outraged old lady against her grasping relatives.

She was far too interested in the whole drama to give up her
own part in it, and, as she subsequently explained to me, she felt it
her duty to remain the partner and co-worker of the poor Curé in
this dangerous task of securing to the poor of Porhoët the fortune
which otherwise would be squandered away on gaming tables and
race-courses.

For this, and many reasons too complicated to analyse, she
decided to accept her share in the trust imposed upon her by her
newly-found friend.

Neither the Marquise nor her son took any notice of Lady Molly
as she presently took leave of Mademoiselle de Genneville, who,

at the last, made her take a solemn oath that she would stand by the Curé and fulfil the wishes of a dying and much-wronged woman.

Much perturbed, monsieur le Curé went away. Lady Molly went several times after that to the château of Porhoët to see the invalid, who had taken a violent fancy to her. In October we had, perforce, to return to England and to work, and the following spring we had news from the Curé that Mademoiselle de Genneville was dead.

3

Lady Molly had certainly been working too hard, and was in a feeble state of health when we reached Porhoët the following 19th of September, less than twenty-four hours before the eventful moment when the old clock would reveal the will and testament of Mademoiselle de Genneville.

We walked straight from the station to the presbytery, anxious to see the Curé and to make all arrangements for to-morrow's business. To our terrible sorrow and distress, we were informed by the housekeeper that the Curé was very seriously ill at the hospital at Brest, whither he had been removed by the doctor's orders.

This was the first inkling I had that things would not go as smoothly as I had anticipated. Miss de Genneville's dispositions with regard to the sensational disclosure of her will had, to my mind, been so ably taken that it had never struck me until now that the Marquise de Terhoven and her precious son would make a desperate fight before they gave up all thoughts of the coveted fortune.

I imagined the Marquis hemmed in on every side; any violence offered against the Curé or Lady Molly when they entered the château in order to accomplish the task allotted to them being visited by the sending of the confession to Monsieur le Procureur de la République, when prosecution for forgery would immediately follow. Damage to the clock itself would be punished in the same way.

But I had never thought of sudden illnesses, of—heaven help us!—poison or unaccountable accidents to either the Curé or to the woman I loved best in all the world.

No wonder Lady Molly looked pale and fragile as, having thanked the housekeeper, we found our way in silence to the convent where we had once again engaged rooms.

Somehow the hospitality shown us last year had lost something of its cordiality. Moreover, our bedrooms this time did not communicate with one another, but opened out independently on to a stone passage.

The sister who showed us upstairs explained, somewhat shamefacedly, that as the Mother Superior had not expected us, she had let the room which was between our two bedrooms to a lady visitor, who, however, was ill in bed at the present moment.

That sixth sense, of which so much has been said and written, but which I will not attempt to explain, told me plainly enough that we were no longer amidst friends in the convent.

Had bribery been at work? Was the lady visitor a spy set upon our movements by the Terhovens? It was impossible to say. I could no longer chase away the many gloomy forebodings which assailed me the rest of that day and drove away sleep during the night. I can assure you that in my heart I wished all eccentric old ladies and their hidden wills at the bottom of the sea.

My dear lady was apparently also very deeply perturbed; any attempt on my part to broach the subject of Miss de Genneville's will was promptly and authoritatively checked by her. At the same time I knew her well enough to guess that all these nameless dangers which seemed to have crept up round her only served to enhance her determination to carry out her old friend's dying wishes to the letter.

We went to bed quite early; for the first time without that delightful final gossip, when events, plans, surmises and work were freely discussed between us. The unseen lady visitor in the room which separated us acted as a wet blanket on our intimacy.

I stayed with Lady Molly until she was in bed. She hardly talked to me whilst she undressed, but when I kissed her "good-night" she whispered almost inaudibly right into my ear:

"The Terhoven faction are at work. They may waylay you and offer you a bribe to keep me out of the château to-morrow. Pretend to fall in with their views. Accept all bribes and place yourself at their disposal. I must not say more now. We are being spied upon."

That my lady was, as usual, right in her surmises was proved within the next five minutes. I had slipped out of her room, and was just going into mine, when I heard my name spoken hardly above a whisper, whilst I felt my arm gently seized from behind.

An elderly, somewhat florid, woman stood before me attired in a dingy-coloured dressing-gown. She was pointing towards my own bedroom door, implying her desire to accompany me to my room. Remembering my dear lady's parting injunctions, I nodded in acquiescence. She followed me, after having peered cautiously up and down the passage.

Then, when the door was duly closed, and she was satisfied that we were alone, she said very abruptly:

"Miss Granard, tell me! you are poor, eh?—a paid companion to your rich friend, what?"

Still thinking of Lady Molly's commands, I replied with a pathetic sigh.

"Then," said the old lady, eagerly, "would you like to earn fifty thousand francs?"

The eagerness with which I responded "Rather!" apparently pleased her, for she gave a sigh of satisfaction.

"You know the story of my sister's will—of the clock?" she asked eagerly: "of your friend's role in this shameless business?"

Once more I nodded. I knew that my lady had guessed rightly. This was the Marquise de Terhoven, planted here in the convent to gain my confidence, to spy on Lady Molly, and to offer me a bribe.

Now for some clever tactics on my part.

"Can you prevent your friend from being at the château to-morrow before one o'clock?" asked the Marquise.

"Easily," I replied calmly.

"How?"

"She is ill, as you know. The doctor has ordered her a sleeping draught. I administer it. I can arrange that she has a strong dose in the morning instead of her other medicine. She will sleep till the late afternoon."

I rattled this off glibly in my best French. Madame la Marquise heaved a deep sigh of relief.

"Ah! that is good!" she said. "Then listen to me. Do as I tell you, and to-morrow you will be richer by fifty thousand francs. Come to the château in the morning, dressed in your friend's clothes. My son will be there; together you will assist at the opening of the secret doors, and when my son has wound up the old clock himself, he will place fifty thousand francs in your hands."

"But Monsieur le Curé?" I suggested tentatively.

"He is ill," she replied curtly.

But as she spoke these three words there was such an evil sneer in her face, such a look of cruel triumph in her eyes, that all my worst suspicions were at once confirmed.

Had these people's unscrupulous rapacity indeed bribed some needy country practitioner to put the Curé temporarily out of the way? It was too awful to think of, and I can tell you that I needed all my presence of mind, all my desire to act my part bravely and intelligently to the end, not to fly from this woman in horror.

She gave me a few more instructions with regard to the services which she and her precious son would expect of me on the morrow. It seems that, some time before her death, Miss de Genneville had laid strict injunctions on two of her most trusted men-servants to remain in the château, and to be on the watch on the eventful 20th day of September of this year, lest any serious violence be done to the English lady or to the Curé. It was with a view to allay any suspicion which might arise in the minds of these two men that the Marquis desired me to impersonate Lady Molly to-morrow, and to enter with him—on seemingly friendly terms—the room where stood the monumental clock.

For these services, together with those whereby Lady Molly was to be sent into a drugged sleep whilst the theft of the will was being carried through, I—Mary Granard—was to receive from Monsieur le Marquis de Terhoven the sum of fifty thousand francs.

All these matters being settled to this wicked woman's apparent satisfaction, she presently took hold of both my hands, shook them warmly, and called me her dearest friend; assured me of everlasting gratitude, and finally, to my intense relief, slipped noiselessly out of my room.

4

I surmised—I think correctly—that Madame la Marquise would spend most of the night with her ear glued to the thin partition which separated her room from that of Lady Molly; so I did not dare to go and report myself and the momentous conversation which I had just had, and vaguely wondered when I should have an opportunity of talking matters over with my dear lady without feeling that a spy was at my heels.

The next morning when I went into her room, to my boundless amazement—and before I had time to utter a word—she moaned audibly, as if in great pain, and said feebly, but very distinctly:

"Oh, Mary! I'm so glad you've come. I feel terribly ill. I haven't had a wink of sleep all night, and I am too weak to attempt to get up."

Fortunately my perceptions had not been dulled by the excitement of the past few hours, and I could see that she was not so ill as she made out. Her eyes sought mine as I approached her bed, and her lips alone framed the words which I believed I interpreted correctly.

"Do as they want. I stay in bed. Will explain later."

Evidently she had reason to think that we were being closely watched; but what I could not understand was, what did she expect would happen if she herself were not present when the opening of the clock door would disclose the will? Did she want me to snatch the document: to bear the brunt of the Terhovens' wrath and disappointment? It was not like her to be afraid of fulfilling a duty, however dangerous that fulfilment might prove; and it certainly was not like her to break a promise given to a dying person.

But, of course, my business was to obey. Assuming that our movements were being watched, I poured out a dose of medicine for my dear lady, which she took and then fell back on her pillows as if exhausted.

"I think I could sleep now, Mary," she said; "but wake me later on; I must be at the château by twelve o'clock, you know."

As one of Lady Molly's boxes was in my room, I had no difficulty in arraying myself in some of her clothes. Thus equipped and closely veiled, still ignorant of my lady's plans, anxious, but determined to obey like a soldier, blindly and unquestioningly, I made my way to the château a little before noon.

An old butler opened the door in answer to my ring, and in the inner hall sat the Marquise de Terhoven, whilst her son was walking agitatedly up and down.

"Ah! here comes my lady," said the Marquise, with easy unconcern. "You have come, my lady," she added, rising and taking my hand, "to perform a duty which will rob my son of a fortune which by right should have been his. We can put no hindrance in your way, under penalty of an appalling disgrace which would then fall on my son; moreover, my late sister has filled this house with guards and spies. So, believe me, you need have no fear. You can perform your duty undisturbed. Perhaps you will not object to my son keeping you company. My precious sister had the door of her room removed before her death and a curtain put in its stead," she concluded with what was intended to be the sneer of a disappointed fortune-hunter, "so the least call from you will bring her spies to your assistance."

Without a word the Marquis and I bowed to one another, then, preceded by the old family butler, we went up the monumental staircase to what I suppose had been the eccentric old lady's room.

The butler drew the *portière* curtain aside and he remained in the corridor whilst we went within. There stood the massive clock exactly as my lady had often described it to me. It was ticking with slow and deep-toned majesty.

Monsieur le Marquis pointed to an armchair for me. He was obviously in a state of terrible nerve-tension. He could not sit still, and his fingers were incessantly clasped and unclasped with a curious, febrile movement, which betrayed his intense agitation.

I was about to make a remark when he abruptly seized my wrist, placed one finger to his lips, and pointed in the direction of the *portière.* Apparently he thought that someone was on the watch outside, but the clock itself was so placed that it could not be seen by anyone who was not actually in the room.

After that we were both silent, whilst that old piece of mechanism ticked on relentlessly, still hiding the secret which it contained.

I would have given two years' salary to know what Lady Molly would have wished me to do. Frankly, I fully expected to see her walk in at any moment. I could not bring myself to believe that she meant to shirk her duty.

But she had said to me, "Fall in with their views," So that when, presently, the Marquis beckoned to me across the room to come and examine the clock, I obeyed readily enough. I felt, by that time, as if my entire body was stuffed with needles and pins, which were pricking my nerves and skin until I could have yelled with the agony of the sensation.

I walked across the room as if in a dream, and looked at the curious clock which, in less than fifteen minutes, would reveal its hidden secret. I suppose cleverer people than poor Mary Granard could enter into long philosophical disquisitions as to this dumb piece of mechanism which held the fate of this ruined, unscrupulous gambler safely within its doors; but I was only conscious of that incessant tick, tick, tick, whilst my eyes literally ached with staring at the door.

I don't know now how it all happened, for, of course, I was taken unawares; but the next moment I found myself quite helpless, hardly able to breathe, for a woolen scarf was being wound round my mouth, whilst two strong arms encircled my body so that I could not move.

"This is only a protection for myself, my dear Miss Granard," a trembling voice whispered in my ear; "keep quite still; no harm will come to you. In ten minutes you shall have your fifty thousand francs in your pocket, and can walk unconcernedly out of the château. Neither your English lady nor Monsieur le Curé can say that they suffered any violence, nor will the clock be damaged. What happens after that I care not. The law cannot wrest the old fool's fortune from me, once I have destroyed her accursed will."

To begin to tell you what passed in my mind then were an impossibility. Did I actually guess what would happen, and what my dear lady had planned? Or was it merely the ingrafted sympathy which exists between her and me which caused me to act blindly in accordance with her wishes?

"Fall in with their views. Take their bribes," she had said, and I—like a soldier—obeyed this command to the letter.

I remained absolutely still, scarcely moving an eyelid as I watched the face of the clock, the minutes speeding on—now three—now five—now ten—

I could hear the Marquis' stertorous breathing close beside me.

Was I dreaming, or did I really see now a dark line—the width of a hair—between the massive double doors of the clock case? Oh, how my pulses throbbed!

That dark line was widening perceptibly. The doors were slowly opening! For the moment I almost felt in sympathy with the blackguard who was on the watch with me. His agitation must have been the most exquisite torture.

Now we could distinctly see the glimmer of white paper—not pressed down by the ponderous weights, but lying loosely just inside the doors; and anon, as the aperture widened, the papers fell out just at my feet.

With a smothered, gurgling exclamation which I will not attempt to describe, the Marquis literally fell on that paper, like a hungry wild beast upon its prey. He was on his knees before me, and I could see that the paper was a square envelope, which, with a trembling hand, he tore open.

It contained a short document whereon the signature "Amédé de Terhoven" was clearly visible. It was the confession of forgery made by the young Marquis just a year ago; there were also a few banknotes: some hundred thousand francs, perhaps. The young man threw them furiously aside, and once more turned to the clock. The doors were wide open, but they revealed nothing save the huge and complicated mechanism of the clock.

Mademoiselle de Genneville—eccentric and far-seeing to the last—had played this gigantic hoax on her scheming relatives.

Whilst they directed all their unscrupulous energies towards trying to obtain possession of her will in one place, she had calmly
put it securely somewhere else.

Meantime, Monsieur le Marquis had sufficient presence of
mind, and, I must own, sufficient dignity, not only to release me
from my bonds but also to offer me the fifty thousand francs which
he had promised me.

"I can wind up the clock now," he said dully, "and you can walk
straight out of this place. No one need know that you impersonated your friend. She, no doubt, knew of this—hoax; therefore we
found the scheme to keep her out of the way so easy of accom-
plishment. It was a grisly joke, wasn't it? How the old witch must
be chortling in her grave!"

Needless to say, I did not take his money. He escorted me downstairs silently, subdued, no doubt, by the spirit of hatred which
had followed him up from the land of shadows.

He even showed no surprise when, on reaching the hall, he was
met by his late aunt's lawyer, Maître Vendôme, and also by Lady
Molly, who had just arrived. Madame la Marquise de Terhoven was
nowhere to be seen.

My dear lady smiled at me approvingly, and when I came near
her she contrived to draw me aside and to whisper hurriedly:

"You have done admirably, Mary. I came to fetch you. But now
that this young blackguard is thoroughly outwitted, we may as well
go, for our work here is done."

The Marquis did not even glance at her as she slightly bowed
her head to him, took leave of Maître Vendôme, and finally walked
out of the château with me.

As soon as we were out in the open air I begged for an explanation.

"Maître Vendôme has Mademoiselle's will," she replied. "She
had enjoined him to read it in the château to-day in the presence
of the three trustees appointed for the poor of Porhoët, who inherit all her wealth."

"And the Terhovens?" I asked.

"They've got his confession back," she said dryly, "and they will
receive an annuity from the trustees."

"And you knew this all along?" I rejoined somewhat reproach-fully.

"Yes, so did the Curé, but Mademoiselle made me swear a most solemn oath not to reveal her secret even to you; she was so afraid of the machinations of the Terhovens. You see," continued Lady Molly, smiling at my eagerness, "Miss de Genneville possessed the ancient key wherewith she could open the clock case at any time. Obviously, even so perfect a piece of mechanism might go wrong, when examination and re-adjustment of the works would be nec-essary. After the family conclave wherein she had announced that her will was hidden in the clock, I—at my next interview with her—begged her to modify this idea, to send her will to her solicitor, but to leave the Terhovens under the impression that it was still lying in its strange hiding place. At first she refused to listen to me or to discuss the subject, but I am happy to say that I finally suc-ceeded in persuading her, with what result you already know."

"But poor Monsieur le Curé!" I ejaculated.

Her bright eyes gleamed with merriment.

"Oh! that was a final little hoax. He himself, poor dear, was afraid lest he might blurt out the whole thing. His illness was partly a sham, and he is quite all right again now, but the doctor at the Brest hospital is a great friend of his, and is keeping him there until all this business has blown over."

"I was the only one who was kept in the dark," I concluded rue-fully.

"Yes, Mary, dear," said my dear lady, gently; "it was a promise, remember. But I never thought that we should get so much excite-ment outside our own professional work."

It certainly had been a non-professional experience; but here, too, as in the detection of crime, her keen intuition had proved more than a match for an unscrupulous blackguard, and certainly on the 20th day of September last I lived through the most excit-ing ten minutes of my life.

A CHRISTMAS TRAGEDY

1

It was a fairly merry Christmas party, although the surliness of our host somewhat marred the festivities. But imagine two such beautiful young women as my own dear lady and Margaret Ceely, and a Christmas Eve Cinderella in the beautiful ball-room at Clevere Hall, and you will understand that even Major Ceely's well-known cantankerous temper could not altogether spoil the merriment of a good, old-fashioned, festive gathering.

It is a far cry from a Christmas Eve party to a series of cattle-maiming outrages, yet I am forced to mention these now, for although they were ultimately proved to have no connection with the murder of the unfortunate Major, yet they were undoubtedly the means whereby the miscreant was enabled to accomplish the horrible deed with surety, swiftness, and—as it turned out afterwards—a very grave chance of immunity.

Everyone in the neighbourhood had been taking the keenest possible interest in those dastardly outrages against innocent animals. They were either the work of desperate ruffians who stick at nothing in order to obtain a few shillings, or else of madmen with weird propensities for purposeless crimes.

Once or twice suspicious characters had been seen lurking about in the fields, and on more than one occasion a cart was heard in the middle of the night driving away at furious speed. Whenever this occurred the discovery of a fresh outrage was sure to follow, but, so far, the miscreants had succeeded in baffling not only the police, but also the many farm hands who had formed themselves into a band of volunteer watchmen, determined to bring the cattle maimers to justice.

We had all been talking about these mysterious events during the dinner which preceded the dance at Clevere Hall; but later on, when the young people had assembled, and when the first strains of "The Merry Widow" waltz had set us aglow with prospective enjoyment, the unpleasant topic was wholly forgotten.

The guests went away early, Major Ceely, as usual, doing nothing to detain them; and by midnight all of us who were staying in the house had gone up to bed.

My dear lady and I shared a bedroom and dressing-room together, our windows giving on the front. Clevere Hall is, as you know, not very far from York, on the other side of Bishopthorpe, and is one of the finest old mansions in the neighbourhood, its only disadvantage being that, in spite of the gardens being very extensive in the rear, the front of the house lies very near the road.

It was about two hours after I had switched off the electric light and called out "Good-night" to my dear lady, that something roused me out of my first sleep. Suddenly I felt very wide-awake, and sat up in bed. Most unmistakably—though still from some considerable distance along the road—came the sound of a cart being driven at unusual speed.

Evidently my dear lady was also awake. She jumped out of bed and, drawing aside the curtains, looked out of the window. The same idea had, of course, flashed upon us both, at the very moment of waking: all the conversations anent the cattle-maimers and their cart, which we had heard since our arrival at Clevere, recurring to our minds simultaneously.

I had joined Lady Molly beside the window, and I don't know how many minutes we remained there in observation, not more than two probably, for anon the sound of the cart died away in the distance along a side road. Suddenly we were startled with a terrible cry of "Murder! Help! Help!" issuing from the other side of the house, followed by an awful, deadly silence. I stood there near

the window shivering with terror, while my dear lady, having already turned on the light, was hastily slipping into some clothes.

The cry had, of course, aroused the entire household, but my
dear lady was even then the first to get downstairs, and to reach
the garden door at the back of the house, whence the weird and
despairing cry had undoubtedly proceeded.

That door was wide open. Two steps lead from it to the terraced walk which borders the house on that side, and along these
steps Major Ceely was lying, face downwards, with arms outstretched, and a terrible wound between his shoulder-blades.

A gun was lying close by—his own. It was easy to conjecture
that he, too, hearing the rumble of the wheels, had run out, gun in
hand, meaning, no doubt, to effect, or at least to help, in the cap-
ture of the escaping criminals. Someone had been lying in wait for
him; that was obvious—someone who had perhaps waited and
watched for this special opportunity for days, or even weeks, in
order to catch the unfortunate man unawares.

Well, it were useless to recapitulate all the various little incidents which occurred from the moment when Lady Molly and the
butler first lifted the Major's lifeless body from the terrace steps
until that instant when Miss Ceely, with remarkable coolness and
presence of mind, gave what details she could of the terrible event
to the local police inspector and to the doctor, both hastily summoned.

These little incidents, with but slight variations, occur in every
instance when a crime has been committed. The broad facts alone
are of weird and paramount interest.

Major Ceely was dead. He had been stabbed with amazing sure-
ness and terrible violence in the back. The weapon used must have
been some sort of heavy, clasp knife. The murdered man was now
lying in his own bedroom upstairs, even as the Christmas bells on
that cold, crisp morning sent cheering echoes through the stillness of the air.

We had, of course, left the house, as had all the other guests.
Everyone felt the deepest possible sympathy for the beautiful young

girl who had been so full of the joy of living but a few hours ago, and was now the pivot round which revolved the weird shadow of tragedy, of curious suspicions and of an ever-growing mystery. But at such times all strangers, acquaintances, and even friends in a house, are only an additional burden to an already overwhelming load of sorrow and of trouble.

We took up our quarters at the "Black Swan," in York. The local superintendent, hearing that Lady Molly had been actually a guest at Clevere on the night of the murder, had asked her to remain in the neighbourhood.

There was no doubt that she could easily obtain the chief's consent to assist the local police in the elucidation of this extraordinary crime. At this time both her reputation and her remarkable powers were at their zenith, and there was not a single member of the entire police force in the kingdom who would not have availed himself gladly of her help when confronted with a seemingly impenetrable mystery.

That the murder of Major Ceely threatened to become such no one could deny. In cases of this sort, when no robbery of any kind has accompanied the graver crime, it is the duty of the police and also of the coroner to try to find out, first and foremost, what possible motive there could be behind so cowardly an assault; and among motives, of course, deadly hatred, revenge, and animosity stand paramount.

But here the police were at once confronted with the terrible difficulty, not of discovering whether Major Ceely had an enemy at all, but rather which, of all those people who owed him a grudge, hated him sufficiently to risk hanging for the sake of getting him out of the way.

As a matter of fact, the unfortunate Major was one of those miserable people who seem to live in a state of perpetual enmity with everything and everybody. Morning, noon and night he grumbled, and when he did not grumble he quarreled either with his own daughter or with the people of his household, or with his neighbours.

I had often heard about him and his eccentric, disagreeable ways from Lady Molly, who had known him for many years. She—like everybody in the county who otherwise would have shunned the old man—kept up a semblance of friendship with him for the sake of the daughter.

Margaret Ceely was a singularly beautiful girl, and as the Major was reputed to be very wealthy, these two facts perhaps combined to prevent the irascible gentleman from living in quite so complete an isolation as he would have wished.

Mammas of marriageable young men vied with one another in their welcome to Miss Ceely at garden parties, dances and bazaars. Indeed, Margaret had been surrounded with admirers ever since she had come out of the schoolroom. Needless to say, the cantankerous Major received these pretenders to his daughter's hand not only with insolent disdain, but at times even with violent opposition.

In spite of this the moths fluttered round the candle, and amongst this venturesome tribe none stood out more prominently than Mr. Laurence Smethick, son of the M.P. for the Pakethorpe division. Some folk there were who vowed that the young people were secretly engaged, in spite of the fact that Margaret was an outrageous flirt and openly encouraged more than one of her crowd of adorers.

Be that as it may, one thing was very certain—namely, that Major Ceely did not approve of Mr. Smethick any more than he did of the others, and there had been more than one quarrel between the young man and his prospective father-in-law.

On that memorable Christmas Eve at Clevere none of us could fail to notice his absence; whilst Margaret, on the other hand, had shown marked predilection for the society of Captain Glynne, who, since the sudden death of his cousin, Viscount Heslington, Lord Ullesthorpe's only son (who was killed in the hunting field last October, if you remember), had become heir to the earldom and its £40,000 a year.

Personally, I strongly disapproved of Margaret's behaviour the night of the dance; her attitude with regard to Mr. Smethick—whose constant attendance on her had justified the rumour that they were engaged—being more than callous.

On that morning of December 24th—Christmas Eve, in fact—the young man had called at Clevere. I remember seeing him just as he was being shown into the boudoir downstairs. A few moments later the sound of angry voices rose with appalling distinctness from that room. We all tried not to listen, yet could not fail to hear Major Ceely's overbearing words of rudeness to the visitor, who, it seems, had merely asked to see Miss Ceely, and had been most unexpectedly confronted by the irascible and extremely disagreeable Major. Of course, the young man speedily lost his temper, too, and the whole incident ended with a very unpleasant quarrel between the two men in the hall, and with the Major peremptorily forbidding Mr. Smethick ever to darken his doors again.

On that night Major Ceely was murdered.

2

Of course, at first, no one attached any importance to this weird coincidence. The very thought of connecting the idea of murder with that of the personality of a bright, good-looking young Yorkshireman like Mr. Smethick seemed, indeed, preposterous, and with one accord all of us who were practically witnesses to the quarrel between the two men, tacitly agreed to say nothing at all about it at the inquest, unless we were absolutely obliged to do so on oath.

In view of the Major's terrible temper, this quarrel, mind you, had not the importance which it otherwise would have had; and we all flattered ourselves that we had well succeeded in parrying the coroner's questions.

The verdict at the inquest was against some person or persons unknown; and I, for one, was very glad that young Smethick's name had not been mentioned in connection with this terrible crime.

Two days later the superintendent at Bishopthorpe sent an urgent telephonic message to Lady Molly, begging her to come to the police-station immediately. We had the use of a motor all the while that we stayed at the "Black Swan," and in less than ten minutes we were bowling along at express speed towards Bishopthorpe.

On arrival we were immediately shown into Superintendent Etty's private room behind the office. He was there talking with Danvers—who had recently come down from London. In a corner of the room, sitting very straight on a high-backed chair, was a youngish woman of the servant class, who, as we entered, cast a quick, and I thought suspicious, glance at us both.

She was dressed in a coat and skirt of shabby-looking black, and although her face might have been called good-looking—for she had fine, dark eyes—her entire appearance was distinctly repellent. It suggested slatternliness in an unusual degree; there were holes in her shoes and in her stockings, the sleeve of her coat was half unsewn, and the braid on her skirt hung in loops all round the bottom. She had very red and very coarse-looking hands, and undoubtedly there was a furtive expression in her eyes, which, when she began speaking, changed to one of defiance.

Etty came forward with great alacrity when my dear lady entered. He looked perturbed, and seemed greatly relieved at sight of her.

"She is the wife of one of the outdoor men at Clevere," he explained rapidly to Lady Molly, nodding in the direction of the young woman, "and she has come here with such a queer tale that I thought you would like to hear it."

"She knows something about the murder?" asked Lady Molly.

"Noa! I didn't say that!" here interposed the woman, roughly, "doan't you go and tell no lies, Master Inspector. I thought as how you might wish to know what my husband saw on the night when the Major was murdered, that's all; and I've come to tell you."

"Why didn't your husband come himself?" asked Lady Molly.

"Oh, Haggett ain't well enough—he—" she began explaining, with a careless shrug of the shoulders, "so to speak—"

"The fact of the matter is, my lady," interposed Etty, "this woman's husband is half-witted. I believe he is only kept on in the garden because he is very strong and can help with the digging. It is because his testimony is so little to be relied on that I wished to consult you as to how we should act in the matter."

"What is his testimony, then?"

"Tell this lady what you have just told us, Mrs. Haggett, will you?" said Etty, curtly.

Again that quick, suspicious glance shot into the woman's eyes. Lady Molly took the chair which Danvers had brought forward for her, and sat down opposite Mrs. Haggett, fixing her earnest, calm gaze upon her.

"There's not much to tell," said the woman, sullenly. "Haggett is certainly queer in his head sometimes—and when he is queer he goes wandering about the place of nights."

"Yes?" said my lady, for Mrs. Haggett had paused awhile and now seemed unwilling to proceed.

"Well!" she resumed with sudden determination, "he had got one of his queer fits on Christmas Eve, and didn't come in till long after midnight. He told me as how he'd seen a young gentleman prowling about the garden on the terrace side. He heard the cry of 'Murder' and 'Help' soon after that, and ran in home because he was frightened."

"Home?" asked Lady Molly, quietly, "where is home?"

"The cottage where we live. Just back of the kitchen garden."

"Why didn't you tell all this to the superintendent before?"

"Because Haggett only told me last night, when he seemed less queer-like. He is mighty silent when the fits are on him."

"Did he know who the gentleman was whom he saw?"

"No, ma'am—I don't suppose he did—leastways he wouldn't say—but—"

"Yes? But?"

"He found this in the garden yesterday," said the woman, holding out a screw of paper which apparently she had held tightly clutched up to now, "and maybe that's what brought Christmas Eve and the murder back to his mind."

Lady Molly took the thing from her, and undid the soiled bit of paper with her dainty fingers. The next moment she held up for Etty's inspection a beautiful ring composed of an exquisitely carved moonstone surrounded with diamonds of unusual brilliance.

At the moment the setting and the stones themselves were marred by scraps of sticky mud which clung to them; the ring obviously having lain on the ground, and perhaps been trampled on for some days, and then been only very partially washed.

"At any rate you can find out the ownership of the ring," commented my dear lady after awhile, in answer to Etty's silent attitude of expectancy. "There would be no harm in that."

Then she turned once more to the woman.

"I'll walk with you to your cottage, if I may," she said decisively, "and have a chat with your husband. Is he at home?"

I thought Mrs. Haggett took this suggestion with marked reluctance. I could well imagine, from her own personal appearance, that her home was most unlikely to be in a fit state for a lady's visit. However, she could, of course, do nothing but obey, and, after a few muttered words of grudging acquiescence, she rose from her chair and stalked towards the door, leaving my lady to follow as she chose.

Before going, however, she turned and shot an angry glance at Etty.

"You'll give me back the ring, Master Inspector," she said with her usual tone of sullen defiance. "'Findings is keepings' you know."

"I am afraid not," replied Etty, curtly; "but there's always the reward offered by Miss Ceely for information which would lead to the apprehension of her father's murderer. You may get that, you know. It is a hundred pounds."

"Yes! I knew that," she remarked dryly, as, without further comment, she finally went out of the room.

3

My dear lady came back very disappointed from her interview with Haggett.

It seems that he was indeed half-witted—almost an imbecile, in fact, with but a few lucid intervals, of which this present day was one. But, of course, his testimony was practically valueless.

He reiterated the story already told by his wife, adding no details. He had seen a young gentleman roaming on the terraced walk

on the night of the murder. He did not know who the young gentleman was. He was going homewards when he heard the cry of "Murder," and ran to his cottage because he was frightened. He picked
up the ring yesterday in the perennial border below the terrace
and gave it to his wife.

Two of these brief statements made by the imbecile were easily
proved to be true, and my dear lady had ascertained this before
she returned to me. One of the Clevere under-gardeners said he had
seen Haggett running home in the small hours of that fateful Christmas morning. He himself had been on the watch for the cattle-
maimers that night, and remembered the little circumstance quite
plainly. He added that Haggett certainly looked to be in a panic.

Then Newby, another outdoor man at the Hall, saw Haggett
pick up the ring in the perennial border and advised him to take it
to the police.

Somehow, all of us who were so interested in that terrible
Christmas tragedy felt strangely perturbed at all this. No names
had been mentioned as yet, but whenever my dear lady and I looked
at one another, or whenever we talked to Etty or Danvers, we all
felt that a certain name, one particular personality, was lurking at
the back of all our minds.

The two men, of course, had no sentimental scruples to worry
them. Taking the Haggett story merely as a clue, they worked diligently on that, with the result that twenty-four hours later Etty
appeared in our private room at the "Black Swan" and calmly informed us that he had just got a warrant out against Mr. Laurence
Smethick on a charge of murder, and was on his way even now to
effect the arrest.

"Mr. Smethick did *not* murder Major Ceely," was Lady Molly's
firm and only comment when she heard the news.

"Well, my lady, that's as it may be!" rejoined Etty, speaking
with that deference with which the entire force invariably addressed my dear lady; "but we have collected a sufficiency of evidence, at any rate, to justify the arrest, and, in my opinion, enough
of it to hang any man. Mr. Smethick purchased the moonstone and
diamond ring at Nicholson's in Coney Street about a week ago. He

was seen abroad on Christmas Eve by several persons, loitering round the gates at Clevere Hall, somewhere about the time when the guests were leaving after the dance, and, again, some few moments after the first cry of 'Murder' had been heard. His own valet admits that his master did not get home that night until long after 2.0 a.m., whilst even Miss Granard here won't deny that there was a terrible quarrel between Mr. Smethick and Major Ceely less than twenty-four hours before the latter was murdered."

Lady Molly offered no remark to this array of facts which Etty thus pitilessly marshalled before us, but I could not refrain from exclaiming:

"Mr. Smethick is innocent, I am sure."

"I hope, for his sake, he may be," retorted Etty, gravely, "but somehow 'tis a pity that he don't seem able to give a good account of himself between midnight and two o'clock that Christmas morning."

"Oh!" I ejaculated, "what does he say about that?"

"Nothing," said the man dryly; "that's just the trouble."

Well, of course, as you who read the papers will doubtless remember, Mr. Laurence Smethick, son of Colonel Smethick, M.P., of Pakethorpe Hall, Yorks, was arrested on the charge of having murdered Major Ceely on the night of December 24th-25th, and, after the usual magisterial inquiry, was duly committed to stand his trial at the next York assizes.

I remember well that, throughout his preliminary ordeal, young Smethick bore himself like one who had given up all hope of refuting the terrible charges brought against him, and, I must say, the formidable number of witnesses which the police brought up against him more than explained that attitude.

Of course, Haggett was not called, but, as it happened, there were plenty of people to swear that Mr. Laurence Smethick was seen loitering round the gates of Clevere Hall after the guests had departed on Christmas Eve. The head gardener, who lives at the lodge actually spoke to him, and Captain Glynne, leaning out of his brougham, was heard to exclaim:

"Hello, Smethick, what are you doing here at this time of night?"

And there were others, too.

To Captain Glynne's credit, be it here recorded, he tried his best to deny having recognized his unfortunate friend in the dark. Pressed by the magistrate, he said obstinately:

"I thought at the time that it was Mr. Smethick standing by the lodge gates, but on thinking the matter over I feel sure that I was mistaken."

On the other hand, what stood dead against young Smethick was, firstly, the question of the ring, and then the fact that he was seen in the immediate neighbourhood of Clevere, both at midnight and again at about two, when some men, who had been on the watch for the cattle-maimers, saw him walking away rapidly in the direction of Pakethorpe.

What was, of course, unexplainable and very terrible to witness was Mr. Smethick's obstinate silence with regard to his own movements during those fatal hours on that night. He did not contradict those who said that they had seen him at about midnight near the gates of Clevere, nor his own valet's statements as to the hour when he returned home. All he said was that he could not account for what he did between the time when the guests left the Hall and he himself went back to Pakethorpe. He realized the danger in which he stood, and what caused him to be silent about a matter which might mean life or death to him could not easily be conjectured.

The ownership of the ring he could not and did not dispute. He had lost it in the grounds of Clevere, he said. But the jeweller in Coney Street swore that he had sold the ring to Mr. Smethick on the 18th of December, whilst it was a well-known and an admitted fact that the young man had not openly been inside the gates of Clevere for over a fortnight before that.

On this evidence Laurence Smethick was committed for trial. Though the actual weapon with which the unfortunate Major had been stabbed had not been found, nor its ownership traced, there was such a vast array of circumstantial evidence against the young man that bail was refused.

He had, on the advice of his solicitor, Mr. Grayson—one of the ablest lawyers in York—reserved his defence, and on that miserable afternoon at the close of the year, we all filed out of the crowded court, feeling terribly depressed and anxious.

4

My dear lady and I walked back to our hotel in silence. Our hearts seemed to weigh heavily within us. We felt mortally sorry for that good-looking young Yorkshireman, who, we were convinced, was innocent, yet at the same time seemed involved in a tangled web of deadly circumstances from which he seemed quite unable to extricate himself.

We did not feel like discussing the matter in the open streets, neither did we make any comment when presently, in a block in the traffic in Coney Street, we saw Margaret Ceely driving her smart dog-cart, whilst sitting beside her, and talking with great earnestness close to her ear, sat Captain Glynne.

She was in deep mourning, and had obviously been doing some shopping, for she was surrounded with parcels; so perhaps it was hypercritical to blame her. Yet somehow it struck me that just at the moment when there hung in the balance the life and honour of a man with whose name her own had oft been linked by popular rumour, it showed more than callous contempt for his welfare to be seen driving about with another man who, since his sudden access to fortune, had undoubtedly become a rival in her favours.

When we arrived at the "Black Swan," we were surprised to hear that Mr. Grayson had called to see my dear lady, and was upstairs waiting.

Lady Molly ran up to our sitting-room and greeted him with marked cordiality. Mr. Grayson is an elderly dry-looking man, but he looked visibly affected, and it was some time before he seemed able to plunge into the subject which had brought him hither. He fidgeted in his chair, and started talking about the weather.

"I am not here in a strictly professional capacity, you know," said Lady Molly presently, with a kindly smile and with a view to helping him out of his embarrassment. "Our police, I fear me, have an exaggerated view of my capacities, and the men here asked me unofficially to remain in the neighbourhood and to give them my advice if they should require it. Our chief is very lenient to me and has allowed me to stay. Therefore, if there is anything I can do—"

"Indeed, indeed there is!" ejaculated Mr. Grayson with sudden energy. "From all I hear, there is not another soul in the kingdom but you who can save this innocent man from the gallows."

My dear lady heaved a little sigh of satisfaction. She had all along wanted to have a more important finger in that Yorkshire pie.

"Mr. Smethick?" she said.

"Yes; my unfortunate young client," replied the lawyer. "I may as well tell you," he resumed after a slight pause, during which he seemed to pull himself together, "as briefly as possible what occurred on December 24th last and on the following Christmas morning. You will then understand the terrible plight in which my client finds himself, and how impossible it is for him to explain his actions on that eventful night. You will understand, also, why I have come to ask your help and your advice. Mr. Smethick considered himself engaged to Miss Ceely. The engagement had not been made public because of Major Ceely's anticipated opposition, but the young people had been very intimate, and many letters had passed between them. On the morning of the 24th Mr. Smethick called at the Hall, his intention then being merely to present his *fiancée* with the ring you know of. You remember the unfortunate *contretemps* that occurred: I mean the unprovoked quarrel sought by Major Ceely with my poor client, ending with the irascible old man forbidding Mr. Smethick the house.

"My client walked out of Clevere feeling, as you may well imagine, very wrathful; on the doorstep, just as he was leaving, he met Miss Margaret, and told her very briefly what had occurred. She took the matter very lightly at first, but finally became more serious, and ended the brief interview with the request that, since he could not come to the dance after what had occurred, he should come and see her afterwards, meeting her in the gardens soon after midnight. She would not take the ring from him then, but talked a good deal of sentiment about Christmas morning, asking him to bring the ring to her at night, and also the letters which she had written him. Well—you can guess the rest."

Lady Molly nodded thoughtfully.

"Miss Ceely was playing a double game," continued Mr. Grayson, earnestly. "She was determined to break off all relationship with Mr. Smethick, for she had transferred her volatile affections to Captain Glynne, who had lately become heir to an earldom and £40,000 a year. Under the guise of sentimental twaddle she got my unfortunate client to meet her at night in the grounds of Clevere and to give up to her the letters which might have compromised her in the eyes of her new lover. At two o'clock a.m. Major Ceely was murdered by one of his numerous enemies; as to which I do not know, nor does Mr. Smethick. He had just parted from Miss Ceely at the very moment when the first cry of 'Murder' roused Clevere from its slumbers. This she could confirm if she only would, for the two were still in sight of each other, she inside the gates, he just a little way down the road. Mr. Smethick saw Margaret Ceely run rapidly back towards the house. He waited about a little while, half hesitating what to do; then he reflected that his presence might be embarrassing, or even compromising to her whom, in spite of all, he still loved dearly; and knowing that there were plenty of men in and about the house to render what assistance was necessary, he finally turned his steps and went home a broken-hearted man, since she had given him the go-by, taken her letters away, and flung contemptuously into the mud the ring he had bought for her."

The lawyer paused, mopping his forehead and gazing with whole-souled earnestness at my lady's beautiful, thoughtful face.

"Has Mr. Smethick spoken to Miss Ceely since?" asked Lady Molly, after a while.

"No; but I did," replied the lawyer.

"What was her attitude?"

"One of bitter and callous contempt. She denies my unfortunate client's story from beginning to end; declares that she never saw him after she bade him 'good-morning' on the doorstep of Clevere Hall, when she heard of his unfortunate quarrel with her father. Nay, more; she scornfully calls the whole tale a cowardly attempt to shield a dastardly crime behind a still more dastardly libel on a defenceless girl."

We were all silent now, buried in thought which none of us would have cared to translate into words. That the *impasse* seemed indeed hopeless no one could deny.

The tower of damning evidence against the unfortunate young man had indeed been built by remorseless circumstances with no faltering hand.

Margaret Ceely alone could have saved him, but with brutal indifference she preferred the sacrifice of an innocent man's life and honour to that of her own chances of a brilliant marriage. There are such women in the world; thank God I have never met any but that one!

Yet am I wrong when I say that she alone could save the unfortunate young man, who throughout was behaving with such consummate gallantry, refusing to give his own explanation of the events that occurred on that Christmas morning, unless she chose first to tell the tale. There was one present now in the dingy little room at the "Black Swan" who could disentangle that weird skein of coincidences, if any human being not gifted with miraculous powers could indeed do it at this eleventh hour.

She now said, gently:

"What would you like me to do in this matter, Mr. Grayson? And why have you come to me rather than to the police?"

"How can I go with this tale to the police?" he ejaculated in obvious despair. "Would they not also look upon it as a dastardly libel on a woman's reputation? We have no proofs, remember, and Miss Ceely denies the whole story from first to last. No, no!" he exclaimed with wonderful fervour. "I came to you because I have heard of your marvellous gifts, your extraordinary intuition. Someone murdered Major Ceely! It was not my old friend Colonel Smethick's son. Find out who it was, then! I beg of you, find out who it was!"

He fell back in his chair broken down with grief. With inexpressible gentleness Lady Molly went up to him and placed her beautiful white hand on his shoulder.

"I will do my best, Mr. Grayson," she said simply.

5

We remained alone and singularly quiet the whole of that evening. That my dear lady's active brain was hard at work I could guess by the brilliance of her eyes, and that sort of absolute stillness in her person through which one could almost feel the delicate nerves vibrating.

The story told her by the lawyer had moved her singularly. Mind you, she had always been morally convinced of young Smethick's innocence, but in her the professional woman always fought hard battles against the sentimentalist, and in this instance the overwhelming circumstantial evidence and the conviction of her superiors had forced her to accept the young man's guilt as something out of her ken.

By his silence, too, the young man had tacitly confessed; and if a man is perceived on the very scene of a crime, both before it has been committed and directly afterwards; if something admittedly belonging to him is found within three yards of where the murderer must have stood; if, added to this, he has had a bitter quarrel with the victim, and can give no account of his actions or whereabouts during the fatal time, it were vain to cling to optimistic beliefs in that same man's innocence.

But now matters had assumed an altogether different aspect. The story told by Mr. Smethick's lawyer had all the appearance of truth. Margaret Ceely's character, her callousness on the very day when her late *fiancé* stood in the dock, her quick transference of her affections to the richer man, all made the account of the events on Christmas night as told by Mr. Grayson extremely plausible.

No wonder my dear lady was buried in thought.

"I shall have to take the threads up from the beginning, Mary," she said to me the following morning, when after breakfast she appeared in her neat coat and skirt, with hat and gloves, ready to go out, "so, on the whole, I think I will begin with a visit to the Haggetts."

"I may come with you, I suppose?" I suggested meekly.

"Oh, yes!" she rejoined carelessly.

Somehow I had an inkling that the carelessness of her mood was only on the surface. It was not likely that she—my sweet, womanly, ultra-feminine, beautiful lady—should feel callously on this absorbing subject.

We motored down to Bishopthorpe. It was bitterly cold, raw, damp, and foggy. The chauffeur had some difficulty in finding the cottage, the "home" of the imbecile gardener and his wife.

There was certainly not much look of home about the place. When, after much knocking at the door, Mrs. Haggett finally opened it, we saw before us one of the most miserable, slatternly places I think I ever saw.

In reply to Lady Molly's somewhat curt inquiry, the woman said that Haggett was in bed, suffering from one of his "fits."

"That is a great pity," said my dear lady, rather unsympathetically, I thought, "for I must speak with him at once."

"What is it about?" asked the woman, sullenly. "I can take a message."

"I am afraid not," rejoined my lady. "I was asked to see Haggett personally."

"By whom, I'd like to know," she retorted, now almost insolently.

"I dare say you would. But you are wasting precious time. Hadn't you better help your husband on with his clothes? This lady and I will wait in the parlour."

After some hesitation the woman finally complied, looking very sulky the while.

We went into the miserable little room wherein not only grinding poverty but also untidiness and dirt were visible all round. We sat down on two of the cleanest-looking chairs, and waited whilst a colloquy in subdued voices went on in the room over our heads.

The colloquy, I may say, seemed to consist of agitated whispers on one part, and wailing complaints on the other. This was followed presently by some thuds and much shuffling, and presently Haggett, looking uncared-for, dirty, and unkempt, entered the parlour, followed by his wife.

He came forward, dragging his ill-shod feet and pulling nervously at his forelock.

"Ah!" said my lady, kindly; "I am glad to see you down, Haggett, though I am afraid I haven't very good news for you."

"Yes, miss!" murmured the man, obviously not quite comprehending what was said to him.

"I represent the workhouse authorities," continued Lady Molly, "and I thought we could arrange for you and your wife to come into the Union to-night, perhaps."

"The Union?" here interposed the woman, roughly. "What do you mean? We ain't going to the Union?"

"Well! but since you are not staying here," rejoined my lady, blandly, "you will find it impossible to get another situation for your husband in his present mental condition."

"Miss Ceely won't give us the go-by," she retorted defiantly.

"She might wish to carry out her late father's intentions," said Lady Molly with seeming carelessness.

"The Major was a cruel, cantankerous brute," shouted the woman with unpremeditated violence. "Haggett had served him faithfully for twelve years, and—"

She checked herself abruptly, and cast one of her quick, furtive glances at Lady Molly.

Her silence now had become as significant as her outburst of rage, and it was Lady Molly who concluded the phrase for her.

"And yet he dismissed him without warning," she said calmly.

"Who told you that?" retorted the woman.

"The same people, no doubt, who declare that you and Haggett had a grudge against the Major for this dismissal."

"That's a lie," asserted Mrs. Haggett, doggedly; "we gave information about Mr. Smethick having killed the Major because—"

"Ah," interrupted Lady Molly, quickly, "but then Mr. Smethick did not murder Major Ceely, and your information therefore was useless!"

"Then who killed the Major, I should like to know?"

Her manner was arrogant, coarse, and extremely unpleasant. I marvelled why my dear lady put up with it, and what was going on in that busy brain of hers. She looked quite urbane and smiling, whilst I wondered what in the world she meant by this story of the workhouse and the dismissal of Haggett.

"Ah, that's what none of us know!" she now said lightly; "some folks say it was your husband."

"They lie!" she retorted quickly, whilst the imbecile, evidently not understanding the drift of the conversation, was mechanically stroking his red mop of hair and looking helplessly all round him.

"He was home before the cries of 'Murder' were heard in the house," continued Mrs. Haggett.

"How do you know?" asked Lady Molly, quickly.

"How do I know?"

"Yes; you couldn't have heard the cries all the way to this cottage—why, it's over half a mile from the Hall!"

"He was home, I say," she repeated with dogged obstinacy.

"You sent him?"

"He didn't do it—"

"No one will believe you, especially when the knife is found."

"What knife?"

"His clasp knife, with which he killed Major Ceely," said Lady Molly, quietly; "see, he has it in his hand now."

And with a sudden, wholly unexpected gesture she pointed to the imbecile, who in an aimless way had prowled round the room whilst this rapid colloquy was going on.

The purport of it all must in some sort of way have found an echo in his enfeebled brain. He wandered up to the dresser whereon lay the remnants of that morning's breakfast, together with some crockery and utensils.

In that same half-witted and irresponsible way he had picked up one of the knives and now was holding it out towards his wife, whilst a look of fear spread over his countenance.

"I can't do it, Annie, I can't—you'd better do it," he said.

There was dead silence in the little room. The woman Haggett stood as if turned to stone. Ignorant and superstitious as she was,

I suppose that the situation had laid hold of her nerves, and that she felt that the finger of a relentless Fate was even now being pointed at her.

The imbecile was shuffling forward, closer and closer to his wife, still holding out the knife towards her and murmuring brokenly:

"I can't do it. You'd better, Annie—you'd better—"

He was close to her now, and all at once her rigidity and nerve-strain gave way; she gave a hoarse cry, and snatching the knife from the poor wretch, she rushed at him ready to strike.

Lady Molly and I were both young, active and strong; and there was nothing of the squeamish *grande dame* about my dear lady when quick action was needed. But even then we had some difficulty in dragging Annie Haggett away from her miserable husband. Blinded with fury, she was ready to kill the man who had betrayed her. Finally, we succeeded in wresting the knife from her.

You may be sure that it required some pluck after that to sit down again quietly and to remain in the same room with this woman, who already had one crime upon her conscience, and with this weird, half-witted creature who kept on murmuring pitiably:

"You'd better do it, Annie—"

Well, you've read the account of the case, so you know what followed. Lady Molly did not move from that room until she had obtained the woman's full confession. All she did for her own protection was to order me to open the window and to blow the police whistle which she handed to me. The police-station fortunately was not very far, and sound carried in the frosty air.

She admitted to me afterwards that it had been foolish, perhaps, not to have brought Etty or Danvers with her, but she was supremely anxious not to put the woman on the alert from the very start, hence her circumlocutory speeches anent the workhouse, and Haggett's probable dismissal.

That the woman had had some connection with the crime, Lady Molly, with her keen intuition, had always felt; but as there was no witness to the murder itself, and all circumstantial evidence was dead against young Smethick, there was only one chance of successful discovery, and that was the murderer's own confession.

If you think over the interview between my dear lady and the Haggetts on that memorable morning, you will realise how admirably Lady Molly had led up to the weird finish. She would not speak to the woman unless Haggett was present, and she felt sure that as soon as the subject of the murder cropped up, the imbecile would either do or say something that would reveal the truth.

Mechanically, when Major Ceely's name was mentioned, he had taken up the knife. The whole scene recurred to his tottering mind. That the Major had summarily dismissed him recently was one of those bold guesses which Lady Molly was wont to make.

That Haggett had been merely egged on by his wife, and had been too terrified at the last to do the deed himself was no surprise to her, and hardly one to me, whilst the fact that the woman ultimately wreaked her own passionate revenge upon the unfortunate Major was hardly to be wondered at, in the face of her own coarse and elemental personality.

Cowed by the quickness of events, and by the appearance of Danvers and Etty on the scene, she finally made full confession.

She was maddened by the Major's brutality, when with rough, cruel words he suddenly turned her husband adrift, refusing to give him further employment. She herself had great ascendency over the imbecile, and had drilled him into a part of hate and of revenge. At first he had seemed ready and willing to obey. It was arranged that he was to watch on the terrace every night until such time as an alarm of the recurrence of the cattle-maiming outrages should lure the Major out alone.

This effectually occurred on Christmas morning, but not before Haggett, frightened and pusillanimous, was ready to flee rather than to accomplish the villainous deed. But Annie Haggett, guessing perhaps that he would shrink from the crime at the last, had also kept watch every night. Picture the prospective murderer watching and being watched!

When Haggett came across his wife he deputed her to do the deed herself.

I suppose that either terror of discovery or merely desire for the promised reward had caused the woman to fasten the crime on another.

The finding of the ring by Haggett was the beginning of that cruel thought which, but for my dear lady's marvellous powers, would indeed have sent a brave young man to the gallows.

Ah, you wish to know if Margaret Ceely is married? No! Captain Glynne cried off. What suspicions crossed his mind I cannot say; but he never proposed to Margaret, and now she is in Australia—staying with an aunt, I think—and she has sold Clevere Hall.

THE BAG OF SAND

1

Of course, I knew at once by the expression of her face that morning that my dear lady had some important business on hand.

She had a bundle in her arms, consisting of a shabby-looking coat and skirt, and a very dowdy hat trimmed with bunches of cheap, calico roses.

"Put on these things at once, Mary," she said curtly, "for you are going to apply for the situation of 'good plain cook,' so mind you look the part."

"But where in the world—?" I gasped in astonishment.

"In the house of Mr. Nicholas Jones, in Eaton Terrace," she interrupted dryly, "the one occupied until recently by his sister, the late Mrs. Dunstan. Mrs. Jones is advertising for a cook, and you must get that place."

As you know, I have carried obedience to the level of a fine art. Nor was I altogether astonished that my dear lady had at last been asked to put one of her dainty fingers in that Dunstan pie, which was puzzling our fellows more completely than any other case I have ever known.

I don't know if you remember the many circumstances, the various contradictions which were cropping up at every turn, and which baffled our ablest detectives at the very moment when they thought themselves most near the solution of that strange mystery.

Mrs. Dunstan herself was a very uninteresting individual: self-righteous, self-conscious and fat, a perfect type of the moneyed middle-class woman whose balance at the local bank is invariably heavier than that of her neighbours. Her niece, Violet Frostwicke, lived with her: a smart, pretty girl, inordinately fond of dainty clothes and other luxuries which money can give. Being totally impecunious herself, she bore with the older woman's constantly varying caprices with almost angelic patience, a fact probably attributable to Mrs. Dunstan's testamentary intentions, which, as she often averred, were in favour of her niece.

In addition to these two ladies, the household consisted of three servants and Miss Cruikshank. The latter was a quiet, unassuming girl who was by way of being secretary and lady-help to Mrs. Dunstan, but who, in reality, was nothing but a willing drudge. Up betimes in the morning, she combined the work of a housekeeper with that of an upper servant. She interviewed the tradespeople, kept the servants in order, and ironed and smartened up Miss Violet's blouses. A Cinderella, in fact.

Mrs. Dunstan kept a cook and two maids, all of whom had been with her for years. In addition to these, a charwoman came very early in the morning to light fires, clean boots, and do the front steps.

On November 22nd, 1907—for the early history of this curious drama dates back to that year—the charwoman who had been employed at Mrs. Dunstan's house in Eaton Terrace for some considerable time, sent word in the morning that in future she would be unable to come. Her husband had been obliged to move to lodgings nearer to his work, and she herself could not undertake to come the greater distance at the early hour at which Mrs. Dunstan required her.

The woman had written a very nice letter explaining these facts, and sent it by hand, stating at the same time that the bearer of the note was a very respectable woman, a friend of her own, who would be very pleased to "oblige" Mrs. Dunstan by taking on the morning's work.

I must tell you that the message and its bearer arrived at Eaton Terrace somewhere about 6.0 a.m., when no one was down except the Cinderella of the house, Miss Cruikshank.

She saw the woman, liked her appearance, and there and then engaged her to do the work, subject to Mrs. Dunstan's approval.

The woman, who had given her name as Mrs. Thomas, seemed very quiet and respectable. She said that she lived close by, in St. Peter's Mews, and therefore could come as early as Mrs. Dunstan wished. In fact, from that day, she came every morning at 5.30 a.m., and by seven o'clock had finished her work, and was able to go home.

If, in addition to these details, I tell you that, at that time, pretty Miss Violet Frostwicke was engaged to a young Scotsman, Mr. David Athol, of whom her aunt totally disapproved, I shall have put before you all the personages who, directly or indirectly, were connected with that drama, the final act of which has not yet been witnessed either by the police or by the public.

2

On the following New Year's Eve, Mrs. Dunstan, as was her invariable custom on that day, went to her married brother's house to dine and to see the New Year in.

During her absence the usual thing occurred at Eaton Terrace. Miss Violet Frostwicke took the opportunity of inviting Mr. David Athol to spend the evening with her.

Mrs. Dunstan's servants, mind you, all knew of the engagement between the young people, and with the characteristic sentimentality of their class, connived at these secret meetings and helped to hoodwink the irascible old aunt.

Mr. Athol was a good-looking young man, whose chief demerit lay in his total lack of money or prospects. Also he was by way of being an actor, another deadly sin in the eyes of the puritanically-minded old lady.

Already, on more than one occasion, there had been vigorous wordy warfare 'twixt Mr. Athol and Mrs. Dunstan, and the latter had declared that if Violet chose to take up with this mountebank, she should never see a penny of her aunt's money now or in the future.

The young man did not come very often to Eaton Terrace, but on this festive New Year's Eve, when Mrs. Dunstan was not expected to be home until long after midnight, it seemed too splendid an opportunity for an ardent lover to miss.

As ill-luck would have it, Mrs. Dunstan had not felt very well after her copious dinner, and her brother, Mr. Nicholas Jones, escorted her home soon after ten o'clock.

Jane, the parlour-maid who opened the front door, was, in her own graphic language, "knocked all of a heap" when she saw her mistress, knowing full well that Mr. Athol was still in the dining-room with Miss Violet, and that Miss Cruikshank was at that very moment busy getting him a whisky and soda.

Meanwhile the coat and hat in the hall had revealed the young man's presence in the house.

For a moment Mrs. Dunstan paused, whilst Jane stood by trembling with fright. Then the old lady turned to Mr. Nicholas Jones, who was still standing on the doorstep, and said quietly:

"Will you telephone over to Mr. Blenkinsop, Nick, the first thing in the morning, and tell him I'll be at his office by ten o'clock?"

Mr. Blenkinsop was Mrs. Dunstan's solicitor, and as Jane explained to the cook later on, what could such an appointment mean but a determination to cut Miss Violet out of the missis's will with the proverbial shilling?

After this Mrs. Dunstan took leave of her brother and went straight into the dining-room.

According to the subsequent testimony of all three servants, the mistress "went on dreadful." Words were not easily distinguishable from behind the closed door, but it seems that, immediately she entered, Mrs. Dunstan's voice was raised as if in terrible anger, and a few moments later Miss Violet fled crying from the dining-room, and ran quickly upstairs.

Whilst the door was thus momentarily opened and shut, the voice of the old lady was heard saying, in majestic wrath:

"That's what you have done. Get out of this house. As for her, she'll never see a penny of my money, and she may starve for aught I care!"

The quarrel seems to have continued for a short while after that, the servants being too deeply awed by those last vindictive words which they had heard to take much note of what went on subsequently.

Mrs. Dunstan and Mr. Athol were closeted together for some time; but apparently the old lady's wrath did not subside, for when she marched up to bed an hour later she was heard to say:

"Out of this house she shall go, and the first thing in the morning, too. I'll have no goings-on with a mountebank like you."

Miss Cruikshank was terribly upset.

"It is a frightful blow for Miss Violet," she said to cook, "but perhaps Mrs. Dunstan will feel more forgiving in the morning. I'll take her up a glass of champagne now. She is very fond of that, and it will help her to get to sleep."

Miss Cruikshank went up with the champagne, and told cook to see Mr. Athol out of the house; but the young man, who seemed very anxious and agitated, would not go away immediately. He stayed in the dining-room, smoking, for a while, and when the two younger servants went up to bed, he asked cook to let him remain until he had seen Miss Violet once more, for he was sure she would come down again—he had asked Miss Cruikshank to beg her to do so.

Mrs. Kennett, the cook, was a kind-hearted old woman. She had taken the young people under her special protection, and felt very vexed that the course of true love should not be allowed to run quite smoothly. So she told Mr. Athol to make himself happy and comfortable in the dining-room, and she would sit up by the fire in the library until he was ready to go.

The good soul thereupon made up the fire in the library, drew a chair in front of it, and—went fast to sleep.

Suddenly something awoke her. She sat up and looked round in that dazed manner peculiar to people just aroused from deep sleep.

She looked at the clock; it was past three. Surely, she thought, it must have been Mr. Athol calling to her which had caused her to wake. She went into the hall, where the gas had not yet been turned off, and there she saw Miss Violet, fully dressed and wearing a hat and coat, in the very act of going out at the front door.

In the cook's own words, before she could ask a question or even utter a sound, the young girl had opened the front door, which was still on the latch, and then banged it to again, she herself having disappeared into the darkness of the street beyond.

Mrs. Kennett ran to the door and out into the street as fast as her old legs would let her; but the night was an exceptionally foggy one. Violet, no doubt, had walked rapidly away, and there came no answer to Mrs. Kennett's repeated calls.

Thoroughly upset, and not knowing what to do, the good woman went back into the house. Mr. Athol had evidently left, for there was no sign of him in the dining-room or elsewhere. She then went upstairs and knocked at Mrs. Dunstan's door. To her astonishment the gas was still burning in her mistress's room, as she could see a thin ray of light filtering through the keyhole. At her first knock there came a quick, impatient answer:

"What is it?"

"Miss Violet, 'm," said the cook, who was too agitated to speak very coherently, "she is gone—"

"The best thing she could do," came promptly from the other side of the door. "You go to bed, Mrs. Kennett, and don't worry."

Whereupon the gas was suddenly turned off inside the room, and, in spite of Mrs. Kennett's further feeble protests, no other word issued from the room save another impatient:

"Go to bed."

The cook then did as she was bid; but before going to bed she made the round of the house, turned off all the gas, and finally bolted the front door.

3

Some three hours later the servants were called, as usual, by Miss Cruikshank, who then went down to open the area door to Mrs. Thomas, the charwoman.

At half-past six, when Mary the housemaid came down, candle in hand, she saw the charwoman a flight or two lower down, also apparently in the act of going downstairs. This astonished Mary not a little, as the woman's work lay entirely in the basement, and she was supposed never to come to the upper floors.

The woman, though walking rapidly down the stairs, seemed, moreover, to be carrying something heavy.

"Anything wrong, Mrs. Thomas?" asked Mary, in a whisper.

The woman looked up, pausing a moment immediately under the gas bracket, the by-pass of which shed a feeble light upon her and upon her burden. The latter Mary recognised as the bag containing the sand which, on frosty mornings, had to be strewn on the front steps of the house.

On the whole, though she certainly was puzzled, Mary did not think very much about the incident then. As was her custom, she went into the housemaid's closet, got the hot water for Miss Cruikshank's bath, and carried it to the latter's room, where she also pulled up the blinds and got things ready generally. For Miss Cruikshank usually ran down in her dressing-gown, and came up to tidy herself later on.

As a rule, by the time the three servants got downstairs, it was nearly seven, and Mrs. Thomas had generally gone by that time; but on this occasion Mary was earlier. Miss Cruikshank was busy in the kitchen getting Mrs. Dunstan's tea ready. Mary spoke about seeing Mrs. Thomas on the stairs with the bag of sand, and Miss Cruikshank, too, was very astonished at the occurrence.

Mrs. Kennett was not yet down, and the charwoman apparently had gone; her work had been done as usual, and the sand was strewn over the stone steps in front, as the frosty fog had rendered them very slippery.

At a quarter past seven Miss Cruikshank went up with Mrs. Dunstan's tea, and less than two minutes later a fearful scream rang through the entire house, followed by the noise of breaking crockery.

In an instant the two maids ran upstairs, straight to Mrs. Dunstan's room, the door of which stood wide open.

The first thing Mary and Jane were conscious of was a terrific smell of gas, then of Miss Cruikshank, with eyes dilated with horror, staring at the bed in front of her, whereon lay Mrs. Dunstan, with one end of a piece of india-rubber piping still resting in her mouth, her jaw having dropped in death. The other end of that piece of piping was attached to the burner of a gas-bracket on the wall close by.

Every window in the room was fastened and the curtains drawn. The whole room reeked of gas.

Mrs. Dunstan had been asphyxiated by its fumes.

4

A year went by after the discovery of the mysterious tragedy, and I can assure you that our fellows at the Yard had one of the toughest jobs in connection with the case that ever fell to their lot. Just think of all the contradictions which met them at every turn.

Firstly, the disappearance of Miss Violet.

No sooner had the women in the Dunstan household roused themselves sufficiently from their horror at the terrible discovery which they had just made, than they were confronted with another almost equally awful fact—awful, of course, because of its connection with the primary tragedy.

Miss Violet Frostwicke had gone. Her room was empty, her bed had not been slept in. She herself had been seen by the cook, Mrs. Kennett, stealing out of the house at dead of night.

To connect the pretty, dainty young girl even remotely with a crime so hideous, so callous, as the deliberate murder of an old woman, who had been as a mother to her, seemed absolutely out of the question, and by tacit consent the four women, who now remained in the desolate and gloom-laden house at Eaton Terrace, forbore to mention Miss Violet Frostwicke's name either to police or doctor.

Both these, of course, had been summoned immediately; Miss Cruikshank sending Mary to the police-station and thence to Dr. Folwell, in Eaton Square, whilst Jane went off in a cab to fetch Mr. Nicholas Jones, who, fortunately, had not yet left for his place of business.

The doctor's and the police-inspector's first thought, on examining the *mise en scène* of the terrible tragedy, was that Mrs. Dunstan had committed suicide. It was practically impossible to

imagine that a woman in full possession of health and strength
would allow a piece of india-rubber piping to be fixed between her
teeth, and would, without a struggle, continue to inhale the poi-
sonous fumes which would mean certain death. Yet there were no
marks of injury upon the body, nothing to show how sufficient
unconsciousness had been produced in the victim to permit of the
miscreant completing his awesome deed.

But the theory of suicide set up by Dr. Folwell was promptly
refuted by the most cursory examination of the room.

Though the drawers were found closed, they had obviously been
turned over, as if the murderer had been in search either of money
or papers, or the key of the safe.

The latter, on investigation, was found to be open, whilst the
key lay on the floor close by. A brief examination of the safe revealed the fact that the tin boxes must have been ransacked, for
they contained neither money nor important papers now, whilst
the gold and platinum settings of necklaces, bracelets, and a tiara
showed that the stones—which, as Mr. Nicholas Jones subsequently
averred, were of considerable value—had been carefully, if somewhat clumsily, taken out by obvious inexperienced hands.

On the whole, therefore, appearances suggested deliberate,
systematic, and very leisurely robbery, which wholly contradicted
the theory of suicide.

Then suddenly the name of Miss Frostwicke was mentioned.
Who first brought it on the *tapis* no one subsequently could say;
but in a moment the whole story of the young girl's engagement to
Mr. Athol, in defiance of her aunt's wishes, the quarrel of the night
before, and the final disappearance of both young people from the
house during the small hours of the morning, was dragged from
the four unwilling witnesses by the able police-inspector.

Nay, more. One very unpleasant little circumstance was de-
tailed by one of the maids and corroborated by Miss Cruikshank.

It seems that when the latter took up the champagne to Mrs.
Dunstan, the old lady desired Miss Violet to come to her room.
Mary, the housemaid, was on the stairs when she saw the young
girl, still dressed in her evening gown of white chiffon, her eyes
still swollen with tears, knocking at her aunt's door.

The police-inspector was busy taking notes, already building up in his mind a simple, if very sensational, case against Violet Frostwicke, when Mrs. Kennett promptly upset all his calculations.

Miss Violet could have had nothing to do with the murder of her aunt, seeing that Mrs. Dunstan was alive and actually spoke to the cook when the latter knocked at her bedroom door after she had seen the young girl walk out of the house.

Then came the question of Mr. Athol. But, if you remember, it was quite impossible even to begin to build up a case against the young man. His own statement that he left the house at about midnight, having totally forgotten to rouse the cook when he did so, was amply corroborated from every side.

The cabman who took him up to the corner of Eaton Terrace at 11.50 p.m. was one witness in his favour; his landlady at his rooms in Jermyn Street, who let him in, since he had mislaid his latchkey, and who took him up some tea at seven o'clock the next morning, was another; whilst, when Mary saw Miss Violet going into her aunt's room, the clock at St. Peter's, Eaton Square, was just striking twelve.

I dare say you think I ought by now to have mentioned the charwoman, Mrs. Thomas, who represented the final, most complete, most hopeless contradiction in this remarkable case.

Mrs. Thomas was seen by Mary, the housemaid, at half-past six o'clock in the morning, coming down from the upper floors, where she had no business to be, and carrying the bag of sand used for strewing over the slippery front-door steps.

The bag of sand, of course, was always kept in the area.

The moment that bag of sand was mentioned Dr. Folwell gave a curious gasp. Here, at least, was the solution to one mystery. The victim had been stunned whilst still in bed by a blow on the head dealt with that bag of sand; and whilst she was unconscious the callous miscreant had robbed her and finally asphyxiated her with the gas fumes.

Where was the woman who, at half-past six in the morning, was seen in possession of the silent instrument of death?

Mrs. Thomas had disappeared. The last that was then or ever has been seen of her was when she passed underneath the dim light

of a by-pass on the landing, as if tired out with the weight which
she was carrying.

Since then, as you know, the police have been unswerving in
their efforts to find Mrs. Thomas. The address which she had given
in St. Peter's Mews was found to be false. No one of that name or
appearance had ever been seen there.

The woman who was supposed to have sent her with a letter of
recommendation to Mrs. Dunstan knew nothing of her. She swore
that she had never sent anyone with a letter to Mrs. Dunstan. She
gave up her work there one day because she found it too hard at
such an early hour in the morning; but she never heard anything
more from her late employer after that.

Strange, wasn't it, that two people should have disappeared out
of that house on that same memorable night?

Of course, you will remember the tremendous sensation that
was caused some twenty-four hours later, when it transpired that
the young person who had thrown herself into the river from Waterloo Bridge on that same eventful morning, and whose body was
subsequently recovered and conveyed to the Thames Police
station, was identified as Miss Violet Frostwicke, the niece of the
lady who had been murdered in her own house in Eaton Terrace.

Neither money nor diamonds were found on poor Miss Violet.
She had herself given the most complete proof that she, at least,
had no hand in robbing or killing Mrs. Dunstan.

The public wondered why she took her aunt's wrath and her
probable disinheritance so fearfully to heart, and sympathised with
Mr. David Athol for the terribly sad loss which he had sustained.

But Mrs. Thomas, the charwoman, had not yet been found.

5

I think I looked an extremely respectable, good plain cook when
I presented myself at the house in Eaton Terrace in response to
the advertisement in the "Daily Telegraph."

As, in addition to my prepossessing appearance, I also asked
very low wages and declared myself ready to do anything except

scour the front steps and the stone area, I was immediately engaged by Mrs. Jones, and was duly installed in the house the following day under the name of Mrs. Curwen.

But few events had occurred here since the discovery of the dual tragedy, now more than a year ago, and none that had thrown any light upon the mystery which surrounded it.

The verdict at the inquest had been one of willful murder against a person known as Mrs. Thomas, the weight of evidence, coupled with her disappearance, having been very heavy against her; and there was a warrant out for her arrest.

Mrs. Dunstan had died intestate. To the astonishment of all those in the know, she had never signed the will which Messrs. Blenkinsop and Blenkinsop had drafted for her, and wherein she bequeathed £20,000 and the lease of her house in Eaton Terrace to her beloved niece, Violet Frostwicke, £1,000 to Miss Cruikshank, and other, smaller, legacies to friends or servants.

In default of a will, Mr. Nicholas Jones, only brother of the deceased, became possessed of all her wealth.

He was a very rich man himself, and many people thought that he ought to give Miss Cruikshank the £1,000 which the poor girl had thus lost through no fault of her own.

What his ultimate intentions were with regard to this no one could know. For the present he contented himself with moving to Eaton Terrace with his family; and, as his wife was a great invalid, he asked Miss Cruikshank to continue to make her home in the house and to help in its management.

Neither the diamonds nor the money stolen from Mrs. Dunstan's safe were ever traced. It seems that Mrs. Dunstan, a day or two before her death, had sold a freehold cottage which she owned near Teddington. The money, as is customary, had been handed over to her in gold, in Mr. Blenkinsop's office, and she had been foolish enough not to bank it immediately. This money and the diamonds had been the chief spoils of her assailant. And all the while no trace of Mrs. Thomas, in spite of the most strenuous efforts on the part of the police to find her.

Strangely enough, when I had been in Eaton Terrace about three days, and was already getting very tired of early rising and hard work, the charwoman there fell ill one day and did not come to her work as usual.

I, of course, grumbled like six, for I had to be on my hands and knees the next morning scrubbing stone steps, and my thoughts of Lady Molly, for the moment, were not quite as loyal as they usually were.

Suddenly I heard a shuffling footstep close behind me. I turned and saw a rough-looking, ill-dressed woman standing at the bottom of the steps.

"What do you want?" I asked sourly, for I was in a very bad humour.

"I saw you scrubbing them steps, miss," she replied in a raucous voice; "my 'usband is out of work, and the children hain't 'ad no breakfast this morning. I'd do them steps, miss, if you'd give me a trifle."

The woman certainly did not look very prepossessing, with her shabby, broad-brimmed hat hiding the upper part of her face, and her skirt, torn and muddy, pinned up untidily round her stooping figure.

However, I did not think that I could be doing anything very wrong by letting her do this one bit of rough work, which I hated, so I agreed to give her sixpence, and left her there with kneeling mat and scrubbing-brush, and went in, leaving, however, the front door open.

In the hall I met Miss Cruikshank, who, as usual, was down before everybody else.

"What is it, Curwen?" she asked, for through the open door she had caught sight of the woman kneeling on the step.

"A woman, miss," I replied, somewhat curtly. "She offered to do the steps. I thought Mrs. Jones wouldn't mind, as Mrs. Callaghan hasn't turned up."

Miss Cruikshank hesitated an instant, and then walked up to the front door.

At the same moment the woman looked up, rose from her knees, and boldly went up to accost Miss Cruikshank.

"You'll remember me, miss," she said, in her raucous voice. "I used to work for Mrs. Dunstan once. My name is Mrs. Thomas."

No wonder Miss Cruikshank uttered a quickly smothered cry of horror. Thinking that she would faint, I ran to her assistance; but she waved me aside and then said quite quietly:

"This poor woman's mind is deranged. She is no more Mrs. Thomas than I am. Perhaps we had better send for the police."

"Yes, miss; p'r'aps you'd better," said the woman with a sigh. "My secret has been weighin' heavy on me of late."

"But, my good woman," said Miss Cruikshank, very kindly, for I suppose that she thought, as I did, that this was one of those singular cases of madness which sometimes cause innocent people to accuse themselves of undiscovered crimes. "You are not Mrs. Thomas at all. I knew Mrs. Thomas well, of course—and—"

"Of course you knew me, miss," replied the woman. "The last conversation you and I had together was in the kitchen that morning, when Mrs. Dunstan was killed. I remember your saying to me—"

"Fetch the police, Curwen," said Miss Cruikshank, peremptorily.

Whereupon the woman broke into a harsh and loud laugh of defiance.

To tell you the truth, I was not a little puzzled. That this scene had been foreseen by my dear lady, and that she had sent me to this house on purpose that I should witness it, I was absolutely convinced. But—here was my dilemma: ought I to warn the police at once or not?

On the whole, I decided that my best plan would undoubtedly be to communicate with Lady Molly first of all, and to await her instructions. So I ran upstairs, scribbled a hasty note to my dear lady, and, in response to Miss Cruikshank's orders, flew out of the house through the area gate, noticing, as I did so, that Miss Cruikshank was still parleying with the woman on the doorstep.

I sent the note off to Maida Vale by taxicab; then I went back to Eaton Terrace. Miss Cruikshank met me at the front door, and told me that she had tried to detain the woman, pending my return; but that she felt very sorry for the unfortunate creature, who obviously was labouring under a delusion, and she had allowed her to go away.

About an hour later I received a curt note from Lady Molly ordering me to do nothing whatever without her special authorisation.

In the course of the day, Miss Cruikshank told me that she had been to the police-station, and had consulted with the inspector, who said there would be no harm in engaging the pseudo Mrs. Thomas to work at Eaton Terrace, especially as thus she would remain under observation.

Then followed a curious era in Mr. Nicholas Jones's otherwise well-ordered household. We three servants, instead of being called at six as heretofore, were allowed to sleep on until seven. When we came down we were not scolded. On the contrary, we found our work already done.

The charwoman—whoever she was—must have been a very hard-working woman. It was marvellous what she accomplished single-handed before seven a.m., by which time she had invariably gone.

The two maids, of course, were content to let this pleasant state of things go on, but I was devoured with curiosity.

One morning I crept quietly downstairs and went into the kitchen soon after six. I found the pseudo Mrs. Thomas sitting at a very copious breakfast. I noticed that she had on altogether different—though equally shabby and dirty—clothes from those she had worn when she first appeared on the doorstep of 180, Eaton Terrace. Near her plate were three or four golden sovereigns over which she had thrown her grimy hand.

Miss Cruikshank the while was on her hands and knees scrubbing the floor. At sight of me she jumped up, and with obvious confusion muttered something about "hating to be idle," etc.

That day Miss Cruikshank told me that I did not suit Mrs. Jones, who wished me to leave at the end of my month. In the afternoon I received a little note from my dear lady, telling me to be downstairs by six o'clock the following morning.

I did as I was ordered, of course, and when I came into the kitchen punctually at six a.m. I found the charwoman sitting at the table with a pile of gold in front of her, which she was counting over with a very grubby finger. She had her back to me, and was saying as I entered:

"I think if you was to give me another fifty quid I'd leave you the rest now. You'd still have the diamonds and the rest of the money."

She spoke to Miss Cruikshank, who was facing me, and who, on seeing me appear, turned as white as a ghost. But she quickly recovered herself, and, standing between me and the woman, she said vehemently:

"What do you mean by prying on me like this? Go and pack your boxes and leave the house this instant."

But before I could reply the woman had interposed.

"Don't you fret yourself, miss," she said, placing her grimy hand on Miss Cruikshank's shoulder. "There's the bag of sand in that there corner; we'll knock 'er down as we did Mrs. Dunstan—eh?"

"Hold your tongue, you lying fool!" said the girl, who now looked like a maddened fury.

"Give me that other fifty quid and I'll hold my tongue," retorted the woman, boldly.

"This creature is mad," said Miss Cruikshank, who had made a vigorous and successful effort to recover herself. "She is under the delusion that not only is she Mrs. Thomas, but that she murdered Mrs. Dunstan—"

"No—no!" interrupted the woman. "I only came back that morning because I recollected that you had left the bag of sand upstairs after you so cleverly did away with Mrs. Dunstan, robbed her of all her money and jewels, and even were sharp enough to imitate her voice when Mrs. Kennett, the cook, terrified you by speaking to Mrs. Dunstan through the door."

"It is false! You are not Mrs. Thomas. The two maids who are here now, and who were in this house at the time, can swear that you are a liar."

"Let us change clothes now, Miss Cruikshank," said a voice, which sounded almost weirdly in my ear in spite of its familiarity, for I could not locate whence it came, "and see if in a charwoman's dress those two maids would not recognise *you*."

"Mary," continued the same familiar voice, "help me out of these filthy clothes. Perhaps Miss Cruikshank would like to resume her own part of Mrs. Thomas, the charwoman."

"Liars and impostors—both!" shouted the girl, who was rapidly losing all presence of mind. "I'll send for the police."

"Quite unnecessary," rejoined Lady Molly coolly; "Detective-Inspector Danvers is just outside that door."

The girl made a dash for the other door, but I was too quick for her, and held her back, even whilst Lady Molly gave a short, sharp call which brought Danvers on the scene.

I must say that Miss Cruikshank made a bold fight, but Danvers had two of our fellows with him, and arrested her on the warrant for the apprehension of the person known as Mrs. Thomas.

The clothes of the charwoman who had so mysteriously disappeared had been found by Lady Molly at the back of the coal cellar, and she was still dressed in them at the present moment.

No wonder I had not recognised my own dainty lady in the grimy woman who had so successfully played the part of a blackmailer on the murderess of Mrs. Dunstan. She explained to me subsequently that the first inkling that she had had of the horrible truth—namely, that it was Miss Cruikshank who had deliberately planned to murder Mrs. Dunstan by impersonating a charwoman for a while, and thus throwing dust in the eyes of the police—was when she heard of the callous words which the old lady was supposed to have uttered when she was told of Miss Violet's flight from the house in the middle of the night.

"She may have been very angry at the girl's escapade," explained Lady Molly to me, "but she would not have allowed her to starve. Such cruelty was out of all proportion to the offence. Then I looked about me for a stronger motive for the old lady's wrath; and, remembering what she said on New Year's Eve, when Violet fled crying from the room, I came to the conclusion that her anger was not directed against her niece, but against the other girl, and against the man who had transferred his affections from Violet Frostwicke to Miss Cruikshank, and had not only irritated Mrs. Dunstan by this clandestine, double-faced love-making, but had broken the heart of his trusting *fiancée*.

"No doubt Miss Cruikshank did not know that the will, whereby she was to inherit £1,000, was not signed, and no doubt she and young Athol planned out that cruel murder between them. The charwoman was also a bag of sand which was literally thrown in the eyes of the police."

"But," I objected, "I can't understand how a cold-blooded creature like that Miss Cruikshank could have allowed herself to be terrorised and blackmailed. She knew that you could not be Mrs. Thomas, since Mrs. Thomas never existed."

"Yes; but one must reckon a little sometimes with that negligible quantity known as conscience. My appearance as Mrs. Thomas vaguely frightened Miss Cruikshank. She wondered who I was and what I knew. When, three days later, I found the shabby clothes in the coal-cellar and appeared dressed in them, she lost her head. She gave me money! From that moment she was done for. Confession was only a matter of time."

And Miss Cruikshank did make full confession. She was recommended to mercy on account of her sex, but she was plucky enough not to implicate David Athol in the recital of her crime.

He has since emigrated to Western Canada.

THE MAN IN THE INVERNESS CAPE

1

I have heard many people say—people, too, mind you, who read their daily paper regularly—that it is quite impossible for anyone to "disappear" within the confines of the British Isles. At the same time these wise people invariably admit one great exception to their otherwise unimpeachable theory, and that is the case of Mr. Leonard Marvell, who, as you know, walked out one afternoon from the Scotia Hotel in Cromwell Road and has never been seen or heard of since.

Information had originally been given to the police by Mr. Marvell's sister Olive, a Scotchwoman of the usually accepted type: tall, bony, with sandy-coloured hair, and a somewhat melancholy expression in her blue-grey eyes.

Her brother, she said, had gone out on a rather foggy afternoon. I think it was the 3rd of February, just about a year ago. His intention had been to go and consult a solicitor in the City—whose address had been given him recently by a friend—about some private business of his own.

Mr. Marvell had told his sister that he would get a train at South Kensington Station to Moorgate Street, and walk thence to Finsbury Square. She was to expect him home by dinner-time.

As he was, however, very irregular in his habits, being fond of spending his evenings at restaurants and music-halls, the sister did not feel the least anxious when he did not return home at the

340

appointed time. She had her dinner in the *table d'hôte* room, and went to bed soon after 10.0.

She and her brother occupied two bedrooms and a sitting-room on the second floor of the little private hotel. Miss Marvell, more-over, had a maid always with her, as she was somewhat of an in-valid. This girl, Rosie Campbell, a nice-looking Scotch lassie, slept on the top floor.

It was only on the following morning, when Mr. Leonard did not put in an appearance at breakfast, that Miss Marvell began to feel anxious. According to her own account, she sent Rosie in to see if anything was the matter, and the girl, wide-eyed and not a little frightened, came back with the news that Mr. Marvell was not in his room, and that his bed had not been slept in that night.

With characteristic Scottish reserve, Miss Olive said nothing about the matter at the time to anyone, nor did she give informa-tion to the police until two days later, when she herself had ex-hausted every means in her power to discover her brother's where-abouts.

She had seen the lawyer to whose office Leonard Marvell had intended going that afternoon, but Mr. Statham, the solicitor in question, had seen nothing of the missing man.

With great adroitness Rosie, the maid, had made inquiries at South Kensington and Moorgate Street stations. At the former, the booking clerk, who knew Mr. Marvell by sight, distinctly remem-bered selling him a first-class ticket to one of the City stations in the early part of the afternoon; but at Moorgate Street, which is a very busy station, no one recollected seeing a tall, red-haired Scotchman in an Inverness cape—such was the description given of the missing man. By that time the fog had become very thick in the City; traffic was disorganised, and everyone felt fussy, ill-tem-pered, and self-centred.

These, in substance, were the details which Miss Marvell gave to the police on the subject of her brother's strange disappearance.

At first she did not appear very anxious; she seemed to have great faith in Mr. Marvell's power to look after himself; moreover, she declared positively that her brother had neither valuables nor money about his person when he went out that afternoon.

But as day succeeded day and no trace of the missing man had yet been found, matters became more serious, and the search instituted by our fellows at the Yard waxed more keen.

A description of Mr. Leonard Marvell was published in the leading London and provincial dailies. Unfortunately, there was no good photograph of him extant, and descriptions are apt to prove vague.

Very little was known about the man beyond his disappearance, which had rendered him famous. He and his sister had arrived at the Scotia Hotel about a month previously, and subsequently they were joined by the maid Campbell.

Scotch people are far too reserved ever to speak of themselves or their affairs to strangers. Brother and sister spoke very little to anyone at the hotel. They had their meals in their sitting-room, waited on by the maid, who messed with the staff. But, in face of the present terrible calamity, Miss Marvell's frigidity relaxed before the police inspector, to whom she gave what information she could about her brother.

"He was like a son to me," she explained with scarcely restrained tears, "for we lost our parents early in life, and as we were left very, very badly off, our relations took but little notice of us. My brother was years younger than I am—and though he was a little wild and fond of pleasure, he was as good as gold to me, and has supported us both for years by journalistic work. We came to London from Glasgow about a month ago, because Leonard got a very good appointment on the staff of the *Daily Post*."

All this, of course, was soon proved to be true; and although, on minute inquiries being instituted in Glasgow, but little seemed to be known about Mr. Leonard Marvell in that city, there seemed no doubt that he had done some reporting for the *Courier*, and that latterly, in response to an advertisement, he had applied for and obtained regular employment on the *Daily Post*.

The latter enterprising halfpenny journal, with characteristic magnanimity, made an offer of £50 reward to any of its subscribers who gave information which would lead to the discovery of the whereabouts of Mr. Leonard Marvell.

But time went by, and that £50 remained unclaimed.

2

Lady Molly had not seemed as interested as she usually was in cases of this sort. With strange flippancy—wholly unlike herself—she remarked that one Scotch journalist more or less in London did not vastly matter.

I was much amused, therefore, one morning about three weeks after the mysterious disappearance of Mr. Leonard Marvell, when Jane, our little parlour-maid, brought in a card accompanied by a letter.

The card bore the name "Miss Olive Marvell." The letter was the usual formula from the chief, asking Lady Molly to have a talk with the lady in question, and to come and see him on the subject after the interview.

With a smothered yawn my dear lady told Jane to show in Miss Marvell.

"There are two of them, my lady," said Jane, as she prepared to obey.

"Two what?" asked Lady Molly with a laugh.

"Two ladies, I mean," explained Jane.

"Well! Show them both into the drawing-room," said Lady Molly, impatiently.

Then, as Jane went off on this errand, a very funny thing happened; funny, because during the entire course of my intimate association with my dear lady, I had never known her act with such marked indifference in the face of an obviously interesting case. She turned to me and said:

"Mary, you had better see these two women, whoever they may be; I feel that they would bore me to distraction. Take note of what they say, and let me know. Now, don't argue," she added with a laugh, which peremptorily put a stop to my rising protest, "but go and interview Miss Marvell and Co."

Needless to say, I promptly did as I was told, and the next few seconds saw me installed in our little drawing-room, saying polite preliminaries to the two ladies who sat opposite to me.

I had no need to ask which of them was Miss Marvell. Tall, ill-dressed in deep black, with a heavy crape veil over her face, and black cotton gloves, she looked the uncompromising Scotchwoman to the life. In strange contrast to her depressing appearance, there sat beside her an over-dressed, much behatted, peroxided young woman, who bore the stamp of *the* profession all over her pretty, painted face.

Miss Marvell, I was glad to note, was not long in plunging into the subject which had brought her here.

"I saw a gentleman at Scotland Yard," she explained, after a short preamble, "because Miss—er—Lulu Fay came to me at the hotel this very morning with a story which, in my opinion, should have been told to the police directly my brother's disappearance became known, and not three weeks later."

The emphasis which she laid on the last few words and the stern look with which she regarded the golden-haired young woman beside her, showed the disapproval with which the rigid Scotchwoman viewed any connection which her brother might have had with the lady, whose very name seemed unpleasant to her lips.

Miss—er—Lulu Fay blushed even through her rouge, and turned a pair of large, liquid eyes imploringly upon me.

"I—I didn't know. I was frightened," she stammered.

"There's no occasion to be frightened now," retorted Miss Marvell, "and the sooner you try and be truthful about the whole matter, the better it will be for all of us."

And the stern woman's lips closed with a snap, as she deliberately turned her back on Miss Fay and began turning over the leaves of a magazine which happened to be on a table close to her hand.

I muttered a few words of encouragement, for the little actress looked ready to cry. I spoke as kindly as I could, telling her that if indeed she could throw some light on Mr. Marvell's present whereabouts it was her duty to be quite frank on the subject.

She "hem"-ed and "ha"-ed for awhile, and her simpering ways were just beginning to tell on my nerves, when she suddenly started talking very fast.

"I am principal boy at the Grand," she explained with great volubility; "and I knew Mr. Leonard Marvell well—in fact—er—he paid me a good deal of attention and—"

"Yes—and—?" I queried, for the girl was obviously nervous.

There was a pause. Miss Fay began to cry.

"And it seems that my brother took this young—er—lady to supper on the night of February 3rd, after which no one has ever seen or heard of him again," here interposed Miss Marvell, quietly.

"Is that so?" I asked.

Lulu Fay nodded, whilst heavy tears fell upon her clasped hands.

"But why did you not tell this to the police three weeks ago?" I ejaculated, with all the sternness at my command.

"I—I was frightened," she stammered.

"Frightened? Of what?"

"I am engaged to Lord Mountnewte and—"

"And you did not wish him to know that you were accepting the attentions of Mr. Leonard Marvell—was that it? Well," I added, with involuntary impatience, "what happened after you had supper with Mr. Marvell?"

"Oh! I hope—I hope that nothing happened," she said through more tears; "we had supper at the Trocadero, and he saw me into my brougham. Suddenly, just as I was driving away, I saw Lord Mountnewte standing quite close to us in the crowd."

"Did the two men know one another?" I asked.

"No," replied Miss Fay; "at least, I didn't think so, but when I looked back through the window of my carriage I saw them standing on the kerb talking to each other for a moment, and then walk off together towards Piccadilly Circus. That is the last I have seen of either of them," continued the little actress with a fresh flood of tears. "Lord Mountnewte hasn't spoken to me since, and Mr. Marvell has disappeared with my money and my diamonds."

"Your money and your diamonds?" I gasped in amazement.

"Yes; he told me he was a jeweller, and that my diamonds wanted re-setting. He took them with him that evening, for he said that London jewellers were clumsy thieves, and that he would love to do the work for me himself. I also gave him two hundred pounds, which he said he would want for buying the gold and platinum required for the settings. And now he has disappeared—and my diamonds—and my money! Oh! I have been very—very foolish—and—"

Her voice broke down completely. Of course, one often hears of the idiocy of girls giving money and jewels unquestioningly to clever adventurers who know how to trade upon their inordinate vanity. There was, therefore, nothing very out of the way in the story just told me by Miss—er—Lulu Fay, until the moment when Miss Marvell's quiet voice, with its marked Scotch burr, broke in upon the short silence which had followed the actress's narrative.

"As I explained to the chief detective-inspector at Scotland Yard," she said calmly, "the story which this young—er—lady tells is only partly true. She may have had supper with Mr. Leonard Marvell on the night of February 3rd, and he may have paid her certain attentions; but he never deceived her by telling her that he was a jeweller, nor did he obtain possession of her diamonds and her money through false statements. My brother was the soul of honour and loyalty. If for some reason which Miss—er—Lulu Fay chooses to keep secret, he had her jewels and money in his possession on the fatal February 3rd, then I think his disappearance is accounted for. He has been robbed and perhaps murdered."

Like a true Scotchwoman she did not give way to tears, but even her harsh voice trembled slightly when she thus bore witness to her brother's honesty, and expressed the fears which assailed her as to his fate.

Imagine my plight! I could ill forgive my dear lady for leaving me in this unpleasant position—a sort of peacemaker between two women who evidently hated one another, and each of whom was trying her best to give the other "the lie direct."

I ventured to ring for our faithful Jane and to send her with an imploring message to Lady Molly, begging her to come and disentangle the threads of this muddled skein with her clever fingers;

but Jane returned with a curt note from my dear lady, telling me not to worry about such a silly case, and to bow the two women out of the flat as soon as possible and then come for a nice walk.

I wore my official manner as well as I could, trying not to betray the 'prentice hand. Of course, the interview lasted a great deal longer, and there was considerably more talk than I can tell you of in a brief narrative. But the gist of it all was just as I have said. Miss Lulu Fay stuck to every point of the story which she had originally told Miss Marvell. It was the latter uncompromising lady who had immediately marched the younger woman off to Scotland Yard in order that she might repeat her tale to the police. I did not wonder that the chief promptly referred them both to Lady Molly.

Anyway, I made excellent shorthand notes of the conflicting stories which I heard; and I finally saw, with real relief, the two women walk out of our little front door.

3

Miss—er—Lulu Fay, mind you, never contradicted in any one particular the original story which she had told me, about going out to supper with Leonard Marvell, entrusting him with £200 and the diamonds, which he said he would have reset for her, and seeing him finally in close conversation with her recognised *fiancé*, Lord Mountnewte. Miss Marvell, on the other hand, very commendably refused to admit that her brother acted dishonestly towards the girl. If he had her jewels and money in his possession at the time of his disappearance, then he had undoubtedly been robbed, or perhaps murdered, on his way back to the hotel, and if Lord Mountnewte had been the last to speak to him on that fatal night, then Lord Mountnewte must be able to throw some light on the mysterious occurrence.

Our fellows at the Yard were abnormally active. It seemed, on the face of it, impossible that a man, healthy, vigorous, and admittedly sober, should vanish in London between Piccadilly Circus and Cromwell Road without leaving the slightest trace of himself or of the valuables said to have been in his possession.

Of course, Lord Mountnewte was closely questioned. He was a young Guardsman of the usual pattern, and, after a great deal of vapid talk which irritated Detective-Inspector Saunders not a little, he made the following statement—

"I certainly am acquainted with Miss Lulu Fay. On the night in question I was standing outside the Troc, when I saw this young lady at her own carriage window talking to a tall man in an Inverness cape. She had, earlier in the day, refused my invitation to supper, saying that she was not feeling very well, and would go home directly after the theatre; therefore I felt, naturally, a little vexed. I was just about to hail a taxi, meaning to go on to the club, when, to my intense astonishment, the man in the Inverness cape came up to me and asked me if I could tell him the best way to get back to Cromwell Road."

"And what did you do?" asked Saunders.

"I walked a few steps with him and put him on his way," replied Lord Mountnewte, blandly.

In Saunder's own expressive words, he thought that story "fishy." He could not imagine the arm of coincidence being quite so long as to cause these two men—who presumably were both in love with the same girl, and who had just met at a moment when one of them was obviously suffering pangs of jealously—to hold merely a topographical conversation with one another. But it was equally difficult to suppose that the eldest son and heir of the Marquis of Loam should murder a successful rival and then rob him in the streets of London.

Moreover, here came the eternal and unanswerable questions: If Lord Mountnewte had murdered Leonard Marvell, where and how had he done it, and what had he done with the body?

I dare say you are wondering by this time why I have said nothing about the maid, Rosie Campbell.

Well, plenty of very clever people (I mean those who write letters to the papers and give suggestions to every official department in the kingdom) thought that the police ought to keep a very strict eye upon that pretty Scotch lassie. For she was very pretty,

and had quaint, demure ways which rendered her singularly attractive, in spite of the fact that, for most masculine tastes, she
would have been considered too tall. Of course, Saunders and
Danvers kept an eye on her—you may be sure of that—and got a
good deal of information about her from the people at the hotel.
Most of it, unfortunately, was irrelevant to the case. She was maid-
attendant to Miss Marvell, who was feeble in health, and who went
out but little. Rosie waited on her master and mistress upstairs,
carrying their meals to their private room, and doing their bed-
rooms. The rest of the day she was fairly free, and was quite so-
ciable downstairs with the hotel staff.

With regard to her movements and actions on that memorable
3rd of February, Saunders—though he worked very hard—could
glean but little useful information. You see, in a hotel of that kind,
with an average of thirty to forty guests at one time, it is extremely
difficult to state positively what any one person did or did not do
on that particular day.

Most people at the Scotia remembered that Miss Marvell dined
in the *table d'hôte* room on that 3rd of February; this she did about
once a fortnight, when her maid had an evening "out."

The hotel staff also recollected fairly distinctly that Miss Rosie
Campbell was not in the steward's room at supper-time that
evening, but no one could remember definitely when she came in.

One of the chambermaids who occupied the bedroom adjoining hers, said she heard her moving about soon after midnight;
the hall porter declared that he saw her come in just before half-
past twelve when he closed the doors for the night.

But one of the ground-floor valets said that, on the morning of
the 4th, he saw Miss Marvell's maid, in hat and coat, slip into the
house and upstairs, very quickly and quietly, soon after the front
doors were opened, namely, about 7.0 a.m.

Here, of course, was a direct contradiction between the chambermaid and hall porter on the one side, and the valet on the other,
whilst Miss Marvell said that Campbell came into her room and
made her some tea long before seven o'clock every morning, including that of the 4th.

I assure you our fellows at the Yard were ready to tear their hair out by the roots, from sheer aggravation at this maze of contradictions which met them at every turn.

The whole thing seemed so simple. There was nothing "to it" as it were, and but very little real suggestion of foul play, and yet Mr. Leonard Marvell had disappeared, and no trace of him could be found.

Everyone now talked freely of murder. London is a big town, and this would not have been the first instance of a stranger—for Mr. Leonard Marvell was practically a stranger in London—being enticed to a lonely part of the city on a foggy night, and there done away with and robbed, and the body hidden in an out-of-the-way cellar, where it might not be discovered for months to come.

But the newspaper-reading public is notably fickle, and Mr. Leonard Marvell was soon forgotten by everyone save the chief and the batch of our fellows who had charge of the case.

Thus I heard through Danvers one day that Rosie Campbell had left Miss Marvell's employ, and was living in rooms in Findlater Terrace, near Walham Green.

I was alone in our Maida Vale flat at the time, my dear lady having gone to spend the week-end with the Dowager Lady Loam, who was an old friend of hers; nor, when she returned, did she seem any more interested in Rosie Campbell's movements than she had been hitherto.

Yet another month went by, and I for one had absolutely ceased to think of the man in the Inverness cape, who had so mysteriously and so completely vanished in the very midst of busy London, when, one morning early in January, Lady Molly made her appearance in my room, looking more like the landlady of a disreputable gambling-house than anything else I could imagine.

"What in the world—?" I began.

"Yes! I think I look the part," she replied, surveying with obvious complacency the extraordinary figure which confronted her in the glass.

My dear lady had on a purple cloth coat and skirt of a peculiarly vivid hue, and of a singular cut, which made her matchless figure look like a sack of potatoes. Her soft brown hair was quite hidden beneath a "transformation," of that yellow-reddish tint only to be met with in very cheap dyes.

As for her hat! I won't attempt to describe it. It towered above and around her face, which was plentifully covered with brick-red and with that kind of powder which causes the cheeks to look a deep mauve.

My dear lady looked, indeed, a perfect picture of appalling vulgarity.

"Where are you going in this elegant attire?" I asked in amazement.

"I have taken rooms in Findlater Terrace," she replied lightly. "I feel that the air of Walham Green will do us both good. Our amiable, if somewhat slatternly, landlady expects us in time for luncheon. You will have to keep rigidly in the background, Mary, all the while we are there. I said that I was bringing an invalid niece with me, and, as a preliminary, you may as well tie two or three thick veils over your face. I think I may safely promise that you won't be dull."

And we certainly were not dull during our brief stay at 34, Findlater Terrace, Walham Green. Fully equipped, and arrayed in our extraordinary garments, we duly arrived there, in a rickety four-wheeler, on the top of which were perched two seedy-looking boxes.

The landlady was a toothless old creature, who apparently thought washing a quite unnecessary proceeding. In this she was evidently at one with every one of her neighbours. Findlater Terrace looked unspeakably squalid; groups of dirty children congregated in the gutters and gave forth discordant shrieks as our cab drove up.

Through my thick veils I thought that, some distance down the road, I spied a horsy-looking man in ill-fitting riding-breeches and gaiters, who vaguely reminded me of Danvers.

Within half an hour of our installation, and whilst we were eating a tough steak over a doubtful table cloth, my dear lady told me that she had been waiting a full month, until rooms in this

particular house happened to be vacant. Fortunately the population in Findlater Terrace is always a shifting one, and Lady Molly
had kept a sharp eye on No. 34, where, on the floor above, lived
Miss Rosie Campbell. Directly the last set of lodgers walked out of
the ground-floor rooms, we were ready to walk in.

My dear lady's manners and customs, whilst living at the above
aristocratic address, were fully in keeping with her appearance.
The shrill, rasping voice which she assumed echoed from attic to
cellar.

One day I heard her giving vague hints to the landlady that her
husband, Mr. Marcus Stein, had had a little trouble with the police about a small hotel which he had kept somewhere near Fitzroy
Square, and where "young gentlemen used to come and play cards
of a night." The landlady was also made to understand that the
worthy Mr. Stein was now living temporarily at His Majesty's
expense, whilst Mrs. Stein had to live a somewhat secluded life,
away from her fashionable friends.

The misfortunes of the pseudo Mrs. Stein in no way marred
the amiability of Mrs. Tredwen, our landlady. The inhabitants of
Findlater Terrace care very little about the antecedents of their
lodgers, so long as they pay their week's rent in advance, and settle
their "extras" without much murmur.

This Lady Molly did, with a generosity characteristic of an
ex-lady of means. She never grumbled at the quantity of jam and
marmalade which we were supposed to have consumed every week,
and which anon reached titanic proportions. She tolerated Mrs.
Tredwen's cat, tipped Ermyntrude—the tousled lodging-house
slavey—lavishly, and lent the upstairs lodger her spirit-lamp and
curling-tongs when Miss Rosie Campbell's got out of order.

A certain degree of intimacy followed the loan of those curling-tongs. Miss Campbell, reserved and demure, greatly sympathised with the lady who was not on the best of terms with the
police. I kept steadily in the background. The two ladies did not
visit each other's rooms, but they held long and confidential conversations on the landings, and I gathered, presently, that the
pseudo Mrs. Stein had succeeded in persuading Rosie Campbell

that, if the police were watching No. 34, Findlater Terrace, at all, it was undoubtedly on account of the unfortunate Mr. Stein's faithful wife.

I found it a little difficult to fathom Lady Molly's intentions. We had been in the house over three weeks, and nothing whatever had happened. Once I ventured on a discreet query as to whether we were to expect the sudden re-appearance of Mr. Leonard Marvell.

"For if that's all about it," I argued, "then surely the men from the Yard could have kept the house in view, without all this inconvenience and masquerading on our part."

But to this tirade my dear lady vouchsafed no reply.

She and her newly acquired friend were, about this time, deeply interested in the case known as the "West End Shop Robberies," which no doubt you recollect, since they occurred such a very little while ago. Ladies who were shopping in the large drapers' emporiums during the crowded and busy sale time, lost reticules, purses, and valuable parcels, without any trace of the clever thief being found.

The drapers, during sale-time, invariably employ detectives in plain clothes to look after their goods, but in this case it was the customers who were robbed, and the detectives, attentive to every attempt at "shop-lifting," had had no eyes for the more subtle thief.

I had already noticed Miss Rosie Campbell's keen look of excitement whenever the pseudo Mrs. Stein discussed these cases with her. I was not a bit surprised, therefore, when, one afternoon at about teatime, my dear lady came home from her habitual walk, and, at the top of her shrill voice, called out to me from the hall:

"Mary! Mary! they've got the man of the shop robberies. He's given the silly police the slip this time, but they know who he is now, and I suppose they'll get him presently. 'Tisn't anybody I know," she added, with that harsh, common laugh which she had adopted for her part.

I had come out of the room in response to her call, and was standing just outside our own sitting-room door. Mrs. Tredwen, too, bedraggled and unkempt, as usual, had sneaked up the area steps, closely followed by Ermyntrude.

But on the half-landing just above us the trembling figure of Rosie Campbell, with scared white face and dilated eyes, looked on the verge of a sudden fall.

Still talking shrilly and volubly, Lady Molly ran up to her, but Campbell met her half-way, and the pseudo Mrs. Stein, taking vigorous hold of her wrist, dragged her into our own sitting-room.

"Pull yourself together, now," she said with rough kindness; "that owl Tredwen is listening, and you needn't let her know too much. Shut the door, Mary. Lor' bless you, m'dear, I've gone through worse scares than these. There! you just lie down on this sofa a bit. My niece'll make you a nice cup o'tea; and I'll go and get an evening paper, and see what's going on. I suppose you are very interested in the shop robbery man, or you wouldn't have took on so."

Without waiting for Campbell's contradiction to this statement, Lady Molly flounced out of the house.

Miss Campbell hardly spoke during the next ten minutes that she and I were left alone together. She lay on the sofa with eyes wide open, staring up at the ceiling, evidently still in a great state of fear.

I had just got tea ready when Lady Molly came back. She had an evening paper in her hand, but threw this down on the table directly she came in.

"I could only get an early edition," she said breathlessly, "and the silly thing hasn't got anything in it about the matter."

She drew near to the sofa, and, subduing the shrillness of her voice, she whispered rapidly, bending down towards Campbell:

"There's a man hanging about at the corner down there. No, no; it's not the police," she added quickly, in response to the girl's sudden start of alarm. "Trust me, my dear, for knowing a 'tec when I see one! Why, I'd smell one half a mile off. No; my opinion is that it's your man, my dear, and that he's in a devil of a hole."

"Oh! he oughtn't to come here," ejaculated Campbell in great alarm. "He'll get me into trouble and do himself no good. He's been a fool!" she added, with a fierceness wholly unlike her usual demure placidity, "getting himself caught like that. Now I suppose we shall have to hook it—if there's time."

"Can I do anything to help you?" asked the pseudo Mrs. Stein. "You know I've been through all this myself, when they was after Mr. Stein. Or perhaps Mary could do something."

"Well, yes," said the girl, after a slight pause, during which she seemed to be gathering her wits together; "I'll write a note, and you shall take it, if you will, to a friend of mine—a lady who lives in the Cromwell Road. But if you still see a man lurking about at the corner of the street, then, just as you pass him, say the word 'Campbell,' and if he replies 'Rosie,' then give *him* the note. Will you do that?"

"Of course I will, my dear. Just you leave it all to me."

And the pseudo Mrs. Stein brought ink and paper and placed them on the table. Rosie Campbell wrote a brief note, and then fastened it down with a bit of sealing-wax before she handed it over to Lady Molly. The note was addressed to Miss Marvell, Scotia Hotel, Cromwell Road.

"You understand?" she said eagerly. "Don't give the note to the man unless he says 'Rosie' in reply to the word 'Campbell.'"

"All right—all right!" said Lady Molly, slipping the note into her reticule. "And you go up to your room, Miss Campbell; it's no good giving that old fool Tredwen too much to gossip about."

Rosie Campbell went upstairs, and presently my dear lady and I were walking rapidly down the badly-lighted street.

"Where is the man?" I whispered eagerly as soon as we were out of earshot of No. 34.

"There is no man," replied Lady Molly, quickly.

"But the West End shop thief?" I asked.

"He hasn't been caught yet, and won't be either, for he is far too clever a scoundrel to fall into an ordinary trap."

She did not give me time to ask further questions, for presently, when we had reached Reporton Square, my dear lady handed me the note written by Campbell, and said:

"Go straight on to the Scotia Hotel, and ask for Miss Marvell; send up the note to her, but don't let her see you, as she knows you by sight. I must see the chief first, and will be with you as soon as possible. Having delivered the note, you must hang about outside as long as you can. Use your wits; she must not leave the hotel before I see her."

There was no hansom to be got in this elegant quarter of the town, so, having parted from my dear lady, I made for the nearest Underground station, and took a train for South Kensington.

Thus it was nearly seven o'clock before I reached the Scotia. In answer to my inquiries for Miss Marvell, I was told that she was ill in bed and could see no one. I replied that I had only brought a note for her, and would wait for a reply.

Acting on my dear lady's instructions, I was as slow in my movements as ever I could be, and was some time in finding the note and handing it to a waiter, who then took it upstairs.

Presently he returned with the message: "Miss Marvell says there is no answer."

Whereupon I asked for pen and paper at the office, and wrote the following brief note on my own responsibility, using my wits as my dear lady had bidden me to do.

"Please, madam," I wrote, "will you send just a line to Miss Rosie Campbell? She seems very upset and frightened at some news she has had."

Once more the waiter ran upstairs, and returned with a sealed envelope, which I slipped into my reticule.

Time was slipping by very slowly. I did not know how long I should have to wait outside in the cold, when, to my horror, I heard a hard voice, with a marked Scotch accent, saying:

"I am going out, waiter, and shan't be back to dinner. Tell them to lay a little cold supper upstairs in my room."

The next moment Miss Marvell, with coat, hat, and veil, was descending the stairs.

My plight was awkward. I certainly did not think it safe to present myself before the lady; she would undoubtedly recollect my face. Yet I had orders to detain her until the appearance of Lady Molly.

Miss Marvell seemed in no hurry. She was putting on her gloves as she came downstairs. In the hall she gave a few more instructions to the porter, whilst I, in a dark corner in the background, was vaguely planning an assault or an alarm of fire.

Suddenly, at the hotel entrance, where the porter was obsequiously holding open the door for Miss Marvell to pass through, I saw the latter's figure stiffen; she took one step back as if involuntarily, then, equally quickly, attempted to dart across the threshold, on which a group—composed of my dear lady, of Saunders, and of two or three people scarcely distinguishable in the gloom beyond—had suddenly made its appearance.

Miss Marvell was forced to retreat into the hall; already I had heard Saunder's hurriedly whispered words:

"Try and not make a fuss in this place, now. Everything can go off quietly, you know."

Danvers and Cotton, whom I knew well, were already standing one each side of Miss Marvell, whilst suddenly amongst this group I recognised Fanny, the wife of Danvers, who is one of our female searchers at the yard.

"Shall we go up to your own room?" suggested Saunders.

"I think that is quite unnecessary," interposed Lady Molly. "I feel convinced that Mr. Leonard Marvell will yield to the inevitable quietly, and follow you without giving any trouble."

Marvell, however, did make a bold dash for liberty. As Lady Molly had said previously, he was far too clever to allow himself to be captured easily. But my dear lady had been cleverer. As she told me subsequently, she had from the first suspected that the trio who lodged at the Scotia Hotel were really only a duo—namely, Leonard Marvell and his wife. The latter impersonated a maid most of the time; but among these two clever people the three characters were interchangeable. Of course, there was no Miss Marvell at all. Leonard was alternately dressed up as man or woman, according to the requirements of his villainies.

"As soon as I heard that Miss Marvell was very tall and bony," said Lady Molly, "I thought that there might be a possibility of her being merely a man in disguise. Then there was the fact—but little dwelt on by either the police or the public—that no one seems ever to have seen brother and sister together, nor was the entire trio ever seen at one and the same time.

"On that 3rd of February Leonard Marvell went out. No doubt he changed his attire in a lady's waiting-room at one of the railway stations; subsequently he came home, now dressed as Miss Marvell, and had dinner in the *table d'hôte* room so as to set up a fairly plausible alibi. But ultimately it was his wife, the pseudo Rosie Campbell, who stayed indoors that night, whilst he, Leonard Marvell, when going out after dinner, impersonated the maid until he was clear of the hotel; then he reassumed his male clothes once more, no doubt in the deserted waiting-room of some railway station, and met Miss Lulu Fay at supper, subsequently returning to the hotel in the guise of the maid.

"You see the game of criss-cross, don't you? This interchanging of characters was bound to baffle everyone. Many clever scoundrels have assumed disguises, sometimes impersonating members of the opposite sex to their own, but never before have I known two people play the part of three. Thus, endless contradictions followed as to the hour when Campbell the maid went out and when she came in, for at one time it was she herself who was seen by the valet, and at another it was Leonard Marvell dressed in her clothes."

He was also clever enough to accost Lord Mountnewte in the open street, thus bringing further complications into this strange case.

After the successful robbery of Miss Fay's diamonds, Leonard Marvell and his wife parted for awhile. They were waiting for an opportunity to get across the Channel and there turn their booty into solid cash. Whilst Mrs. Marvell, *alias* Rosie Campbell, led a retired life in Findlater Terrace, Leonard kept his hand in with West End shop robberies.

Then Lady Molly entered the lists. As usual, her scheme was bold and daring; she trusted her own intuition and acted accordingly.

When she brought home the false news that the author of the shop robberies had been spotted by the police, Rosie Campbell's obvious terror confirmed her suspicions. The note written by the latter to the so-called Miss Marvell, though it contained nothing in any way incriminating, was the crowning certitude that my dear lady was right, as usual, in all her surmises.

And now Mr. Leonard Marvell will be living for a couple of years at the tax-payers' expense; he has "disappeared" temporarily from the public eye.

Rosie Campbell—*i.e.* Mrs. Marvell—has gone to Glasgow. I feel convinced that two years hence we shall hear of the worthy couple again.

THE WOMAN IN THE BIG HAT

1

Lady Molly always had the idea that if the finger of Fate had pointed to Mathis' in Regent Street, rather than to Lyons', as the most advisable place for us to have a cup of tea that afternoon, Mr. Culledon would be alive at the present moment.

My dear lady is quite sure—and needless to say that I share her belief in herself—that she would have anticipated the murderer's intentions, and thus prevented one of the most cruel and callous of crimes which were ever perpetrated in the heart of London.

She and I had been to a matinée of "Trilby," and were having tea at Lyons', which is exactly opposite Mathis' Vienna café in Regent Street. From where we sat we commanded a view of the street and of the café, which had been very crowded during the last hour.

We had lingered over our toasted muffin until past six, when our attention was drawn to the unusual commotion which had arisen both outside and in the brilliantly lighted place over the road.

We saw two men run out of the doorway, and return a minute or two later in company with a policeman. You know what is the inevitable result of such a proceeding in London. Within three minutes a crowd had collected outside Mathis'. Two or three more constables had already assembled, and had some difficulty in keeping the entrance clear of intruders.

But already my dear lady, keen as a pointer on the scent, had hastily paid her bill, and, without waiting to see if I followed her or not, had quickly crossed the road, and the next moment her graceful form was lost in the crowd.

I went after her, impelled by curiosity, and presently caught sight of her in close conversation with one of our own men. I have always thought that Lady Molly must have eyes at the back of her head, otherwise how could she have known that I stood behind her now? Anyway, she beckoned to me, and together we entered Mathis', much to the astonishment and anger of the less fortunate crowd.

The usually gay little place was indeed sadly transformed. In one corner the waitresses, in dainty caps and aprons, had put their heads together, and were eagerly whispering to one another whilst casting furtive looks at the small group assembled in front of one of those pretty alcoves, which, as you know, line the walls all round the big tea-room at Mathis'.

Here two of our men were busy with pencil and note-book, whilst one fair-haired waitress, dissolved in tears, was apparently giving them a great deal of irrelevant and confused information.

Chief Inspector Saunders had, I understood, been already sent for; the constables, confronted with this extraordinary tragedy, were casting anxious glances towards the main entrance, whilst putting the conventional questions to the young waitress. And in the alcove itself, raised from the floor of the room by a couple of carpeted steps, the cause of all this commotion, all this anxiety, and all these tears, sat huddled up on a chair, with arms lying straight across the marble-topped table, on which the usual paraphernalia of afternoon tea still lay scattered about. The upper part of the body, limp, backboneless, and awry, half propped up against the wall, half falling back upon the outstretched arms, told quite plainly its weird tale of death.

Before my dear lady and I had time to ask any questions, Saunders arrived in a taxicab. He was accompanied by the medical officer, Dr. Townson, who at once busied himself with the dead man, whilst Saunders went up quickly to Lady Molly.

"The chief suggested sending for you," he said quickly; "he was 'phoning you when I left. There's a woman in this case, and we shall rely on you a good deal."

"What has happened?" asked my dear lady, whose fine eyes were glowing with excitement at the mere suggestion of work.

"I have only a few stray particulars," replied Saunders, "but the chief witness is that yellow-haired girl over there. We'll find out what we can from her directly Dr. Townson has given us his opinion."

The medical officer, who had been kneeling beside the dead man, now rose and turned to Saunders. His face was very grave.

"The whole matter is simple enough, so far as I am concerned," he said. "The man has been killed by a terrific dose of morphia—administered, no doubt, in this cup of chocolate," he added, pointing to a cup in which there still lingered the cold dregs of the thick beverage.

"But when did this occur?" asked Saunders, turning to the waitress.

"I can't say," she replied, speaking with obvious nervousness. "The gentleman came in very early with a lady, somewhere about four. They made straight for this alcove. The place was just beginning to fill, and the music had begun."

"And where is the lady now?"

"She went off almost directly. She had ordered tea for herself and a cup of chocolate for the gentleman, also muffins and cakes. About five minutes afterwards, as I went past their table, I heard her say to him. 'I am afraid I must go now, or Jay's will be closed, but I'll be back in less than half an hour. You'll wait for me, won't you?'"

"Did the gentleman seem all right then?"

"Oh, yes," said the waitress. "He had just begun to sip his chocolate, and merely said 'S'long,' as she gathered up her gloves and muff and then went out of the shop."

"And she has not returned since?"

"No."

"When did you first notice there was anything wrong with this gentleman?" asked Lady Molly.

"Well," said the girl with some hesitation, "I looked at him once or twice as I went up and down, for he certainly seemed to have fallen all of a heap. Of course, I thought that he had gone to sleep, and I spoke to the manageress about him, but she thought that I ought to leave him alone for a bit. Then we got very busy, and I paid no more attention to him, until about six o'clock, when most afternoon tea customers had gone, and we were beginning to get the tables ready for dinners. Then I certainly did think there was something wrong with the man. I called to the manageress, and we sent for the police."

"And the lady who was with him at first, what was she like? Would you know her again?" queried Saunders.

"I don't know," replied the girl; "you see, I have to attend to such crowds of people of an afternoon, I can't notice each one. And she had on one of those enormous mushroom hats; no one could have seen her face—not more than her chin—unless they looked right under the hat."

"Would you know the hat again?" asked Lady Molly.

"Yes—I think I should," said the waitress. "It was black velvet and had a lot of plumes. It was enormous," she added, with a sigh of admiration and of longing for the monumental headgear.

During the girl's narrative one of the constables had searched the dead man's pockets. Among other items, he had found several letters addressed to Mark Culledon, Esq., some with an address in Lombard Street, others with one in Fitzjohn's Avenue, Hampstead. The initials M. C., which appeared both in the hat and on the silver mount of a letter-case belonging to the unfortunate gentleman, proved his identity beyond a doubt.

A house in Fitzjohn's Avenue does not, somehow, suggest a bachelor establishment. Even whilst Saunders and the other men were looking through the belongings of the deceased, Lady Molly had already thought of his family—children, perhaps a wife, a mother—who could tell?

What awful news to bring to an unsuspecting, happy family, who might even now be expecting the return of father, husband, or son, at the very moment when he lay murdered in a public place, the victim of some hideous plot or feminine revenge!

As our amiable friends in Paris would say, it jumped to the eyes that there was a woman in the case—a woman who had worn

a gargantuan hat for the obvious purpose of remaining unidentifi-
able when the question of the unfortunate victim's companion that
afternoon came up for solution. And all these facts to put before
an expectant wife or an anxious mother!

As, no doubt, you have already foreseen, Lady Molly took the
difficult task on her own kind shoulders. She and I drove together
to Lorbury House, Fitzjohn's Avenue, and on asking of the man-
servant who opened the door if his mistress were at home, we were
told that Lady Irene Culledon was in the drawing-room.

Mine is not a story of sentiment, so I am not going to dwell on
that interview, which was one of the most painful moments I recollect having lived through.

Lady Irene was young—not five-and-twenty, I should say—*petite* and frail-looking, but with a quiet dignity of manner which
was most impressive. She was Irish, as you know, the daughter of
the Earl of Athyville, and, it seems, had married Mr. Mark Culledon
in the teeth of strenuous opposition on the part of her family, which
was as penniless as it was aristocratic, whilst Mr. Culledon had
great prospects and a splendid business, but possessed neither
ancestors nor high connections. She had only been married six
months, poor little soul, and from all accounts must have idolised
her husband.

Lady Molly broke the news to her with infinite tact, but there it
was! It was a terrific blow—wasn't it?—to deal to a young wife—
now a widow; and there was so little that a stranger could say in
these circumstances. Even my dear lady's gentle voice, her persuasive eloquence, her kindly words, sounded empty and conventional in the face of such appalling grief.

2

Of course, everyone expected that the inquest would reveal
something of the murdered man's inner life—would, in fact, allow
the over-eager public to get a peep into Mr. Mark Culledon's secret orchard, wherein walked a lady who wore abnormally large

velvet hats, and who nourished in her heart one of those terrible grudges against a man which can only find satisfaction in crime.

Equally, of course, the inquest revealed nothing that the public did not already know. The young widow was extremely reticent on the subject of her late husband's life, and the servants had all been fresh arrivals when the young couple, just home from their honeymoon, organised their new household at Lorbury House.

There was an old aunt of the deceased—a Mrs. Steinberg—who lived with the Culledons, but who at the present moment was very ill. Someone in the house—one of the younger servants, probably—very foolishly had told her every detail of the awful tragedy. With positively amazing strength, the invalid thereupon insisted on making a sworn statement, which she desired should be placed before the coroner's jury. She wished to bear solemn testimony to the integrity of her late nephew, Mark Culledon, in case the personality of the mysterious woman in the big hat suggested to evilly disposed minds any thought of scandal.

"Mark Culledon was the one nephew whom I loved," she stated with solemn emphasis. "I have shown my love for him by bequeathing to him the large fortune which I inherited from the late Mr. Steinberg. Mark was the soul of honour, or I should have cut him out of my will as I did my other nephews and nieces. I was brought up in a Scotch home, and I hate all this modern fastness and smartness, which are only other words for what I call profligacy."

Needless to say, the old lady's statement, solemn though it was, was of no use whatever for the elucidation of the mystery which surrounded the death of Mr. Mark Culledon. But as Mrs. Steinberg had talked of "other nephews," whom she had cut out of her will in favour of the murdered man, the police directed inquiries in those various quarters.

Mr. Mark Culledon certainly had several brothers and sisters, also cousins, who at different times—usually for some peccadillo or other—seemed to have incurred the wrath of the strait-laced old lady. But there did not appeal to have been any ill-feeling in the family owing to this. Mrs. Steinberg was sole mistress of her fortune. She might just as well have bequeathed it *in toto* to some hospital as to one particular nephew whom she favoured, and the various relations were glad, on the whole, that the money was going to remain in the family rather than be cast abroad.

The mystery surrounding the woman in the big hat deepened as the days went by. As you know, the longer the period of time which elapses between a crime and the identification of the criminal, the greater chance the latter has of remaining at large.

In spite of strenuous efforts and close questionings of every one of the employees at Mathis', no one could give a very accurate description of the lady who had tea with the deceased on that fateful afternoon.

The first glimmer of light on the mysterious occurrence was thrown, about three weeks later, by a young woman named Katherine Harris, who had been parlour-maid at Lorbury House when first Mr. and Lady Irene Culledon returned from their honeymoon.

I must tell you that Mrs. Steinberg had died a few days after the inquest. The excitement had been too much for her enfeebled heart. Just before her death she had deposited £250 with her banker, which sum was to be paid over to any person giving information which would lead to the apprehension and conviction of the murderer of Mr. Mark Culledon.

This offer had stimulated everyone's zeal, and, I presume, had aroused Katherine Harris to a realisation of what had all the while been her obvious duty.

Lady Molly saw her in the chief's private office, and had much ado to disentangle the threads of the girl's confused narrative. But the main point of Harris's story was that a foreign lady had once called at Lorbury House, about a week after the master and mistress had returned from their honeymoon. Lady Irene was out at the time, and Mr. Culledon saw the lady in his smoking-room.

"She was a very handsome lady," explained Harris, "and was beautifully dressed."

"Did she wear a large hat?" asked the chief.

"I don't remember if it was particularly large," replied the girl.

"But you remember what the lady was like?" suggested Lady Molly.

"Yes, pretty well. She was very, very tall, and very good-looking."

"Would you know her again if you saw her?" rejoined my dear lady.

"Oh, yes; I think so," was Katherine Harris's reply.

Unfortunately, beyond this assurance the girl could say nothing very definite. The foreign lady seems to have been closeted with Mr. Culledon for about an hour, at the end of which time Lady Irene came home.

The butler being out that afternoon it was Harris who let her mistress in, and as the latter asked no questions, the girl did not volunteer the information that her master had a visitor. She went back to the servants' hall, but five minutes later the smoking-room bell rang, and she had to run up again. The foreign lady was then in the hall alone, and obviously waiting to be shown out. This Harris did, after which Mr. Culledon came out of his room, and, in the girl's on graphic words, "he went on dreadful."

"I didn't know I 'ad done anything so very wrong," she explained, "but the master seemed quite furious, and said I wasn't a proper parlour-maid, or I'd have known that visitors must not be shown in straight away like that. I ought to have said that I didn't know if Mr. Culledon was in; that I would go and see. Oh, he did go on at me!" continued Katherine Harris, volubly. "And I suppose he complained to the mistress, for she give me notice the next day."

"And you have never seen the foreign lady since?" concluded Lady Molly.

"No; she never come while I was there."

"By the way, how did you know she was foreign? Did she speak like a foreigner?"

"Oh, no," replied the girl. "She did not say much—only asked for Mr. Culledon—but she looked French like."

This unanswerable bit of logic concluded Katherine's statement. She was very anxious to know whether, if the foreign lady was hanged for murder, she herself would get the £250.

On Lady Molly's assurance that she certainly would, she departed in apparent content.

3

"Well! we are no nearer than we were before," said the chief, with an impatient sigh, when the door had closed behind Katherine Harris.

"Don't you think so?" rejoined Lady Molly, blandly.

"Do you consider that what we have heard just now has helped us to discover who was the woman in the big hat?" retorted the chief, somewhat testily.

"Perhaps not," replied my dear lady, with her sweet smile; "but it may help us to discover who murdered Mr. Culledon."

With which enigmatical statement she effectually silenced the chief, and finally walked out of his office, followed by her faithful Mary.

Following Katherine Harris's indications, a description of the lady who was wanted in connection with the murder of Mr. Culledon was very widely circulated, and within two days of the interview with the ex-parlour-maid another very momentous one took place in the same office.

Lady Molly was at work with the chief over some reports, whilst I was taking shorthand notes at a side desk, when a card was brought in by one of the men, and the next moment, without waiting either for permission to enter or to be more formally announced, a magnificent apparition literally sailed into the dust-covered little back office, filling it with an atmosphere of Parma violets and russia leather.

I don't think that I had ever seen a more beautiful woman in my life. Tall, with a splendid figure and perfect carriage, she vaguely reminded me of the portraits one sees of the late Empress of Austria. This lady was, moreover, dressed to perfection, and wore a large hat adorned with a quantity of plumes.

The chief had instinctively risen to greet her, whilst Lady Molly, still and placid, was eyeing her with a quizzical smile.

"You know who I am, sir," began the visitor as soon as she had sunk gracefully into a chair; "my name is on that card. My appearance, I understand, tallies exactly with that of a woman who is supposed to have murdered Mark Culledon."

She said this so calmly, with such perfect self-possession, that I literally gasped. The chief, too, seemed to have been metaphorically lifted off his feet. He tried to mutter a reply.

"Oh, don't trouble yourself, sir!" she interrupted him, with a smile. "My landlady, my servant, my friends have all read the description of the woman who murdered Mr. Culledon. For the past twenty-four hours I have been watched by your police, therefore I have come to you of my own accord, before they came to arrest me in my flat. I am not too soon, am I?" she asked, with that same cool indifference which was so startling, considering the subject of her conversation.

She spoke English with a scarcely perceptible foreign accent, but I quite understood what Katherine Harris had meant when she said that the lady looked "French like." She certainly did not look English, and when I caught sight of her name on the card, which the chief had handed to Lady Molly, I put her down at once as Viennese. Miss Elizabeth Löwenthal had all the charm, the grace, the elegance, which one associates with Austrian women more than with those of any other nation.

No wonder the chief found it difficult to tell her that, as a matter of fact, the police were about to apply for a warrant that very morning for her arrest on a charge of willful murder.

"I know—I know," she said, seeming to divine his thoughts; "but let me tell you at once, sir, that I did not murder Mark Culledon. He treated me shamefully, and I would willingly have made a scandal just to spite him; he had become so respectable and strait-laced. But between scandal and murder there is a wide gulf. Don't you think so, madam," she added, turning for the first time towards Lady Molly.

"Undoubtedly," replied my dear lady, with the same quizzical smile.

"A wide gulf which, no doubt, Miss Elizabeth Löwenthal will best be able to demonstrate to the magistrate to-morrow," rejoined the chief, with official sternness of manner.

I thought that, for the space of a few seconds, the lady lost her self-assurance at this obvious suggestion—the bloom on her cheeks seemed to vanish, and two hard lines appeared between her fine eyes. But, frightened or not, she quickly recovered herself, and said quietly:

"Now, my dear sir, let us understand one another. I came here for that express purpose. I take it that you don't want your police to look ridiculous any more than I want a scandal. I don't want detectives to hang about round my flat, questioning my neighbours and my servants. They would soon find out that I did not murder Mark Culledon, of course; but the atmosphere of the police would hang round me, and I—I prefer Parma violets," she added, raising a daintily perfumed handkerchief to her nose.

"Then you have come to make a statement?" asked the chief.

"Yes," she replied; "I'll tell you all I know. Mr. Culledon was engaged to marry me; then he met the daughter of an earl, and thought he would like her better as a wife than a simple Miss Löwenthal. I suppose I should be considered an undesirable match for a young man who has a highly respectable and snobbish aunt, who would leave him all her money only on the condition that he made a suitable marriage. I have a voice, and I came over to England two years ago to study English, so that I might sing in oratorio at the Albert Hall. I met Mark on the Calais-Dover boat, when he was returning from a holiday abroad. He fell in love with me, and presently he asked me to be his wife. After some demur, I accepted him; we became engaged, but he told me that our engagement must remain a secret, for he had an old aunt from whom he had great expectations, and who might not approve of his marrying a foreign girl, who was without connections and a professional singer. From that moment I mistrusted him, nor was I very astonished when gradually his affection for me seemed to cool. Soon after, he informed me, quite callously, that he had changed his mind, and was going to marry some swell English lady. I didn't care much, but I wanted to punish him by making a scandal, you understand. I went to his house just to worry him, and finally I decided to bring an action for breach of promise against him. It would have upset him, I know; no doubt his aunt would have cut him out of her will. That is all I wanted, but I did not care enough about him to murder him."

Somehow her tale carried conviction. We were all of us obviously impressed. The chief alone looked visibly disturbed, and I could read what was going on in his mind.

"As you say, Miss Löwenthal," he rejoined, "the police would have found all this out within the next few hours. Once your connection with the murdered man was known to us, the record of your past and his becomes an easy one to peruse. No doubt, too," he added insinuatingly, "our men would soon have been placed in possession of the one undisputable proof of your complete innocence with regard to that fateful afternoon spent at Mathis' café."

"What is that?" she queried blandly.

"An alibi."

"You mean, where I was during the time that Mark was being murdered in a tea shop?"

"Yes," said the chief.

"I was out for a walk," she replied quietly.

"Shopping, perhaps?"

"No."

"You met some one who would remember the circumstance— or your servants could say at what time you came in?"

"No," she repeated dryly; "I met no one, for I took a brisk walk on Primrose Hill. My two servants could only say that I went out at three o'clock that afternoon and returned after five."

There was silence in the little office for a moment or two. I could hear the scraping of the pen with which the chief was idly scribbling geometrical figures on his blotting pad.

Lady Molly was quite still. Her large, luminous eyes were fixed on the beautiful woman who had just told us her strange story, with its unaccountable sequel, its mystery which had deepened with the last phrase which she had uttered. Miss Löwenthal, I felt sure, was conscious of her peril. I am not sufficiently a psychologist to know whether it was guilt or merely fear which was distorting the handsome features now, hardening the face and causing the lips to tremble.

Lady Molly scribbled a few words on a scrap of paper, which she then passed over to the chief. Miss Löwenthal was making visible efforts to steady her nerves.

"That is all I have to tell you," she said, in a voice which sounded dry and harsh. "I think I will go home now."

But she did not rise from her chair, and seemed to hesitate as if fearful lest permission to go were not granted her.

To her obvious astonishment—and, I must add, to my own—the chief immediately rose and said, quite urbanely:

"I thank you very much for the helpful information which you have given me. Of course, we may rely on your presence in town for the next few days, may we not?"

She seemed greatly relieved, and all at once resumed her former charm of manner and elegance of attitude. The beautiful face was lit up by a smile.

The chief was bowing to her in quite a foreign fashion, and in spite of her visible reassurance she eyed him very intently. Then she went up to Lady Molly and held out her hand.

My dear lady took it without an instant's hesitation. I, who knew that it was the few words hastily scribbled by Lady Molly which had dictated the chief's conduct with regard to Miss Löwenthal, was left wondering whether the woman I loved best in all the world had been shaking hands with a murderess.

4

No doubt you will remember the sensation which was caused by the arrest of Miss Löwenthal, on a charge of having murdered Mr. Mark Culledon, by administering morphia to him in a cup of chocolate at Mathis' café in Regent Street.

The beauty of the accused, her undeniable charm of manner, the hitherto blameless character of her life, all tended to make the public take violent sides either for or against her, and the usual budget of amateur correspondence, suggestions, recriminations and advice poured into the chief's office in titanic proportions.

I must say that, personally, all my sympathies went out to Miss Löwenthal. As I have said before, I am no psychologist, but I had seen her in the original interview at the office, and I could not get rid of an absolutely unreasoning certitude that the beautiful Viennese singer was innocent.

The magistrate's court was packed, as you may well imagine, on that first day of the inquiry; and, of course, sympathy with the accused went up to fever pitch when she staggered into the dock, beautiful still, despite the ravages caused by horror, anxiety, fear, in face of the deadly peril in which she stood.

The magistrate was most kind to her; her solicitor was unimpeachably assiduous; even our fellows, who had to give evidence against her, did no more than their duty, and were as lenient in their statements as possible.

Miss Löwenthal had been arrested in her flat by Danvers, accompanied by two constables. She had loudly protested her innocence all along, and did so still, pleading "Not guilty" in a firm voice.

The great points in favour of the arrest were, firstly, the undoubted motive of disappointment and revenge against a faithless sweetheart, then the total inability to prove any kind of alibi, which, under the circumstances, certainly added to the appearance of guilt.

The question of where the fatal drug was obtained was more difficult to prove. It was stated that Mr. Mark Culledon was director of several important companies, one of which carried on business as wholesale druggists.

Therefore it was argued that the accused, at different times and under some pretext or other, had obtained drugs from Mr. Culledon himself. She had admitted to having visited the deceased at his office in the City, both before and after his marriage.

Miss Löwenthal listened to all this evidence against her with a hard, set face, as she did also to Katherine Harris's statement about her calling on Mr. Culledon at Lorbury House, but she brightened up visibly when the various attendants at Mathis' café were placed in the box.

A very large hat belonging to the accused was shown to the witnesses, but, though the police upheld the theory that that was the headgear worn by the mysterious lady at the café on that fateful afternoon, the waitresses made distinctly contradictory statements with regard to it.

Whilst one girl swore that she recognised the very hat, another was equally positive that it was distinctly smaller than the one she recollected, and when the hat was placed on the head of Miss Löwenthal, three out of the four witnesses positively refused to identify her.

Most of these young women declared that though the accused, when wearing the big hat, looked as if she might have been the lady in question, yet there was a certain something about her which was different.

With that vagueness which is a usual and highly irritating characteristic of their class, the girls finally parried every question by refusing to swear positively either for or against the identity of Miss Löwenthal.

"There's something that's different about her somehow," one of the waitresses asserted positively.

"What is it that's different?" asked the solicitor for the accused, pressing his point.

"I can't say," was the perpetual, maddening reply.

Of course the poor young widow had to be dragged into the case, and here, I think, opinions and even expressions of sympathy were quite unanimous.

The whole tragedy had been inexpressibly painful to her, of course, and now it must have seemed doubly so. The scandal which had accumulated round her late husband's name must have added the poignancy of shame to that of grief. Mark Culledon had behaved as callously to the girl whom clearly he had married from interested, family motives, as he had to the one whom he had heartlessly cast aside.

Lady Irene, however, was most moderate in her statements. There was no doubt that she had known of her husband's previous entanglement with Miss Löwenthal, but apparently had not thought fit to make him accountable for the past. She did not know that Miss Löwenthal had threatened a breach of promise action against her husband.

Throughout her evidence she spoke with absolute calm and dignity, and looked indeed a strange contrast, in her closely fitting tailor-made costume of black serge and tiny black toque, to the more brilliant woman who stood in the dock.

The two great points in favour of the accused were, firstly, the vagueness of the witnesses who were called to identify her, and, secondly, the fact that she had undoubtedly begun proceedings for breach of promise against the deceased. Judging by the latter's letters to her, she would have had a splendid case against him, which fact naturally dealt a severe blow to the theory as to motive for the murder.

On the whole, the magistrate felt that there was not a sufficiency of evidence against the accused to warrant his committing her for trial; he therefore discharged her, and, amid loud applause from the public, Miss Löwenthal left the court a free woman.

Now, I know that the public did loudly, and, to my mind, very justly, blame the police for that arrest, which was denounced as being as cruel as it was unjustifiable. I felt as strongly as anybody on the subject, for I knew that the prosecution had been instituted in defiance of Lady Molly's express advice, and in distinct contradiction to the evidence which she had collected. When, therefore, the chief asked my dear lady to renew her efforts in that mysterious case, it was small wonder that her enthusiasm did not respond to his anxiety. That she would do her duty was beyond a doubt, but she had very naturally lost her more fervent interest in the case.

The mysterious woman in the big hat was still the chief subject of leading articles in the papers, coupled with that of the ineptitude of the police who could not discover her. There were caricatures and picture post-cards in all the shop windows of a gigantic hat covering the whole figure of its wearer, only the feet, and a very long and pointed chin, protruding from beneath the enormous brim. Below was the device, "Who is she? Ask the police?"

One day—it was the second since the discharge of Miss Löwenthal—my dear lady came into my room beaming. It was the first time I had seen her smile for more than a week, and already I had guessed what it was that had cheered her.

"Good news, Mary," she said gaily. "At last I've got the chief to let me have a free hand. Oh, dear! what a lot of argument it takes to extricate that man from the tangled meshes of red tape!"

"What are you going to do?" I asked.

"Prove that my theory is right as to who murdered Mark Culledon," she replied seriously; "and as a preliminary we'll go and ask his servants at Lorbury House a few questions."

It was then three o'clock in the afternoon. At Lady Molly's bidding, I dressed somewhat smartly, and together we went off in a taxi to Fitzjohn's Avenue.

Lady Molly had written a few words on one of her cards, urgently requesting an interview with Lady Irene Culledon. This she handed over to the man-servant who opened the door at Lorbury House. A few moments later we were sitting in the cosy boudoir. The young widow, high-bred and dignified in her tight-fitting black gown, sat opposite to us, her white hands folded demurely before her, her small head, with its very close coiffure, bent in closest attention towards Lady Molly.

"I most sincerely hope, Lady Irene," began my dear lady, in her most gentle and persuasive voice, "that you will look with all possible indulgence on my growing desire—shared, I may say, by all my superiors at Scotland Yard—to elucidate the mystery which still surrounds your late husband's death."

Lady Molly paused, as if waiting for encouragement to proceed. The subject must have been extremely painful to the young widow; nevertheless she responded quite gently:

"I can understand that the police wish to do their duty in the matter; as for me, I have done all, I think, that could be expected of me. I am not made of iron, and after that day in the police court—"

She checked herself, as if afraid of having betrayed more emotion than was consistent with good breeding, and concluded more calmly:

"I cannot do any more."

"I fully appreciate your feelings in the matter," said Lady Molly, "but you would not mind helping us—would you?—in a passive way, if you could, by some simple means, further the cause of justice."

"What is it you want me to do?" asked Lady Irene.

"Only to allow me to ring for two of your maids and to ask them a few questions. I promise you that they shall not be of such a nature as to cause you the slightest pain."

For a moment I thought that the young widow hesitated, then, without a word, she rose and rang the bell.

"Which of my servants did you wish to see?" she asked, turning to my dear lady as soon as the butler entered in answer to the bell.

"Your own maid and your parlour-maid, if I may," replied Lady Molly.

Lady Irene gave the necessary orders, and we all sat expectant and silent until, a minute or two later, two girls entered the room. One wore a cap and apron, the other, in neat black dress and dainty lace collar, was obviously the lady's maid.

"This lady," said their mistress, addressing the two girls, "wishes to ask you a few questions. She is a representative of the police, so you had better do your best to satisfy her with your answers."

"Oh!" rejoined Lady Molly pleasantly—choosing not to notice the tone of acerbity with which the young widow had spoken, nor the unmistakable barrier of hostility and reserve which her words had immediately raised between the young servants and the "representative of the police"— "what I am going to ask these two young ladies is neither very difficult nor very unpleasant. I merely want their kind help in a little comedy which will have to be played this evening, in order to test the accuracy of certain statements made by one of the waitresses at Mathis' tea shop with regard to the terrible tragedy which has darkened this house. You will do that much, will you not?" she added, speaking directly to the maids.

No one can be so winning or so persuasive as my dear lady. In a moment I saw the girls' hostility melting before the sunshine of Lady Molly's smile.

"We'll do what we can, ma'am," said the maid.

"That's a brave, good girl!" replied my lady. "You must know that the chief waitress at Mathis' has, this very morning, identified the woman in the big hat who, we all believe, murdered your late master. Yes!" she continued, in response to a gasp of astonishment which seemed to go round the room like a wave, "the girl seems quite positive, both as regards the hat and the woman who wore it. But, of course, one cannot allow a human life to be sworn away without bringing every possible proof to bear on such a statement, and I am sure that everyone in this house will understand that we don't want to introduce strangers more than we can help into this sad affair, which already has been bruited abroad too much."

She paused a moment; then, as neither Lady Irene nor the maids made any comment, she continued:

"My superiors at Scotland Yard think it their duty to try and confuse the witness as much as possible in her act of identification. They desire that a certain number of ladies wearing abnormally large hats should parade before the waitress. Among them will be, of course, the one whom the girl has already identified as being the mysterious person who had tea with Mr. Culledon at Mathis' that afternoon.

"My superiors can then satisfy themselves whether the waitress is or is not so sure of her statement that she invariably picks out again and again one particular individual amongst a number of others or not."

"Surely," interrupted Lady Irene, dryly, "you and your superiors do not expect my servants to help in such a farce?"

"We don't look upon such a proceeding as a farce, Lady Irene," rejoined Lady Molly, gently. "It is often resorted to in the interests of an accused person, and we certainly would ask the co-operation of your household."

"I don't see what they can do."

But the two girls did not seem unwilling. The idea appealed to them, I felt sure; it suggested an exciting episode, and gave promise of variety in their monotonous lives.

"I am sure both these young ladies possess fine big hats," continued Lady Molly with an encouraging smile.

"I should not allow them to wear ridiculous headgear," retorted Lady Irene, sternly.

"I have the one your ladyship wouldn't wear, and threw away," interposed the young parlour-maid. "I put it together again with the scraps I found in the dusthole."

There was just one instant of absolute silence, one of those magnetic moments when Fate seems to have dropped the spool on which she was spinning the threads of a life, and is just stooping in order to pick it up.

Lady Irene raised a black-bordered handkerchief to her lips, then said quietly:

"I don't know what you mean, Mary. I never wear big hats."

"No, my lady," here interposed the lady's maid; "but Mary means the one you ordered at Sanchia's and only wore the once—the day you went to that concert."

"Which day was that?" asked Lady Molly, blandly.

"Oh! I couldn't forget that day," ejaculated the maid; "her ladyship came home from the concert—I had undressed her, and she told me that she would never wear her big hat again—it was too heavy. That same day Mr. Culledon was murdered."

"That hat would answer our purpose very well," said Lady Molly, quite calmly. "Perhaps Mary will go and fetch it, and you had better go and help her put it on."

The two girls went out of the room without another word, and there were we three women left facing one another, with that awful secret, only half-revealed, hovering in the air like an intangible spectre.

"What are you going to do, Lady Irene?" asked Lady Molly, after a moment's pause, during which I literally could hear my own heart beating, whilst I watched the rigid figure of the widow in deep black crape, her face set and white, her eyes fixed steadily on Lady Molly.

"You can't prove it!" she said defiantly.

"I think we can," rejoined Lady Molly, simply; "at any rate, I mean to try. I have two of the waitresses from Mathis' outside in a cab, and I have already spoken to the attendant who served you at Sanchia's, an obscure milliner in a back street near Portland Road. We know that you were at great pains there to order a hat of certain dimensions and to your own minute description; it was a copy of one you had once seen Miss Löwenthal wear when you met her at your late husband's office. We can prove that meeting, too. Then we have your maid's testimony that you wore that same hat once, and once only, the day, presumably, that you went out to a concert—a statement which you will find it difficult to substantiate—and also the day on which your husband was murdered."

"Bah! the public will laugh at you!" retorted Lady Irene, still defiantly. "You would not dare to formulate so monstrous a charge!"

"It will not seem monstrous when justice has weighed in the balance the facts which we can prove. Let me tell you a few of these, the result of careful investigation. There is the fact that you knew of Mr. Culledon's entanglement with Miss Elizabeth Löwenthal, and did your best to keep it from old Mrs. Steinberg's knowledge, realising that any scandal round her favourite nephew would result in the old lady cutting him—and therefore you—out of her will. You dismissed a parlour-maid for the sole reason that she had been present when Miss Löwenthal was shown into Mr. Culledon's study. There is the fact that Mrs. Steinberg had so worded her will that, in the event of her nephew dying before her, her fortune would devolve on you; the fact that, with Miss Löwenthal's action for breach of promise against your husband, your last hope of keeping the scandal from the old lady's ears had effectually vanished. You saw the fortune eluding your grasp; you feared Mrs. Steinberg would alter her will. Had you found the means, and had you dared, would you not rather have killed the old lady? But discovery would have been certain. The other crime was bolder and surer. You have inherited the old lady's millions, for she never knew of her nephew's earlier peccadillos.

"All this we can state and prove, and the history of the hat, bought, and worn one day only, that same memorable day, and then thrown away."

A loud laugh interrupted her—a laugh that froze my very marrow.

"There is one fact you have forgotten, my lady of Scotland Yard," came in sharp, strident accents from the black-robed figure, which seemed to have become strangely spectral in the fast gathering gloom which had been enveloping the luxurious little boudoir. "Don't omit to mention the fact that the accused took the law into her own hands."

And before my dear lady and I could rush to prevent her, Lady Irene Culledon had conveyed something—we dared not think what—to her mouth.

"Find Danvers quickly, Mary!" said Lady Molly, calmly. "You'll find him outside. Bring a doctor back with you."

Even as she spoke Lady Irene, with a cry of agony, fell senseless in my dear lady's arms.

The doctor, I may tell you, came too late. The unfortunate woman evidently had a good knowledge of poisons. She had been determined not to fail; in case of discovery, she was ready and able to mete out justice to herself.

I don't think the public ever knew the real truth about the woman in the big hat. Interest in her went the way of all things. Yet my dear lady had been right from beginning to end. With unerring precision she had placed her dainty finger on the real motive and the real perpetrator of the crime—the ambitious woman who had married solely for money, and meant to have that money even at the cost of one of the most dastardly murders that have ever darkened the criminal annals of this country.

I asked Lady Molly what it was that first made her think of Lady Irene as the possible murderess. No one else for a moment had thought her guilty.

"The big hat," replied my dear lady with a smile. "Had the mysterious woman at Mathis' been tall, the waitresses would not, one and all, have been struck by the abnormal size of the hat. The wearer must have been *petite*, hence the reason that under a wide brim only the chin would be visible. I at once sought for a *small* woman. Our fellows did not think of that, because they are men."

You see how simple it all was!

SIR JEREMIAH'S WILL

1

Many people have asked me whether I knew when, and in what circumstances, Lady Molly joined the detective staff at Scotland Yard, who she was, and how she managed to keep her position in Society—as she undoubtedly did—whilst exercising a profession which usually does not make for high social standing.

Well, of course, there is much that I have known all along about my dear lady—just as much, in fact, as her aristocratic friends and relations did—but I had promised her not to let the general public know anything of her private life until she gave me leave to do so.

Now things have taken a different turn, and I can tell you all I know. But I must go back some years for that, and recall to your mind that extraordinary crime known in those days as the Baddock Will Case, which sent one of the most prominent and popular young men in Society to penal servitude—a life sentence, mind you, which was considered to be remarkably lenient by a number of people who thought that Captain de Mazareen ought to have been hanged.

He was such a good-looking young soldier in those days. I specially remember him at the late Queen's funeral—one of the tallest men in the British Army, and with that peculiar charm of manner which, alas! one has ceased to associate with young Englishmen nowadays. If to these two undeniable advantages you add the one that Hubert de Mazareen was the dearly loved grandson of Sir Jeremiah Baddock, the multi-millionaire shipowner of Liverpool, you will realize how easy it was for that young Guardsman to ingratiate himself with every woman in Society, and more particularly with every mamma who had a marriageable daughter.

But Fate and Love have a proverbial knack of making a muddle of things. Captain de Mazareen, with a bevy of pretty and eligible girls from whom to select a wife, chose to fall in love with the one woman in the whole of England who, in his grandfather's opinion, should have remained a stranger, even an enemy, to him.

You remember the sad story—more than a quarter of a century old now—of Sir Jeremiah's unhappy second marriage with the pretty French actress, Mlle. Adèle Desty, who was then over thirty years younger than himself. He married her abroad, and never brought her to England. She made him supremely wretched for about three years, and finally ran away with the Earl of Flintshire, whom she had met at Monte Carlo.

Well! it was with a daughter of that same Earl of Flintshire, Lady Molly Robertson-Kirk, that Captain Hubert de Mazareen fell desperately in love. Imagine Sir Jeremiah's feelings when he heard of it.

Captain Hubert, you must know, had resigned his commission in 1902 at his grandfather's request, when the latter's health first began to fail. He had taken up his permanent abode at Appledore Castle, Sir Jeremiah's magnificent home in Cumberland, and, of course, it was generally understood that ultimately he would become possessed of the wealthy shipowner's millions as well as of the fine property, seeing that his mother had been Sir Jeremiah's only child by the latter's first marriage.

Lord Flintshire's property was quite close to Appledore; but, needless to say, old Sir Jeremiah never forgave his noble neighbour the cruel wrong he had suffered at his hands.

The second Lady Baddock, afterwards Countess of Flintshire, has been dead twenty years. Neither the county nor the more exclusive sets of London ever received her, but her daughter Molly, who inherited all her beauty and none of her faults, was the idol of her father, and the acknowledged queen of county and town Society

You see, it was the ancient, yet ever new, story of Cappelletti and Montecchi over again, and one day Captain Hubert de Mazareen had to tell Sir Jeremiah that he desired to marry the daughter of his grandfather's most cruel enemy.

What the immediate result of that announcement was no one could say. Neither Sir Jeremiah nor Captain Hubert de Mazareen would have allowed servants or dependents to hear a word of disagreement that might have passed between them, much less to suspect that an unpleasant scene had occurred.

Outwardly everything went on as usual at Appledore Castle for about a fortnight or so, after which Captain Hubert went away one day, ostensibly for a brief stay in London; but he never re-entered the doors of the Castle until after the dark veil of an appalling tragedy had begun to descend on the stately old Cumberland home.

Sir Jeremiah bore up pretty well for a time, then he had a slight paralytic stroke and became a confirmed invalid. The postmaster at Appledore declared that after that many letters came, addressed to Sir Jeremiah in Captain Hubert's well-known handwriting and bearing the London postmark; but presumably the old gentleman felt bitterly irreconcilable towards his grandson, for Captain de Mazareen was never seen at the Castle.

Soon the invalid grew more and more eccentric and morose. He ordered all the reception rooms of his magnificent home to be closed and shuttered, and he dismissed all his indoor servants, with the exception of his own male attendant and an old married couple named Bradley, who had been in his service for years, and who now did the little work that was required in what had once been one of the most richly appointed country mansions in England.

Bitter resentment against his once dearly loved grandson, and against the man who had robbed him of his young wife twenty-five years ago, seemed to have cut off the old man from contact with the outside world.

Thus matters stood until the spring of 1903, when Sir Jeremiah announced one morning to the three members of his household that Mr. Philip Baddock was coming to stay at the Castle, and that a room must be got ready immediately.

Mr. Philip Baddock came that same evening. He was a young man of quite ordinary appearance: short, rather dark, with the somewhat uncouth manners suggestive of an upbringing in a country parsonage.

His arrival created no little excitement in the neighbourhood. Who was Mr. Philip Baddock, and where did he come from? No one had ever heard of him before, and now—after a very brief time spent at the Castle—he seemed to be gradually taking up the position which originally had belonged to Captain Hubert.

He took over the command of the small household, dismissing Sir Jeremiah's personal attendant after a while and engaging another. He supervised the outdoor men, reducing the staff both in the gardens and the stables. He sold most of the horses and carriages, and presently bought a motor-car, which he at once took to driving all over the country.

But he spoke to no one in the village, and soon, in answer to inquiries by one or two of Sir Jeremiah's faithful friends and cronies, the reply came regularly from Mr. Philip Baddock that the invalid was disinclined for company. Only Doctor Thorne, the local practitioner, saw the patient. Sir Jeremiah, it was understood, was slowly sinking towards the grave; but his mind was quite clear, even if his temper was abnormal.

One day Mr. Philip Baddock made inquiries in the village for a good chauffeur. George Taylor presented himself, and was at once told off to drive the car as quickly as possible to Carlisle, to the office of Mr. Steadman, solicitor, and to bring that gentleman back to the Castle as soon as he could come.

The distance from Appledore to Carlisle is over fifty miles. It was seven o'clock in the evening before George Taylor was back, bringing Mr. Steadman with him.

The solicitor was received at the Castle door by old Bradley, and at Sir Jeremiah's door by Felkin, the new attendant, who showed him in. The interview between the invalid and Mr. Steadman lasted half an hour, after which the latter was driven back to Carlisle by George Taylor.

That same evening a telegram was sent off by Mr. Philip Baddock to Captain de Mazareen in London, containing the few words:

"Sir Jeremiah very ill. Come at once."

Twenty-four hours later Captain Hubert arrived at Appledore Castle—too late, however, to see his grandfather alive.

Sir Jeremiah Baddock had died an hour before the arrival of his once so tenderly cherished grandson, and all hopes of a reconciliation had now been mercilessly annihilated by death.

The end had come much more suddenly than Doctor Thorne had anticipated. He had seen the patient in the morning and thought that he might last some days. But when Sir Jeremiah had heard that Captain de Mazareen had been sent for he had worked himself into a state of such terrible agitation that the poor, over-taxed brain and heart finally gave way.

2

The events of those memorable days—in the early spring of 1904—are so graven on my memory that I can recount them as if they happened yesterday.

I was maid to Lady Molly Robertson-Kirk at the time. Since then she has honoured me with her friendship.

Directly after Captain Hubert's first estrangement from his grandfather she and I came down to Cumberland and lived very quietly at Kirk Hall, which, as you know, is but a stone's throw from Appledore.

Here Captain Hubert paid my dear lady several visits. She had irrevocably made up her mind that their engagement was to be indefinitely prolonged, for she had a vague hope that, sooner or later, Sir Jeremiah would relent towards the grandson whom he had loved so dearly. At any rate there was a chance of it whilst the marriage had not actually taken place.

Captain de Mazareen, mind you, was in no sense of the word badly off. His father had left him some £25,000, and Lady Molly had a small private fortune of her own. Therefore I assure you that there was not a single mercenary thought behind this protracted engagement or Captain Hubert's desire for a reconciliation with his grandfather.

The evening that he arrived at Appledore in response to Mr. Philip Baddock's telegram Lady Molly met him at the station. He sent his luggage on to Kirk Hall, and the two young people walked together as far as the Elkhorn Woods, which divide the Earl of Flintshire's property from Appledore itself.

Here they met Mr. Steadman, the solicitor, who had motored over from Carlisle in response to an urgent summons from Sir Jeremiah Baddock, but whose car had broken down about two hundred yards up the road.

It seems that the chauffeur had suggested his walking on through the woods, it being an exceptionally fine and mild spring evening, with a glorious full moon overhead, which lit up almost every turn of the path that cuts through the pretty coppice.

Lady Molly had given me rendezvous at the edge of the wood, so that I might accompany her home after she had taken leave of Captain Hubert. It seems that the latter knew Mr. Steadman slightly, as we saw the two men shake hands with one another, then, after a few words of conversation, turn off to walk together through the wood. We then made our way back silently to Kirk Hall.

My dear lady was inexpressibly sad. She appreciated very deeply the love which Captain Hubert bore for his grandfather, and was loath to see the final annihilation of all her hopes of an ultimate reconciliation between the two men.

I had dressed Lady Molly for dinner, and she was just going downstairs when Captain de Mazareen arrived at the Hall.

He announced the sad news of his grandfather's death and looked extremely dejected and upset.

Of course, he stayed at the Hall, for Mr. Philip Baddock seemed quite to have taken command at Appledore Castle, and Captain Hubert did not care to be beholden to him for hospitality.

My dear lady asked him what had become of Mr. Steadman.

"I don't know," he replied. "He started to walk with me through the wood, then he seemed to think that the tramp would be too much for him, and that the car could be put right very quickly. He preferred to drive round, and was quite sure that he would meet me at the Castle in less than half an hour. However, he never turned up."

Lady Molly asked several more questions about Sir Jeremiah, which Captain Hubert answered in a listless way. He had been met at the door of the Castle by Mr. Philip Baddock, who told him that the old gentleman had breathed his last half an hour before.

I remember that we all went to bed that night feeling quite unaccountably depressed. It seemed that something more tragic than the natural death of a septuagenarian hovered in the air of these remote Cumberland villages.

The next morning our strange premonitions were confirmed. Lord Flintshire, my dear lady, and Captain Hubert were sitting at breakfast when the news was brought to the Hall that Mr. Steadman, the Carlisle solicitor, had been found murdered in the Elkhorn Woods earlier in the morning. Evidently he had been stunned, and then done to death by a heavily-loaded stick or some similar weapon. When he was discovered in the early hours of the morning, he had, apparently, been dead some time. The local police were at once apprised of the terrible event, which created as much excitement as the death of the eccentric old millionaire at Appledore Castle.

Everyone at Kirk Hall, of course, was keenly interested, and Captain de Mazareen went over to Appledore as soon as he could in order to place his information at the service of the police.

It is a strange fact, but nevertheless a true one, that when a deadly peril arises such as now threatened Captain de Mazareen, the person most in danger is the last to be conscious of it.

I am quite sure that Lady Molly, the moment she heard that Mr. Steadman had been murdered in the Elkhorn Woods, realized that the man she loved would be implicated in that tragedy in some sinister manner. But that is the intuition of a woman—of a woman who loves.

As for Captain Hubert, he went about during the whole of that day quite unconscious of the abyss which already was yawning at his feet. He even discussed quite equably the several valuable bits of information which the local police had already collected, and which eventually formed a portion of that damning fabric of circumstantial evidence which was to bring him within sight of the gallows.

Earlier in the day, Mr. Philip Baddock sent him a stiff little note, saying that, as Captain de Mazareen was now the owner of Appledore Castle, he (Philip Baddock) did not desire to trespass a moment longer than was necessary on his relative's hospitality, and had arranged to stay at the village inn until after the funeral, when he would leave Cumberland.

To this Captain Hubert sent an equally curt note saying that, as far as he knew, he had no say in the matter of anyone coming or going from the Castle, and that Mr. Philip Baddock must, of course, please himself as to whether he stayed there or not.

So far, of course, the old gentleman's testamentary dispositions were not known. He had made a will in 1902 bequeathing Appledore and everything he possessed unconditionally to his beloved grandson, Hubert de Mazareen, whom he also appointed his sole executor. That will was lodged with Mr. Truscott, who had been solicitor to the deceased practically until the last moment, when Mr. Steadman, a new arrival at Carlisle, had been sent for.

Whether that will had been revoked or not Mr. Truscott did not know; but, in the course of the afternoon, Lord Flintshire, whilst out driving, met the local superintendent of police, who told him that Mr. Steadman's senior partner—a Mr. Fuelling—had made a statement to the effect that Sir Jeremiah had sent for Mr. Steadman the day before his death and given instructions for the drafting of a new will whereby the old gentleman bequeathed Appledore and everything he possessed to his beloved grandson, Hubert de Mazareen, but only on the condition that the latter did not marry the daughter or any other relative of the Earl of Flintshire. In the event of Hubert de Mazareen disregarding this condition at any future time of his life, Sir Jeremiah's entire fortune was to devolve on Philip Baddock, sole issue of testator's second marriage, with Adèle Desty. The draft of this will, added Mr. Fuelling, was in Mr. Steadman's pocket ready for Sir Jeremiah's signature on that fateful night when the unfortunate young solicitor was murdered.

The draft had not been found in the murdered man's pocket. A copy of it, however, was in Mr. Fuelling's safe. But as this will had never been signed by the deceased the one of 1902 remained valid, and Captain Hubert de Mazareen remained unconditionally his grandfather's sole heir.

3

Events crowded thick and fast on that day—one of the most miserable I have ever lived through.

After an early tea, which my dear lady had alone in her little boudoir, she sent me down to ask Captain Hubert to come up and speak to her. He did so at once, and I went into the next room—which was Lady Molly's bedroom—to prepare her dress for the evening.

I had, of course, discreetly closed the door of communication between the two rooms, but after the first five minutes, Lady Molly deliberately reopened it, from which I gathered that she actually wished me to know what was going on.

It was then a little after four o'clock. I could hear Captain de Mazareen's voice, low-toned and infinitely tender. He adored my dear lady, but he was a very quiet man, and it was only by the passionate tensity of his attitude when he was near her that a shrewdly observant person could guess how deeply he cared. Now, through the open door, I could see his handsome head bowed very low, so that he could better look into her upturned eyes. His arms were round her, as if he were fighting the world for the possession of her, and would never let her go again. But there were tears in her eyes.

"Hubert," she said after a while, "I want you to marry me. Will you?"

"Will I?" he whispered, with an intensity of passionate longing which seemed to me then so unutterably pathetic that I could have sat down and had a good cry.

"But," rejoined Lady Molly earnestly, "I mean as soon as possible—to-morrow, by special licence. You can wire to Mr. Hurford to-night, and he will see about it the first thing in the morning. We can travel up to town by the night train. Father and Mary will come with me. Father has promised, you know, and we can be married to-morrow . . . I think that would be the quickest way."

There was a pause. I could well imagine how astonished and perturbed Captain Hubert must be feeling. It was such a strange request for a woman to make at such a time. I could see by the expression of his eyes that he was trying to read her thoughts. But she looked up quite serenely at him, and, frankly, I do not think that he had the slightest inkling of the sublime motive at the back of her strange insistence.

"You prefer to be married in London rather than here?" he asked quite simply.

"Yes," she replied; "I desire to be married in London to-morrow."

A few moments later my dear lady quietly shut the door again, and I heard and saw no more; but half an hour later she called me. She was alone in her boudoir, bravely trying to smile through a veil of tears. Captain Hubert's footsteps could still be heard going along the hall below.

Lady Molly listened until the final echo of that tread died away in the distance; then she buried her sweet face on my shoulder and sobbed her very heart out.

"Get ready as quickly as you can, Mary," she said to me when the paroxysm had somewhat subsided. "We go up to town by the 9.10."

"Is his lordship coming with us, my lady?" I asked.

"Oh, yes!" she said, whilst a bright smile lit up her face. "Father is simply grand . . . and yet he knows."

"Knows what, my lady?" I queried instinctively, for Lady Molly had paused, and I saw a look of acute pain once more darken her soft, grey eyes.

"My father knows," she said, slowly and almost tonelessly, "that half an hour ago the police found a weighted stick in the Elkhorn Woods not far from the spot where Mr. Steadman was murdered.

The stick has the appearance of having been very vigorously cleaned and scraped recently in spite of which fact tiny traces of blood are still visible on the leaden knob. The inspector showed my father that stick. I saw it too. It is the property of Captain Hubert de Mazareen, and by to-morrow, at the latest, it will be identified as such."

There was silence in the little boudoir now: a silence broken only by the sound of dull sobs which rose from my dear lady's over-burdened heart. Lady Molly at this moment had looked into the future, and with that unerring intuition which has since been of such immense service to her she had already perceived the grim web which Fate was weaving round the destiny of the man she loved.

I said nothing. What could I say? I waited for her to speak again.

The first words she uttered after the terrible pronouncement which she had just made were:

"I'll wear my white cloth gown to-morrow, Mary. It is the most becoming frock I have, and I want to look my best on my wedding day."

4

Captain Hubert de Mazareen was married to Lady Molly Robertson-Kirk by special licence on April 22nd, 1904, at the Church of St. Margaret, Westminster. No one was present to witness the ceremony except the Earl of Flintshire and myself. No one was apprised of the event at the time, nor, until recently, did any-one know that Lady Molly of Scotland Yard was the wife of De Mazareen the convict.

As you know, he was arrested at Appledore railway station the following morning and charged with the willful murder of Alexander Steadman, solicitor, of Carlisle.

Everything was against him from the first. The draft of the will which Mr. Steadman was taking up to Sir Jeremiah for signature supplied the motive for the alleged crime, and he was the last person seen in company with the murdered man.

The chauffeur, George Taylor, who had driven to Carlisle to fetch Mr. Steadman, and brought him back that evening, explained how two of his tyres burst almost simultaneously after going over a bit of broken road close to the coppice. He had suggested to Mr. Steadman the idea of walking through the wood, and, as he had not two fresh tyres with him, he started pushing his car along, as the village was not more than half a mile away. He never saw Mr. Steadman again.

The stick with which the terrible deed had been committed was the most damning piece of evidence against the accused. It had been identified as his property by more than one witness, and was found within twenty yards of the victim, obviously cleaned and scraped, but still bearing minute traces of blood. Moreover, it had actually been seen in Captain Hubert's hand by one or two of the porters when he arrived at Appledore Station on that fatal night, was met there by Lady Molly, and subsequently walked away with her previous to meeting Mr. Steadman on the edge of the wood.

Captain de Mazareen, late of His Majesty's Household Brigade, was indicted for the willful murder of Alexander Steadman, tried at the next assizes, found guilty, and condemned to be hanged. The jury, however, had strongly recommended him to mercy owing to his hitherto spotless reputation, and to the many services he had rendered his country during the last Boer War. A monster petition was sent up to the Home Office, and the sentence was commuted to twenty years' penal servitude.

That same year, Lady Molly applied for, and obtained, a small post on the detective staff of the police. From that small post she has worked her way upwards, analysing and studying, exercising her powers of intuition and of deduction, until at the present moment she is considered, by chiefs and men alike, the greatest authority among them on criminal investigation.

The Earl of Flintshire died some three years ago. Kirk Hall devolved on a distant cousin, but Lady Molly has kept a small home at Kirk ready for her husband when he comes back from Dartmoor.

The task of her life is to apply her gifts, and the obvious advantages at her disposal as a prominent member of the detective force, to prove the innocence of Captain Hubert de Mazareen, which she never doubted for a moment.

But it was sublime, and at the same time deeply pathetic, to see the frantic efforts at self-sacrifice which these two noble-hearted young people made for one another's sake.

Directly Captain Hubert realised that, so far as proving his innocence was concerned, he was a lost man, he used every effort to release Lady Molly from the bonds of matrimony. The marriage had been, and was still, kept a profound secret. He determined to plead guilty to murder at his trial, and then to make a declaration that he had entrapped Lady Molly into a marriage, knowing at the time that a warrant was out for his arrest, and hoping, by his con-nection with the Earl of Flintshire, to obtain a certain amount of leniency. When he was sufficiently convinced that such a course was out of the question, he begged Lady Molly to bring a nullity suit against him. He would not defend it. He only wished to set her free.

But the love she bore him triumphed over all. They did keep their marriage a secret, but she remained faithful to him in every thought and feeling within her, and loyal to him with her whole soul. Only I—once her maid, now her devoted friend—knew what she suffered, even whilst she threw herself heart and mind into her work.

We lived mostly in our little flat in Maida Vale, but spent some delightful days of freedom and peace in the little house at Kirk. Hither—in spite of the terrible memories the place evoked—Lady Molly loved to spend her time in wandering over the ground where that mysterious crime had been committed which had doomed an innocent man to the life of a convict.

"That mystery has got to be cleared up, Mary," she would re-peat to me with unswerving loyalty, "and cleared up soon, before Captain de Mazareen loses all joy in life and all belief in me."

5

I suspect you will be interested to hear something about Appledore Castle and about Mr. Philip Baddock, who had been so near getting an immense fortune, yet had it snatched from him before his very eyes.

As Sir Jeremiah Baddock never signed the will of 1904, Captain de Mazareen's solicitors, on his behalf, sought to obtain probate of the former one, dated 1902. In view of the terrible circumstances connected with the proposed last testamentary dispositions of the deceased, Mr. Philip Baddock was advised to fight that suit.

It seems that he really was the son of Sir Jeremiah by the latter's second marriage with Mlle. Desty, but the old gentleman, with heartless vengefulness, had practically repudiated the boy from the first, and absolutely refused to have anything to do with him beyond paying for his maintenance and education, and afterwards making him a goodly allowance on the express condition that Philip—soon to become a young man—never set his foot on English soil.

The condition was strictly complied with. Philip Baddock was born abroad, and lived abroad until 1903, when he suddenly appeared at Appledore Castle. Whether Sir Jeremiah, in a fit of tardy repentance, had sent for him, or whether he risked coming of his own accord, no one ever knew.

Captain de Mazareen was not, until that same year 1903, aware of the existence of Philip Baddock any more than was anybody else, and he spent his last days of freedom in stating positively that he would not accept the terms of the will of 1902, but would agree to Sir Jeremiah's fortune being divided up as it would have been if the old gentleman had died intestate. Thus Philip Baddock, the son, and Hubert de Mazareen, the grandson, received an equal share of Sir Jeremiah's immense wealth, estimated at close upon £2,000,000 sterling.

Appledore was put up for sale and bought in by Mr. Philip Baddock, who took up his residence there and gradually gained for himself a position in the county as one of the most wealthy magnates in the north of England. Thus he became acquainted with the present Lord Flintshire, and, later on, met my dear lady. She neither sought nor avoided his acquaintance, and even went once to a dinner party at Appledore Castle.

That was lately, on the occasion of our last stay at Kirk. I had gone up to the Castle in the brougham so that I might accompany

Lady Molly home, and had been shown into the library, whither my dear lady came in order to put on her cloak.

While she was doing so Mr. Philip Baddock came in. He had a newspaper in his hand and seemed greatly agitated.

"Such extraordinary news, Lady Molly," he said, pointing to a head-line in the paper. "You know, of course, that the other day a convict succeeded in effecting his escape from Dartmoor?"

"Yes, I knew that," said my dear lady, quietly.

"Well, I have reason to—to suppose," continued Mr. Baddock, "that that convict was none other than my unfortunate nephew, De Mazareen."

"Yes?" rejoined Lady Molly, whose perfect calm and serene expression of face contrasted strangely with the obvious agitation of Philip Baddock.

"Heaven knows that he tried to do me an evil turn," rejoined the latter after a while; "but of course I bear him no grudge, now that the law has given me that which he tried to wrench from me— a just share of my father's possessions. Since he has thrown himself on my mercy—"

"Thrown himself on your mercy!" ejaculated my dear lady, whose face had become almost grey with a sudden fear. "What do you mean?"

"De Mazareen is in my house at the present moment," replied Mr. Baddock, quietly.

"Here?"

"Yes. It seems that he tramped here. I am afraid that his object was to try and see you. He wants money, of course. I happened to be out in the woods this afternoon, and saw him.

"No, no!" added Philip Baddock quickly, in response to an instinctive gasp of pain from Lady Molly; "you need not have the slightest fear. My nephew is as safe with me as he would be in your own house. I brought him here, for he was exhausted with fatigue and want of food. None of my servants know of his presence in the house except Felkin, whom I can trust. By to-morrow he will have rested. . . . We'll make a start in the very early morning in my car; we'll get to Liverpool before midday. De Mazareen shall wear

Felkin's clothes—no one will know him. One of the Baddock steamers is leaving for Buenos Ayres the same afternoon, and I can arrange with the captain. You need not have the slightest fear," he repeated, with simple yet earnest emphasis; "I pledge you my word that De Mazareen will be safe."

"I should like to thank you," she murmured.

"Please don't," he rejoined with a sad smile. "It is a great happiness to me to be able to do this. . . . I know that you—you cared for him at one time. . . . I wish you had known and trusted me in those days—but I am glad of this opportunity which enables me to tell you that, even had my father signed his last will and testament, I should have shared his fortune with De Mazareen. The man whom you honoured with your love need never have resorted to crime in order to gain a fortune."

Philip Baddock paused. His eyes were fixed on Lady Molly with unmistakable love and an appeal for sympathy. I had no idea that he cared for her—nor had she, I am quite sure. Her heart belonged solely to the poor, fugitive convict, but she could not fail, I thought, to be touched by the other man's obvious sincerity and earnestness.

There was silence in the room for a few moments. Only the old clock in its Sheraton case ticked on in solemn imperturbability.

Lady Molly turned her luminous eyes on the man who had just made so simple, so touching a profession of love. Was she about to tell him that she was no longer free, that she bore the name of the man whom the law had ostracised and pronounced a criminal— who had even now, by this daring attempt at escape, added a few years to his already long term of punishment and another load to his burden of shame?

"Do you think," she asked quietly, "that I might speak to Captain de Mazareen for a few moments without endangering his safety?"

Mr. Baddock did not reply immediately. He seemed to be pondering over the request. Then he said:

"I will see that everything is safe. I don't think there need be any danger."

He went out of the room, and my dear lady and I were left alone for a minute or two. She was so calm and serene that I marvelled at her self-control, and wondered what was going on in her mind.

"Mary," she said to me, speaking very quickly, for already we could hear two men's footsteps approaching the library door, "you must station yourself just outside the front door; you understand? If you see or hear anything suspicious come and warn me at once."

I made ready to obey, and the next moment the door opened and Mr. Philip Baddock entered, accompanied by Captain Hubert.

I smothered the involuntary sob which rose to my throat at sight of the man who had once been the most gallant, the handsomest soldier I had ever seen. I had only just time to notice that Mr. Baddock prepared to leave the room again immediately. At the door he turned back and said to Lady Molly:

"Felkin has gone down to the lodge. If he hears or sees anything that seems suspicious he will ring up on the telephone;" and he pointed to the apparatus which stood on the library table in the centre of the room.

After that he closed the door, and I was left to imagine the moments of joy, mingled with acute anguish, which my dear lady would be living through.

I walked up and down restlessly on the terrace which fronts the Castle. The house itself appeared silent and dark: I presume all the servants had gone to bed. Far away on my right I caught the glimmer of a light. It came from the lodge where Felkin was watching. From the church in Appledore village came the sound of the clock striking the hour of midnight.

How long I had been on the watch I cannot say, when suddenly I was aware of a man's figure running rapidly along the drive towards the house. The next moment the figure had skirted the Castle, apparently making for one of the back doors.

I did not hesitate a moment. Having left the big front door on the latch, I ran straight in and made for the library door.

Already Mr. Philip Baddock had forestalled me. His hand was on the latch. Without more ado he pushed open the door and I followed him in.

Lady Molly was sitting on the sofa, with Captain Hubert beside her. They both rose at our entrance.

"The police!" said Mr. Baddock, speaking very rapidly. "Felkin has just run up from the lodge. He is getting the car ready. Pray God we may yet be able to get away."

Even as he spoke the front door bell sounded with a loud clang, which to me had the sound of a death knell.

"It is too late, you see," said my dear lady, quietly.

"No, not too late," ejaculated Philip Baddock, in a rapid whisper. "Quick! De Mazareen, follow me through the hall. Felkin is at the stables getting the car ready. It will be some time before the servants are roused."

"Mary, I am sure, has failed to fasten the front door," interrupted Lady Molly, with the same strange calm. "I think the police are already in the hall."

There was no mistaking the muffled sound of feet treading the thick Turkey carpet in the hall. The library had but one exit. Captain Hubert was literally in a trap. But Mr. Baddock had not lost his presence of mind.

"The police would never dream of searching my house," he said; "they will take my word that De Mazareen is not here. Here!" he added, pointing to a tall Jacobean wardrobe which stood in an angle of the room. "In there, man, and leave the rest to me!"

"I am afraid that such a proceeding would bring useless trouble upon you, Mr. Baddock," once more interposed Lady Molly; "the police, if they do not at once find Captain de Mazareen, will surely search the house."

"Impossible! They would not dare!"

"Indeed they would. The police know that Captain de Mazareen is here."

"I swear they do not," rejoined Mr. Baddock. "Felkin is no traitor, and no one else—"

"It was I who gave information to the police," said Lady Molly, speaking loudly and clearly. "I called up the superintendent on the telephone just now, and told him that his men would find the escaped convict hiding at Appledore Castle."

"You!" ejaculated Mr. Baddock, in a tone of surprise and horror, not unmixed with a certain note of triumph. "You?"

"Yes!" she replied calmly. "I am of the police, you know. I had to do my duty. Open the door, Mary," she added, turning to me.

Captain Hubert had not spoken a word so far. Now, when the men, led by Detective-Inspector Etty, entered the room, he walked with a firm step towards them, held out his hands for the irons, and with a final look at Lady Molly, in which love, trust, and hope were clearly expressed, he passed out of the room and was soon lost to sight.

My dear lady waited until the heavy footfalls had died away; then she turned with a pleasant smile to Mr. Philip Baddock:

"I thank you for your kind thoughts of me," she said, "and for your noble efforts on behalf of your nephew. My position was a difficult one. I hope you will forgive the pain I have been obliged to bring upon you."

"I will do more than forgive, Lady Molly," he said earnestly, "I will venture to hope."

He took her hand and kissed it. Then she beckoned to me and I followed her into the hall.

Our brougham—a hired one—had been waiting in the stable-yard. We drove home in silence; but half an hour later, when my dear lady kissed me good night she whispered in my ear:

"And now, Mary, we'll prove him innocent."

THE END

One or two people knew that at one time Lady Molly Robertson-Kirk had been engaged to Captain Hubert de Mazareen, who was now convict No. 97, undergoing a life sentence for the murder of Mr. Steadman, a solicitor of Carlisle, in the Elkhorn woods in April, 1904. Few, on the other hand, knew of the secret marriage solemnised on that never-to-be-forgotten afternoon, when all of us present in the church, with the exception of the bridegroom himself, were fully aware that proofs of guilt—deadly and irrefutable—were even then being heaped up against the man to whom Lady Molly was plighting her troth, for better or for worse, with her mental eyes wide open, her unerring intuition keen to the fact that nothing but a miracle could save the man she loved from an ignoble condemnation, perhaps from the gallows.

The husband of my dear lady, the man whom she loved with all the strength of her romantic and passionate nature, was duly tried and convicted of murder. Condemned to be hanged, he was reprieved, and his sentence commuted to penal servitude for life.

The question of Sir Jeremiah's estate became a complicated one, for his last will and testament was never signed, and the former one, dated 1902, bequeathed everything he possessed unconditionally to his beloved grandson Hubert.

After much legal argument, which it is useless to recapitulate here, it was agreed between the parties, and ratified in court, that the deceased gentleman's vast wealth should be disposed of as if he had died intestate. One half of it, therefore, went to Captain Hubert de Mazareen, grandson, and the other half to Philip Baddock, the son. The latter bought Appledore Castle and resided there, whilst his nephew became No. 97 in Dartmoor Prison.

Captain Hubert had served two years of his sentence when he made that daring and successful escape which caused so much sensation at the time. He managed to reach Appledore, where he was discovered by Mr. Philip Baddock, who gave him food and shelter and got everything ready for the safe conveyance of his unfortunate nephew to Liverpool and thence to a port of safety in South America.

You remember how he was thwarted in this laudable attempt by Lady Molly herself, who communicated with the police and gave up convict No. 97 into the hands of the authorities once more.

Of course, public outcry was loud against my dear lady's action. Sense of duty was all very well, so people argued, but no one could forget that at one time Captain Hubert de Mazareen and Lady Molly Robertson-Kirk had actually been engaged to be married, and it seemed positively monstrous for a woman to be so pitiless towards the man whom she must at one time have loved.

You see how little people understood my dear lady's motives. Some went so far as to say that she had only contemplated marriage with Captain Hubert de Mazareen because he was then, presumably, the heir to Sir Jeremiah's fortune; now—continued the gossips—she was equally ready to marry Mr. Philip Baddock, who at any rate was the happy possessor of one half of the deceased gentleman's wealth.

Certainly Lady Molly's conduct at this time helped to foster this idea. Finding that even the chief was inclined to give her the cold shoulder, she shut up our flat in Maida Vale and took up her residence at the little house which she owned in Kirk, and from the windows of which she had a splendid view of stately Appledore Castle nestling among the trees on the hillside.

I was with her, of course, and Mr. Philip Baddock was a frequent visitor at the house. There could be no doubt that he admired her greatly, and that she accepted his attentions with a fair amount of graciousness. The county fought shy of her. Her former engagement to Captain de Mazareen was well known, and her treachery to him—so it was called—was severely censured.

Living almost in isolation in the village, her whole soul seemed wrapped in thoughts of how to unravel the mystery of the death of Mr. Steadman. Captain de Mazareen had sworn in his defence that the solicitor, after starting to walk through the Elkhorn woods with him, had feared that the tramp over rough ground would be too much for him, and had almost immediately turned back in order to regain the road. But the chauffeur, George Taylor, who was busy with the broken-down car some two hundred yards up the road, never saw Mr. Steadman again, whilst Captain de Mazareen arrived at the gates of Appledore Castle alone. Here he was met by Mr. Philip Baddock, who informed him that Sir Jeremiah had breathed his last an hour before.

No one at the Castle recollected seeing a stick in Captain Hubert's hand when he arrived, whilst there were several witnesses who swore that he carried one at Appledore Station when he started to walk with her ladyship. The stick was found close to the body of the solicitor; and the solicitor, when he met with his terrible death, had in his pocket the draft of a will which meant disinheritance to Captain de Mazareen.

Here was the awful problem which Lady Molly had to face and to solve if she persisted in believing that the man whom she loved, and whom she had married at the moment when she knew that proofs of guilt were dead against him, was indeed innocent.

2

We had spent all the morning shopping in Carlisle, and in the afternoon we called on Mr. Fuelling, of the firm of Fuelling, Steadman and Co., solicitors.

Lady Molly had some business to arrange in connection with the purchase of an additional bit of land to round off her little garden at Kirk.

Mr. Fuelling was courteous, but distinctly stiff, in his manner towards the lady who was "connected with the police," more especially when—her business being transacted—she seemed inclined to tarry for a little while in the busy solicitor's office, and to lead conversation round to the subject of the murder of Mr. Steadman.

"Five years have gone by since then," said Mr. Fuelling, curtly, in response to a remark from Lady Molly. "I prefer not to revive unpleasant memories."

"You, of course, believed Captain de Mazareen guilty?" retorted my dear lady, imperturbably.

"There were circumstances—" rejoined the solicitor, "and—and, of course, I hardly knew the unfortunate young man. Messrs. Truscott and Truscott used to be the family solicitors."

"Yes. It seemed curious that when Sir Jeremiah wished to make his will he should have sent for you, rather than for his accustomed lawyer," mused Lady Molly.

"Sir Jeremiah did not send for me," replied Mr. Fuelling, with some acerbity, "he sent for my junior, Mr. Steadman."

"Perhaps Mr. Steadman was a personal friend of his."

"Not at all. Not at all. Mr. Steadman was a new arrival in Carlisle, and had never seen Sir Jeremiah before the day when he was sent for and, in a brief interview, drafted the will which, alas! proved to be the primary cause of my unfortunate young partner's death."

"You cannot draft a will in a brief interview, Mr. Fuelling," remarked Lady Molly, lightly.

"Mr. Steadman did so," retorted Mr. Fuelling, curtly. "Though Sir Jeremiah's mind was as clear as crystal, he was very feeble, and the interview had to take place in a darkened room. That was the only time my young partner saw Sir Jeremiah. Twenty-four hours later they were both dead."

"Oh!" commented my dear lady with sudden indifference. "Well! I won't detain you, Mr. Fuelling. Good afternoon."

A few moments later, having parted from the worthy old solicitor, we were out in the street once more.

"The darkened room is my first ray of light," quoth Lady Molly to me, with a smile at her own paradoxical remark.

When we reached home later that afternoon we were met at the garden gate by Mr. Felkin, Mr. Philip Baddock's friend and agent, who lived with him at Appledore Castle.

Mr. Felkin was a curious personality; very taciturn in manner but a man of considerable education. He was the son of a country parson, and at the time of his father's death he had been studying for the medical profession. Finding himself unable to pursue his studies for lack of means, and being left entirely destitute, he had been forced to earn his living by taking up the less exalted calling of male nurse. It seems that he had met Mr. Philip Baddock on the Continent some years ago, and the two young men had somehow drifted into close acquaintanceship. When the late Sir Jeremiah required a personal nurse-attendant Mr. Philip Baddock sent for his friend and installed him at Appledore Castle.

Here Mr. Felkin remained, even after the old gentleman's death. He was nominally called Mr. Baddock's agent, but really did very little work. He was very fond of shooting and of riding, and spent his life in the pursuit of these sports, and he always had plenty of money to spend.

But everyone voted him a disagreeable bear, and the only one who ever succeeded in making him smile was Lady Molly, who always showed an unaccountable liking for the uncouth creature. Even now, when he extended a somewhat grimy hand and murmured a clumsy apology at his intrusion, she greeted him with warm effusiveness and insisted on his coming into the house.

We all turned to walk along the little drive, when Mr. Baddock's car came whizzing round the corner of the road from the Village. He pulled up at our gate, and the next moment had joined us in the drive.

There was a very black look in his eyes, as they wandered restlessly from my dear lady's face to that of his friend. Lady Molly's little hand was even then resting on Mr. Felkin's coat-sleeve; she had been in the act of leading him herself towards the house, and did not withdraw her hand when Mr. Baddock appeared upon the scene.

"Burton has just called about those estimates, Felkin," said the latter, somewhat roughly; "he is waiting at the Castle. You had better take the car—l can walk home later on."

"Oh! how disappointing!" exclaimed Lady Molly, with what looked uncommonly like a pout. "I was going to have such a cosy chat with Mr. Felkin—all about horses and dogs. Couldn't you see that tiresome Burton, Mr. Baddock?" she added ingenuously.

I don't think that Mr. Baddock actually swore, but I am sure he was very near doing so.

"Burton can wait," said Mr. Felkin, curtly.

"No, he cannot," retorted Philip Baddock, whose face was a frowning mirror of uncontrolled jealousy; "take the car, Felkin, and go at once."

For a moment it seemed as if Felkin would refuse to obey. The two men stood looking at each other, measuring one another's power of will and strength of passion. Hate and jealousy were clearly written in each pair of glowering eyes. Philip Baddock looked defiant, and Felkin taciturn and sulky.

Close to them stood my dear lady. Her beautiful eyes literally glowed with triumph. That these two men loved her, each in his own curious, uncontrolled way, I, her friend and confidant, knew very well. I had seen, and often puzzled over, the feminine attacks which she had made on the susceptibilities of that morose lout Felkin. It had taken her nearly two years to bring him to her feet. During that time she had alternately rendered him happy with her smiles and half mad with her coquetries, whilst Philip Baddock's love for her was perpetually fanned by his ever-growing jealousy.

I remember that I often thought her game a cruel one. She was one of those women whom few men could resist; if she really desired to conquer she invariably succeeded, and her victory over Felkin seemed to me as purposeless as it was unkind. After all, she was the lawful wife of Captain de Mazareen, and to rouse hatred between two friends for the sake of her love, when that love was not hers to give, seemed unworthy of her. At this moment, when I could read deadly hatred in the faces of these two men, her cooing laugh grated unpleasantly on my ear.

"Never mind, Mr. Felkin," she said, turning her luminous eyes on him. "Since you have so hard a taskmaster, you must do your duty now. But," she added, throwing a strange, defiant look at Mr. Baddock, "I shall be at home this evening; come and have our cosy chat after dinner."

She gave him her hand, and he took it with a certain clumsy gallantry and raised it to his lips. I thought that Philip Baddock would strike his friend with his open hand. The veins on his temples were swollen like dark cords, and I don't think that I ever saw such an evil look in anyone's eyes before.

Strangely enough, the moment Mr. Felkin's back was turned my dear lady seemed to set herself the task of soothing the violent passions which she had willfully aroused in the other man. She invited him to come into the house, and, some ten minutes later, I heard her singing to him. When, later on, I went into the boudoir to join them at tea, she was sitting on the music stool whilst he half bent over her, half knelt at her feet; her hands were clasped in her lap, and his fingers were closed over hers.

He did not attempt to leave her side when he saw me entering the room. In fact, he wore a triumphant air of possession, and paid her those little attentions which only an accepted lover would dare to offer.

He left soon after tea, and she accompanied him to the door. She gave him her hand to kiss, and I, who stood at some little distance in the shadow, thought that he would take her in his arms, so yielding and gracious did she seem. But some look or gesture on her part must have checked him, for he turned and walked quickly down the drive.

Lady Molly stood in the doorway gazing out towards the sunset. I, in my humble mind, wondered once again what was the purport of this cruel game.

3

Half an hour later she called to me, asked for her hat, told me to put on mine and to come out for a stroll.

As so often happened, she led the way towards the Elkhorn woods, which in spite, or perhaps because, of the painful memories they evoked, was a very favourite walk of hers.

As a rule the wood, especially that portion of it where the unfortunate solicitor had been murdered, was deserted after sunset.

The villagers declared that Mr. Steadman's ghost haunted the clearing, and that the cry of the murdered man, as he was being foully struck from behind, could be distinctly heard echoing through the trees.

Needless to say, these superstitious fancies never disturbed Lady Molly. She liked to wander over the ground where was committed that mysterious crime which had sent to ignominy worse than death the man she loved so passionately. It seemed as if she meant to wrench its secret from the silent ground, from the leafy undergrowth, from the furtive inhabitants of the glades.

The sun had gone down behind the hills; the wood was dark and still. We strolled up as far as the first clearing, where a plain, granite stone, put up by Mr. Philip Baddock, marked the spot where Mr. Steadman had been murdered.

We sat down on it to rest. My dear lady's mood was a silent one; I did not dare to disturb it, and, for a while, only the gentle "hush—sh—sh" of the leaves, stirred by the evening breeze, broke the peaceful stillness of the glade.

Then we heard a murmur of voices, deep-toned and low. We could not hear the words spoken, though we both strained our ears, and presently Lady Molly arose and cautiously made her way among the trees in the direction whence the voices came, I following as closely as I could.

We had not gone far when we recognised the voices, and heard the words that were said. I paused, distinctly frightened, whilst my dear lady whispered a warning "Hush!"

Never in all my life had I heard so much hatred, such vengeful malignity expressed in the intonation of the human voice as I did in the half-dozen words which now struck my ear.

"You will give her up, or—"

It was Mr. Felkin who spoke. I recognised his raucous delivery, but I could not distinguish either of the two men in the gloom.

"Or what?" queried the other, in a voice which trembled with either rage or fear—perhaps with both.

"You will give her up," repeated Felkin, sullenly. "I tell you that it is an impossibility—do you understand?—an impossibility for me to stand by and see her wedded to you, or to any other man for the matter of that. But that is neither here nor there," he added after a slight pause. "It is with you I have to deal now. You shan't have her—you shan't—I won't allow it, even if I have to—"

He paused again. I cannot describe the extraordinary effect this rough voice coming out of the darkness had upon my nerves. I had edged up to Lady Molly, and had succeeded in getting hold of her hand. It was like ice, and she herself was as rigid as that piece of granite on which we had been sitting.

"You seem bubbling over with covert threats," interposed Philip Baddock, with what was obviously a sneer; "what are the extreme measures to which you will resort if I do not give up the lady whom I love with my whole heart, and who has honoured me to-day by accepting my hand in marriage?"

"That is a lie!" ejaculated Felkin.

"What is a lie?" queried the other, quietly.

"She has not accepted you—and you know it. You are trying to keep me away from her—arrogating rights which you do not possess. Give her up, man, give her up. It will be best for you. She will listen to me—I can win her all right—but you must stand aside for me this time. Take the word of a desperate man for it, Baddock. It will be best for you to give her up."

Silence reigned in the wood for a few moments, and then we heard Philip Baddock's voice again, but he seemed to speak more calmly, almost indifferently, as I thought.

"Are you going now?" he asked. "Won't you come in to dinner?"

"No," replied Felkin, "I don't want any dinner, and I have an appointment for afterwards."

"Don't let us part ill friends, Felkin," continued Philip Baddock in conciliatory tones. "Do you know that, personally, my feeling is that no woman on earth is worth a serious quarrel between two old friends, such as we have been."

"I'm glad you think so," rejoined the other drily. "S'long."

The cracking of twigs on the moss-covered ground indicated that the two men had parted and were going their several ways.

With infinite caution, and holding my hand tightly in hers, my dear lady made her way along the narrow path which led us out of the wood.

Once in the road we walked rapidly, and soon reached our garden gate. Lady Molly had not spoken a word during all that time, and no one knew better than I did how to respect her silence.

During dinner she tried to talk of indifferent subjects, and never once alluded to the two men whom she had thus willfully pitted one against the other. That her calm was only on the surface, however, I realised from the fact that every sound on the gravel path outside caused her to start. She was, of course, expecting the visit of Mr. Felkin.

At eight o'clock he came. It was obvious that he had spent the past hour in wandering about in the woods. He looked untidy and unkempt. My dear lady greeted him very coldly, and when he tried to kiss her hand she withdrew it abruptly.

Our drawing-room was a double one, divided by *portière* curtains. Lady Molly led the way into the front room, followed by Mr. Felkin. Then she drew the curtains together, leaving me standing behind them. I concluded that she wished me to stay there and to listen, conscious of the fact that Felkin, in the agitated mood in which he was, would be quite oblivious of my presence.

I almost pitied the poor man, for to me—the listener—it was at once apparent that my dear lady had only bidden him come tonight in order to torture him. For about a year she had been playing with him as a cat does with a mouse; encouraging him at times with sweet words and smiles, repelling him at others with coldness not unmixed with coquetry. But to-night her coldness was unalloyed; her voice was trenchant, her attitude almost one of contempt.

I missed the beginning of their conversation, for the curtains were thick and I did not like to go too near, but soon Mr. Felkin's voice was raised. It was harsh and uncompromising.

"I suppose that I am only good enough for a summer's flirtation?" he said sullenly, "but not to marry, eh? The owner of Appledore Castle, the millionaire, Mr. Baddock, is more in your line—"

"It certainly would be a more suitable match for me," rejoined Lady Molly, coolly.

"He told me you had formally accepted him," said the man, with enforced calm; "is that true?"

"Partly," she replied.

"But you won't marry him!"

The exclamation seemed to come straight from a heart brimful of passion, of love, of hate, and of revenge. The voice had the same intonation in it which had rung an hour ago in the dark Elkhorn woods.

"I may do," came in quiet accents from my dear lady.

"You won't marry him," repeated Felkin, roughly.

"Who shall prevent me?" retorted Lady Molly, with a low, sarcastic laugh.

"I will."

"You?" she said contemptuously.

"I told him an hour ago that he must give you up. I tell you now that you shall not be Philip Baddock's wife."

"Oh!" she interposed. And I could almost see the disdainful shrug of her shoulders, the flash of contempt in her expressive eyes.

No doubt it maddened him to see her so cool, so indifferent, when he had thought that he could win her. I do believe that the poor wretch loved her. She was always beautiful, but never more so than to-night when she had obviously determined finally to dismiss him.

"If you marry Philip Baddock," he now said, in a voice which quivered with uncontrolled passion, "then within six months of your wedding-day you will be a widow, for your husband will have ended his life on the gallows."

"You are mad!" she retorted calmly.

"That is as it may be," he replied. "I warned him to-night, and he seems inclined to heed my warning; but he won't stand aside if you beckon to him. Therefore, if you love him, take my warning. I may not be able to get you, but I swear to you that Philip Baddock shan't either. I'll see him hanged first," he added, with gruesome significance.

"And you think that you can force me to do your bidding by such paltry threats?" she retorted.

"Paltry threats? Ask Philip Baddock if my threats are paltry. He knows full well that in my room at Appledore Castle, safe from thievish fingers, lie the proofs that he killed Alexander Steadman in the Elkhorn woods. Oh! I wouldn't help him in his nefarious deeds until he placed himself in my hands. He had to take my terms or leave the thing alone altogether, for he could not work without me. My wants are few, and he has treated and paid me well. Now we are rivals, and I'll destroy him before I'll let him gloat over me.

"Do you know how we worked it? Sir Jeremiah would not disinherit his grandson—he steadily refused to make a will in Philip Baddock's favour. But when he was practically dying we sent for Alexander Steadman—a newcomer, who had never seen Sir Jeremiah before—and I impersonated the old gentleman for the occasion. Yes, I!" he repeated with a coarse laugh, "I was Sir Jeremiah for the space of half an hour, and I think that I played the part splendidly. I dictated the terms of a new will. Young Steadman never suspected the fraud for a single instant. We had darkened the room for the comedy, you see, and Mr. Steadman was destined by Baddock and myself never to set eyes on the real Sir Jeremiah.

"After the interview Baddock sent for Captain de Mazareen; this was all part of his plan and mine. We engineered it all, and we knew that Sir Jeremiah could only last a few hours. We sent for Steadman again, and I myself scattered a few dozen sharp nails among the loose stones in the road where the motorcar was intended to break down, thus forcing the solicitor to walk through the woods. Captain de Mazareen's appearance on the scene at that particular moment was an unrehearsed effect which nearly upset all our plans, for had Mr. Steadman stuck to him that night, instead of turning back, he would probably be alive now, and Baddock and I would be doing time somewhere for attempted fraud. We should have been done, at any rate.

"Well! you know what happened. Mr. Steadman was killed. Baddock killed him, and then ran straight back to the house, just in time to greet Captain de Mazareen, who evidently had loitered on his way. But it was I who thought of the stick, as an additional precaution to avert suspicion from ourselves. Captain de Mazareen was carrying one, and left it in the hall at the Castle. I cut my own hand and stained the stick with it, then polished and cleaned it up, and later, during the night, deposited it in the near neighbourhood of the murdered body. Ingenious, wasn't it? I am a clever beggar, you see. Because I was cleverer than Baddock he could not do without me, and because he could not do without me I made him write and sign a request to me to help him to manufacture a bogus will and then to murder the solicitor who had drawn it up. And I have hidden that precious document in the wing of Appledore Castle which I inhabit; the exact spot is known only to myself. Baddock has often tried to find out, but all he knows is that these things are in that particular wing of the house. I have the document, and the draft of the will taken out of Mr. Steadman's pocket, and the short bludgeon with which he was killed—it is still stained with blood— and the rags with which I cleaned the stick. I swear that I will never make use of these things against Philip Baddock unless he drives me to it, and if you make use of what I have just told you I'll swear that I have lied. No one can find the proofs which I hold. But on the day that you marry Baddock I'll place them in the hands of the police."

There was silence in the room. I could almost hear the beating of my own heart, so horrified, so appalled was I at the horrible tale which the man had just told to my dear lady.

The villainy of the whole scheme was so terrible, and at the same time so cunning, that it seemed inconceivable that human brain could have engendered it. Vaguely in my dull mind I wondered if Lady Molly would have to commit bigamy before she could wrench from this evildoer's hands the proofs that would set her own husband free from his martyrdom.

What she said I did not hear, what he meant to retort I never knew, for at that moment my attention was attracted by the sound of running footsteps on the gravel, followed by a loud knock at our front door. Instinctively I ran to open it. Our old gardener was standing there hatless and breathless.

"Appledore Castle, miss," he stammered, "it's on fire. I thought you would like to know."

Before I had time to reply I heard a loud oath uttered close behind me, and the next moment Felkin dashed out of the drawing-room into the hall.

"Is there a bicycle here that I can take?" he shouted to the gardener.

"Yes, sir," replied the old man; "my son has one. Just in that shed, sir, on your left."

In fewer seconds than it takes to relate, Felkin had rushed to the shed, dragged out the bicycle, mounted it, and I think that within two minutes of hearing the awful news, he was bowling along the road, and was soon out of sight.

4

One wing of the stately mansion was ablaze when, a quarter of an hour later, my dear lady and I arrived upon the scene. We had come on our bicycles not long after Mr. Felkin.

At the very moment that the weird spectacle burst fully upon our gaze, a loud cry of horror had just risen from the hundred or so people who stood watching the terrible conflagration, whilst the local fire brigade, assisted by Mr. Baddock's men, were working with the hydrants. That cry found echo in our own throats as we saw a man clambering, with the rapidity of a monkey, up a long ladder which had been propped up against a second floor window of the flaming portion of the building. The red glow illumined the large, shaggy head of Felkin, throwing for a moment into bold relief his hooked nose and straggly beard. For the space of three seconds perhaps he stood thus, outlined against what looked like a glowing furnace behind him, and the next instant he had disappeared beyond the window embrasure.

"This is madness!" came in loud accents from out the crowd in the foreground, and before one fully realised whence that voice had come, Mr. Philip Baddock was in his turn seen clambering up that awful ladder. A dozen pairs of hands reached him just in time to drag him back from the perilous ascent. He fought to free himself, but the firemen were determined and soon succeeded in bringing him back to level ground, whilst two of them, helmeted and well-equipped, took his place upon the ladder.

The foremost had hardly reached the level of the first story when Felkin's figure once more appeared in the window embrasure above. He was staggering like a man drunk or fainting, his shaggy hair and beard were blown about his head by the terrible draught caused by the flames, and he waved his arms over his head, giving the impression to those below, who gazed horrified, that he was either possessed or dying. In one hand he held what looked like a great, long bundle.

We could see him now put one leg forward, obviously gathering strength to climb the somewhat high window ledge. With a shout of encouragement the two firemen scrambled up with squirrel-like agility, and the cry of "They're coming! they're coming! Hold on, Felkin!" rose from a hundred excited throats.

The unfortunate man made another effort. We could see his face clearly now in the almost blinding glow which surrounded him. It was distorted with fear and also with agony.

He gave one raucous cry, which I do believe will echo in my ears as long as I live, and with a superhuman effort he hurled the bundle which he held out of the window.

At that same moment there was a terrific hissing, followed by a loud crash. The floor beneath the feet of the unfortunate man must have given way, for he disappeared suddenly in a sea of flames.

The bundle which he had hurled down had struck the foremost fireman on the head. He lost his hold, and as he fell he dragged his unfortunate comrade down with him. The others ran to the rescue of their comrades. I don't think they were seriously hurt, but what happened directly after among the crowd, the firemen, or the burning building, I cannot tell you. I only know that at the moment when Felkin's figure was, for the second time, seen in the frame of the glowing window, Lady Molly seized my hand and dragged me forward through the crowd.

Her husband's life was hanging in the balance, just as much as that of the miserable wretch who was courting a horrible death for the sake of those proofs which—as it was proved afterwards—Philip Baddock tried to destroy by such drastic means.

The excitement round the ladder, the fall of the two firemen, the crashing in of the floor and the gruesome disappearance of Felkin caused so much excitement in the crowd that the bundle which the unfortunate man had thrown remained unheeded for the moment. But Philip Baddock reached the spot where it fell thirty seconds after Lady Molly did. She had already picked it up, when he said harshly:

"Give me that. It is mine. Felkin risked his life to save it for me."

Inspector Etty, however, stood close by, and before Philip Baddock realised what Lady Molly meant to do, she had turned quickly and placed the bundle in the inspector's hands.

"You know me, Etty, don't you?" she said rapidly.

"Oh, yes, my lady!" he replied.

"Then take the utmost care of this bundle. It contains proofs of one of the most dastardly crimes ever committed in this country."

No other words could have aroused the enthusiasm and caution of Etty in the same manner.

After that Philip Baddock might protest, might rage, storm, or try to bribe, but the proofs of his guilt and Captain de Mazareen's innocence were safe in the hands of the police, and bound to come to light at last.

But, as a matter of fact, Baddock neither stormed nor pleaded. When Lady Molly turned to him once more he had disappeared.

You know the rest, of course. It occurred too recently to be recounted. Philip Baddock was found the next morning with a bullet through his head, lying on the granite stone which, with cruel hypocrisy, he himself had erected in memory of Mr. Steadman whom he had so foully murdered.

The unfortunate Felkin had not lied when he said that the proofs which he held of Baddock's guilt were conclusive and deadly.

Captain de Mazareen obtained His Majesty's gracious pardon after five years of martyrdom which he had borne with heroic fortitude.

I was not present when Lady Molly was once more united to the man who so ardently worshipped and trusted her, and to whose love, innocence, and cause she had remained so sublimely loyal throughout the past few years.

She has given up her connection with the police. The reason for it has gone with the return of her happiness, over which I—her ever faithful Mary Granard—will, with your permission, draw a veil.

Coachwhip Publications

CoachwhipBooks.com

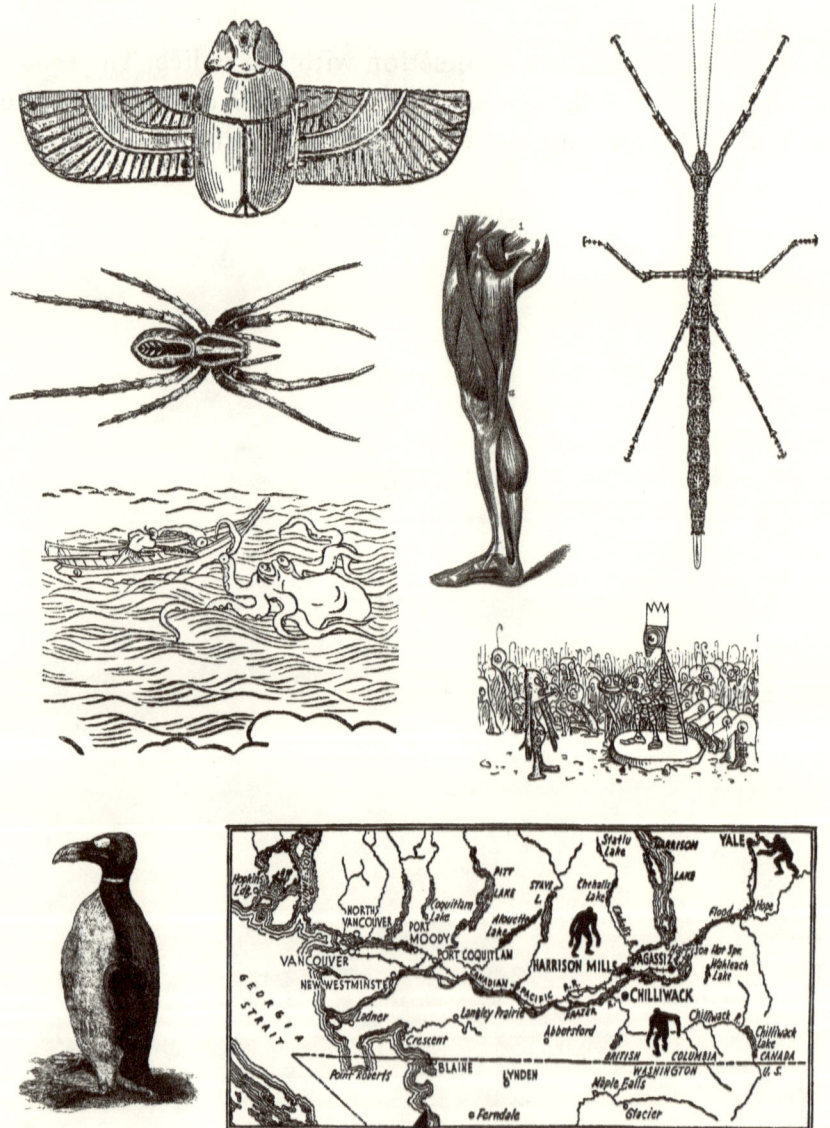

2 DETECTIVES

ASTRO, THE MASTER OF MYSTERIES
GELETT BURGESS

DR. XAVIER WYCHERLEY, THE MIND-READER
MAX RITTENBERG

ASTRO, THE MASTER OF MYSTERIES /
DR. XAVIER WYCHERLEY, THE MIND-READER

ISBN 1-61646-103-9

AVERAGE JONES/
DR. FURNIVALL, PHYSICIAN-DETECTIVE

ISBN 1-61646-098-9

THE CHRONICLES OF ADDINGTON PEACE /
LUTHER TRANT, PSYCHOLOGICAL DETECTIVE

ISBN 1-61646-097-0

THE COMPLETE ADVENTURES OF

ROMNEY PRINGLE

R. Austin Freeman &
John J. Pitcairn

(as by Clifford Ashdown)

The Complete Adventures of
Romney Pringle

ISBN 1-61646-090-3

12 Cases for Max Carrados

ISBN 1-61646-018-0

www.ingramcontent.com/pod-product-compliance
Lightning Source LLC
Chambersburg PA
CBHW031030030726
47497CB00004B/1079

* 9 7 8 1 6 1 6 4 6 1 1 2 6 *